A Spy in Exile

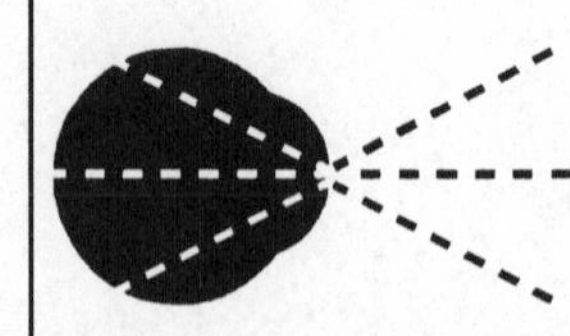

A Spy in Exile

A THRILLER

Jonathan de Shalit

Translated by Steven Cohen

THORNDIKE PRESS

A part of Gale, a Cengage Company

Farmington Hills, Mich • San Francisco • New York • Waterville, Maine
Meriden, Conn • Mason, Ohio • Chicago

Thorndike Press, a part of Gale, a Cengage Company.

Thorndike Press® Large Print Peer Picks.
The text of this Large Print edition is unabridged.
Other aspects of the book may vary from the original edition.
Set in 16 pt. Plantin.

**LIBRARY OF CONGRESS CIP DATA ON FILE.
CATALOGUING IN PUBLICATION FOR THIS BOOK
IS AVAILABLE FROM THE LIBRARY OF CONGRESS**

ISBN-13: 978-1-4328-6559-7 (hardcover alk. paper)

Published in 2019 by arrangement with Emily Bestler Books/Atria, an imprint of Simon & Schuster, Inc.

Printed in Mexico
1 2 3 4 5 6 7 23 22 21 20 19

A Spy in Exile

1

June 2014

Soothed by the sound coming from the Audi's wide tires on the asphalt, Ya'ara reclined in the backseat of the car and closed her eyes. The vehicle's interior, insulated from the blistering late afternoon sun by the tinted windows, was chilly. Two tight-lipped young men, who Ya'ara assumed were members of the Shin Bet security service's VIP Protection Unit, were sitting in the front seats. The call from the prime minister's office had come through some two hours earlier. *The prime minister would like to meet with you,* said Mai, or was it Kim — whatever, it was one of those typical names for young women working for older senior officials. *Today, right away,* the secretary said. *We'll send a car to get you.*

She had spotted the black Audi from a mile away, and the guy who was waiting for her stood out like a sore thumb, too. After all, you didn't see very many young men hanging around a college campus in dark glasses and a dark jacket on a blistering hot day in June, even if the sun was sinking steadily toward the blue strip of sea on the horizon at the far end of Einstein Street.

They were northward bound from the Morasha Junction, with gilt-edged clouds visible to the west and the loam-earth fields glowing orange. In this light, of almost-sunset, the orchards had taken on a purple-black hue, and Ya'ara couldn't help but marvel at the scene. In the twilight that encapsulated the drive, the landscape appeared profound and filled with splendor, a German expressionist painting. And yet, it was Israel.

Almost a year had gone by since she'd played her part in flushing out of one of Israel's most dangerous traitors. Ya'ara had been on unpaid leave when Michael Turgeman recruited her for the team set up by former Mossad chief Aharon Levin. It hadn't ended well. The hunt had been swift and dizzying. The team had managed to identify the traitor within just a few months. He was an aide close to the prime minister. She hadn't been alone in urging Levin to kill the man immediately, but Levin refused and ordered the team not to touch him.

Ya'ara decided when the man chose to run that there were times when justice must be written in blood. Alon Regev, the advisor who had crossed the line, was on his way to a deserted beach north of Ashkelon, where a rescue boat courtesy of the Russian intelligence service was waiting for him. He didn't make it to the rendezvous point. He died on his way there in a road accident, and his extraction team slipped away silently through the black waters.

Ya'ara was never accused of killing Regev. The papers reported the accident; the police closed the case. But Aharon Levin made sure she couldn't go back to the Mossad after that. He'd told her that she was aggressive, undisciplined, unpredictable, and too prone to violence. And he didn't keep his opinions to himself.

Ya'ara didn't want to go back anyway. She felt stifled by all the regulations and procedures and orders and approvals. She didn't want to be smothered. She wanted to breathe. She traveled in South America for four months, crossing the continent from southern Chile to Ecuador on a large motorcycle. Her lover Hagai was waiting for her at the airport on her return, and his eyes filled with tears as he told her he couldn't take it any longer, that it was over between them. She collected her books, photography equipment, and clothes from the house on the *moshav* and moved back to Tel Aviv, into a room in an apartment rented by Einat, a girl she knew from the unit. She hardly felt a thing when Hagai broke things off, other than a slight sense of relief and the knowledge that that's just the way things were. Thirty-four years old and living with a roommate in a dilapidated two-bedroom apartment in the old part of the northern end of the city. Yes, she could have done a little better for herself, but she didn't really care. She went back to university, for her final semester toward a bachelor's degree in film. She had certainly taken her time.

Now the academic year was winding down and editing of her final project was coming to an end. The short film she had written and directed was taking shape before her eyes, assuming depth and character, a life of its own. The leads were a man and woman in their thirties. They had first met years ago, and now they had met again, by chance. The chemistry between them was immediate and powerful. They went to a large, shuttered apartment in Netanya. Wine, Turkish coffee, dates, a sharp Gouda cheese, arak. The man and woman went from one bed to the next, spending each night in a different room, and with each passing day the shutters opened a little more to allow the sunlight to flood the room and the sea breeze to dry their bodies. The couple hardly spoke. There was something somber yet captivating about the movie. Ya'ara was pleased with it. There was something truly compelling about the emerging relationship that she saw on the screen. She felt she had achieved something real, something that touched on an element of the secrets that exist between a man and a woman. She was looking forward to screening it but now, out of nowhere, she was on her way to see the prime minister.

The large Audi turned eastward on Route 57. The wide-open stretch of sky that Ya'ara could see through the windshield was already dark. The car slowed down and turned left into a *moshav.* Ya'ara didn't catch sight of the name as they drove through the gate, nor did she manage to spot the wooden sign that customarily stood alongside the checkpoints at the entrances to the *moshavim* in the area. It annoyed her. She felt rusty. *This wouldn't have happened a few years ago,* she scolded herself silently.

"Where are we?" she asked the two security service agents sitting in the front. The one in the passenger seat responded without even turning around: "We'll be there in a minute."

Cheeky bastard, she thought. The car slowed in front of an electric gate, which slid open to reveal a narrow driveway hidden by large trees with thick black-green foliage. Less than a minute went by before they stopped in front of a house whose concealed lighting exposed the ocher shade of its walls, the color of earth or clay. A security guard armed with a short-barreled M16 assault rifle approached, nodded to the men in front, and opened the right rear door of the vehicle.

"Come with me, please." As they crossed the threshold into the house, the guard asked: "Are you armed?"

"Me? Of course not!"

"I have to check you anyway."

"Listen up." Ya'ara's voice turned icy. "I don't know your name, but the prime minister was the one who summoned me here. I didn't ask to see him. You can check my bag, but we haven't known each other long enough for me to let you run your hands over me. If that's a problem, you can tell your two friends to take me back home."

From deep within the house a voice called out, "It's okay, Eitan. I trust this girl." Ya'ara recognized the prime minister's resonant voice from both television and the numerous times she had sat in on briefings seeking to secure his approval for specific operations. As she turned toward the sound of his voice, she saw the figure of the prime minister, dressed in a black polo shirt, following in its wake toward her. He approached with an outstretched hand. "I see that the rumors are true. You really are someone who's not to be messed with." As he shook her hand, he said, "Ya'ara, I know that we've met before. You aren't someone who is easily forgotten."

As Ya'ara let go of the prime minister's hand, she wondered why her meeting was taking place at a large, secluded villa rather than in his office. "This home belongs to a family member who resides abroad most of the year," the prime minister said, appearing to read her mind as he escorted her into the house, initially through a spacious guest area and then into a large and dimly lit study. "He's placed it at my disposal, and I use it when I want to meet someone discreetly, without disturbances from anyone, without any filming or recording, without any records anywhere."

He led Ya'ara to a sitting area illuminated by a yellowish light from a free-standing lamp. The beam from a second lamp formed a circle of light on the large desk. The rest of the room was shrouded in darkness. Darkness and Chopin's Concerto No. 2. They sat in identical leather armchairs, and an elderly woman emerged seemingly out of nowhere bearing a tray with two cups of coffee, a jug of cold water, and a small plate of cookies. "Thank you, Bracha," the prime minister said. "Please close the door. If we need anything, we'll give you a shout."

As soon as the old woman closed the door behind her, he leaned toward Ya'ara and said, "I'll get straight to the point."

Ya'ara nodded, her eyes fixed on those of the prime minister.

"I need — the state of Israel needs — to put together a new capability. A capability, in fact, that we possessed in the past but which has eroded in recent years. We need a small, highly skilled strike force that can operate in absolute secrecy, completely detached from the state. A strike force that can act swiftly, resolutely, aggressively, free of the restraints of procedures and approvals and legal advisors. Finally, it must be a strike force that the state of Israel — and I — can, if necessary, deny."

After a long, silent moment, the prime minister rose from his armchair, walked over to a dark wooden sideboard, and returned with a bottle of fine single-malt scotch. "Can I pour one for you, too? Bracha looks after me, offers me and my guests nothing other than coffee and cold water. But we're adults, right? For a conversation like this, we're allowed something a little stronger, aren't we? But not too much, of course."

Ya'ara loved scotch. She added a few drops of cold water to the measure the prime minister had poured for her. "It brings out additional flavors," she said, and the prime minister nodded.

"Well," he continued, at ease in his armchair again, "I'm looking for a black horse to help pull the chariot. Are you familiar with Plato's Chariot Allegory?"

"Yes," she admitted. "Sort of . . ."

"There are numerous interpretations of the dialogue of Socrates and Phaedrus," the prime minister went on, and Ya'ara wondered if he had read the allegory in the original Greek, "and all of those with which I'm familiar present the black horse, the wild one, as a beast that needs to be controlled and tamed. Just as reason should have the upper hand over animal urges."

He sipped his whiskey for a moment, then set it on the table and leaned forward. "I think differently. I think that a country striving for survival requires two kinds of horses to pull its chariot. An absolute must. The one, a white horse, is reason, the appropriate measures of law and order. The second is a black horse, wild, aggressive, subversive, which has to be reined in all the time. I believe — no, Ya'ara — I'm *convinced* that our intelligence services, and particularly those that operate beyond the borders of the state, need to be our black horse. The elected government can then lead the way by means of the two horses. The white horse is vital, essential. Without it, the chariot would have no direction. But in a world as complex and stormy as ours, we also need a black horse that will lead us to the places we wouldn't get to without it."

He leaned back in his chair, his face falling into shadow. "Once upon a time, in the early days, our intelligence services were a black horse. Over the years, they've grown — too much perhaps — more organized and structured, with hierarchies and bureaucracy, regulations, procedures. We've reaped benefits from the process, but these restrictions have created a gap that needs to be filled. And for that, I need you. I need you to be my black horse."

Ya'ara was of two minds about the prime minister's interpretation of Plato's allegory.

The prime minister had admitted, too, that his interpretation might be a unique one. But while she didn't know much about Greek philosophy she did understand what the prime minister was saying. She sipped her whiskey, her ever-present string of pearls glistening in the hollow of her throat, and asked: "What exactly do you have in mind?"

"I have been briefed on your career and on your last operation. I'm aware of everything that led up to the exposure of the traitor Alon Regev, who fortunately worked for my predecessor and not for me, because then I would have killed him myself," the prime minister responded. "I'm not convinced that the course of action selected by the president was the right one, but that's all in the past now." He leaned forward again. "And, I've been told of your role in Regev's exposure, and I believe that it was you who put the affair to bed." He smiled tightly as he said, "You've been described to me as violent and wild. There you go — I'm telling you straight to your face."

He reached for his whiskey again. "There's probably some truth to that, some part of you that matches the description. But I'm also familiar with things you did working for Mossad — the extraordinary things you did as a field operative. This is what I know from your former commanders: You're brave, you're highly intelligent, you understand what motivates people, how to lead them. You have that strength. And you love that world of secrecy. You love it and it brings out such strength in you. I also know about your sister and the profound effect her story had on you."

Ya'ara remained silent as the prime minister listed her virtues, and at the mention of her sister, too. She knew there had to be more to come.

"I need you back in service," the prime minister said. "Not the Mossad. I want you to set up a unit that'll operate by a different set of rules. Like I said — swiftly, highly aggressive, highly professional, with a willingness to take risks. The world is changing quickly, and we need a force that can act even quicker. You'll pick your own people, and you'll work completely detached from any and every government body. You'll be ruthless and violent if necessary, but you'll operate only against the targets I provide, in the name of the government of Israel."

"And what if I believe you're using me to take care of personal issues, or to promote a political agenda of some kind?" Ya'ara asked.

"There you go — that's exactly why I want you," the prime minister said with obvious self-satisfaction, like someone who had taken a bet with himself and won. "You're meeting privately with the prime minister of Israel, face-to-face, yet show no fear of me at all. You don't flinch in the slightest before slamming your fist into someone's face."

"Sir, I respect you and the position you hold, but I have to ask such questions. Without flinching. Otherwise I'm not the one to do this work for you."

"Ya'ara, I'm not trying to establish a private militia or political assassination unit. I will never pass on directives you cannot tolerate. And, no matter what, the final decision whether or not to act will always be yours. I will never expect you to do anything that doesn't sit well with you or your team. The bottom line is that the darkest deeds have to be carried out by the purest individuals."

"Don't fool yourself, sir, I'm far from pure, but I can tell the difference between right and wrong, and I try my best to make the right choices. But what you've heard is true. There's a wild side to me, one that has me walking a fine line. And, because I'm a patriot, I'm willing to cross that line sometimes, too. This means you have to be prepared for surprises, sir. I may not be who or what you think I am."

"I'm willing to take the risk. And in any event, I still maintain the right to deny everything. Just so you know, if you and your unit get into trouble, we won't be able to come to your assistance. You'll be out there on your own. Totally alone." His face looked suddenly tired. "You're taking on a heavy burden. Of isolation, of anonymity. There won't be any medals or glowing reports in your file — it will just be you, and the things you know. And the rest of your life will all be on hold." He raised his eyes to hers as he asked his final question, "Will you do it, Ya'ara?"

She sat silent long enough to not appear too eager, long enough to mourn her unfinished film for a moment, then she said, "It'll take me some time to recruit a team and train them. It's not going to happen overnight. You should know that."

"I understand, but don't forget that we're at war. I want you to do this right, but from now on, the rules of war apply."

The night sky was as black as ink. The orange glow of the coastal plain, the product of lights and smog, appeared in the distance. She was sitting again in the rear of the large black Audi, which was driving her back to

Tel Aviv. Her motorcycle was waiting for her outside the university. *My new life is about to begin,* Ya'ara thought to herself almost gleefully. She didn't know how long this specific chapter would last. She didn't know if she'd come out on the other side in one piece. All she knew was that she had a big adventure ahead of her.

She had tied up a few technical details with the prime minister before leaving. His personal lawyer, Shaul Ben-Atar, was going to put everything in place. The front companies, the bank accounts. Keep it as simple as possible, the prime minister had said, sharing a lifetime of experience with her in just a few words. *Keep it simple.* His voice had changed when he began to talk about operational realities. "No matter what, this will get complicated. So, build the unit and operate it in the most practical way you can come up with — the most focused way. What should always be clear to you, the thing that requires constant clarity, is the objective. The individual you're after must always remain in your sights. Always in the center."

2

WANTED: MEN AND WOMEN FOR HAZARDOUS JOURNEY
CONSTANT DANGER, LONG MONTHS OF COMPLETE DARKNESS,
SAFE RETURN DOUBTFUL, SMALL WAGES
SENSE OF DIGNITY AND SATISFACTION IN EVENT OF SUCCESS

Ya'ara looked at the ad she had composed, and it pleased her. It was a paraphrase of the recruitment ad published in 1913 by polar explorer and adventurer Sir Ernest Shackleton during his preparations for the expedition that eventually brought him eternal glory. Funny how that renowned expedition was one that failed at its very outset. Shackleton had aspired to be the first man to cross Antarctica on foot. But the ship in which Shackleton and his crew set out became trapped in pack ice in the frozen South Sea, and they were forced to abandon the vessel. Lost in an endless sea of ice, their quest took on a new objective. Instead of crossing the continent, they were now forced to save themselves. Considering the harsh weather conditions, the vast distance from any other sign of human life, and the awful solitude, they appeared doomed from the very start; but Shackleton, in a display of remarkable leadership that command schools and colleges still teach today, managed to save his crew, every last one of them.

At the time, Shackleton's odd and tantalizing ad elicited a flood of some five thousand responses. *I wonder,* Ya'ara thought to herself, *if anyone's going to respond to the strange challenge more than a century later.* Ya'ara posted the ad on two internet message boards and one of the social networks. Her plan was to recruit most of her team by means of the age-old method of "a friend brings a friend," but she also wanted to poke the digital domain to see if it could cough up some interesting candidates for her.

She didn't need that many. Six, eight at most. Certainly no more for the initial setting-up stage. When working with such a small number of individuals, each and every one of them is significant. Any one of them could make the difference. *I'm starting to think in American English,* she thought, wincing. That language finds its way into everything. Like beach sand.

Sitting and waiting for Aslan at a small bar in the Levinsky Market, Ya'ara felt completely at ease. She had absolute faith in him, held his capabilities in very high regard, and enjoyed being in his company. She had no doubts at all — she wanted him to join the enterprise, she wanted him with her.

As always, he materialized unnoticed. His catlike ability to do so scared the life out of most people, but she was accustomed by now to seeing him appear before her, seemingly out of thin air, a powerful and silent tiger, his smile lighting up his face.

"I can see you've set up a command center there," Aslan said, his eyes alluding to the open silver iPad and the brand-new iPhone that was connected to the device with a cable. "How did you get your hands on that model so quickly? The launch was just a week ago."

"Aslan," she responded, speaking his name with uncharacteristic warmth and standing to embrace him. Droplets of water trickled down the sides of a glass of milky arak filled with ice — a part of the command center. "Can I order one for you, too?"

Aslan took the seat across the table from her, and Ya'ara gestured to the waitress to bring another arak to the table. She sized him up. His slim, muscular body appeared relaxed. His face, as always, was tanned. And in his eyes, she caught distinct glimmers of joy.

"You look great," she declared. "Even though you're old," she added with a smile that belied her words. Aslan was one of those people who never seem to age.

"I can only hope that when you get to my age, you'll be able to do even half of what I do," he said.

Aslan devoted most of his time to extreme sports — mountain climbing, rafting, skydiving, anything and everything dangerous, remote, and in beautiful surroundings.

"I have neither the inclination nor the ability to compete with you." Ya'ara showed him the ad. "Would you respond?" she asked.

"Without a doubt. Crazy ad. Perfect for people like me."

Ya'ara told him about her meeting with the prime minister. Aslan didn't have to ask.

It was plain to see that she had taken the job. “It’s like a start-up,” she said. “We can work on it for a few years, until things become too institutionalized. And when that happens, we can make an exit. We’ll pass on the reins to someone responsible and stable, and move on from there.”

“We, we, we. And who is this we you’re talking about?”

“You know I’m talking about you. I want us to do this together. I’m asking you,” she added when she saw his gaze harden. “Someone has to do it. You recall our talks about what we’d do were we given the chance to rebuild everything. I’d like to think you were being serious, that we were serious. Because this is it, we have the opportunity to do so now. And opportunities like this come around maybe once in a lifetime. We’ve got hold of its tail. Let’s not let it slip away. We’ve got the chance to ride on the back of a tiger.”

Aslan leaned forward and listened. She knew she had his attention. Ya’ara enthusiastically outlined the stages she envisioned. First, the recruitment stage. They need to recruit swiftly and aggressively. And then the training stage. We’ll begin abroad from the outset, she said, her eyes fixed on him. The entire team. In the field. We have the required budget. We'll teach them at the same time how to construct a cover persona. A personal cover story for each of the field operatives. And a cover for the team. And then the missions stage. We'll begin operating, establishing a dark presence. She seemed to be enveloped by an inner light of enthusiasm as she spoke, and Aslan looked at her and smiled. He was familiar with her other sides, too — the gloomy sides, the dark ones, those that danced with despair and with pain. He loved those sides of her just as much.

"We already have an operations base, a small apartment, not far from here, on Y. L. Peretz Street. And a company. We're the International Dried Fruit Import and Export Company."

"Dried fruit?"

"Why not?"

"True. Why not?"

"So what do you say?" she asked without shifting her gaze.

"Look, you know I love action. And this country is still embroiled in its wars. And wherever there's a fight to be fought, you can count me in, on the good side. But I've been elsewhere these past few years. You know about all the things I do. These are the years in which I can still experience things. Even I'm not getting any younger."

"I'm not asking you to stop. But I'm offering you a partnership, or some kind of partnership at least. You can still go on your travels. But between them, you'll be with me, with the unit. You'll be a part-time field operative. Your experience is important to me, your knowledge. You keep me balanced. You're more level-headed than I am. I need your advice and experience. And more so" — she paused for a moment and stared at him from the depths of her blue-gray eyes — "I need a brother in arms. Give as much as you can give. But tell me that you're with me."

Aslan had known he was going to say yes to her already on the phone, when they had made the arrangement to meet at the bar. He didn't know then what he'd be agreeing to, but he sensed it wasn't going to be just a simple get-together. And now, as she sat there looking at him, her fingertips almost touching his hand, he sipped on his arak and said, "Okay. I'm in. As much as I can be. We'll do it together." He sighed. "If only my son could meet someone like you."

"Uri's twenty-two, and I'm an old woman of thirty-four, and he has a girlfriend. You showed me pictures of her."

"I know, I know. And you're so young that

it hurts. You have no right to talk about being old. And Uri will still go through many more girlfriends until he finds someone who suits him."

"He has all the time in the world. Come, let's drink to the young ones, whose entire lives lie ahead of them."

3

Their furniture shopping at IKEA took less than two hours. Ya'ara had come armed with a detailed list of everything they needed to turn the apartment into a work base. She had quickly marked off several options for each item they required in the catalog and now bounded joyfully up the escalator. At that moment, he thought she seemed younger than ever.

"You're like a war machine," Aslan remarked in wonder.

"More like a shopping machine. I hate these kinds of places," she confessed. "They frighten me. Get in quickly and get out even faster — that's what I say. And don't buy what you hadn't decided was necessary before getting here. Otherwise you're just playing into their hands."

Their next stop was a business that dealt in safes.

And then they purchased an espresso

machine. "Definitely essential," Aslan agreed.

Afterward at a bar they went through their lists of contacts again, writing down the name of every friend or acquaintance who they thought might be able to suggest a suitable candidate. And they also searched through their memories for potential members of the unit they were getting off the ground.

"What exactly are we looking for?" Ya'ara had asked shortly before, as they poured themselves grappa from the bottle kept especially for her in the freezer behind the counter. *Something inside her has broken free, has changed,* Aslan thought to himself once more. Their meetings in the past had always taken place at trendy wine bars or in hotel lobbies. But here, too, in the Levinsky Market, Ya'ara — with her hair tied up and the string of pearls around her neck — looked at home. He kept his impressions to himself and responded: "Women and men. The team must be diverse. That's the way to survive on the streets."

"Obviously. Exceptional women and men. We're setting up a very small team. Six to eight individuals. They have to be special."

"Smart, intelligent," Aslan said.

"Smart and intelligent people are a dime a dozen," she commented.

"Brave. Streetwise. Who can work as part of a team, but can also operate alone. Individuals who like to be alone. Who are happy to be so."

"Yes," Ya'ara responded pensively. "Individuals who understand that solitude is strength. That their world is full even without people around them all the time. Know what I mean?" And Aslan thought for a moment that she was talking about herself, but quickly brushed the notion aside and nodded in agreement. He understood. "But I love having a good friend by my side," she added, looking into his eyes.

"And the ability to operate under a foreign identity, of course," he said.

"Absolute trustworthiness," Ya'ara said. "They always have to report only the truth, and in full."

"There isn't a man or woman out there without secrets."

"True. But when it comes to matters concerning an operation, albeit something indirect or marginal, we must be able to trust them completely. Not for one second will I work with someone who isn't willing to tell me the whole truth." Ya'ara knew that sometimes she herself refrained from speaking the whole truth. But when circumstances require doing so, *it's not the same thing as lying,* she thought defiantly.

"And patriotism," Aslan added.

"That's our starting point. That's a must. We aren't mercenaries. And the ability to listen. To show empathy. Good interpersonal skills."

"Perseverance. Thoroughness."

"The ability to carry things out to the end. The very end. The ability to cross the threshold, to cross the Rubicon. To breach the mission."

"Now you sound like the guys from the Office. 'To breach the mission.' What the hell does that mean anyway?"

"A lot of good things have come out of the Office. Including innovations in the language. You know, the Office made me what I am today."

"I'm not so sure. No one invented you. You made yourself."

"It seems to me sometimes that our natures are like Michelangelo's sculptures. He said, you know, that his sculptures were already there, in the marble, and that he merely exposed them. Allowed them to emerge from the stone."

"When you ramble on like that, you lose me," Aslan responded with a smile, even though Ya'ara knew he understood exactly what she meant. "Please, continue."

"They need to be determined. Iron-willed. Imaginative. We're looking for creativity. The ability to perform at a high level. Optimism. I think that's crucial — optimism. They must believe they're going to succeed even if they find themselves up against a wall." She kept track of the required traits with her fingers.

"With a list like this," Aslan said, laughing, "we aren't going to find anyone. Just look at us. We aren't people like that."

"Obviously no one can be perfect, no one can boast all the right qualities and abilities, but there has to be a critical mass. The right people for us will possess enough of these qualities — and more. Just so you know, I haven't told you even half of what I want yet."

"*Basta, genug, no más* — enough! How about you tell me your top five, the five things you define as the most critical, so I don't have to spend the day on this barstool?"

Ya'ara sipped on her grappa. A small wrinkle appeared on her forehead as she pondered Aslan's question.

"Do I have to name only five?"

"Yes."

"Okay then, here goes — absolute trustworthiness, good interpersonal skills, a cool head, the ability to carry things through, optimism, and a void to fill."

"A void to fill? That's new."

"You're going to say it's just another one of my strange notions. But yes, a void to fill, a deficiency. We all have to be lacking something. A hole of sorts in our soul, a void we're constantly trying to fill. Everything we do seeks to make up for that void, that deficiency. To find an answer for it."

"I don't feel I'm lacking anything," Aslan said, his eyes glinting, his teeth gleaming white.

Ya'ara thought about it for a moment. "Perhaps you're the exception to the rule," she said. "Perhaps you're so good at what you do because you're at peace with yourself. But I'm brilliant at what I do because of my empty spaces." She went silent. "It's too early for such candor," she continued with a smile. "It's not even ten in the morning yet. But I think I'm right. We'll look for people who are missing a part of their soul."

"And yet they must still be trustworthy, stable, cool-headed, and all that."

"Yes."

"And aside from that, you named six traits. I asked for five."

"A deficiency isn't a trait. It's something that needs to be filled. You can't count that."

"Okay, I'll give you that one."

"I was thinking, Aslan, that we'll have to take into account just how far the people have already come in their lives. We need to find individuals who have come a long way. Who've had to deal with difficulties, with meager beginnings or with significant changes, who've already taken a beating, who've come out on top. People who've learned how to win."

"And we'll be doing all this without a recruiting department, without psychologists, without a list of names of former members of the military's special forces or dean's list university graduates . . ."

"Exactly. Just you and me. We're the recruiters and the psychologists and the personnel department and the veteran field operatives. That's just the point."

"God help us," Aslan sighed, pouring himself another shot of grappa.

"It can't hurt to have Him on our side. I'm kind of counting on it."

4

They had gathered at a spacious holiday cabin, its living room window offering a view through a curtain of rain of the Western Galilee mountains, steep, towering, and cleaved by deep valleys, large rock formations rising from the earth like lost islands in a thick and tangled sea of greenery.

There were eight of them — Ya'ara and Aslan, and the six women and men they had recruited over the previous four months. It was the first time everyone had met, and they were sitting in a circle in absolute silence. Ya'ara sized them up one by one before opening her mouth to speak.

"Shalom," she began. "As you all already know, my name's Ya'ara Stein. And this guy next to me here is Aslan. Amnon Aslan actually, but only his mother still calls him Amnon. Thank you for coming. You'll be assigned to your rooms later this afternoon. Meanwhile, we'll start getting to know one another a little. It may take some time. And then we'll discuss the training that lies ahead and the preparations required beforehand. As I've already informed you, the training will take place abroad. In Berlin. It's going to be cold there for sure, but then again you've been promised a long journey in the dark. The cabins here are ours for five days. Today we'll be dining on the sandwiches we've brought along with us. From tomorrow, you'll be divided into pairs and each pair will be responsible in turn for preparing a light lunch and, primarily, a sumptuous dinner. The winners get free air tickets to Europe . . . and the losers get the same."

She looked around the circle, giving each of her cadets a measured smile before continuing. "Let's begin with me telling you something about myself. And then you'll each have a turn to do the same. Any questions?"

Six pairs of eyes remained focused on her. No, there were no questions.

"About a year and a half ago, I murdered someone. While on active duty. He was a dangerous man. A piece of filth, to be exact, and I have no doubt that he deserved to die. But he still shows up in my nightmares." An icy chill seemed to blow through the room. One of the cadets took a deep breath. Other than that — absolute silence.

"But let me go back to the beginning. I was born in Russia. In a small town in Siberia. I was eight when we immigrated to Israel. I grew up in Kiryat Haim and we were immigrants and we were poor. As a young girl, I was a dreamer, and I devoured books in Hebrew and in Russian. My parents struggled to make friends with their new homeland, but I loved the Israeli sunshine and the wonderful fragrances at the end of winter, in those areas where there were still orchards. I can remember the endless noise of the trucks and cars on the road to Haifa. My mother told me stories about Siberia and our life there, and she taught me how to read and write in Russian. I soon lost my accent. I'm not proud of that. I had a brother and a sister. But my sister, Tatiana, who was two years older than me, disappeared when she was sixteen. She simply didn't return home from school one day. Her story didn't make waves. Only in the neighborhood, but not in the press. Perhaps because we were new immigrants, or maybe due to rumors that she left home of her own accord. Some twenty years have gone by and, still, no one knows — *I* don't know — what happened to her. Not a day goes by without my thinking of her."

Ya'ara paused for a moment to sip from the bottle of water on the floor next to her. There was absolute silence in the room. The light coming through the large windows was weak, pale.

"The police conducted an investigation, of course. But they came up with nothing, not a single lead. And a few months later, the case fell by the wayside. Inquiries that my parents tried to make yielded nothing. But they couldn't do much and had very few resources. I was a child and also couldn't do anything really. Other than travel the entire world in my imagination to find her. And I did, of course. I found her every time. My mother spoke about her until her dying day. She passed away without knowing what happened to her older daughter. That's my story, and my pain, and I have no intention of talking about it again. And none of you will breathe a word about my sister and her fate ever again — at least not to me."

Ya'ara looked at the group of people sitting around her, held silent and still by her words.

"My parents sent me to a boarding school in Jerusalem. I served in the army for four years and was recruited by the Mossad immediately thereafter. I spent eight years as a field operative. It suited me. Your training course will give you a good idea what that entails. Prolonged periods abroad. Lots of living on the street. Long nights spent on stakeout. Tracking people. Getting close to people. Initiating contact with them. Disappearing from your friends, your family. Making up stories and offering excuses, until they've had enough and simply forget about you. Meeting guys and watching them shy away and back off because you aren't ever there, and they don't know where you are, and they can never call you, only you them, sometimes, and they don't know who you're with and what you're up to. And you do things you didn't believe were possible at all, and realize that this is what you can do when *all* your capabilities and character traits come into play. And you become addicted to this feeling of excitement and sense of 'I can do anything.' Omnipotence — that's how I'd describe it. A sense of superiority, of great power.

"I had to get away from it all. I needed to be just like everyone else at least once. I took a year off to study, and then added another two years of unpaid leave. And I studied what I had always dreamed of studying — film. It was wonderful, and it was liberating. My final project is almost complete, and no, you can't see it, not now. Maybe down the road at some point, if I finish it. But only if you promise to be particularly generous and kind."

One of the young women in the circle spoke up. "You didn't say what you did in the army," she said.

"Military intelligence," Ya'ara answered curtly.

"What you told us at the start, about the murder," the young woman continued. "You said it happened a year and a half ago. Weren't you at university at the time?"

"I was summoned. I dropped everything and reported for duty. I took another break from my studies, and I'm not even going to tell you about the trouble I had with the faculty administration," she added with a smile that vanished in a flash. "When it all ended, I needed some space and time to myself. I traveled in South America and then the U.S. for a few months. My boyfriend left me. We were going to get married, but I couldn't promise him that I wouldn't ever disappear again.

"My disappearances were a part of me, not just a part of my job. You don't get used to something like that. So he left," she said in a clear voice that also held a warning.

One of the cadets thought he saw a tear in her eye, but realized it might be the light playing tricks on him.

"And here we are together now, you and I — and Aslan," Ya'ara continued. "I'm looking forward to it, to what lies ahead. We'll take a ten-minute break now and afterward you'll all have a chance to introduce yourselves. Over and above the profile dossiers we have on all of you, I'm expecting you to be totally open and honest. Ann, you'll be first. And after you, Sayid."

5

They were milling around the hot water urn, making themselves Turkish coffee in paper cups. Or Taster's Choice. Milk, a sachet of sugar. The refreshments also included halva cookies.

"I didn't expect this," one of the cadets said. "I didn't think we'd be talking like this. From the heart, with such intensity. I was pretty stunned by what Ya'ara told us, that story about her sister."

"Yes, I need to rethink what I'm going to say," Ann responded. "I thought it would be something like reading out my CV — date and place of birth, school, university, hobbies — a checklist of sorts."

"I'm not sure if I'm up for this. It seems a bit too much, don't you think? Touchy-feely manipulation."

"I don't know. There's something very impressive about it."

"Everybody's going back in. You ready to go?"

The smell of wet earth enveloped them, with rain falling continually and the air turning cooler. The strong wind was blowing the raindrops onto the covered porch. Ann wrapped her arms around herself, clutching the thick, warm sweater that clung to her long and slender torso. She felt alert and happy. She had the sense that she had finally found the thing she had always been looking for. She wondered how she could express that feeling in words, voice it in a manner that everyone would understand.

"Okay, shalom, my name is Ann McFarlane." Her voice, with its rolling accent, sounded deep and low. She appeared a little embarrassed, but her shyness was accompanied by a beautiful smile. "As you can hear, I'm from England. I came to Israel about three years ago, which feels such a long time ago but also like yesterday. Everything here seems new to me, and I'm never sure if I'm doing the right thing. So please forgive me from now on. It's not that I'm clumsy or awkward or just a bit dim . . . I'm simply new here.

"I was born and raised in York, in the north of England. My mother is a stage actress, and still quite the diva today. She wasn't around much for me as a child because she was on stage in the evenings — or with her lovers. As I learned later. Or her theater group was on tour, in London and many other cities in the UK. My father is a branch manager for Barclays Bank. My relationship with him was always an easier one. He's conservative, always in a gray suit, but he has a great sense of humor. Even as a child I wasn't able to understand the connection between them. They were like two strangers in the same house. But I knew he loved her, my sweet father, and she broke his heart so many times. I'm still in touch with him, a lot less with her. It's much easier when you live overseas, I mean here," she concluded.

"I'm not Jewish," she continued after a deep breath. She felt as if she had dropped a bomb in the room but there was no reaction from the others, who simply kept their eyes on her. "I'm here because of love . . . I love . . . No. To be precise, I'm in love. Still in love. With Daniel. We've known each other for seven years now, almost eight. We met at Oxford. I was studying mathematics and the philosophy of science. Daniel was doing his PhD in history. He's a professor today at Tel Aviv University, and he's the most adorable lecturer in Israel."

"Are you married?" asked one of the young women in the circle, who couldn't restrain herself.

"We had a big English wedding. With around eighty guests, perhaps. And yes, I know, that's considered a small wedding in Israel." Ann smiled. "Shortly afterward we returned to Israel. Lucky for me, I pick up languages easily. I think my Hebrew is not too bad. I hope so. Otherwise it would have been hell. I also speak French and German. And I know Latin from university. I was in Israel just once before then, with Daniel, and it was one big party. After the wedding, we came for good, forever. And that's a completely different feeling. There's something more to that, a commitment of sorts. I suddenly feel I have a responsibility. Daniel is important to me. His family is now my family, too. And they're important to me as well. I look at you and I feel closer to you than I ever felt to my friends at Balliol College. And I don't even know you yet." Ann no longer looked embarrassed. Her cheeks had taken on a slight flush, and her beauty was suddenly breathtaking.

"I have one brother. He's two years younger than me. He also left York. He's an English literature student at Dublin University. He also followed his heart. You see, the English aren't as cold as people say they are. Love, that's what it's all about. There's a movie like that. Hugh Grant is prime minister. For those who like romantic comedies."

"Tell me, Ann, did you do anything with the mathematics? Did you ever work in the field?"

"I wasn't sure if I wanted to continue studying toward a PhD or find a job in the City, with an investment firm. To do mathematical analyses of the activity on stock exchanges around the world. I earned a living doing something completely different during my studies. I was a model. Mostly photo shoots. But in the summer, when I wasn't at university, I did shows, too. To be honest, I hated it. It was easy money, but there I was just a pretty face, legs. It was as if my brain didn't count for anything. My personality, too. And there's always going to be someone younger, prettier, thinner in the room, and you show up thousands of times only to be selected occasionally. And you're surrounded by lowlifes, too. You need to be able to handle them. I can be a bitch or a badass when I need to be. In any event, I decided I would never work in that field again." Ann smiled, as if to make light of her words.

"So here I am now, with you. I asked Ya'ara why she offered me a place on the team, and I don't know if I'm allowed to say . . ." Ya'ara looked at her and nodded. "Ya'ara said: Because you're a fanatic. You're absolute. I was very surprised by what she said. I've never seen myself as someone like that. I'm hoping the training will allow me to discover things about myself. Anyway, I wanted to tell you something, and I'm not even sure if I'm expressing it very well. This group, the things that lie ahead for us together, even the rain — they all give me a sense that I've come to a place that's me. It's strange, because I'm not from here. But I've never felt so, so at ease as I feel right now. So significant."

6

An email notification appeared on the screen of Ya'ara's iPhone. She moved away a little from the group, which was gathered once again around the refreshments table, and opened the email. A chill went down her spine. Matthias. She hadn't heard from him in four years. Another one of those connections that had vanished from her life after she left the Mossad. Connections that had slowly died off would be a more accurate term. Matthias Geller was the head of the BND's Hamburg station. Clearly aware of the inherent potential of naval personnel and businessmen in terms of reporting on events outside Germany, the country's Federal Intelligence Service operated a station in the huge port city. Matthias was a vastly experienced naval captain who was recruited by the BND at a relatively advanced age. It didn't take more than a single brief glance to know that he was a hard and seasoned man of the sea. He had captained huge merchant ships and was said to have docked at every major port in the world, associating effortlessly with hard men like him who chose to live on large oceangoing vessels and remain months on end away from home. Following an abbreviated training period, he rose very quickly through the ranks of the intelligence service. Within three years, he was already overseeing the Hamburg station. To his handful of friends he said with sober irony at the time that his rapid — meteoric, some would say — rise through the ranks had also heralded the termination of his advancement within the organization. He wasn't going anywhere from there. He knew that the Hamburg post would be his final position in the BND. As head of the service's naval station, he was in the position that suited him best. He couldn't picture himself sitting behind a desk at BND headquarters, or at any other station either, any station that didn't specialize in the sea. He loved the ships, the smell that permeated the ports, the people whose lives were tied to the ocean highways. That rumble, deep and powerful, emanating from the belly of a ship as it sets sail from the harbor. The odor of fuel and machine oil, mixing with the smell of sea salt. The screeching of seagulls, the wake of foam trailing behind the ship. The smell of wet seaweed.

When Ya'ara first met him, he was already forty-five years old. The Mossad wanted to get to a Russian submarine that was lost in the Baltic Sea, to retrieve secret equipment that had also been supplied to one of the Arab states. Matthias was the German intelligence service's representative in the operation. And with Matthias's help, Ya'ara and her team reached the site on board a large ship captained by one of his agents.

Eight or nine years had gone by since, and they had run into each other now and then during that time. On one occasion, they were again together on the deck of a large ship, waiting as always for the signal to set their operation in motion. The call came in on the satellite phone in the middle of the night. Matthias passed the handset to Ya'ara, who was standing next to him. He saw the blood drain from her face and heard her say, in English, a cold formality in her voice, "Thank you for letting me know. No, I can't be there right away. We're in the midst of negotiations. Ask them to wait for me." She turned to Matthias, buried her head in his chest, and he felt her entire body shake as she sobbed. He stroked her head. They stood like that for several long minutes, the ship cruising slowly in a circular pattern, maintaining its position in the waiting area, the crashing of the sea against the hull rising like a distant echo to the bridge high above. Her tremors finally subsided, and Ya'ara pulled away from him. She wiped away her tears on the sleeve of her sweater, and the apologetic smile she then offered tore his heart. "My mother's dead," she said. "I didn't know it would hurt this much."

He held her hand, which suddenly went limp, and they stood like that without a word. "I'm ruining your sweater," she said a few minutes later, rubbing the tear stains with her hand. He poured her some cognac from the metal hip flask he always carried in his pocket, and there, in silence, facing the purple sea, the sky above dotted with large stars, they stood motionless. Only when it was all over, with the white helicopter approaching the deck with a deafening sound, did they raise a silent toast to the memory of Ya'ara's mother. Only then did she let go of Matthias's hand, move toward the helicopter that was hovering about a meter above the deck, throw her bag through its open door, and grab hold of the hand of a crew member, who pulled her inside. As the helicopter rose and turned sharply to the west, she noticed that Matthias had his eyes fixed on her, his long, light hair disheveled.

They met several more times over the years, unexpectedly becoming friends. Matthias appreciated her operational mind-set, her grit and courage, but it was the wild and dangerous side he saw in her that brought them closer. Her tenacious ferocity was the thing that drew him to her. Since that single occasion, he had never seen her break down like that again, but he knew that the potential to do so existed inside her, that there was an element of softness under the tempered steel. He thought sometimes that she reminded him of something in himself, something that had existed once but was now gone. Matthias and Ya'ara were in direct breach of procedures when they exchanged phone numbers and email addresses and remained in touch now and then. And when they met up, they were like two open and honest individuals whose profound affinity failed to have any bearing on their daily lives. Matthias viewed Ya'ara as a younger sister, and he wasn't quite sure how she saw him. Still, their connection had faded in recent years. Ya'ara was focused on her film studies, and Matthias felt too old, a part of a different era. And now, out of the blue, his email lit up on her screen. She could picture him as she read his words. His light-colored hair a mess. His face tanned and lined. A man who had spent many a day under the strong sun. Dressed as always in the same thick black sweater.

The email was almost laconic. "Dear Ya'ara," it said. "Forgive me for disappearing. I need to see you as soon as possible. Uncle Matthias is about to get married and he needs your blessing. Let me know where and when. Does tomorrow work?"

Uncle Matthias is about to get married. *That's what it sounds like when a German tries to be funny,* Ya'ara thought. He doesn't need my blessing, he needs help. Urgently. Otherwise he wouldn't have suggested tomorrow.

"Dearest Uncle, I've missed you. Of course we can meet. How does the Dan Carmel Hotel sound? Let me know when you'll be arriving. Your fiancée knows by now that you're not easy, right? You can't let her be shocked and surprised. Warm hug. See you."

Ya'ara had no idea what kind of help Matthias needed. Had he gotten himself into trouble, and how? She decided not to think about it. Their now-tenuous connection wasn't going to allow her to make a wise guess. Anyway, she'd know soon enough. Matthias, she assumed, would be in Israel within twenty-four hours.

7

When he rose from his seat, the others saw a short, thin, young-looking man. He had a handsome and gentle face, with light eyes. He smiled and his smile wasn't directed at anyone in particular. "My name is Sayid. Sayid Cohen-Tsedek," he said. "I was born in Algeria, in the city of Algiers. My mother died when I was a child. My two older sisters married and immigrated to Canada. They're both still living in a suburb of Montreal. After my sisters had left, my father, may he rest in peace, contracted that awful disease and died within less than three months. I was left alone. I was one of the last Jews in the city. All the others were old. I didn't want to stay there and I didn't want to join my sisters. They're my beloved sisters, but I knew there was nothing for me in Montreal, where I'd always be the little brother, always under their wing. I gathered all my papers and certificates. I asked the university for a certified English and French translation of my curriculum and grade records. I handed the keys of the house to the elderly synagogue caretaker. Perhaps he'd be able to sell it once I was gone. I went to the Jewish cemetery and said goodbye to my parents. And afterward, carrying two suitcases, I boarded a ship bound for Marseilles. From there I continued to Paris by train, took a room in a small hotel in the Seventh Arrondissement, and then reported to the Israeli Consulate. A week and a half later, I landed at Ben-Gurion Airport. I wanted to kiss the ground of the Land of Israel, but there was only a jet bridge displaying advertisements for a bank that led from the airplane to the terminal. I was a young man, just twenty-two. It was the year 2000. That's a good year to begin a new life."

Sayid stopped for a moment and looked at the faces of the other cadets. They appeared to be a single tight-knit entity, and he didn't know if he'd find his place among them. He hoped he would. His Israeli experience thus far had been a complex one. He loved the country and inhaled its sacred air deep into his lungs. But his gentleness had been shattered time and again by the aggressiveness of his surroundings. As a child, he had learned a little Hebrew from his father, but it wasn't enough. So he studied his heart out at the language school and his Hebrew was now fluent, and often elegant. But he hadn't managed to shake his accent and was often mistaken for an Arab.

"People think I'm an Arab," he continued. "Because of my accent. Because of my name. And perhaps because of my appearance. And it's true. I am an Arab. An Arabic Jew. And an Israeli. I'd like to explain myself. A Jew who comes from France has no qualms when it comes to saying he's French. And the same goes for a Jew who has immigrated from Russia or the United States. But Jews who have immigrated from Arab countries are afraid to identify with the countries from which they came. They may say they're Egyptians or Iraqis; but when people in Israel say that, they're talking about ethnicity, not a country. And they certainly won't say they're Arabs. Because the Arabs are our enemy, and because Arab culture in Israel is looked down upon. But I feel Arab . . . Arab as well as Jewish. Arabic is my mother tongue. It's the language I spoke to my parents, the language in which I think, and my culture is Arabic, too. Arabic and French. So I am an Arab. But I was born a Jew, and I want to be a Jew, and I could read from the Torah already by the age of four. In Algeria, I went with my father to synagogue every Friday and every Saturday, until there were simply so few Jews left that it shut down. Now, I've been an Israeli for fourteen years.

"I studied economics at Constantine University. What was supposed to be a shortened military service turned into a four-year stint in uniform. I enrolled afterward in various supplementary courses to complete my BA, and then went on to obtain my master's in economics. You can just imagine how difficult it is to get credit for courses you studied at an Algerian university. Having my bachelor's degree recognized was out of the question, of course. Over the past six years, I worked for First International Bank's Research Department, and God only knows how and why I quit a steady and stable job in favor of Ya'ara's madness.

"Frankly, I told Ya'ara that if my parents were still alive, I wouldn't have joined, because I wouldn't have been able to explain myself to them. I wouldn't have been able to justify my choice. But as things are, on my own, I am willing to dive headfirst into an empty pool. Besides," he added with a smile, "I was told I could meet nice girls here."

"Honey, you really have come to the wrong place for that," one of the young women in the circle responded. "Serious, intelligent — yes, for sure. But nice?! Us? You shouldn't count on that."

"What's your name? Nufar, right? I'm sorry. I was kidding. Although you're surely not as fearsome as you'd like to make out."

Nufar gave him a stern look, but Sayid noticed the smile she was trying to suppress.

8

"I'm Nufar Ben-Bassat, from Ramat Hasharon. Everyone's clearly laying their cards on the table, so here are mine: My father was a contractor, the owner of a large construction company, Ben-Bassat and Brothers, you may have heard of it, although there weren't any brothers, my father was an only child. He built primarily in Petah Tikva, Kfar Saba, Kfar Yona. These days he spends his time in Hadarim Prison, serving a three-year sentence for tax offenses. He always worked long days, but one day he came home early and told us — me, my mother, and my sister — that he had messed up. His face was gray, and his voice, which was always rich and full of life, was dead. His voice was the thing that made me realize that everything wasn't going to be just fine. You see, I had always looked up to him, ever since I was a young girl. My friends used to say he looked like he just stepped out of a television commercial. He always drove a big car, an American car. Back then, when it happened, he owned a black Cadillac, which my mother hated and refused to travel in. But he was proud of his projects. When we were kids, he used to take us on weekends to his construction sites, to show us what he was building, and how the work was progressing. He was proud of his company's reputation. 'We set a standard for others,' he'd say.

"My mother's a judge. Still is today, on the bench of the Herzliya Magistrate's Court. We looked like the model family. Well-established. Educated and wealthy parents who had acquired status in the world. And as for me, I did as they expected of me, I studied what they thought I should study, and I completed my economics degree at Tel Aviv University with distinction. I was on a summer break from my studies toward an MBA at INSEAD at the time. I felt I was on top of the world, studying in the best business school in Europe. And my sister, Tamar, was a recently released air force officer, just two months away from her big trip to the Far East. Our mother had been on duty that day at the court for remand hearings. She always returned home a little frazzled from days like that, and our father came through the door like a dead man, a walking dead man. He asked us to come and sit down with him in the living room; my sister offered him a glass of water and he just waved it off. I don't really know why I'm telling you all of this, in such detail, but if everyone shares in . . . So anyway, my father, the squeaky clean and straight-as-an-arrow contractor, Ben-Bassat, told us he was in trouble. Really serious trouble. Certain factors had left the company facing a crisis, and the accountants did indeed warn him, but it wasn't their company, damn it, it was his company, he explained. He had to come to its rescue. The investigators, he told us, had shown up at the company's offices with a warrant that same day, in the early hours of the morning, and had seized computers and papers. His lawyer had already put him in touch with a firm that specialized in white-collar crimes. He couldn't look my mother in the eye, and she just sat there holding his hand, with her own eyes fixed on some imaginary point in the distance. Two people incapable of looking at each other. Her face was pale, as if she, too, had joined the world of the walking dead.

"As for me, I ran away. I went back to France. I mumbled something about suspending my studies, about putting them on hold until everything had blown over, but my father said I had to continue, that it was a once-in-a-lifetime opportunity, and besides, the process would be a long one and he had the best lawyers working for him. He allowed me to go back to INSEAD, ordered me even, but the truth is I ran away. I couldn't deal with his fall from grace, with my mother's shame.

"The whole thing dragged on for two years — the investigation, the trial, the conviction. The rejected appeal. I had to beg for financial aid because his assets were frozen. The good life had come to an end, and I worked while I was studying. I returned to Israel before the entire process was over. The day he went to jail, he wanted me alone to escort him. Tamar was back in the East, on another trip, I knew it would have been too much for her, and my mother went to work that morning, as if it was just another regular day, her face pale and her hair tied back. Like she was the one going to jail and not him. She barely said goodbye to him. I accompanied him. They only allow you in up to a certain point in the jail, and my father went on alone from there. It's like in the movies, the sound of the steel door clanging shut and the bolt sliding into place to lock it. I sat in my car and cried. I sat there, in the prison parking lot, crying for two hours — until the shift changed and there were too many people watching for me to stay. I haven't shed a tear since."

Sayid was surprised how much he wanted to reach out for Nufar's hand, to console her. He wondered how she'd react if he did — probably not well. So he remained still, in the silent circle.

"I live alone these days in Tel Aviv. My computer games and I. I have the soul of a geek. I've always been good with computers, and I became a PlayStation addict from the moment the very first model was launched. I don't think I've kicked the habit just yet and I hope it doesn't show. That's what I did in the army, too — messed with computers. Or as the news would say, I 'participated in cyberattacks on the information infrastructure of Israel's adversaries.' " She smiled, and Ya'ara noticed it was a tight smile, almost a grimace.

Nufar continued, "There wasn't a term for it back then. After I left the military, I went to work for an investment firm by the name of IIG, or rather I worked there up until two weeks ago. It's a small firm with large portfolios — they only handle investments upward of one million dollars. I was responsible for keeping people like me out of their computers. Our offices . . . their offices are located in a Bauhaus building on Ahad Ha'am Street. I felt like I was suffocating there.

"My father is due to be released from prison in nine months, assuming he's granted parole after serving two-thirds of his sentence. I visit him every week. Every Wednesday. Stepping into the prison after spending a day at a plush and discreet office in the heart of Tel Aviv is like entering another world, a completely opposite one."

"You haven't told us anything about your personal life," someone said in a quiet voice.

"My personal life, right. A psychological cliché to the point of embarrassment. I had an affair for two years with someone twenty years older than me. He paints and also teaches painting. And he's even pretty good at it. If you've visited a museum in recent years, you've probably come across one of his works, but his name isn't important right now. We split up two months ago. It was a real love story, but it had to end. He wanted us to be just us, to forget the rest of the world. He used to say he didn't need anything but me. It sounds romantic, and I got swept along for a while, but I soon realized that my overriding emotion about our relationship was fear. And it wasn't just his possessiveness that scared me. I was afraid of surrendering to it, of remaining in that same state of togetherness with him forever, in this seemingly wonderful world he'd created for me, which was actually miserable and closed and destructive."

"But what brought you *here*?" murmured the young woman across from her in the circle.

Ya'ara didn't know whether Nufar had heard the question, but she appeared to shrug it off, and her voice was steady when she said: "I needed to restore meaning to my life. I felt like everything had faded into nothing. My family — the one I had or perhaps didn't have — had come apart at the seams, my job had lost all its appeal, and my relationship was going nowhere."

Nufar's eyes dropped to the floor and her voice went soft. "I hope I'll be good at what we'll be doing, and I hope I can be a good team member. I've been on my own for too long — even when I was in a relationship. I want to be a part of this unit. I want to be a part of something that doesn't have a profit-and-loss line at the end. And I want, finally, to win."

Ya'ara hid a smile as she watched heads

around the circle nod in unconscious agreement.

9

Ya'ara's heart skipped a beat as she spotted the weather-beaten figure of Matthias at the far end of the hotel lobby. She walked toward him, and he saw her, too, that same familiar smile spreading across his face. She thought for a second about shaking his hand, but they quickly found themselves wrapped in a warm embrace, Ya'ara momentarily enveloped by his large frame.

"Matthias, it's been so long."

"And you, even more beautiful — if that's at all possible."

Matthias noted to himself that Ya'ara looked thinner than she had the last time he saw her, a wrinkle of concern now distinctly visible between her eyes. Yes, she had become a serious and grown-up woman. The young girl who once was seemed to have stepped aside.

He wondered if the change had been good for her, if the altered expression on her face was evidence of accumulated experience or something else. Without doubt, however, her beauty had turned more profound — and now possessed shades of determination. The same pearl necklace glistened around her neck, and only a single strand of rebellious hair somewhat softened the cool veneer she displayed to the world. But not to him.

He wondered, for a moment, if the strand of hair was also the product of a calculated act, but quickly dismissed the notion. She was Ya'ara Stein; he knew her. He knew how she worked — and why. He had seen her break and bounce back, bounce back quicker than anyone else he knew, as if she were made of particularly durable material. But he sensed she was happy to see him, and he knew for sure that the emotion was mutual and sincere.

"Let's get out of here," she said. "We'll go to a pub, by the port. You'll feel at home there." She winked at him as if to say that an old sea dog like him could only feel at home close to the waves. And actually, there might have been some truth in that.

Ya'ara was in the habit of leaving her motorcycle at home on rainy days. Matthias had been on the back of the bike with her before, on the streets of Berlin and in Tel

Aviv. He felt relieved when he saw they were walking toward a four-wheeled vehicle, and he offered a silent prayer of gratitude to the goddess of transportation who kept Ya'ara from riding a motorcycle in the wet. She might have grown up after all.

"So you're in trouble, huh, Matthias?" Ya'ara said as she started the car and watched him settle into the seat next to her. He had finally dropped the fixed expression on his face that said everything was just fine, and she could see how concerned he really was.

"Yes, big trouble," he responded plainly. "I need your help."

The pub was dimly lit — *just as such places are supposed to be,* thought Ya'ara, who was actually somewhat familiar with the specific establishment. And at that twilight hour, it was empty, too. Two glasses of Leffe, a half liter each, stood on the counter in front of them. It could have been a movie set.

"Before we begin," she said, "you should know that I'm no longer working for the company." The "company" was the customary term for the Mossad, BND, CIA, and basically every intelligence organization out there. "I've been sort of freelancing of late, and my capabilities are very limited. There you have it" — she gestured at herself — "what you see is what you get."

"And that's a great deal," Matthias responded. "In some ways, it may be better like this. I'm going to tell you a story, and I want you to tell me what you think. Be tough on me. Not the softy you always are." He smiled.

"Some two years ago, I met a young woman by the name of Martina Müller. She was twenty-seven when we met. There was something refreshing about her, something cheeky and full of energy, something that attracted me. I know it sounds like a cliché, but she was different from all the other women I've met. We met by chance, at one of the bars nearby the port. She was there with a group of friends, all university students, and she stayed on after they left."

Matthias was a man who had always safeguarded his solitude. He had never married, his serious relationships with women had been few and far between, and he had always been frighteningly discreet about them. It suited his life as a man of the sea, and it also suited the clandestine life he made for himself thereafter. And truth be told, it sat well with his character — withdrawn, hard, and averse to the luxuries in life. Although he spoke somewhat lightheartedly about his acquaintanceship with Martina, Ya'ara knew that the mere fact that he was sharing it with her was out of the ordinary. She gazed at him and waited for the rest.

"We struck up a relationship," he continued. "I'm no longer at an age at which I feel required to inform headquarters about every new person I meet. I don't need the pencil pushers from Pullach — sorry, they're based in Berlin now — meddling in my personal life. You know I'm not one to enter into a committed relationship lightly; but despite her age, Martina proved to be charming and mature, and the connection between us soon turned serious. She even shared my love for the sea, although she always said she preferred the forest. Martina was working — or rather is working — toward her PhD in political science. She was researching the radical left of the 1960s and '70s. She had delved very deeply into the subject and her life was her doctoral thesis. She herself was born after all that madness had died down, and she would often ask me to tell her about the period. About what things were really like. I told her that I was far removed from all that was happening at the time. I was a high school student in a small town on the shores of the

Baltic Sea, and I joined the naval academy as soon as I could. After graduation, I lived mostly aboard ships. But she loved to sit with me in front of the big fireplace, cuddled up together on the sofa, and drink cognac or schnapps and tell me about the things she had come across in the archives and ask me questions. I was enchanted by her enthusiasm, even if the subject matter was of no particular interest to me. Yes, we moved in together four months into our relationship. She moved some clothes and a lot of books into my house. And her black laptop too, of course."

"And you still haven't informed headquarters about this now-serious relationship?"

"Exactly. Initially, I didn't say anything because I didn't want to, and afterward I refrained from doing so because it was already too late by then; and honestly, no one has the right to poke his or her nose into my bedroom. Martina, obviously, was unaware of the work I do. I told her I was a customs official, and she simply sighed and said: 'It's not enough for me to be in love with an old man, but he also has to be a pencil pusher. A civil servant. Oh, well, I'm a little screwed up, that's just me.' She could be so charming — even when she was teasing me. She was a serious young woman, but she was also blessed with a childlike mischievousness that made me feel young again. I was head-over-heels in love, Ya'ara. I hadn't felt like that in a very long time."

"So what happened, Matthias? Why do you keep talking in the past tense?"

Matthias gestured to the bartender to refill their glasses.

"Because it all ended out of the blue," he said. "One evening, just a month ago, we were both sitting in the library and reading, and she turned to look at me with tears in her eyes. I noticed that she wasn't wiping them away, was letting them trickle down her cheeks, and then she said: 'Matthias, I'm going, I'm leaving you.' I didn't understand what she was saying, I thought she was talking about an upcoming trip, I really didn't grasp what was happening. 'I'm leaving, Matthias. I have to, I've got no choice.' 'Why, sweetheart?' I asked. 'What's happened? We love one another, we feel good together.' And then something about her appeared to stiffen and harden, something in her posture, in the look in her eyes. Like she had sealed herself shut in an instant. 'None of that matters,' she replied. 'It counts for nothing. It means nothing.'

"Right then, Ya'ara, she seemed to be an entirely different person. She went into the bedroom and emerged again with a sports bag full of her things. I was still sitting there, feeling like some invisible force had pinned me to my armchair. She gave me a kiss here, under my eye, and walked out of the house. She doesn't have a car, she always got around by bicycle or by train. She used to say it was greener, good for the environment. But that night I saw that a car came to get her. I spotted it from the window but I was too much in shock to catch its license plate number. I went back to my armchair and sat, surrounded by my books, until morning came. I haven't seen her since."

"Did you look for her?"

"Yes, I went to the university. I asked about her. They, too, hadn't seen her over the past few days. And when I went back at a later stage to ask again, they informed me that she hadn't been there in several weeks. And then I ran her name through the office computer."

"You mean you hadn't ever run a check on her? You let her move in without ever making sure she was who she said she was?"

"You know something, Ya'ara? It simply didn't occur to me to do that. She worked her way into my heart, and I didn't want to put her or our relationship under a microscope. I wanted to shake off my natural suspiciousness and all the caution I'd been trained to exercise. And it seemed like the right thing to do, because we simply fulfilled one another, or so I thought at least. She told me that her parents were dead, and you know I come from a small family. You must understand, despite the age difference, we were well suited. I trusted her. I didn't want to contaminate our connection by running a check through the BND computers.

"But when I did, I learned that we had nothing on her. Nothing at all. She had never interested us. We didn't have a dossier on her. And truthfully? It's not surprising. There are eighty million Germans out there. How many of them have dossiers? We're not the Stasi. We're not even the security service. So I wasn't surprised to learn that she didn't appear in our records. I was simply longing for her. And that longing accompanied me day after day. All day long. It didn't disappear or diminish. I looked for her because if I could see her name on my computer screen, it would be a little like seeing her again. Like our connection hadn't been severed completely. Do you understand?"

Ya'ara nodded.

"But her name wasn't there. My computer screen remained blank. No search results. I ran a check through the security service's database, too. A good friend there allowed me to use his computer. It goes against regulations, and requires coordination and forms and approvals, but he's a friend, and we do those kinds of things sometimes. Nothing. She hadn't strayed into the sights of our friends in Cologne either. Believe me, purely out of longing I began browsing through the Interior Ministry's system. Just for a chance to see her picture from her ID card, her passport. And there I found her. She looked a little confused in her passport pictures — no makeup, like in a mug shot, coarse and hard. The pictures there show not even the hint of a smile, just a blank stare.

"I continued my search through the Interior Ministry database. I found the records relating to her parents, Angela and Rolfe. Rolfe Müller, Angela Rohl. Angela Rohl. The name Rohl sounded familiar to me. A simple web search. Angela Rohl. Turns out that Angela Rohl was the daughter of Klaus Reiner Rohl, the left-wing journalist and publisher. And Gertrude Meyer. I was familiar with the name Rohl, and I was surprised that Martina had never mentioned her grandfather. I assumed she must have had her reasons. I didn't recognize the name

Gertrude Meyer, but still it troubled me. I checked online and then through the archives of *Die Welt.* Gertrude Meyer never actually graced the headlines, but she did earn a certain degree of infamy — she was the Baader-Meinhof Gang's finance chief. When the authorities flushed out Andreas Baader and Ulrike Meinhof, they apprehended Gertrude, too. She was slapped with a six-year prison sentence and served four and a half years behind bars. According to an article I read about her marriage, she did express remorse for her actions, albeit halfheartedly, but that's no mitigation for her crimes.

"Are you getting what I'm telling you?" he snapped, "I, the head of the Hamburg station of the Federal Intelligence Service, fell head over heels in love with the granddaughter of a member of the most brutal and notorious band of terrorists in the history of the Federal Republic of West Germany."

"It doesn't mean a thing, Matthias," Ya'ara said. "Why should you care? She is her own person, she's not her grandmother. Martina is two generations away from the whole story. How could it have any significance?"

"It's like, it's like you falling in love with the grandson of George Habash's finance chief. Or your son hooking up with the daughter of whatshisname, Rabin's assassin . . ."

"Yigal Amir."

"Yes, Yigal Amir." The name of Rabin's killer sounded odd in Matthias's German accent.

"It's not the same, and even if it is, it doesn't matter. What does it matter if Martina is the granddaughter of a terrorist, or not even a terrorist, the woman who managed the finances of a terror group? It's like being an accountant. And it doesn't reflect badly on her. Or on you. Maybe she didn't tell you because she was ashamed of them."

"You know that's not true. But it's not just that. Her disappearance is troubling. My senses went to sleep somewhat when I was with her, but I'm wide awake now. And my intuition or my instincts . . . or, perhaps, some small detail I picked up on, is telling me that something is very wrong. This is not merely the bruised ego of an aging man. I smell danger."

"Matthias, isn't this the time to hang your head and humbly report the whole story to Berlin and let them figure out what's going on?"

"Theoretically, yes. In keeping with procedures, that would be the right thing to do.

That's what I'd expect from others. But you have to understand, Ya'ara, it's not something I can do. If there's nothing to it, I don't want them saying that lovesick old Matthias has started to see demons in places where demons have never been."

Ya'ara muttered something in Hebrew about blowing things out of proportion, and Matthias frowned in response. "Forget it, it's nothing," Ya'ara said. "Go on."

"And if there is anything to what I'm saying," he continued, "it would spell the end for me. I got caught up like a fool in something I should never have begun in the first place. Not only did I fall pathetically in love, but out of all the young girls in the world, I had to choose the granddaughter of a dedicated member of the most despicable group of terrorists to operate on German soil since World War II. And, worse, I have no idea what's going on, despite the fact that she was telling me the history of her family for nights on end in front of a blazing fire. Someone could easily come along and put two and two together and suspect me of cooperating with her."

Ya'ara grimaced at him. From her vantage point, she could see that he hadn't thought this through to the bottom yet. If she had gotten this as a case, it wouldn't take her long to wonder whether Matthias, stuck in a dead-end job, felt rejected by those in the inner circle and, when this beautiful young woman came along, allowed her to twist him around her little finger and make him do things he shouldn't do.

"Ya'ara," he said, "Do you think there is a chance that she's a Soviet honey pot? Do you think the SVR would mount an operation to recruit a frustrated officer from the German intelligence service . . . ?"

Ya'ara shook her head and took his hand. "Matthias, Matthias, I think you've gone way too far now. There's nothing here, other than merely a gut feeling, and other than the fact that out of all the young and beautiful women in Germany you really did unknowingly choose the one with a rather dubious family heritage. Apart from that, there's nothing to support your gut feeling. We have to get our hands on the facts. Without the facts, we're just going to make ourselves paranoid. A type of paranoia spiced with melancholy. A surefire recipe for going off the rails."

Matthias liked the fact that Ya'ara had started to speak in the plural. He knew she was on his side and already hooked, ready to help him. For the first time in weeks he knew he wasn't alone in his predicament.

"Look," she said to him, "I can be in Germany with a small team by next week. We'll find her. She hasn't disappeared off the face of the earth. And as soon as we know where she is, we'll begin looking into what she is doing. But Germany is your territory and you have to find us a lead to follow. You said you have a good friend in the security service. They can locate cellular telephones, pinpoint where computers connect to the internet, track credit cards, review the records of the border control system and airline passenger lists. Enlist his help. Ask him to run all those checks discreetly, without opening an official case file for now. Tell him you're acting on a hunch, that you don't want to stir things up without anything to support your notion. He'll help you. First things first, though, good friends help each other out. They hold back their questions for another time. And sometimes we don't ask at all."

She chose to return to the Dan Carmel via the road that ran alongside the sea rather than drive through the city's downtown area. They made their way there in silence. The road wound steeply and, looking in the rearview mirror, she could see the old buildings turning ever smaller. Twisted pine trees painted the streets a dark green, and she thought about how close they were to the place where she had grown up. Close and far away, too. When she stopped outside the hotel, she stepped out of the car to say good-bye. There was a sudden sense of awkwardness between them. The next steps were clearly going to alter their relationship. Ya'ara pulled herself together first. She smiled. "Don't worry," she said. "We'll take care of it. Everyone goes through times like this. It's your turn now. And you're not alone. When lone wolves band together, nothing can stand in their way. We're already winning, even if it doesn't look like it now." There had always been something very tenderhearted about him, but now she was seeing Matthias in a moment of helplessness for the very first time. And witnessing him like that only made her even fonder of him. *Sometimes the flaws and shortcomings are actually the things we love the most,* she thought, somewhat to her surprise, as she made her way back to her cadets.

10

"You're out of your mind," Aslan said.

"Maybe," Ya'ara responded. "But we have no alternative."

"Taking six cadets whose names we barely know and throwing them headfirst into an affair that may be connected to terrorism or Russian espionage, with the German intelligence service unknowingly providing you with the leads to follow, leads that the Germans themselves may subsequently take an interest in and then very soon be onto you . . ." Aslan sighed. "Ya'ara, creative thinking is not another word for suicide."

"Look, Aslan, this is an amazing opportunity. We're not in the charity business here. Regardless of my fondness for Matthias, you and I have already agreed to throw them into the deep end and to conduct the training overseas from day one. So this is it — the deep end."

"Yes, the deep end . . . but there's a difference between conducting the training gradually, in a structured manner, with drills, drills, and more drills, and safety margins that allow for error, and an orderly process of debriefing and drawing conclusions and learning lessons, and what you're proposing now. You're taking a group of skilled individuals — some of whom, by the way, are pretty deeply scarred — and you're asking them to fly an F-16 before they've even learned the fundamental principles of flight."

"That's not entirely accurate. We'll be there, and Matthias will be somewhere in the background, too. That's three professionals. You and I will oversee their activities, provide real-time instruction, carry out debriefings on street corners or cafés, and send them out to press ahead with their missions and tasks with the two of us right there, with them. Paradoxically, it gives us something of an advantage, too. They're so green, they truly have no clue what they're doing, so they won't be operating conventionally. If anyone's on the lookout, they may not even notice them at all, since they won't be following all the familiar patterns."

"Amateurism is never an advantage. It doesn't do the job."

"I know, but there is something to it

nevertheless. We're breaking the mold. That's why we're setting up this unit. To be different. Besides, we need to begin establishing ties with people like Matthias — outsiders — who can serve as our angels in the future. Our secret guardians. And despite what I said earlier, Matthias is a friend. Period. Let's try for a chance to do something out of friendship rather than just our own self-interest."

"The only good thing that could possibly come out of this is for this entire crazy project of ours to blow up in our faces at the very start. And then, with time off for good behavior, we may be released sooner than expected."

"Don't be so morbid. It doesn't suit you."

"I'm always up for trying new things," Aslan said, his eyes glinting with a smile. "How can I put it? I'm game for anything humanly possible." Ya'ara looked at him in surprise, but the narrowed eyes that looked back at her suggested that he could be teasing her. She relaxed.

11

"Ya'ara's news, that we're leaving for Germany this Thursday evening already, is somewhat disconcerting. Disconcerting, but exciting, too. But perhaps that's why we're all here." Batsheva Kessler cast a serious gaze over her new group of friends. She appeared confident, like someone in control of her audience. "I'm probably the responsible adult among us. You're the young and wild ones who've gathered on a mountaintop in Western Galilee on a rainy winter's day," she said, looking at them, "whereas I, in all likelihood, have come from somewhere a little different." She took a deep breath. "So let me begin with the age thing. I'm forty-four years old. And although I sometimes feel half that, there's no denying your real age when you're a grandmother," she added with a smile. The other members of the group in the circle around her looked genuinely stunned. "A grandmother?" one of the young men whispered particularly loudly. “I don’t believe it,” Nufar said. “It’s not possible.”

“I married at the age of twenty, immediately after completing my national service, and Neria, my eldest, became a father at the age of twenty-two. That’s just the way we do things.”

“How many children do you have?”

“Just three. Neria, the eldest, who served in the Seventh Armored Brigade Reconnaissance Company and is now studying history at university. Yishai, who’s coming to the end of his service as a combat engineer. Assaf, you were an officer in the Combat Engineering Corps, right? And my baby, Michal, who’s no longer a baby at all. She’s in eleventh grade now. They can all look after themselves, and besides, their father is always around. I’ll always be their mother. Nothing could ever change that. But right now, I’m allowing myself to think and also to say out loud: I deserve it. I deserve the chance to live for myself again, too, and for what I believe in. I can’t carry on being there for everyone all the time. I’ve always been a good girl. A model of stability since the age of twenty. I studied law, but also married, and fell pregnant, and took care of our apartment, and made sure I got on both with my parents and with his, and with him, too, and fell pregnant again.

"Four years at university, and with a big tummy for almost two of them. Just try to imagine that. And then an internship, and opening my own law office, and Friday night dinners, and Saturday lunches, and Passover meals for more than thirty people since the age of twenty-five, and the intensity of the work involved in insurance claims. From claims filed by Holocaust survivors through to damages claims. When it comes to claims relating to the Holocaust, things can get very complicated. Emotionally charged. I became profoundly involved in that particular area of work. I was drawn to it as one is drawn to forbidden fruit. It haunted me at night, but I pressed on. And just so you know, behind damages claims — and those relating to medical negligence in particular — lies an entire world of suffering and hardship. And the work trips abroad were always brief, hurried, with always a million things to deal with on my return, more cases and more claims and more court hearings, and getting things ready for Shabbat, and always night flights so I could land at Ben-Gurion Airport in the early hours of the morning and be home in time to get Michal ready for school, with a stolen hour at the Louvre or Steidel or MOMA, just to feel human for a moment before returning to the rat race. So I said to Ya'ara: Count me in. No matter what they say. We have a country to fight for and I have a role to play. Secret agent, of course. But if possible, with a large pair of sunglasses and a silver-plated pistol in my handbag."

Batsheva was a tall and handsome woman, but that hadn't stopped her from wearing very fashionable and beautiful high-heeled shoes. And anyone who knew anything about shoes knew, too, that they were frighteningly expensive ones. The dark red silk of her dress complemented her. She wasn't wearing a wedding ring, but the diamond earrings she had on were spectacular.

"My parents were born in Czechoslovakia," she continued, "and my Czech is excellent. At the age of sixteen, and a year later at seventeen, too, I did some work in Prague and Budapest for Nativ, the liaison organization that maintained contact with Jews living in the Eastern Bloc during the Cold War and encouraged immigration to Israel — under the guise of being there to visit family and tour around. I was there during the final days of the Iron Curtain. I was naïve and enthusiastic enough to do foolish things, and the honorable gentlemen at Nativ were simply insane. Taking a young girl and allowing her to carry out secret tasks, to convey instructions and relay money. They had no limits and were certainly not God-fearing individuals. I, by the way, was and still am." She smiled again, clearly aware of the impression her words were making.

"I'd like to confess to something," she continued in a soft voice. "Outwardly, I may appear to be someone who treads a fine line, the religious woman who's constantly seeking her limits. Perhaps it suits me to have people see me in that way, but I know there are still barriers that I haven't dared to cross. Those barriers are important, I respect them and they mean a lot to me. My way of life is a part of me; my faith, and please excuse the dramatics, is a guiding light in my life. The value system according to which I was raised and have raised my own children is not something I wish to challenge — on the contrary. But now I want to do something I've never dared to do before."

She looked around the room, lingering briefly on Sayid.

"I believe that my faith needs to be expressed not only in the form of leading a religious life. I need to do something real for the sake of our existence here. My husband and children have served in the army, and still do so. Religious women can't serve in combat roles in the army. But here, I can. And it feels right for me." She paused, and her eyes clouded over with sadness. "I'm sorry, I'm usually a lot clearer and more eloquent." She shook her head, as if she was shaking off drops of water. "Anyway, we're about to get going, and that's the main thing. I'm happy to be here, with you, and I'll keep you all in line. Like I said, it's my job to be the responsible adult."

She straightened her dress and the gleam returned to her beautiful eyes. "I'm done," Batsheva said.

12

Ya'ara stood outside, listening to the ebb and flow of the world around her. The sky was a purplish shade of blue, solitary raindrops still fell from the leaves of the plants, and rivulets of rainwater trickled across the ground, their soft murmurings clearly audible from every direction. The concrete path shone with moisture, and she was enveloped by the intoxicating odor of earth and water and rain-washed vegetation. Her thoughts carried her back to the field operatives course she had undergone years ago at the Mossad. She remembered how excited and amazed she had felt to know that she was in, that she belonged. She knew her cadets were feeling the same right now. Two of them had gone to the nearby village to purchase groceries for dinner. The others had dispersed to their respective rooms. She wondered if her urgency was justified. Was she doing the right thing by insisting on getting to Berlin as soon as Thursday evening and thereby cutting short the weeks of preparation that she and Aslan had worked out so meticulously? *It'll do the cadets the world of good,* she thought. A chance for them from the very beginning to get used to the fact that things move quickly, that plans change, that they need to think on the move. Yes, but you're trying to rationalize it, she responded, conducting an internal debate with herself. If rocking the cadets' boat like this from the very outset was the right thing to do, you would have planned it that way. But that's not the real reason. The truth is you want to be in the field already. We have to act swiftly. She who hesitates is lost.

More so than anything else, she sensed the same prickling of danger that Matthias felt. Something wasn't right. Yes, it appeared on the surface to be nothing more than an affair between a middle-aged man and a younger woman, a failed romance that had come to an expected and inevitable end. But something was telling her to think otherwise. Coincidences of that nature simply don't exist. Neither the Law of Large Numbers nor any other law at all could explain how the station chief of an intelligence service and the granddaughter of a terrorist would suddenly fall in love. And even if the love affair had blossomed purely by chance and was indeed real, Ya'ara couldn't come to terms with Martina's sudden disappearance. *I want to be in Germany already,* she thought. She had kept her distance from active fieldwork for too long, and training her group of rookies was only something that simulated the real thing in the interim — even if the order had come from above. She closed her eyes and pictured the figure of Matthias, not as he was in the present but rather as she remembered him from their first encounter, when he, unlike many others, had seen and recognized her worth. *Martina's twenty-nine years old,* she thought. I'm just five years older than her. Was their love affair really so ludicrous, doomed to failure? She remembered that night when she and Matthias had almost crossed that line — from colleagues to lovers. Who backed off first? The answer wasn't all that clear all of a sudden.

"Coming in for a coffee?" She almost jumped out of her skin at the sound of the voice, but managed to maintain her composure. Aslan had crept up on her again unnoticed.

"One of these days you're going to give me a heart attack. You need to give me a heads-up when you're approaching. You can't keep doing that."

"That's just me, you know."

"You're unbearable." She calmed down. "Let's get something hot to drink, I'm freezing."

"Good idea. And the cadets meanwhile can show us what they can cook."

13

"So what do you think?"

They were driving down the steep, winding road toward Deir al-Asad, hoping to find an open mini-market or grocery store.

"About what?"

"About all of this. About the group. About how quickly things are moving. About the fact that we're going to be in another country in three days' time."

The tone of his voice was soft, almost intimate. She kept the conversation on official lines.

"I'm still thinking things over. Despite all the dramatic stories."

"It's like we've been selected based on our personal tragedies."

"Or the manner in which we overcame them."

"So you're not just a pretty face . . ."

"Assaf, or whatever your name may be, don't come on to me like that. It's offensive."

"My name's Assaf Tidhar. I apologize. It just popped out automatically. To tell you the truth, you don't look like a woman who can be won over with clichés."

"Do you mean to say some can be? Okay, I'll ask: What kind of woman do I look like?"

"What can I say? You don't want me to say it, but how can I not? You have a face that isn't easily forgotten, you're sort of elegant, a little stern-faced . . ."

"Stern-faced?! Seriously?"

"Well, a little — like those women in the movies, with their hair pulled back, glasses with thick black frames, blouses modestly buttoned to the very top . . ."

"You aren't going to keep this up, right? As I see things, you're not good-looking enough to be that stupid."

"You're right. I don't know what's got into me. I don't usually talk such nonsense. So please, tell me about yourself."

Helena remained silent for a short while. She was focused on the road, the sharp curves. She was an excellent driver.

"I'm Helena, but that you already know. Helena Stepanov. My family immigrated to Israel from Russia — which you can hear in my accent, perhaps. Although I've been here since the age of seven. We lived in St.

Petersburg before moving to Israel."

"Do you remember anything from there?"

"Of course. And I've been back to visit three, no, four times since. It's a beautiful and hard city," she sighed. "Were you born in Israel?" She glanced at him, his fair hair blowing wild in the wind. She suspected it was always like that.

"Yes. At Kibbutz Gonen. I left the country for the first time only after my military service. I did the big postarmy trip and ended up staying in South America for almost eight years. I worked as a bodyguard for businessmen in Panama, and then in Mexico, before taking over the running of one of the companies' security divisions."

"Why did you come back?"

"It's a long story. But without any drama. It just seemed to be a dead end. Too much money. Too many women. How can one live like that?"

"Do you always respond in this manner? Always resort to cynicism? But I won't bother you right now. We need to find somewhere open. Can you cook?"

"I make a wonderful mushroom soup. That's exactly what I'm going to make this evening. A mushroom soup befitting a winter's day. As long as we can find some mushrooms, of course." He looked around as if he was thinking about stopping and heading out into the woods around them to pick the wild variety. At that specific moment in time, Helena thought he seemed almost tolerable.

"Unlike you, I'm not much of a cook at all. I can make just a few things I learned from my grandmother. My mother didn't cook at all. She worked at the academy from morning till late in the evening. She hasn't changed. I was required to excel in many areas, but was spared the need to shine at cooking."

"I just hope we aren't going to be tested on our kitchen skills, on our ability to produce a three-course gourmet meal," Assaf said, cautiously adding: "You said your mother worked at the academy . . . ?"

"Not that kind of an academy. An institute. The Weizmann Institute, Assaf, the Weizmann Institute. Israelis are so ignorant sometimes. Those associations are simply insulting. My mother is a well-known scientist and I've never met her standards."

Helena refrained from looking at Assaf and focused her gaze on the road, her nose pointing straight ahead in defiance, her eyes ablaze, her lower lip aquiver. But she bit down on it and managed to conceal the subtle tremor.

■ ■ ■ ■

Assaf's mushroom soup was as wonderful as he had promised. Helena prepared a beef stroganoff from a recipe she found online. "If you're as good in the field as you are in the kitchen, we'll be just fine," Ya'ara commented. "But more important, what's for dessert?"

"You're not going to believe it. We came back with a hundred Mallomars."

"A hundred?!"

"Based on ten per person, with a few extras for anyone who may feel deprived."

"We'd better get our act together — and quickly. Otherwise it's not going to end well at all."

Batsheva tried to remember the last time she had eaten one of those chocolate-coated marshmallow treats, while Aslan leaned over to Ya'ara and whispered, "We'll meet later and have a drink. An adult dessert."

"Lucky you're here," she replied in a low voice. "It's not going to be easy."

14

London, December 1947

Yosef Raphael left his studio. He was wearing a thick sweater, and over it a long woolen coat, which he quickly buttoned up to ward off the biting and unexpected cold. His studio was equipped with a good coal heater, and he hadn't felt the chill that was lurking outdoors. His hair sparkled with marble dust, and he ran his hand over his head in a well-practiced motion, brushing it out. A shower of shimmering stone particles rained down around him, and for a brief moment he appeared to have a halo of light as he made his way along the sidewalk. He was a very handsome man, and knew it, too, comfortably accepting the perks and privileges that came his way as a result. It hadn't always been the case. He wasn't particularly aware of his good looks when he was younger, and he was certainly oblivious to the effect they had on other people, women and men alike.

As a young man at Slade, the renowned school of fine art, he couldn't understand the fuss he created, and besides, he wanted others to take an interest in him because of his sculptures, his ideas, and not his looks. Over the years, however, he became accustomed to the effect he created, which stemmed presumably from a combination of everything — his outlandish and immensely powerful works of art, his abundant charisma, his intellectual depth, and his resolute face, its features the epitome of masculine beauty. His studio had once served as a small foundry and he loved its concrete floor, the steel beams that supported the ceiling, the open expanse, and the light that shone through the high windows. The surrounding area had grown since into a bustling neighborhood, complete with a mixture of small businesses and apartment buildings — a colorful and disadvantaged neighborhood in the heart of a gray city that was still licking its wounds from a war that had left it scarred and in ruins. A train passed over the street on a bridge leading to the west. Steam rose from vents in the sidewalk, evidence of the vast and winding world of the underground rail network, of the deep and narrow tunnels, of the escalators descending into dim-lit caverns, the masses of people bunched together, moving like a single entity along the narrow platforms, waiting for the gust of air and then the lights that heralded an approaching train. *There's an entire world living down there,* Raphael thought, an almost ghostly world. The cold was turning his breath into vapor. It was two in the afternoon, but the light was pale. It would be evening soon, Christmas was approaching, but it wouldn't be one of joy and festivities this year; *victory, too, exacts a heavy price,* he thought, not just defeat.

Elhanan was already waiting for him at the pub adjacent to Camden Town Station, a large glass of Guinness on the table in front of him.

"I can't seem to stomach that stuff," Raphael said as he approached the table.

"It's instead of food, and allows me to skip lunch."

"Oh, well, the things we must do for the state in the making."

"How's the sculpturing coming along? Making progress?" Elhanan asked in an effort to show interest.

"I'm doing something different now," Raphael said, hanging his coat over the back of the chair next to him. "I'm working with white marble, and through it I'm trying to capture the traditions of Greek sculpture, classical sculpture. You see, I am indeed going back to the roots, albeit not the roots as you imagine them. It'll work well for the figure of Absalom as I picture him. The image of the rebel. Spectacular beauty, a youthful and muscular physique. No, the fundamentals of the Canaanites won't work this time. It's most definitely not going to be a Canaanite sculpture. My *Absalom* will be something different. Beautiful and menacing."

Elhanan's thoughts began to wander. "I suppose the state's going to need artists, too," he said, consoling himself, "not only fighters, construction engineers, and farmers. I'd like to come to your studio one day, to see what you're doing."

"Whenever you like." Raphael reached under his sweater to retrieve a large brown envelope. "Here, she gave this to me yesterday. She said she's doing what she's doing primarily to exact revenge on her neglectful husband. And less so for us. She doesn't particularly like Jews, she made a point of saying."

"Doesn't like Jews, yet spends the night with you when her husband is away at their country estate. Does she not know you're a Jew?"

"Of course she knows. Only she says I don't look like one. And besides, it's further retribution against her husband, he's a big anti-Semite."

She screws her husband by having a Jew screw her, Elhanan thought, reflecting on the warped nature of the human psyche but keeping the workings of his mind to himself. He had no intention of sharing his notions with Raphael. He's probably too delicate for such vulgarity. He's an artist, after all. But thanks to him, they have access to the British Foreign Office's most confidential documents, and that's the main thing. It's vital that they know what those bastards are planning, when and how they plan to withdraw from the Land of Israel, which forces will pull out and when, what they intend to leave behind for the Arabs, what they plan to do with their substantial weapons depots. *Bringing Raphael back to London was a smart move,* Elhanan thought. *He has the perfect cover, he's well connected, and he thinks right.*

"Elhanan" was second in command to "Yanai," who had set up and headed the European division of SHAI, the Haganah's intelligence and counterespionage service. Ben-Gurion himself had given the order:

We need to establish an intelligence infrastructure throughout the world that in due course will become part of the intelligence service of the State of Israel, after the state is established. "You must gather information," the old man said in his booming voice during the secret meeting at SHAI headquarters. "You have to acquire arms and get them to Israel, you need to construct a network of discreet connections for the sake of the Zionist cause!" Ben-Gurion slammed his hand down on the table. "War has many faces," he continued, his large head tilted forward, "and you will dig your trenches in the Arab states, in the soil of Europe, and in India and China, too, if necessary!" *India and China, yeah, right,* thought Elhanan, who was sitting behind Isser Harel, ready to carry out any order his commander might choose to whisper in his ear. India and China. There Ben-Gurion goes again, getting all carried away. "I'll be expecting your first reports within three months," he said, before collecting his papers and exiting the room in haste, his aide, a young Shimon Peres, following quickly in his wake.

Ben-Gurion didn't simply bark out orders, he had every intention of seeing them carried out, too. And indeed, within less than a month, he, Yanai, and three additional SHAI agents boarded a boat from Haifa to Brindisi, from where they went on to Paris by train. He knew that a small group from the intelligence service's Arab division was making its way at the same time to Beirut, via Europe, but he wasn't up to speed with all the details. Compartmentalization was a principle they adhered to very strictly. And now he was here with Raphael, just one soldier in an increasingly broad network throughout Europe.

Night had fallen by the time Raphael returned to his studio. A strong odor of smoke blended with the icy dampness that encapsulated his meager possessions, like an invisible cloak. After making sure that the bolt on the iron door was firmly in place, he walked over to a large block of wood standing in the corner of the room. He picked up a long, thin nail and inserted it into a small hole in the wood. The block split into two, revealing a hidden cache. Raphael reached into the inside pocket of his coat to retrieve the thick package wrapped in paper that Elhanan had given him. It contained fifteen hundred pounds sterling, a huge sum. His job was to deliver the package at the beginning of the following week to an Irish contact in Liverpool, as part of a deal to purchase submachine guns and ammunition that Elhanan had orchestrated from afar. He was looking forward to the trip. He was hoping to meet in nearby Leeds with Henry Moore, who was already at the height of his powers and fame as a sculptor, and had even staged a large retrospective exhibition at the Museum of Modern Art in New York the year before. Knowing he'd have to make a trip to northern England in the days to come, Raphael had already sent a letter to Moore in which he mentioned a talk given by the renowned artist that he had attended as a student at Slade. The lecture had left Raphael profoundly shaken, and he still remembered it well, some fifteen years later. The manner in which Moore had described his perception of space, the way in which he had spoken about getting a true sense of the material his hands were shaping, had touched his heart.

Raphael walked over to the shrouded object in the middle of the studio. He removed its protective cloth covering and looked at the figure of the young man that had started to emerge from the stone. The figure was his height, five foot ten, and was slowly taking shape from within a spectacular block of white marble. Yosef Raphael was as familiar with the piece of stone as he was with his own body, and the near-complete sculpture was more precious to him than anything he had ever done before. He knew that elsewhere he would never have had the substantial amount of time he needed to shape the sculpture he had dreamed of. Certainly not in the Land of Israel, where his current work might have been condemned as anachronistic. Out of context in terms of place and time. But he was like a man in love. The stone, his marble, boasted semitranslucent particles that shimmered in the light. It was perfect. The torso he had already sculpted was long, thin, and muscular. The unmistakable body of a young man, but with something delicate and heartwarming about his posture. His face, too, was a thing of divine beauty, almost feminine, apart from the large and straight nose, which added a sense of determination and decisiveness to his features. Long curls adorned his face and fell to his shoulders, their softness clearly evident in the white marble. His feet were bare, the muscles in his right calf flexed and prominent. A combination of impending movement and the self-confidence of a body at ease. Was the young man's ultimate fate evident in the sculpture? His terrible end? Yosef Raphael wasn't sure. He looked at the serene beauty of the sculpted young man. He knew that everything was already there, in the marble. *Absalom, Absalom.*

15

They made their way to Berlin in a variety of ways. Two on an Air Berlin flight direct to Tegel Airport. One on a flight to Frankfurt, and from there by train. And another one along the same route the following morning. Two traveled by train from Prague. One arrived via Amsterdam. And one via Brussels. Eight Israelis out of thousands who entered Europe that same day.

Ya'ara and Aslan had come to a decision beforehand concerning the main premise of their cover stories. It was the exact opposite of what they had learned and put into practice in the past. They, and the small unit they were setting up, would operate under the cover of genuine identities. It had been done before, but this time it was their only alternative: With the means at their disposal, and up against a world of increasingly sophisticated security measures, they wouldn't be able to construct watertight fictional identities. Their respective cover stories would be their real stories. They'd have real biographies, they'd have real parents and brothers and friends, their pictures would appear in school yearbooks, on university student rolls, they'd have Facebook accounts and they'd create a presence on Google. But from now on, they'd have to live perforated lives, real lives with self-made holes into which they'd be able to disappear. There'd be no rigid adherence to a fixed daily agenda, a tight framework. Their occupations would allow them to travel far and wide, to be mobile. And they would try in the midst of it all to live as far under the radar as possible. To attract as little attention as possible. To leave behind as few records as possible, within the boundaries of reason. The kind of life that Aslan and Ya'ara had been living all those years anyway. Ya'ara Stein's Facebook account was a smokescreen, just for show. Her presence on the web was minimal, boring even. When they came into contact with their objects, of course, the cadets would be able to be whoever they chose to be. After all, they weren't going to tell an Al Qaeda member or Iranian nuclear scientist that they were Israeli. But when coming into contact with official authorities, wherever they were asked to present state-issued documents, at border crossings, land registry offices, and bank safety deposit vaults, they would be who they truly were. They'd simply have to offer feasible explanations if instructed to do so. And never having to do so would be best, to let their actions and appearance and the context in which they'd chosen to operate be self-explanatory, without the need for words. The best cover story is the one that doesn't have to be told, Ya'ara said during the briefing to her cadets, when she instructed them to compile their background stories in Berlin.

In truth, the first few months in Berlin aren't very complicated at all. It was easy to blend in among the thousands of other young Israelis who had made the city their home. They, too, each for their own reasons, each in their own way, wanted to try and to taste, and all of them almost always went down the same road. German language studies, finding an apartment, checking out employment options. This one as a lawyer, that one as an investment consultant, another as an artist and the one who's planning to write the Israeli *Lonely Planet* on Berlin. The challenge would come when they'd have to cement their covers for an extended stay, or to support frequent visits from Israel. Not that they'd ask many questions. But if they did ask, they'd better have a good response.

Ya'ara had an idea, a glimmer of an idea, regarding how she could further solidify her team's presence in Europe, but there were still many loose ends to tie up. And most important, she needed to enlist the support of someone who had helped her before. She had learned over the years that the world was still full of people who loved Israel. People who had a sympathetic attitude — adoration and admiration sometimes — toward the State of Israel and the youths who served the country as clandestine fighters. Religion quite often was the basis for their support. Sometimes it stemmed from feelings of guilt for the wrongdoings of their parents' and grandparents' generations during World War II. In other instances, their support was motivated by an appreciation of strength, strength that those quiet and impressive Israelis epitomized. But even more frequently, it was rooted in a profound recognition of the justness of the Israeli cause, despite the occupation, despite the heavy-handedness, despite all the screw-ups along the way. Because at the heart of the matter, Israel's story, in their eyes, was a just one. For the most part, it was a combination of some or all of the motivating factors. And when this fundamental support sparked the emergence and development of a close personal bond with the Israeli handler, to a sense of intimacy and adventure, and feelings of friendship and loyalty, there wasn't a thing they weren't willing to do. Because what does this life offer us, ultimately, if not a handful of individuals to whom we're tied by delicate and rare threads of love and true friendship? That was Ya'ara's theory at least, even though those feelings were often foreign to her. Her friendships were professional, for the most part. Every deviation was ultimately rerouted back to her chosen track. And Ya'ara knew that while training the cadets and turning them into intelligence combatants, they would also have to work together to develop this critical network of covert partners, who could play their part, each in his or her own way, in the campaign they would be leading.

The infrastructure was already in place. A modest film production office, a branch of the production company she opened to serve their purpose in Israel, too. In the initial stage, the office would deal with script development, but later would go on to produce films by Israeli artists based in

Berlin, and Germany in general. The Israel-Germany story after all was a fertile ground for ideas, the shadow of the past featured so powerfully in the present. Fragments of stories were scattered throughout the large expanse of the country, highly talented individuals craved expression, the second and third generations were standing in line, the conflicting identities, the attraction and the shame, the tranquil ground was still trembling under their feet. The office would serve as a location for meetings and preparations, and it would function as their base until they moved on, elsewhere, with a different cover story.

16

Berlin, December 2014

They met at Café Einstein on Unter den Linden. The wide thoroughfare was already filled with decorations ahead of the approaching Christmas holiday. The thousands of tiny lights flickered to life on the bare trees, people hurried along the sidewalk, their heads tucked into their coats in an effort to find relief from the bitter, biting cold. Hanging in the air was a hint of the smell of hot wine, spiced with cloves and cinnamon, and Ya'ara remembered just how much she loved that time of the year in Europe, the cold and colorful weeks of December. She was shocked to see how tired Matthias looked when she spotted him. His hunched figure seemed to stand out in direct contrast to the festive holiday mood, the large, tough man now appearing tired and vulnerable. He smiled when he caught sight of her, wrapped in her white coat, and embraced her warmly, crushing her against the coarse sweater he was wearing.

"You look wonderful," he said, sizing her up.

"And you look like someone who needs a rest. You look like a wreck, Matthias."

"Why, thank you, young lady, you've always been generous with your compliments."

"You don't want empty words from me, do you?"

"It wouldn't hurt sometimes, to hear false flattery. But you're right. I haven't heard a thing from Martina yet. Sometimes I tell myself that I'm just feeling hurt, that she got up and left without any explanation, turned her back on me as if I meant nothing to her. An aging man with a bruised ego. But then in creeps this sense that something sinister is going on, and I can't seem to figure it out."

"Are you sleeping?" Ya'ara asked with genuine concern. "It looks like you haven't slept a wink since our meeting in Haifa."

"I'm sleeping too little. Time is moving too slowly. Perhaps the holiday season will give me a chance to relax a little, to put things into perspective."

"Where are you for Christmas?"

"I may go to Alexandra. She suspects

there's something up with me; I wasn't my usual self when we last spoke on the phone. I blamed it on stress at work, but she said, 'I've known you since you were born, Matthias, you can tell tales to others, but not to me.' "

Ya'ara knew that Alexandra had raised Matthias after the death of their parents, serving not only as a big sister but as a solid and stable home base. From the little he had revealed to her about himself, up until this last episode with Martina at least, she knew that Alexandra was the closest person to him in the entire world.

"You're lucky to have a sister like Alexandra. You're not a big talker, but from the stories you've told me I can tell that she's a lovely woman. Perhaps it's time we finally met, and then I can get to know you a little better, too?"

Matthias chose to ignore Ya'ara's remark. "Anyway," he said, "I spoke to my friend at the BfV, our domestic intelligence service. I gave him all the phone numbers for Martina that I'm aware of. He'll see what he can do. He'll have to violate about a hundred regulations and fifty laws along the way. He'll be in big trouble if he's caught. I told him he could blame it all on me, say that I was the one to initiate an unofficial investigation, based solely on a general hunch, and that's why I didn't want to trouble the entire system and run everything through the formal channels. But you're pretty familiar with us by now, and that's something the Germans are not willing to accept. Order must rule. And the Federal Office for the Protection of the Constitution certainly cannot track phones and print call records without cause and without due process of law."

"But he'll do it, right?"

"Yes, he'll do it. For me."

Matthias sensed that Ya'ara's attention had drifted momentarily. Her eyes had fixed on a woman walking along the sidewalk in front of the café. She was wrapped in a long, dark gray woolen coat. Her light-colored hair was uncovered. She moved off into the distance, her hand sliding over her hair, a gold earring glinting in her left ear.

"Do you know her?"

"No, no," Ya'ara responded with an element of nonchalance designed to hide the elevated pulse in her neck. "I thought for a moment that she looked familiar, but it was only my imagination playing tricks on me." That's what she must look like now, twenty years later. Like that woman. Ya'ara almost got up to follow her, even though a second look told her that the eyes were different. Not the same sparkling catlike eyes of her sister, Tatiana. She shook her head, forcing herself to focus on Matthias and return to the business of Martina, who had disappeared on him now and not twenty years ago.

She steadied her voice and asked, "Have you checked the records from border crossings?"

"Yes. Nothing. But that doesn't mean anything. She could have left Germany in a thousand different ways without ever having used a passport. She could fly to any country that's party to the Schengen Agreement, she could board a ferry to Scandinavia or the Baltic states, she could travel by car or train to Austria, the Netherlands, Belgium, Poland, anywhere, without being checked, and aside from flights on airlines that insist on seeing some kind of identification nevertheless, she could leave Germany without ever having to present an ID document at all."

"You said a car picked her up when she left."

"Yes, but I didn't catch its license plate number."

"But you saw something, right? Make? Color? The number of people inside?"

"There was only one person in the car. The driver. A young man, I think. Well, that's what he looked like from the back at least. It may have been an old Land Rover. But Toyota also makes cars like that. Very similar to the Land Rovers. Sand-colored. It looked like a military vehicle was taking her away from me. Only the color, a light brown, almost yellow, remains imprinted in my memory. It really could have been a military vehicle, were we in the desert. Our army's military vehicles are camouflaged in dark shades of brown and green. The car that came to collect Martina looked somewhat like one of those off-road vehicles you see in ads for cigarettes or alcohol from the 1970s. Know what I mean?"

"How old am I, Matthias?"

"Okay, never mind. I keep forgetting that you're such a youngster."

"Are you going back to Hamburg this evening already?"

"Yes. I need to get back to the station. I'll head to my sister in Basel only on the eve of the holiday. Lined up for me until then are more discussions on the work plan for 2015. We need to prepare a detailed proposal for the bosses in Berlin. They're killing me, those discussions. Our planning procedures are so cumbersome and bureaucratic. The world's changing all the time anyway. What's the point of making such detailed plans?"

"Are you sure you're a German, darling?"

"I'm not so sure any longer."

"I hope that your friend at the BfV comes up with something. Another option, of course, would be to stake out her office at the university and her previous apartment, from before she moved in with you. Perhaps I could make contact with her colleagues from the faculty, or with her dissertation advisor. But those would be shots in the dark, and I don't have enough people to do so. I need a sign of life from her. A single point on the radar screen."

"Ya'ara," Matthias said, staring at her in earnest, the flesh under his eyes dark and puffy, "I don't know what to say . . . Having you see me like this, so helpless, is hard for me. I don't know myself like this either, yet here we are . . . But having you here cheers me up. You don't beat around the bush. And you're optimistic. It's a little pathetic to draw courage from someone twenty years younger, but . . ."

Ya'ara was clearly embarrassed by his candor. She almost scolded him. "Matthias," she said, "the roles have been reversed before. Friends don't busy themselves with such considerations. They come when you need them. And the age difference between us is getting smaller all the time."

Matthias wanted to say that the laws of mathematics made that impossible, that the age difference between them couldn't change. But he remained silent. *Maybe there is something to what she's saying,* he thought. There's more than one way to reduce such differences.

"Call when you hear something," Ya'ara said, before standing up, kissing him on the cheek, and disappearing into the night that had fallen on the city like a dark carpet.

17

Ann and Helena entered the pub rosy cheeked from the cold. With a band of fur wrapped around her head, Ann painted a very fetching and refined picture. And when Helena took off her thin down jacket, the eyes of the other occupants of the establishment were drawn to her striking looks, too. Although each was accustomed to the effect she stirred and the attention that followed, their joint presence carried special weight. Ann was beautiful. Helena offered a different kind of beauty. She had a large, hooked nose, unyielding and aggressive. The scar appearing alongside her right eye stretched across that delicate bit of skin between the eye and her temple. Her features were bold, and her lips thicker than those commonly described as beautiful. But her skin was dark and velvety, and contrasted spectacularly with her fair hair. Some swore they had seen flecks of gold in her brown eyes.

Her scar, too, was a touching feature. Ann was certainly more beautiful, but Helena's looks conjured up images of the mythological figure for whom she was named. A woman for whom kings went to war.

They found seats at the far end of the pub. The amber shades of the drinks placed before them twinkled under the hot lights, as if to herald the approaching holiday. They chose to sit side by side, with a view from afar of the entrance.

"Always position yourselves in a manner that offers maximum control and information under the circumstances," Ya'ara had told them, and they were implementing her advice.

Ya'ara had outlined the task ahead for the entire team, telling them it was a real mission, not an exercise. "It may be nothing," she said, "and if so, we would have tried our hand at locating someone, a young woman in this instance, who simply got up and disappeared one day. But there may be something to it, and then it could get dangerous. We need to assume the worst-case scenario, and be extremely cautious. Moreover, we're a team with very little experience."

"To say the least," Sayid commented quietly.

"You're right," Aslan responded. "So we'll do things slowly. In slow motion. We'll review and analyze your proposals together, we'll take breaks whenever possible to assess the situation. Your cover stories will be close to the truth and they'll have to be well prepared, accurate, and detailed. Practice them with one another, to make sure you really know how to tell them. We've been given a rare opportunity, to practice in a real operational environment, and we intend to take advantage of it."

Ya'ara tasked Helena and Ann with making contact with Martina's university, with her professor, with a friend or a classmate, too, perhaps. "To initiate contact," she called it. Under a foreign identity of course. With the addition of a convincing explanation. She asked them to consider whether it would be best to initiate direct contact with the faculty administration, with her professor in person, or whether they should rather make contact via a third person, someone who would refer them to him. She also asked them to analyze the advantages and disadvantages of the different approaches — "the direct approach or the indirect approach," as she had put it — and she requested at least three proposals for each. "Start by defining your ultimate objective," she said.

"To locate Martina Müller," Ann said.

"To find her and figure out what she's up to, what she's planning," Helena added.

"Let me suggest something a little different," Ya'ara said, looking directly at her two cadets. "Locating Martina, learning if she poses a risk, figuring out the essence of that risk, and thwarting it. That's the ultimate objective. And the mission then stems from that: finding updated information on Martina by means of people with whom she has ties. The university is our anchor point. That's where you'll start. The task may branch out from there."

"We should have a method, a modus operandi," Ann said.

"Very true," Ya'ara said, hiding her admiration. "That falls under the category of planning principles. Quality planning is one of the most important things you will learn in the coming months. Devote more time to thinking and planning, and your actions further down the line will be more systematic and provide better results. Dedicate an hour and earn a day, something like that. But don't get me wrong. You don't need sophisticated props or an academic environment. Operational planning doesn't have to be done around a fancy conference table or on a drawing board. And you can't turn it into a never-ending saga either. You need to be efficient and purposeful. Sometimes we'll have a week to plan, sometimes just a few minutes. That shouldn't make any difference to you. You will need to run through the same thought processes, just a whole lot quicker. And you can do it in a hotel lobby, on a street corner, or while walking through a park. What matters is how the mind works, not the scenery or the surrounding conditions. We're not performing rituals. We need to be focused and purposeful in what we do."

"I don't feel like being focused or purposeful now," Ann said lazily. She stretched and stifled a yawn. "I want to drink a little, feel happy, and go to bed."

"Did you speak to Daniel today?"

"No, I didn't get a chance to, and then suddenly it was too late. We've been here for only a week but sometimes I miss him so much, like there's a hole in my heart."

Helena squeezed Ann's hand, a gentle gesture of support. "Yes, it's going to be tough, being cut off from home and the ones we love. I don't know how Assaf will last, he has two small children."

"And Batsheva? She has a daughter in

high school. No, we don't really know what lies ahead of us. And we certainly won't know where it'll stem from."

"Where what will stem from?"

"The longing."

Helena remained silent in agreement. She sipped her cocktail, which was rich in brandy and spices.

"And you, Helena, you haven't told me. Have you left someone at home?"

"Yes and no. We don't have to talk about it now. I like being here with you like this. Only the present, without the past. I don't need bad thoughts now."

Ann sought out Helena's eyes. And when their gazes met, she saw Helena smiling through her tears.

"You're sweet," Helena's lips mouthed without a sound.

18

"Ya'ara, we're onto something!" Matthias said, distinct excitement in his voice.

They had met on the crowded platform of the express train from Hamburg. Ya'ara wrapped her arms around herself. It was difficult all of a sudden for her to make physical contact with Matthias, and he simply grasped her cold hands gently, as if to warm them.

"I don't have much time," he said, "I need to be on the train back to Hamburg in fifty-three minutes."

The manner in which he informed her of his schedule made her smile. Precision was in their blood; they were raised on it from birth. Even Matthias, the hardened sea captain with the sun-etched face, was a stickler for precision.

"Then we'll sit here, in the bar."

And once again two half-liter glasses of dark amber liquid were placed on the table in front of them, but neither of them drank much this time. They had more pressing matters to attend to, and Ya'ara's tastes when it came to alcohol tended to lie elsewhere anyway.

After ensuring there was no one nearby who might be listening in, Matthias got straight to the point, without any preamble. "I got a call last night from Tomas, my friend at the BfV, and we went out this morning for a run together by the lake," he said. "He did it. He located Martina's cellphone, and another phone she could be using, too, perhaps. As you know, the BfV have their special ways and means."

"Can he triangulate them? Offer a pin-point location for Martina's phone and the second device he suspects she's using?"

"Martina's phone, the one we know for certain is hers, hardly ever moves. While the second phone, or the person using it rather, is quite active, moving from place to place. In the evenings, however, it appears to be at a location some thirty kilometers east of Bremen. A rural area. Forestland and agricultural farms. But there is a limit to what Tomas can do, to the number of queries he can submit. He isn't even doing it on his own computer. It's complicated. And dangerous. He's already done a lot more than I could have hoped for. He really is a good friend. One more thing — a number of calls were made from Martina's phone to numbers we were able to identify, but they were to a taxi station, the train ticket office, and a pizzeria in one of Bremen's suburbs."

"That's excellent! So you know the precise location of the telephone that Martina seems to be using, and that means you also know where Martina herself is."

"Not exactly. Like I said, it's the countryside. The network cells in the area are very big. The location that Tomas was able to provide isn't pinpoint accurate, but instead encompasses a number of cellular network cells. We're talking about an area of almost sixty square kilometers."

"Don't you have a way of getting a more precise location?"

"Yes, our intelligence service has the capability to do so, but that would require implementing measures that are probably beyond Tomas's means, and I don't want to submit an official request on the matter. I can't do that."

"That's what we're here for. You must have brought a map with you."

Matthias retrieved two maps from his briefcase, one of the city of Bremen and a second of the surrounding area. He moved the beer glasses aside and spread the maps out over the table. "Here," he said, using a pen to mark several streets around Bremen's central train station. "This is the area in which Martina's cellphone was activated, and this is also where the other phone we think she's using was turned on. And this is the area," he continued, marking out a relatively large expanse on the second map, "where that second phone has appeared for the past five evenings."

Ya'ara thought quietly for a few moments before commenting in a somewhat philosophical tone, "It's time for some fieldwork. There's no substitute, unfortunately, for pounding the beat."

Matthias agreed. Despite all the technological innovations, you need ultimately to get physically close to your object of interest. Wiretapping, reviewing communications, and cyber work were all existing tools. But when it came to people, you needed to be able to touch them. Matthias preferred not to calculate how many years of his life he had wasted on fruitless efforts and plays in the field. But he couldn't think of a single achievement, not even one successful operation, that hadn't involved the most basic kind of fieldwork — surveillance, tailing, the questioning of passersby and neighbors, and initiating contact with the person of interest. Work that required patience, perseverance, waiting, scandalous quantities of bad coffee, lots of alcohol in dingy bars, rubbing shoulders and coming into contact with people you wouldn't necessarily choose as your best friends, or even distant acquaintances.

"Matthias," Ya'ara said, "you have exactly four minutes to make your train. Keep seeing what you can do from Hamburg. I'll see what I can do with my team." Again she chose not to tell him she was working with rookies. They both stood up, and Matthias held out his hand to her. She took it, but they soon sank into a warm embrace, and Matthias was caught by surprise by the fragrance of daffodils she exuded.

19

The small conference room of the production company's office in Berlin was windowless. The posters hanging on the walls conveyed the desired impression — a start-up company with artistic aspirations. Ya'ara fixed those present with a thoughtful look, which turned incisive and resolute. There were some who noticed her gray eyes take on a shade of blue.

"We're going into the field in four teams," she said. "We'll be working in pairs. Groups of three or four will attract attention in that remote region. Operating as couples provides the best cover. A couple speaks for itself. No explanations needed."

"The women here outnumber the men," Nufar remarked. "One of the couples will have to be two women."

"Lo and behold, a math genius! INSEAD was worth it just for that. Education pays," Ya'ara retorted, but in a way that brought a smile to Nufar's face. "Sayid. You'll be working with me. Batsheva with Aslan. Nufar and Ann together. Assaf, you'll be with Helena, but no cooking for you this time. The objective — to try to find something, as trivial as it may seem, that could count as progress, within these sixty square kilometers. Yes, we're moving from Berlin to Bremen. As quickly as possible. Get used to it, that's how things work in the life you've chosen for yourselves. Aslan will brief you on the basic principles of the task and figure out the means of communication between us. He'll pick out a rendezvous point, if needed, in downtown Bremen. We can find additional locations when we get there, and broaden our options in the area in which we'll be operating. For each couple, Aslan will also determine at what point you'll hire a car, and from which company. Following Aslan's briefing we'll split into couples, prepare cover stories for our relationships, and come up with a reason for being in the cold countryside in the middle of the December freeze. And we'll stock up on equipment — cameras, binoculars, something extra for warmth, whatever we need. We'll meet here tomorrow at nine to go over the cover stories and basic plans. The floor is yours, Aslan."

■ ■ ■ ■

Assaf and Helena were the first to leave the production office. One of the rules was not to enter or exit the office in large groups.

"I still need to fully digest Aslan's briefing," Assaf said. "So many details."

"I'm a little freaked out by the fact that we don't know exactly what we're supposed to be looking for."

"That's the point. We won't know until we're in the field. Like Ya'ara said, sometimes the field itself shows you what you're looking for. I'm guessing she knows what she's talking about. It worked for me in the army."

"Yes. It appears that way indeed. But all that talk about legwork, pounding the beat, like we're detectives or something in a Raymond Chandler novel. You know him, right?" She looked at Assaf quizzically.

"There's more to me than meets the eye," Assaf responded, pretending momentarily to be offended before flashing a wide smile.

"That remains to be seen," Helena retorted.

"Oh, really? So you're handing out grades now, I see. Tough girl. Would you like me to give you a reading list?"

"I have no intention of trying to make an impression on you," she replied sternly, widening her steps, "and you don't need to make an impression on me. I like you, Assaf, even though it's hard to say you're doing yourself a good service. But I'm not keen on getting into a constant battle of wits and accomplishments. And I think we've already had this conversation. Let's drop the nonsense and focus on our preparations. Come, let's have a coffee, gather our thoughts, think about the task at hand, and get ourselves ready for this."

Assaf nodded without a word, rubbing his hand over the back of his exposed neck in embarrassment. He felt a sudden pang of longing for Tali, his gentle wife, and Shira and Nimrod, who gazed at their father with adoring eyes, and for a fleeting second he wondered not only about what they were doing at that very moment in Israel, but also what he was doing there, in ice-cold Berlin, while the people dearest to him were in the heart of the Sharon region, perhaps coming to terms already with his absence.

Nufar was behind the wheel of the silver Opel Insignia. Ann was sitting next to her, with a map spread out on her lap and a telephone with an open navigation app in her hand. Destination: Bremen. Nufar drove skillfully, maneuvering through the complex network of roads that led them out of Berlin and westward. Her mind was on the briefing they received from Ya'ara before they left.

"You know," she said to Ann, "there was something about the way she briefed us."

"I was thinking about that while we were talking," Ann responded. "She took us through everything one step at a time. Asked us the right questions, to make sure we know what we're about to do, or rather, that we know the boundaries within which we have to conduct ourselves. It felt more like an emotional coaching session than a briefing."

"I don't think she buys into that kind of thing. What do you call it? Chicken soup for the soul?"

"That's just the Americans. But beside the point. I have no idea what lies ahead for us. And I don't really know what we're going to do there. We've been assigned to an area, we'll carry out a sweep, and if we get lucky we'll see something. I don't even know what that something is. Nevertheless, Ya'ara instills confidence."

"We need to go over our cover story again. Are we a couple?"

"That's nobody's business," Ann replied vehemently, and Nufar burst out laughing.

"You sound very authentic! That anger at the invasion of your privacy." Nufar gave Ann an affectionate pat on the knee, her left hand gripping the steering wheel.

"It really is nobody's business," Ann said. "But under the assumption that we're going to have to be in this car together at all sorts of strange hours in the middle of nowhere, we're going to have to come up with an explanation that'll keep prying eyes and minds off our back. So yes, a romantic relationship could be the most plausible explanation."

"You're very lovely, but no offense, I'm not into that kind of thing. As a cover story, okay. But in real life, it's men only for me. Or should I say, once I get over the slight bout of nausea I was left with from the last one." Nufar put her foot on the gas and moved into the lane to her left, leaving behind the large Mercedes she passed.

"I'm the same. Men only for me, too. Daniel only, that is," Ann said softly, and Nufar glanced at her and coaxed more speed out of the car.

"I'm impressed. What does the speedometer say?" Ann's hand gripped the handle fixed above the door out of habit, but her face showed no signs of stress.

"One-seventy. Great car, this Opel."

"Slow down a little, please."

Nufar moved back into the middle lane.

"I toured around a lot while studying in France," she said, her eyes systematically checking the car's mirrors. "We studied like crazy on weekends, but traveled all through France during the holidays. Spain, too. San Sebastian. Barcelona. And even Germany, along the wine route. But I've never been in the northern part of the country."

"It's gloomy here. Everything's flat and gray. And those clouds."

Nufar drove on, in silence.

"You know," Ann said contemplatively, "all these cover stories that we've had to prepare, it's like playing in the theater, right? Whenever my mother stepped out onto the stage, she was walking into a story." The landscape flashed by at a dizzying speed, appearing blurred at the edges of their fields of vision. "I hated that," she added quietly, "the ease with which she became someone else."

Nufar was focused on the road signs that pointed out the exit to Bremen city center. "Okay," she said, "we're a couple. That's our cover story. No need to make a big deal of it."

20

East of Bremen, December 2014

Saturated with water, the fields were dark and heavy in the pale light of the murky December afternoon. Black earth, deep furrows, and rotting straw everywhere she looked, with towering leafless trees forming a dab of color on the edges of her field of vision. Several grim-looking farmhouse buildings appeared on the other side of the winding road. Tall electricity poles crossed through the fields to the right. Black rainclouds were moving rapidly toward them. *What a lovely day,* Ya'ara thought. She glanced at Sayid, who was sitting to her right, his chin on his chest, his eyes shut. Ya'ara drove sedately, her eyes scanning the vast expanses. It felt as if the sky had gathered thick above them, and they were bearing its considerable and oppressive weight. A fine rain began to fall again and Ya'ara turned on the wipers. Sayid woke suddenly from his slumber and was quick to sit up straight in his seat.

"Sorry, I fell asleep."

"It's okay. But follow the map now. Here, we're here," Ya'ara said, reaching over to point out the road they were on, her eyes still focused straight ahead. "Another three kilometers to the junction."

Despite Google Maps and its user-friendly function, Ya'ara chose to work at the same time with a regular printed version as well. It may have been out of habit, but she liked being able to mark things on the map, and for some reason it gave her a better sense of orientation. She had reiterated to her cadets that computers, after all, can always crash, and GPS units lose their signal at the most crucial moments. But she was well aware, too, of the distinct and decisive advantages of computerized, multilayered maps. *I'm probably the last generation that will use large, cumbersome ones printed on paper,* she thought to herself.

"It really is like the very end of the world here," Sayid said, his eyes scanning the vast expanse spread out in front of them. "If Martina really is here, I wonder what she's doing. What does one do in this depressing place?"

"It's a place in which to disappear, so you

can assume that's exactly what she's doing."

"Maybe she simply wanted to escape Berlin. Maybe she needed peace and quiet to be able to write her doctoral thesis. Maybe she met someone who grew up here and she's come to spend the holiday with his family, a farming family. Pig breeders."

"Maybe. You could very well be right, even when it comes to the little piglets she's now looking after, enjoying the country life. But if that's the story, then something doesn't fit. You don't just disappear without an explanation. You don't turn off your phone and switch to a nameless one. You don't cut yourself off from the world. You don't research the subject of terror in the 1970s and fall in love with a senior officer in the federal republic's intelligence service. And yet, there could still be an innocent explanation for it all. There usually is one."

"But you don't believe there is," Sayid determined.

"Maybe," Ya'ara responded, clearly unwilling to say another word on the subject. Her eyes were fixed on the road ahead.

Large chandeliers encircled by an airy white fabric hung from the lofty glass ceiling in the lobby of the Radisson Blu Hotel. A purplish light illuminated the bottom section of the bar situated in the center of the high atrium. Not far from the beer taps, two men in suits sat side by side, engaged in a lively conversation. Sitting in the corner of the lobby were several Japanese tourists, with two open silver laptops on the table and a crumpled and half-eaten club sandwich falling to pieces on a plate next to them. The entire team was assembled around two tables that had been pushed together on the gray oval carpet, on the other side of the bar.

"Has everyone settled into their hotel rooms?" Aslan asked.

They all nodded.

"Excellent. So each of us has a bed to sleep in. That's a start."

"A double bed even," Batsheva remarked. Helena looked at her, somewhat perplexed.

"We're operating under deluxe conditions. Don't get used to it," Aslan said, before following up his statement with a question that didn't require a response: "And you all have an idea by now of the layout and look of the area assigned to you, right?"

The heads all nodded again in confirmation.

"Have any of you already seen anything that seemed unusual, out of the ordinary?"

"Everything seems unusual and out of the ordinary to me," Assaf responded. "How do they live here in this winter?"

"Something concrete. Anyone?"

The room remained silent.

"Ya'ara and I have reviewed satellite images of the area. Not military grade resolution, just Google, but satisfactory nevertheless. We're going to do a sweep from house to house, farm to farm, to get a general impression. Fortunately, it's a very sparsely populated area, parts of which are swampland or under water. Aside from the clusters of isolated homes, it includes just two small villages. Two teams will start with them. The others will begin a sweep of the farms."

"At this point," Ya'ara followed on from him, "I want us to conduct the sweeps from afar. Surveillance only. You can, of course, go to a farm with some cover story, and try to get a look at what's happening there from up close. But I'd like to keep that possible COA for a later stage."

"What's COA?" Helena asked.

"Course of action. There are several possible courses of action for every task — surveillance, entry under a cover story, a telephone inquiry with a cover story, a review of databases. Ultimately, however, after weighing up the various considerations and scenarios, you need to choose one course of action that is perfectly suited to the task at hand. And that becomes your SCOA, your selected course of action. In our case, we aren't focused just yet and our manpower is limited. At this stage, too much interaction with the area and its inhabitants constitutes an unnecessary risk. We'll start with surveillance from a distance. And that, too, as you'll learn, has its drawbacks. You'll have to be ready to offer a convincing explanation for wandering through the fields or having stopped at the side of a deserted country road. You should always be able to say where you've come from, where you're heading, why you're wandering around with binoculars and cameras. A simple explanation is preferable, and it's best if your presence speaks for itself. So that whoever sees you doesn't even ask questions at all, not of himself or of you, because you'd have blended in with the familiar setting. You'll attract no special interest, and simply be swallowed up in the background. But sometimes you'll have to explain yourselves, and if you have an explanation at the ready, it'll influence the way you look, your self-confidence, what you project toward your surroundings. So don't be lazy. Don't rely solely on your ability to improvise. Have something ready in advance. You'll always have to improvise no matter what, but leave that for all those instances for which it's impossible to make plans. If something happens, you won't regret a single minute of the time you've invested in planning ahead."

"I need to ask something."

"Yes, Assaf," Ya'ara said. Their respective definitions of the word "need" clearly differed.

"Everything we're doing — the inquiries, the surveillance — is it a drill or really a genuine operation? Because at no stage have you explained how we're even connected to this German story. That's it, I think." Although he tried to make light of his words, his question clearly required a great deal of effort on his part.

"My answer is directed at you, Assaf, but at you, too," Ya'ara said, looking up and casting her eyes over the others one by one. "You won't always be filled in on everything. You won't have all the information, and the circumstances and scenarios we give you will be incomplete and partial. That's the nature of this work. You're all thinking people, but it's not your job to question the mission."

"Even if it's an illegal one?" Helena piped up.

"What's that about all of a sudden? What are you — a left-wing peace activist? A member of Yesh Gvul? Breaking the Silence? Aren't you Helena Stepanov, the distinguished and decorated military officer? Because that's what your CV says." Ya'ara spoke with a slight but distinct tone of impatience in her voice.

"I'm only asking," Helena started to say, and Ya'ara was quick to respond: "We're here for one reason, to safeguard Israel's security. Every task assigned to you is designed, indirectly or directly, to serve that purpose. That's how you were chosen. As individuals who are willing and able to operate with that purpose in mind. But maybe we were wrong. If any of you are still harboring doubts, there's the door."

The only door there led from the hotel outside, into Germany's dark and drenched grayness. Helena tried to keep her head up, while Nufar said in a loud whisper, "I don't understand what all these questions are about," and Batsheva nodded. It seemed as if no one else had anything more to say, and some of the cadets were wondering how the conversation had reached this point. Aslan had already cleared his throat to continue when Sayid's voice suddenly rang out loud and clear.

"But can't we ask and want to know the truth without necessarily having doubts?" he asked, his question sparked not only by curiosity but by a real desire to know, to understand, too.

"Not here," Ya'ara responded. "Certainly not now."

Aslan spoke at last, seeking to break the tense silence that had fallen on the room. "Let's get back to business," he said. "I've made you copies of the satellite images. I've marked all the houses I want you to cover. Each one has a number, so that we can refer to them if necessary on the phone. Go to bed early tonight. Rest well. Tomorrow's going to be a long day."

"And a cold one," Ya'ara added with a smile. "Dress appropriately." Perhaps she had come down too hard on the cadets, she thought.

"I hope my answers satisfied you," she said later to Sayid in the car.

"I understand what's expected of us," Sayid said, staring through the window at the artificial lights shining in the night. His eyes sought out the moon.

"Okay, that's enough for me. I just hope you don't snore."

"Me? No way," he replied, trying to smile.

"No offense. We're not just roommates. We're going to be together a lot from now. Feel at ease with me."

"Okay, okay," he sighed. "I'm learning. I'm learning."

21

"Awake?"

Ann's phone vibrated in conjunction with the brief tone that accompanied the incoming WhatsApp message. The question came with a smiley face emoji.

"Barely. I'm wiped out. A long day."

"Here, too. I've missed you."

Ann smiled wearily to herself. A warm and pleasant sensation spread through her chest. Her stomach contracted in shame. She wanted to ask Helena how things were going with Assaf, but chose to tread lightly. "Maybe we'll have time for a beer tomorrow," she wrote.

"Hope so."

"I'm falling asleep. Good night."

"Good night, sweetie."

22

Lincoln, New Hampshire, October 2013, One Year Earlier

It was a warm day by any standards, and Ya'ara took off the thick shirt she was wearing and made do with just the T-shirt she had on underneath. With her hands on her hips, she stood there in awe not only of the uncharacteristic weather, with the temperature approaching twenty degrees Celsius in mid-October, but also of the stretch of country in which she found herself. She couldn't and didn't want to get used to the colors, which seemed more real and primal than any others she had ever known. The sky was blue and big, the sun's rays shone golden, and the mountains appeared to be on fire. Ridge after ridge was ablaze in shades of yellow, orange, and red — the spectacular fall forests of the White Mountains in the throes of a beautiful Indian summer. Ya'ara stood there gazing at all that beauty alone and didn't miss the company of anyone.

Ya'ara had been making her way along the lengthy Appalachian Trail for the past six weeks, northward from the Deep South of the United States. It was never her intention to hike the entire trail. All she wanted was peace and quiet. A most welcome peace and quiet following the turbulent months of the beginning of the year, the breathless months of the pursuit. Because after the reprimands and her swift departure from the Mossad, Ya'ara felt there was just one thing left for her to do: She packed a backpack and flew to South America. From Chile to Peru and from Peru to Bolivia. And from there, on a series of flights, on shoddy airplanes that appeared to get smaller from one flight to the next, she made her way to Kentucky. There she purchased a dark blue used Buick and set out, on narrow roads and dirt tracks. From time to time, she parked the car and took off into the mountains for a few days on foot.

Sometimes she found someone to drive the car to the next point on the trail. But despite the random encounters, she preferred to walk alone. She was with herself. Breathing deeply. Her legs burning with effort. Her lungs filling with sharp, clean air.

After a few days of hiking, she progressed to the next point. She loved the long drives along the side roads, which offered her glimpses of what she thought was the real America. Sometimes she remained in her hotel for a full day, spoiling herself with a hot bath and idle reading, followed by dinner at the best restaurant she could find in the area. There weren't many of those around. Most were diners, which played loud country music and served huge portions of food. Women and men, many of considerable size, sat at nearby tables, drinking whole pitchers of beer or Coke in one-liter glasses. Couples held hands and appeared in love. Sometimes, when they saw she was on her own, men would approach her and try to strike up a conversation. But her cool demeanor and icy stare deterred them. Only once, one evening in North Carolina, did a group of young men hassle her in a diner parking lot and try to block her path to her vehicle. They encircled her and one of them pushed her in the shoulder. Another reached for her crotch. She was forced to break his arm and crush the eye socket of another guy who threw a punch at her face. With two screaming heroes in a heap on the asphalt, the other thugs backed off, hurling awful verbal abuse. She got into the car and drove away, her body trembling with rage.

The northern states through which the trail passed, Vermont and New Hampshire, seemed friendlier. She knew that could change in an instant, but she was surrounded by warmth and serenity, and she gave in to that warmth, wrapped herself in it.

She reached the town of Lincoln, New Hampshire, in the late afternoon. She had walked a distance of about twenty kilometers that day, along the length of a stream in full flood, its waters raging with small rapids and sharp twists and turns. She was surprised, when she looked at her map, to discover that a stream so torrid and vibrant had no name. She thought for a moment about naming it herself, a private name, but changed her mind. It's good to be in a world in which some things remain nameless. The forest around her was golden and quiet and she hiked slowly. After some three hours of walking lost in thought, she stopped for a breather. She dozed while resting up against a thick tree trunk, its bark a silver-white, surrendering to the warm sunbeams that found their way through the trees. She was awakened by a loud noise. A powerful beating of wings. She opened her eyes and saw a huge pheasant, its head a glossy shade of green, its body covered with reddish brown feathers splashed with black dots, rising from the brush and disappearing among the trees of the forest. A chill rose from the stream that flowed nearby, whirlpools of water swirling on its banks among the yellow reeds. She knew right there and then that she would never forget that pheasant and the beating of its wings that woke her. She stood up and started walking.

A gas station attendant in Lincoln recommended she eat at the Gypsy Café. She found it easily. It was hard not to spot its storefront, which was painted a deep blue and decorated with myriad other colors, too. It was dusk, and apart from a couple sitting at the bar, there were no other diners there. A motherly waitress told her that the kitchen would open in ten minutes and that she could look through the menu and relax in the meantime. Feel at home, dear, the waitress said to her. It'll be worth the short wait. Our food is wonderful.

The menu seemed awfully eclectic. Food from a wide variety of places around the world, one dish per country. An Indian dish, a Moroccan dish, a Japanese dish, a Cuban dish. And so on. The Philippines, Turkey, Mexico, Italy. *Nothing good's going to come from this,* she thought, consoling herself with the pleasant sensation in her muscles after the long hike, and with the warmth coursing through her thanks to the red wine she had ordered, a Californian Zinfandel with a ridiculous name — Black Chicken — which tasted surprisingly deep, rich, and smooth. She ordered two small dishes and was pleased to discover just how flavorful and original they turned out to be. She ate slowly and chose to surrender to the moment and savor this strange and friendly place, with its abundance of tastes and colors. She watched the shadows lengthen through the large window overlooking the street. Evening had come and night was about to fall over the White Mountains of New Hampshire. She was pouring herself another glass of wine when into the restaurant stepped an elderly woman, slender, her white hair cut short. The restaurant owner and three waitresses greeted her with applause. The woman smiled, her blue eyes shining with glee. Forty-eight, forty-eight, forty-eight, they chanted out loud before escorting her to a table not far from Ya'ara's, also overlooking the street, now cloaked in the darkness of the October night. Ya'ara looked up, silently greeting her new neighbor. The woman, for her part, responded with a joyous smile. Ya'ara noticed her hiking boots, very similar to the ones on her own feet, strong high-top Timberlands, their leather soft and supple from extensive use. The soles of Ya'ara's boots appeared almost new in comparison.

"What's the forty-eight all about?" she asked.

The elderly woman responded, and her deep voice was exactly the kind of voice that Ya'ara was expecting to hear. Her pronunciation was that of an educated woman. *She may have been a university lecturer,* Ya'ara thought to herself.

"The White Mountains have forty-eight peaks that rise above four thousand feet. For the last ten years, since my retirement, I've been climbing them, one after the other. I scaled the final peak today. A cause for celebration, I thought."

Ya'ara was genuinely impressed. "That's amazing," she said. "What a quest! I'm Ya'ara, by the way," she added, conversing with her fellow diner across two tables.

"I'm Ruth."

"Pleased to meet you. Did you climb alone today?"

"Yes. I usually hike alone. Although I do have a son, who lives in Connecticut, and he joins me sometimes. He's in good shape and likes to climb. But he couldn't make it this time."

Ya'ara felt her blood boil. What a "wonderful" son she must have if he can't even find the time to come and share her festive moment, her crowning glory after a decade of climbing. She was really angry at him, but she said to herself: What do you really know? You don't know her, and you certainly don't know him. It's got nothing to do with you anyway. Take it easy.

But she couldn't let it go. She ached for the noble and lonely woman sitting opposite her.

"I feel fortunate to have stumbled upon such a special occasion," Ya'ara said. "Will you allow me to order us something to drink?"

Ruth paused, and then nodded. "Yes. Why not?" she said. "Thank you."

"Whiskey perhaps? Or cognac?"

"Cognac sounds good. Gladly."

Ya'ara ordered a round of Courvoisier. A plump, fair-haired waitress served them the cognac, which glowed in the two large glasses in deep shades of brown and gold. She and Ruth, each at their respective tables, raised their glasses. "To the most impressive mountain climber I know," Ya'ara toasted.

"To a beautiful passerby from a foreign land," Ruth responded.

At the back of the restaurant, deep in the kitchen, the owner smiled contentedly to herself.

They spoke throughout dinner, Ya'ara trying three more small dishes with curiosity and gusto. *I'm eating like a famished tigress,* she thought, explaining herself apologetically to Ruth: "I walked for several hours today. The fresh air must have given me an appetite."

"Oh, my dear," Ruth respond with obvious fondness, a large, deep bowl of pasta on the table in front of her. "It's healthy, to burn energy, to listen to what your senses are telling you. To eat heartily."

Ruth asked, and Ya'ara told her that she was from Israel, that she was a novice filmmaker, and that she'd been traveling alone for the past six months.

Ruth said she was a retired clinical psychologist, who had studied in Boston and had then worked for many years in west Massachusetts. She didn't mention her husband. "You can guess how old I am. Older than sixteen and beyond seventy-six."

Ya'ara estimated she was approaching eighty. *I really hope,* she thought, *to be so content with myself when I'm her age.*

The glasses of cognac emptied slowly. After stepping outside, Ya'ara waved goodbye one last time to Ruth, who was sitting at the window, her figure illuminated and appearing at ease. A golden glow spilled onto the sidewalk, and fragmented, melodic sounds were still coming from inside the restaurant. The blue façade had turned black by then, but tiny lights shone on its surface. Ya'ara wrapped herself in her coat, shivering for a fraction of a second from the night chill and saying to herself, I'll be back here. She wasn't one to forget places in which she had found peace.

23

East of Bremen, December 2014

Batsheva and Aslan walked side by side down the narrow pathway that ran along the top of the earth embankment bordering the swamp. The sky was an opaque metallic gray. Reeds and grasses rose from the murky water. The farmhouses on the other side of the swamp appeared deserted.

"Do you see the trees there?" Aslan asked, gesturing in the direction of a grove of bare trees at the far end of the embankment.

Batsheva nodded.

"We'll head for them and get into position. We should have a good view of the farm from there."

"When I imagined how all of this would be, I pictured a parallel world of cocktail parties, with elegant Prada shoes and purses, not mud trails and staking out secluded farms in the freezing cold," she moaned, hoping she was doing so gracefully. But Aslan was all about business.

"Things can change from one day to the next," he said. "Sometimes you're a CEO and sometimes you're a bus driver. One day you're playing craps in a casino and the next you're an ornithologist trying to observe waterfowl in a swamp. You do what works best for the operational circumstances."

It was their third day in that dank and gloomy area and this was the seventh farm they were checking. They hadn't noticed anything out of the ordinary at the first six. At five of them they spotted children, playing. Three showed signs of agricultural activity, with trucks offloading goods and filling up with farm produce. On their way to the seventh farm they saw families returning with Christmas trees tied to the roofs of their cars. Smoke billowed from the chimneys of the homes, and Batsheva could picture blazing, stone fireplaces casting an orange glow over the large rooms.

The two hours that had just gone by felt like an eternity to her. She looked at Aslan, patiently surveying the area with the binoculars. He had made himself comfortable on the hard earth and was covered with branches, appearing to have grown out of the ground together with the trees around him. She was simply frozen and on edge.

She looked again through the notebook she was using to record Aslan's comments. There weren't many. She placed the guide to the birds of northern Germany next to her, on a stone-cold rock covered in lichen, with the book open to the page on the white-tailed eagle. The shutters of the farmhouse they were facing were closed. She could make out the chimney rising skyward from the far wall of the house, but there was no smoke. The leveled dirt yard between the farm buildings appeared desolate. A blue VW Golf and a mud-splattered all-terrain vehicle were parked near one of the buildings. A dog was barking somewhere in the distance. The rain was falling in large, fat drops. The earth around the farm was black and saturated with water, and Batsheva felt no less drenched herself.

"It's odd," Aslan whispered. "There are cars here, but no other signs of life. I can hear the dog barking, but I have no idea where its barking is coming from. I get the sense that there are people around, but where are they? And if they are here, then why are the shutters closed?"

"Give me the binoculars for a moment," Batsheva said. She scanned the area, trying to spot some movement, but the rain was clouding her field of vision.

"There's something about this place that I don't like," Aslan said.

"What was that? Did you hear that noise?"

They went silent, and for a second or two all they heard was the call of a bird.

"Be dead still for a moment."

The sounds in the distance were clearer and more distinguishable this time. Gunfire — without doubt. A rapid series of shots. Short bursts. Three rounds. Four. And then a different kind of sound. Louder. Consecutive. Ten or eleven rounds in succession. And then silence. A strong gust of wind showered them with annoying, stinging drops of rain, and also carried more sounds of gunshots, duller now, as if they were being borne on a wave, the noise rising with the peak and then dying, and suddenly rising again, clearer and louder.

Batsheva asked Aslan if he could identify the weapon types according to the sound of the shots. "Yes," he said, "the initial shots sounded like they were coming from an assault rifle, and then the consecutive shots, the louder ones, sounded like someone emptying the magazine of a pistol. But I can't be sure. You'll learn to identify things like that, too. I'm not sure where the shots were coming from. Perhaps from the other side of the embankment that borders the farm from that direction. Do you see?"

Batsheva nodded.

"As we noticed when we got here, the ground begins to fall away beyond the earth embankment, and there's another grove of trees where the fields end a few hundred meters away. The shots may have come from there, from a lower-lying area, and that's a blind spot for us right now. The topography and wind may be affecting the way we are hearing the sounds, which are sometimes dull. Dull and confusing."

"Maybe it's hunters?"

"Maybe. But going out to hunt in weather like this makes about as much sense as going out bird watching." Aslan paused to think. "And I don't think hunters shoot like that. In bursts. And they certainly don't fire handguns."

"But you can't be sure it was a handgun."

"True. I can't say for sure."

"Tell me something, are we in any kind of danger? Being here, I mean, while they're shooting?"

"It's far away. We'll remain here in hiding for a little longer. Maybe we'll get to see something." Aslan looked at his watch. "The sun won't be setting for another hour or so. We'll hang around for another forty-five minutes, and then go back to where we left the car. We don't want to get stuck here in the dark."

"I'm the cadet and you're my commander. I'm sure you'll look after both of us," Batsheva said in a tone that sought to remain calm.

"Of course, Batsheva, don't worry."

24

Bremen, December 2014

The group had assembled at a steakhouse near the port. They were seated at a large table in the restaurant's private room. Big, tasteless steaks, a tomato salad, and baked potatoes with butter and sour cream on the side.

"At least the wine is okay," Nufar said, "insofar as German wine can be good."

"There we are, the Frenchwoman has spoken," Assaf said, alluding to the prestigious university at which Nufar had studied.

"The Germans actually make some excellent wines," Ya'ara said. "But in the same way they've excluded the German painters from the history of art, the French don't have any time for good wines produced elsewhere either."

"Anyway," Batsheva commented, "it's not like we can say we're at a Michelin-starred restaurant."

"I don't believe the Maredo restaurants ever professed to be so. They haven't even come close to a Michelin star," Assaf said, playing his part in the culinary discussion.

"I'm not eating a thing here," Batsheva said. "If I'm going to sin, then I'm certainly not going to do so for a third-rate steak. I don't believe my life depends on making that kind of sacrifice. Maybe some salad." She picked up a withered leaf of lettuce with her fork.

"Okay, my gourmet friends," Ya'ara ended the conversation. "We have work to do. I want to hear the reports from the teams. Aslan, please mark every home or cluster of homes under discussion. We have to be systematic. Ann, would you like to get started?"

They had managed over the past three days to cover almost all of the homes located in the area defined by the cellular network cells that came up in the investigation carried out by Matthias's friend from the federal security service. It wasn't enough. Ya'ara knew that the fact that a specific house didn't look suspicious didn't necessarily mean that it could be discounted. First of all, they might not have gotten a good enough look. Second, something out of the ordinary that could have raised questions might have occurred at one of the locations an hour before they got there or half an hour after they left. Third, Martina might have been at a certain location, but might also have been keeping a low profile and out of sight. But you have to start somewhere, after all, and in the absence of additional intelligence, the scouting and surveillance were the best things she could think of. *And besides,* she thought, *it's excellent training for the cadets.* Fortunately, they had yet to have to deal with questioning by police. But one of the pairs, Assaf and Helena, had already encountered a most troublesome adversary, one who could soon turn into a dangerous enemy — a sharp and suspicious old woman who had latched on to them and started asking too many questions. They were forced to back off and take up a position in a less favorable surveillance spot.

Thus far, the team had managed to identify three structures that had aroused some suspicion. They had already returned to two of them, for further remote observation, but were unable to gather any additional concrete information. She was planning on checking out the third home the following day. And now there was this report from Aslan and Batsheva about a fourth house

— the secluded farm, the shuttered windows, the cars in the yard, and primarily, primarily, the sounds of gunfire.

"To me it sounded like there was someone doing shooting practice in the woods," Aslan said. "And luckily Batsheva heard something. If she hadn't, I probably would have missed it."

"It's still too early to jump to conclusions. It may have been hunters nevertheless. Or someone practicing with a weapon for which he has a license. Maybe there's something like a military academy or sport shooting club in the area, where there's an orderly firing range that we didn't see on the maps or in the satellite images. But you certainly came across something out of the ordinary that needs to be investigated further. You said there were two vehicles parked in the yard. Did you manage to get a look at the license plates?"

"No."

"You said the Golf was blue. And the jeep?"

"It was mostly dirty. But appeared to be a shade of khaki under all the mud. Right, Batsheva?"

"I'd say more of a sandy color. The vehicle was lighter than the mud covering it."

"Did you recognize the make?" Ya'ara asked.

"It may have been a Cherokee or Toyota," Batsheva responded.

"We weren't able to say for certain," Aslan clarified. "I'm not sure."

"We'll go back to that same farm tomorrow," Ya'ara said. "Sayid and I will join you. We'll figure out who'll be doing what and with whom shortly. The remaining two couples will complete their tasks as originally planned. And I'd like you, Helena and Assaf, to go and have another look at this house," she pointed out a location on the satellite image. "That's the home we've marked as number forty-seven. Okay?"

Helena and Assaf confirmed that they understood. Ya'ara wrote something in her notebook.

"Okay, Aslan, stay here with me now. We'll go to that bar at the end of the street. And make plans for tomorrow. The rest of you — home. To your hotels, in other words. To sleep. You don't even realize just how tired you are. Sayid, you can get a proper sleep now, rather than just a nap in the car or on stakeout."

Sayid hung his head. Ya'ara immediately felt a pang of contrition. You're forgetting that they're just cadets, she scolded herself.

They aren't your comrades in arms from the unit. Not yet. Taking them out into the field so soon has caused you to forgo that necessary distinction. You have to make sure, she continued with a certain degree of severity, that in your enthusiasm for the operation you don't leave your charges behind. It takes them time to get used to the cover stories, to the intimacy imposed on small teams working together, to remarks that cross the customary line and could easily offend someone. Especially a gentle soul like Sayid. You've thrown him into the deep end, so don't be surprised to see him struggling somewhat to stay afloat and swim. It's perfectly legitimate. He's coping, and that's the main thing. His gentleness has the support of his strong character from within. It's only a matter of adapting. It takes a little time. It's fine.

25

Moscow, GRU Headquarters, December 2014

All the relevant parties were assembled in the plush bureau of General Sergei Ivanov, the head of the agency's foreign operations unit. Ivanov, a former commander of a division of special forces, had moved to military intelligence just four years earlier. His daring and guile served him well in his current post, too. The military intelligence agency, the GRU, had worked for decades beyond the borders of the Soviet Union, in parallel with the KGB in its various incarnations. That was the way in which the Soviet leaders, Lenin, and Stalin thereafter, were able to divide and rule, and to ensure that no single organization gained exclusive power. And the GRU continued to operate outside the empire even after Stalin's departure, employing methods that were not typical of a military intelligence agency, and this same tradition accompanied Russia into the twenty-first century, too.

Ivanov had never really felt comfortable in his gilt-edged bureau. He had always been more at home in a rangers' tent or camouflaged foxhole. But GRU headquarters were located in a palace from the days of czars, and he was now one of the organization's senior commanders. The palace's splendor had indeed faded and crumbled over the years, but the bureaus were still immense, with gold work adorning their ceilings, and colorful timeworn carpets enhancing the brown wooden floors that shone with polish. He had learned to pretend to be one of the family. Right now, he was fully focused on the words coming from his colleague's mouth.

Colonel Denis Kovanyov, a short, thin, gray-haired and pale-faced man, was addressing the restricted forum: "I'm pleased to inform you that the forces in Ireland and Germany are almost ready for action. The Irish team will arrive in England immediately after Christmas, and then split up and operate simultaneously in London, Birmingham, and Manchester. Three pubs, three bombs. The German team will also split up, and its members will lie in wait on New Year's Eve near the homes of three senior bank officials — the CEO of Commerzbank, the CEO of DZ Bank, and the deputy CEO of Deutsche Bank. As you know, the CEO of Deutsche Bank has been under tight security ever since the incident involving the extortion attempt by the Serbian gang, and it's impossible to get to him directly, and certainly not with the forces at our disposal. That's why we're targeting his deputy. In Italy, I regret to say, we aren't making as much progress. Apparently, abducting a president these days is a lot more complicated than it was almost forty years ago. So we're working on an alternative operation, too, aimed at the director of the central bank. An abduction would be our best option, but it appears to be too complex at this stage. We'll make do with a targeted killing."

General Ivanov glanced to his right and saw the astonished face of the head of the research department. Before the current meeting, he hadn't been privy to the operation, and he had been invited to the present assembly only by virtue of a personal and adamant instruction from the GRU chief, and much to the displeasure of the head of the foreign operations unit. "He must be in on things," the GRU chief had ruled. "Europe is going to go up in flames and he has to understand why. If he doesn't get to see the overall picture, all the research under his purview will be distorted and misleading."

"But we agreed to involve as few people as possible," Ivanov argued angrily.

"Correct, and I'm adding another one. Just one," his superior officer said, thus ending the discussion.

"What are you up to?" whispered the head of the research department, General Professor Vasily Lavarov, seemingly conversing with himself only.

"Does it remind you of anything?" asked Ivanov, who heard his question.

"Yes, it does. It reminds me of the madness that gripped Europe in the 1970s."

He saw a faint smile appear on the face of Ivanov, who also raised one of his eyebrows. Lavarov switched from the second to the first person, but it did nothing to dull the intensity of the shock in his voice.

"Are we reconstructing the chaos that prevailed then? Is that what we're doing?"

The rest of the room's occupants remained silent.

"From what you've described," Lavarov continued, "it appears we're re-creating the IRA's terror attacks in Thatcher's England, the murders committed by the Baader-

Meinhof Gang in Germany, and the abductions and assassinations carried out by the Red Brigades in Italy."

"You've hit the nail on the head," Ivanov drily confirmed.

"But to what end? What's the idea behind this theater of blood?"

Ivanov explained, his voice cool and didactic. "We're at a point in time," he said, "at which we need to remind the Europeans of our ability to cause damage. They've grown accustomed to a comfortable and secure life. Yes, they can see the early manifestations of the Islamic threat, and they're adopting certain measures to counter it, as partial and as panicky as they may be. But they've forgotten about us. We've become taken for granted. Taken for granted!" Ivanov reiterated, raising his voice and slamming his palm down on the table. The water in the glass next to him shook. "Look at how they dare to respond when we show even just the first signs of realizing our most basic rights in Crimea and eastern Ukraine. They have no regard for our interests. They belittle them, and treat us as second rate at best, like a nation that may have been a superpower at some point in the past but has now become a marginal player. We can't allow things to go on like that. They need to be reminded of what could happen if we're pushed into a corner. We have no intention of setting Europe ablaze. On the contrary. We'll have the ability to contain the madness that erupts. That's the only way to show them just how crucial we are to the stability and quiet to which they are so addicted. But before then, they're going to have to wake up. To understand just how easy it would be to go back to the nightmare they experienced back then."

"But what's going to happen if they find out that we were behind all those terror attacks and assassinations and abductions?"

"I realize it's hard for you to digest what I've just said. That's the whole point. We want them to *suspect* that we're involved. That we're connected to the incidents and that we can stop them. That we're the only ones with any sway over this wave of terror that's going to sweep across Europe like a nightmare. They need to come to terms with our power to take Europe — the entire world — back to a time to which none of them wants to return. To ensure success, however, our actions have to remain in the shadows, we have to be like ghosts. So we're working with proxies, others to do our work. We have genuine Irish and German and

Italian agents. And if rumors arise to say that Russian intelligence officers could have some pull, and perhaps even put an end to it, even better. And if the rumors don't sprout unaided, our psychological warfare personnel will put things right."

"It's a crazy idea!"

General Ivanov looked at him with a cold glint in his eyes. "You have the right to express your thoughts in person to the individual who came up with the idea," Ivanov said. "You're familiar with his address. The Kremlin, Red Square, Moscow. The guards will be happy to allow you in. No need to worry."

"Surely he didn't mean the things we're doing."

"I have to say, to his credit, that he added the sting to the plan we formulated. He instructed us to also try to recruit individuals who have a personal connection to the generation of terrorists that operated back then, some forty years ago. The team in Ireland includes three men who were members of the IRA at the time. They're in their sixties today, but just as tough and dedicated. And we also recruited the sons of veterans of the Catholic Republican Army. The granddaughter of the woman who handled the financial side of Klaus Baader and Ulrike Meinhof's activities is part of the team that's operating in Germany, alongside someone who at the time was a young and devilishly talented man, and one of the group's ideologists. Today he's a sixty-seven-year-old revolutionary. In Italy, too, we've managed to recruit two women who were once members of the Red Brigades in Turin and are now involved again in underground activity. Can you see the poetic beauty in all of this? Not to mention the affection of the masses for the children of the famous. Only this time, the famous will be notorious terrorists."

Lavarov remained silent.

"That's the genius of this operation," Ivanov continued. "The more convincing we are about our ability to do damage, the less damage we will ultimately need to inflict. The sooner they get the message, the sooner we'll be able to restore order. All we have to do is present them with the alternatives — a violent, fragmented Europe in the throes of madness once again, or a world in which we are treated with respect and appreciation. A pretty simple choice, right? But in order for them to make the correct choice, they first need to be shown the price of making a mistake. And our message has to be clear, clear and forcefully convincing.

A collective flashback to the horrors of the 1970s will make things clear. And if it doesn't, the glimpse of the bloody past will become a prolonged look. The infrastructure is almost ready, and things will begin within a few days." Ivanov turned to look at his subordinate.

"Good work," he said to Colonel Kovanyov. "Precision is essential. Don't deviate from your plans. The operation has to be a model of perfection. Polished like the Bolshoi Ballet. Let it be clear to one and all that there is someone pulling the strings and orchestrating every move."

All the occupants of the room stood up to leave. The general gestured to Lavarov to remain behind. They were left alone.

"You look as pale as death," the general said to him. "You should rest for a day or two. Take care of yourself."

26

East of Bremen, December 2014

From their position in the small clearing in the forest, they were hidden from the nearby road. The farm was about nine hundred meters away as the crow flies, but out of sight due to the steep incline of the terrain. Aslan surveyed the area meticulously while the others followed him with their eyes.

"There were three, or maybe four, people here," he said. "Can you see the trampled grass? Those are tracks left by several pairs of shoes." He slowly approached the embankment of rocks and earth. Beyond it were the woods, dense and uninviting. "I believe this embankment has taken a fair deal of gunfire."

"Can you see any bullets?" Ya'ara asked.

"No, but look at the shards of rock. They appear fresh. Completely white." He looked down at the ground in silence. "There may have been targets here. These holes in the ground appear to indicate so. The earth here is loose so the signs are a little unclear. But I think these are marks left by spikes that were pushed into the earth and later removed."

"There are glass fragments here, too," Sayid said quietly. "I'm no expert, but it looks like they haven't been here for very long. They're clean, without a layer of mud or dirt."

"If they were shooting here, where do you think they were firing from?"

"From exactly where you are standing now, Ya'ara. It's no more than fifteen meters. I think they fired from there in this direction, toward the embankment. They were shooting at targets and maybe beer bottles. Or wine."

"I don't see any spent cartridges . . ."

Aslan joined her, his eyes scanning the ground. "If they were standing here," he mumbled, "then the casings must have flown off to the right." He walked to the side, a meter or so away, and kicked at the earth with his shoe. And again. And one more time. Nothing. Just moist earth. "I'm pretty sure that the embankment here took gunfire. And I think it was the shooting that we heard yesterday. I think they must have collected the spent cartridges. That's why we aren't finding anything."

"If they picked up the casings, they must be hiding something. They're professionals. Or there's a professional who's instructing them," Ya'ara said.

"Isn't it dangerous to draw conclusions from the fact that there are no spent cartridges lying around?" Batsheva commented. "Excuse me for talking like a lawyer, but a lack of evidence isn't really evidence."

"You're right," Aslan replied, "but there appears to be shrapnel here from gunfire. And that's something real. Concrete. And when you add that to the fact that there are no cartridges, it looks a little suspicious. No, it's not evidence for a court of law, but it's something that requires further investigation."

"We should get out of here," Ya'ara said. "If they were here yesterday, they might come back today. And if our assumptions are correct, then they are armed and we aren't. It's best we don't run into them here."

"If there's a group of armed people here, perhaps we should pass on the entire matter to the German intelligence service?" Sayid wondered out loud.

"Maybe," Ya'ara responded, "but we need

a few more particulars and facts before calling in the cavalry."

"The what?"

"It's just an expression," Ya'ara said. "What I meant was we need more proof before we mobilize forces to this shithole." She omitted the fact that if their suspicions turned out to be justified, Matthias had become entangled in a far more dangerous affair than initially believed. Yes, perhaps this was precisely the right time to end the subterfuge and silence, but if Matthias was caught up in something of this nature, it would spell the end for him in his organization. She didn't want to let go so easily.

"We'll circle around and go to the surveillance point we were at yesterday. Then if they are on their way here, we won't run into them and we'll be able to see if anything's happening at the farm."

"I'm freezing to death. We'll warm up a little if we move," Batsheva commented. Her entire appearance indicated a readiness to spring into action right there and then. Even in her hiking boots she looked like someone who was in the habit of wearing high heels and socializing at parties. But Sayid, who took a long look at her, saw something more. On their way back, he asked if they should continue to memorize the relevant pages in the bird guide as Ya'ara had instructed.

"Remember," Ya'ara said, "a good cover story is one that includes elements of truth. I expect you not only to know the birds, but to love them as well. If anyone asks, the only thing that brought us here was a burning desire to discover the nesting areas of the birds of Germany. We're ornithologists, after all."

Aslan held the binoculars to his eyes and raised his hand to command the attention of the others.

"The door's opening," he whispered.

Ya'ara, Batsheva, and Sayid froze on the spot, hoping that the vegetation and branches were truly offering adequate cover. Ya'ara peered intently through her binoculars. The two cadets strained their eyes.

Six figures emerged from the farmhouse, one after the other. "Four men and two women," Ya'ara said. Three men and one woman walked toward the barn. The remaining man and woman headed for the all-terrain vehicle parked in the yard.

"Can you make out their faces?"

"Barely. Certainly not well enough to positively identify them elsewhere."

"Okay, they're both blond, and they're

both wearing boots and khaki green jackets. They look like hunters."

The woman sat behind the wheel. The man got in next to her and slammed the door. The sound of the engine was loud enough to be heard by the group observing them through the trees. The vehicle growled, leaped forward, made a U-turn, and exited the farm compound in the direction of the road. Ya'ara shivered as a cold gust of wind slammed into the thicket.

"Just a moment, they're leaving the barn now," Aslan whispered. The reddish barn door opened outward and two of the men closed it carefully behind them.

"Are you seeing what I'm seeing?" Ya'ara asked.

Aslan nodded.

"I can't see a thing," Batsheva whispered to Sayid.

One of the men was holding several steel rods that were fitted at one end with white pieces of cardboard. The man was struggling to manage them all, and for a moment it looked as if he was about to drop them. He tried to steady them, and almost managed to do so, but suddenly they started to wobble violently and the man almost fell to the ground.

"The wind must be blowing them

around."

The man bent down, placed the rods on the ground, rearranged them, and then gathered them up again, tightly together.

Swinging on the shoulder of the second man were two assault rifles.

"Kalashnikovs," Ya'ara said.

The two men headed away from them down the slope. They appeared to be walking toward the woods.

"More shooting practice?"

"We'll hear soon enough. I wonder where the other two are."

And just as if someone had heard Aslan's question, the barn door opened again and a man and woman emerged. The man looked middle-aged. His hair was white and long, and tied back. He had something that appeared to be a pistol in his hand. He and the woman followed in their friends' footsteps. Ya'ara and Aslan kept track of them with the binoculars until they disappeared.

Aslan went quiet, and then asked: "Tell me something, Ya'ara, is Martina a blonde?"

Ya'ara responded softly, almost in a whisper. "Her hair in the pictures with Matthias is dark. Black. After finding pictures of her grandmother, ones that appeared in the press when she was arrested, I could see the resemblance between them. Truth be told, her grandmother looked a lot like Ulrike Meinhof herself. She dressed like her, at least, and they had similar hair, too. The only thing missing in the pictures of Martina are the horn-rimmed glasses."

"When you briefed us, back in Berlin," Batsheva suddenly said, "you said something about the vehicle that came to collect Martina from Matthias's home."

Ya'ara tensed up.

"You said Matthias described it as a militarylike vehicle, more suited to the desert than to the German army; you said it was a light color."

"Like a vehicle from a cigarette commercial," Sayid added.

"That's definitely a significant detail," Ya'ara said, still speaking softly. "I should have thought of it myself. Yes, under all that mud it's covered in, that vehicle is the color of sand."

"Shhhh," Aslan quieted them.

Short bursts of gunfire could be heard on the wind.

27

Leeds, December 1947

Raphael took a deep breath and tightened the scarf around his neck. Night had already fallen and he could feel the cold in his bones. His head was spinning. He took another deep breath in an effort to calm himself. His exhilaration was spiritual in nature, but accompanied by physical signs, too. A real difficulty in breathing and a rapid pulse that throbbed in his temple. He had almost forgotten his meeting the previous night with the Irish arms dealer at that dingy pub nearby the Liverpool port. Coursing through him at that moment were his impressions from his lengthy meeting with the great sculptor Henry Moore. Raphael had initiated the meeting by means of a brief letter sent from London, and Moore's reply, a single sentence on a thick greeting card of fine quality, was reservedly polite:

I'd be happy to meet with you when you come to Leeds, young sculptor.

Raphael was offended at first by the arrogant tone — young sculptor. But he later came to his senses and said to himself: He's right, after all, I really am a young sculptor. I come from the periphery, from an arid strip of land at the far end of the Mediterranean Sea. Groveling before one of the greatest sculptors of the time, perhaps the greatest of them all. So yes, young sculptor. Make your pilgrimage. Sit at the feet of the master. You may learn something.

Moore himself opened the door, dressed in a buttoned-up cardigan, a pleasant smile lighting up his face. He led Raphael into a small living room, warning him on their way there that he didn't have much time, three-quarters of an hour at the most, as he needed to return to his work in the studio. The forty-five minutes turned into ninety, and then Moore suggested they continue their conversation in the studio, which was located in a separate structure at the back of the house. Moore didn't only speak, but listened, too, the young man's sharp intelligence, original ideas, and powerful personality capturing his heart. Moore showed him the large white piece of stone on which he was working and asked for Raphael's thoughts on how to proceed with its shaping. Raphael studied the stone from all sides and spoke his mind. Moore's response surprised him. He handed Raphael a hammer and chisel and said, "Your suggestion is interesting, very interesting. Come on, get working. But carefully," he added with a smile.

Even in the dark streets of Leeds he could still feel the dust of the stone in his nose, on his teeth, and in the cavity of his mouth — and he was savoring every grain of it. The dust was proof that it hadn't been a dream. He really had worked with Henry Moore, even if not for very long. He, Yosef Raphael, who was born in Salonika and emigrated to the Land of Israel, had shaped the same piece of stone on which the great English sculptor was working, had carefully carved out his ideas pertaining to its inherent potential. At one point, Moore said to him: Come, allow me. And he took the hammer and chisel from his hands and picked up where the young Raphael had left off, along the same lines. Raphael observed the older sculptor's hands in amazement, steady and strong, yet gentle at the same time, as if he were sculpting lines in a poem. At one point, while Moore was working doggedly and patiently on the stone, Raphael made tea for them.

When they parted a few hours later, the celebrated artist shook his hand and said they would keep in touch. I'm curious to see your works, he said to him. At the earliest opportunity, when I'm in London. Raphael was beside himself. Moore's hand was strong and warm, rough and hard, a sculptor's hand, with the marble and stone dust now a part of its skin. The following day, too, on the morning train that carried him southward, Raphael could still feel its touch on the tips of his fingers.

28

East of Bremen, December 2014

"Listen up,"Ya'ara said to Matthias, her ice-cold hand barely able to grip the telephone. "I need your friend to try to locate Martina's phone now, right now. Both her phones, the one that belongs to her and the one we were able to identify. I think we saw her leaving a farm east of Bremen, and I'm assuming she's on her way to Bremen itself. If you can provide me with a reference point, or even a contained area in which one of her phones appears, we can try to locate her and see what she's doing."

"Are you certain it's her? What drew you to that particular farm, Ya'ara? What's going on there? Is she alone?"

"Matthias, I need you to act right now. Immediately. I'll be able to tell you more later. But we have an opportunity, and we need to act fast. Get back to me."

She ended the conversation, hoping she

had managed to convey the sense of urgency to Matthias. "Let's get out of here. I want us to get to the center of Bremen as quickly as possible. Aslan, alert the other two teams, please. We need as many pairs of eyes as we can get. Sayid, let's go. We're out of here. Aslan, I'll drive.

Matthias called back just as they were about to drive into the parking lot of the large department store, the Kaufhof, in the city center.

"Her phone was located between Osterdeich, Lüneburger Strasse, and Celler Strasse. Are you familiar with them?"

Ya'ara repeated the street names out loud, and Aslan, a map of the city spread out on his knees, signaled that he was searching for them. The streets Matthias had given them formed an enclosed rectangle of sorts. That was the defined area.

Matthias was still on the line. After asking if Ya'ara needed any help, he moved on to a more personal line of questioning. "Tell me, Yaara," he asked, the tone of his voice betraying the emotion he was trying to conceal, "are you sure it's Martina? Is she okay? Has something happened to her?"

"I think it's her, Matthias. I can't be sure. She looks fine, healthy and in one piece, but I think she's mixed up in something bad."

They met in a small public park, near a church. The cold was intense and the icy wind coming from the north chilled them to the bone. Ya'ara briefed the teams. She gave them a description of the man and woman they had seen at the farm. The description was partial, since they had seen them only from afar and through binoculars. She also described the two men who were seen emerging from the barn with the weapons and targets, and the man and woman who had followed them. But Martina was the main objective. Each pair was assigned to a portion of the search area. "Check out every location that is open to the public," she told them. "Every hotel, pub, café, restaurant, subway station, department store, any place where several people can sit together in a group without arousing suspicion. Lucky for us, there aren't many people out in this weather, and those who are stand out, particularly if they're not hurrying from one place to the next."

She thought for a moment and then added: "A meeting is only one possibility. They could be out buying things they need, food, equipment. So keep an eye on the stores, too. If any of you see anyone who looks even vaguely like her, call me or Aslan right away. The area we need to scout isn't very big, that's the only plus. On the other hand, the phone location was correct only at the time we received it. That was some time ago; she may not be here any longer. They may not be here any longer. They may have split up. Let's go. Keep your eyes open. That's all we can do."

Nufar was the one who called. "I think we've spotted them," she said softly, overcoming her excitement. "We're looking right now at a woman and man who fit the descriptions you gave us. Based on Martina's picture, she resembles the young woman we can see at the café. I'm not 100 percent certain, and she's blond as well. Strawberry blond. She may have dyed her hair. And the man she's with is older. They're in a café called Ambiente, at 69 Osterdeich. We first spotted the vehicle. A light-colored Land Rover covered in mud. Parked on a street perpendicular to Osterdeich, about three hundred meters from the café. And then we spotted them."

"Excellent. Keep them under surveillance

and don't go into the café. I'll be right there."

Ya'ara called Aslan and asked him to assemble the other cadets at a nearby location. Then she joined Ann and Nufar, who were keeping their eyes on the café from the opposite sidewalk. They had their hands in their coat pockets and their breath was turning to vapor in the freezing air. Ya'ara was the only one of the three who appeared unaffected by the cold. The large, well-lit windows offered them a good view of the couple, which was now a trio, sitting inside the café. The young woman was undoubtedly the young woman they had seen leaving the farmhouse, and the young man resembled the young man who was with her, and they were sitting and talking now with a third man, an older man, with graying hair and a pale complexion. Ya'ara sensed that it had to be Martina. The young woman resembled the photograph of Martina that Matthias had sent to her, despite the very different expression she had on her face, stern and stiff. She displayed the image from Matthias on the screen of her iPhone and showed it to the two cadets.

"What do you think? Is it her?"

"I think so," Nufar responded. Ann nodded.

"Nufar, you speak German, right?"

"Two years of intensive studies at INSEAD, another language, so yes. Pretty well."

"And your German, Ann, is good, as I recall. You studied it both at high school and at university. I know you've all been instructed to keep your distance, but I'd like you both to go into the café now. Try to sit as close as you can to our friends. Try to hear what they're talking about."

"And take pictures?" Ann asked.

"Only if you can do so without lifting the phone off the table. And without a flash. I don't want to scare them. And make sure the camera's shutter sound is muted."

"What do we do if they get up and leave?"

"Just stay where you are, in the café. They mustn't see any signs of attention from you. We'll be in position around the café and keep track of them when they come out. Go in and report back. Good luck."

Ya'ara received a WhatsApp message from Nufar three minutes later. All the team's communication — phone calls, as well as text messages — was done in English, under false names.

"We couldn't get an adjacent table," the message read, although Ya'ara could see so for herself already. "Struggling to hear the conversation. Sounds like the older man is giving them instructions. They're speaking in German, but the older man has a foreign accent. Annabel thinks she can hear something East European in his German." Annabel was Ann's nickname.

Ann sent a WhatsApp message with a photo of the three. The image was sharp and Ya'ara looked at the blond girl's face and tried to picture her with black hair. Yes, she was almost certain at that point that they were looking at Martina. She studied the older man's face, zooming in on him. Despite his slight build, his face appeared heavy and awkward. High cheekbones. Slightly slanted eyes. She thought she could make out tiny pockmarks on his face, acne scars, perhaps, but it might just have been the graininess of the enlarged image. She couldn't see the face of the younger man. He was sitting with his back to Ann.

Ya'ara called Aslan. "Send Helga to me," she said. "I suggest you get into position with a car for their return to the Land Rover. Take Bethany with you. Seymour will join me. We'll follow our new friend." Helga was Helena, Bethany was Batsheva, and Seymour was Sayid.

"Gotcha."

■ ■ ■ ■

Helena showed up a few minutes later, her eyes aglow below the brim of the woolen hat that was covering her head.

Ya'ara showed her the picture Ann had taken. "Ann thinks he's foreign. She can hear something East European in his accent. Look at his eyes. A bit of Tatar mixed in with the Slavic, right?"

"It's hard to say," Helena responded hesitantly.

"It's important for us to know if he's Russian. I have a gut feeling about this, and I have no idea where it's coming from, but I think it's important. Look, the meeting between the three will come to an end at some point. Whether he leaves the café alone or with the other two, I want you to engage him, not physically, but to get up close to him and ask him in Russian if he knows the way to the train station. I want to see how he responds."

"And what do I do if he doesn't respond? Or if he gives me directions?"

"If he doesn't respond to the Russian, try asking in English. If he responds and tells you the way, head off in the direction he has indicated. Act naturally. If he says he doesn't know, or ignores you, ask someone else on the street. I want him to see you approach others. Begin in Russian with them, too, and switch to broken German if they don't understand, and then English. And follow the directions you're given until you're out of sight. And then go back to your hotel. And that will be it as far as you're concerned for this stage of the operation: no more surveillance for you after such a close encounter. Look, see that bus station across the street? Get into position there and don't lose sight of the door to the café. I'll give you a heads-up when he's about to leave if I have the chance. I'm sure he'll put his coat on before heading out into this cold. That should give me enough time to warn you. But even if I don't manage to, you'll see him leaving and you'll approach him. Okay?"

Ya'ara saw the three of them stand up. The older man shook hands with his younger companions, who then sat down again. He walked over to the coat rack at the back of the café. Ya'ara called Helena. "He's on his way out. Alone. Get ready."

"I'm not hanging up," Helena responded. "You may be able to hear."

"Excuse me, sir," Helena said in Russian.

"Could you perhaps tell me how to get to the nearest train station?"

He answered her at once, without a moment's hesitation. "Keep on straight. See that traffic light ahead? Take a left there and it's a five- or maybe ten-minute walk. You'll see it in the distance after you turn the corner."

Russian. Russian. He spoke Russian. Ya'ara's head was a whirlwind of thoughts.

She turned to Sayid, who had joined her in the meantime. "Come, let's follow him. But stay back. We'll walk together. Remember, we're a couple."

The Russian, as Ya'ara had already dubbed him to herself, set off at a reasonable pace, not too fast, and not slow either. He stopped from time to time to peer into a storefront window, although Ya'ara knew he wasn't looking into the store itself but only at the images of the people reflected in the glass along with him. He turned left at the corner, and then right at the very next corner. Ya'ara and Sayid followed almost at a run, to avoid losing him. And then Ya'ara stopped suddenly, pulling Sayid toward her. She held his face in her hands and kissed him on the lips. Her eyes closed only partially, and at the edge of her field of vision she saw the Russian approach them, pass by, and move on.

"He backtracked," she whispered to Sayid, who didn't understand what was happening. "The Russian backtracked in an effort to see if he's being followed. Our kiss may have led him to erase us from his list of potential followers, but he won't be fooled if he sees us anywhere near him again. All his alarm bells will start ringing." She made sure she was out of sight of the Russian and called Aslan. "Forget the two younger ones," she said to him, meaning that he abandon the surveillance of the café. "Ivan's heading back your way. Take him. I think he's trying to see if he's being followed. Tread cautiously."

Aslan and Batsheva quickly exchanged the warmth of the rental car for the iciness of the street. Aslan understood that the name Ivan belonged to the older man who had been at the table with the two younger individuals in the café. His eyes roamed St. Jurgen Strasse until he spotted him in the distance, approaching Heidelberger Strasse and turning right. Aslan wanted to break into a run to reduce the gap between them, but his experience held him back. Ivan then started to slow down as an illuminated tram station came into his view. "He's going to get on to the next tram," Aslan said to

Batsheva. "I want you to get on with him. I'll be following you. Remain on the tram for one more stop after he gets off. Don't get off with him, because he'll mark you. I'll stay on him after he gets off."

"And what do I do?"

"Depends on what he does. I'll instruct you in keeping with the situation. Okay?" Her hiking boots brought a look of satisfaction to his face. "Better than high heels. Off you go."

He returned to the car and watched Batsheva join the small group of people huddled together at the illuminated tram station. A minute later, tram No. 3 pulled up at the station. Batsheva got on first. She didn't even glance at Ivan, who got on behind her. *Good girl,* Aslan thought as he pulled off slowly, maintaining a safe distance from the tram, allowing another vehicle to come between them.

"He's about to get off," read Batsheva's WhatsApp message ahead of the fourth stop. Aslan stopped at the side of the road, holding back a little. The tram stopped and Ivan alighted, turned right, and began heading in the direction they had just come from. He cast his eyes down the dimly lit street and walked on for about twenty meters before stepping into a small grocery store, the light from its storefront windows flooding the sidewalk. Aslan didn't believe the miserable grocery store was the real reason Ivan had traveled four stops on the tram. He called Batsheva.

"Are you off the tram?"

"Yes. I'm at the station. Quietly freezing."

"What did he do on the tram?"

"He remained standing even though there were vacant seats. Standing and looking out at the road through the rear window. But it's not like he pressed himself up against the glass or something like that. It all looked very natural." Aslan hoped that Ivan hadn't spotted him trailing the tram. Under normal circumstances, they would have trailed the tram using two cars at least, with one car, the closest one, ready to pass the tram as it approached its next stop. But this wasn't normal surveillance and trailing. It was a one-on-one battle, and under such circumstances, victory is secured with the help of experience, awareness, and luck. Mostly luck.

Ivan left the store carrying a small bag and continued heading in the opposite direction from the traffic. Aslan allowed him to pass by, waited for about twenty seconds, and then exited the car, gently shut the door, and started following him. All of a sudden, Ivan stepped into the street and raised his hand. Aslan saw what Ivan had already seen just a second earlier — a taxi coming down the street, its illuminated number indicating it was free. The taxi stopped and Ivan got into the backseat. Aslan, who was still on the sidewalk, was caught in its headlights as it pulled off again. And only after the taxi had moved off into the distance did Aslan allow himself to turn around and keep his eyes on it for as long as he could. He watched it signal left and turn into a wider and busier street, before disappearing with Ivan inside. At that moment, Aslan knew they had lost him. He said a silent prayer of thanks nevertheless to Ya'ara, who had given him fair warning. Thanks to her, he had kept his distance from Ivan, thereby preventing him perhaps from discovering that he was being followed. Ivan, in all likelihood, would spend the next half hour checking to see if he was under surveillance, and then give himself the all-clear. He would believe that all was okay. But all wasn't okay. A professional field operative meeting with two young individuals, at least one of whom had left her regular life and disappeared. People living on a remote farm where there were weapons, where they were carrying out improvised firing practice, where they made sure they collected the spent cartridges thereafter. There was nothing okay about it at all.

29

"Have you spoken to Matthias?"

Ya'ara and Aslan were sitting in the dimly lit bar of the Swissotel. The cadets had been released for the evening and the two of them were meeting to review and analyze the information they had gathered thus far.

"Yes, I've spoken to him," Ya'ara said, stifling a yawn, her face pale and drawn. "He's still hung up on knowing if Martina is okay. He's refusing to face the facts — his girlfriend is mixed up in something radical and dangerous, with a Russian intelligence official running things. He still sees her through the eyes of a middle-aged lover, which is what he was in fact."

"Do I detect a hint of jealousy?" Aslan asked in amazement.

"God, what kind of a question is that?" Aslan shrugged his shoulders and Ya'ara decided to leave the internal debate about her feelings for some other time. "I sent him the picture of Ivan. We'll see if he comes up with an ID."

"We've done some pretty good work so far, but perhaps it's time now to bring in the police, special forces, God knows who, to conduct a raid on the farm, arrest everyone there, seize the weapons, and put an end to this whole thing, which doesn't paint a very pretty picture right now."

"I'm not sure if the information we have is enough to convince them to take action," Ya'ara said, ignoring the bits she didn't want to hear. "And besides, if they apprehend Martina, her relationship with Matthias will come to light. And that would mean the end of his career."

"Maybe it's inevitable. He got himself into this mess by behaving like a fool. And now he has to pay the price."

"Matthias aside, if we bring in the police at this stage, they'll only dispatch a patrol car with two polite officers, and then they won't find a thing at the farm. That, or the small army there will simply eliminate them."

"But even a visit from a patrol car would deter them. They'd realize they've been exposed and they'd put a hold on whatever they're planning — if anything at all."

"And what if they don't necessarily think

like you? It could spark them into action. Make them bring things forward. What we really need is incriminating material. We can't make do with tenuous scraps of information and conspiracy theories." *And I do still want to try to save Matthias,* she thought.

"What do you suggest?"

"We need to get into the farm."

"There are six of them. The chances of their all being away from the farm at the same time are slim. They were today, but we don't have sufficient time or the resources to wait for the farm to be empty again."

"You're right. And today, too, four of them were just a ten-minute walk away."

"We could try to waylay them if they were to return unexpectedly from the firing range."

"I don't like the sound of that," Ya'ara said. "If they're coming back from the range, they'll be armed. I don't want any of us to have to encounter them under such circumstances. We'll wait until we see four of them leaving, and then we'll try to draw the other two out. We can manufacture a window of opportunity for a quick search through the living quarters."

"What do we do if there's a dog at the

farm, or dogs?" Aslan asked. "I heard barking on our first stakeout."

"A good piece of meat could do the trick . . ."

"That's a gamble. A well-trained dog won't fall for that."

"Okay, so I don't have answers for everything. We'd be risking it. But you're right, the operational conditions are undoubtedly extreme."

"Ultimately, Ya'ara, we're here to train cadets. Don't you think we've gone too far?"

"I think it's a lot more than a training exercise. I think we've stumbled onto something big."

Aslan looked out the window. Outside was as dark as the bar in which they were sitting. He wasn't someone who tended to overthink things, yet he couldn't help but wonder if their improvised operation wasn't going to turn suddenly into a quagmire, and if it wasn't time now to fill in their mysterious superiors on what they had been up to. After all, no one was expecting them to come to the aid of a German intelligence officer. Or perhaps they actually were. His acquaintanceship with Ya'ara and the time they had spent working side by side in the past hadn't confused him or led him to believe that he truly knew her. He loved her, but he didn't know her, not to the core. He looked again now at her determined chin. He knew she was going to press on with or without him. With him would be best.

"Listen," he said, "the Christmas festivities are just four days away. I don't think the timing is coincidental. My guess is that if they're planning something, it will go down on Christmas or New Year's Eve. A terror attack during a period that is all about celebration and family and tradition could really rock the boat. So let's give ourselves another two days. And if we aren't able to come up with anything, we'll find a way to spark the police into action."

"Agreed. I'm buying the last drink."

"Cheers, my bro," she said, softly and with a great deal of affection, after their drinks were served.

"To you, my sister," Aslan responded, clinking glasses with her and downing his whiskey in one gulp.

30

Helena and Batsheva stood outside the front door of the farmhouse. They had already been waiting an entire day for an opportunity to come their way, but to no avail. The night before, following a day of no results, the teams had assembled in a gloomy mood. That's just the way it is, Aslan had said, informing them that he had wasted half his life waiting endlessly and coming up empty-handed. "Tomorrow's another day," he added. This time it was Assaf who said: "Nice one, Scarlett O'Hara."

And then that morning, four of the farm's occupants — the two women and two of the men — left the house and made their way to the cars. Martina and the second woman got into the Land Rover, the two men into the Golf. The vehicles pulled out of the farmyard one after the other, got onto the narrow road, and headed west, in the direction of the village. Aslan, who was waiting with Assaf near the intersection, saw them speed by and reported back to Ya'ara. It was the only access road to the farm, and Aslan and Assaf remained in position there, ready to catch sight of the vehicles on their way back. If the infiltration team was still in the farmhouse, they would need to alert them and also try to block or detain them at the same time. Stopping a traveling car is never easy. Ya'ara, Nufar, and Ann, who were still on stakeout duty, informed Batsheva and Helena that four of the farm's residents had left, and the two began walking toward the house. Sayid had taken up a position between the farm and the makeshift shooting range. His job was to warn of approaching strangers from the direction of the woods. The likelihood of anyone approaching from there was slim, but Ya'ara was adamant about not leaving such a wide sector unmanned. If someone were to come and ask what I'm doing there, Sayid had thought, I'd have no convincing story to tell. There I'll be, sticking out like a sore thumb in the middle of a black swamp somewhere in northern Germany. Ya'ara insisted that he come up with a cover story, so as not to find himself at a loss for words at crunch time. "Don't go easy on yourself," she said. "Think of something. And let me know." In the end, he took along a notebook bound in a leatherlike fabric that he had bought on first arriving in Berlin for the purpose of recording ideas and thoughts about life, about the city, general impressions and the like, obviously nothing related to the training and activity awaiting them. The notebook was still empty, and not because he had run out of ideas and thoughts. He simply wasn't able to muster the desire or energy to put them down in writing. And now it was going to serve as the notebook of a budding artist who had gone out to sketch a drab and monotonous nature coming together in oblique lines to a vanishing point on the horizon. He really loved to draw. Perhaps it was time to develop a second career, just in case. Let them prove him wrong, he remonstrated with himself, adding a quick sketch of the branches of the beech tree in the shadow of which he was hiding, gaining confidence and conviction ahead of his task.

Helena knocked vigorously on the door of the farmhouse with Batsheva by her side. It was only after she had knocked for a third time, pounding a beat that conveyed a sense of desperation or urgency, that they heard footsteps approaching, and standing in the doorway was a bearded young man with black-rimmed glasses balanced on his nose.

"Thank God there's someone here," Helena began in English, breathing heavily and appearing somewhat embarrassed. "Do you speak English?" Batsheva was standing next to her, her face smeared with several streaks of black oil. She had tears in her eyes.

"You must help us, *bitte,*" Helena continued, without giving him a chance to respond, and pretending to know only a handful of German words. "We fell into a ditch, or should I say our vehicle skidded into a ditch, and we can't get it out. The wheels got stuck deep in the mud, and the more we tried, the deeper the car sank." The shoes they were wearing, too pretty and elegant for rescue missions, were indeed covered in disgusting black mud.

"We're on our way to Bremen," Batsheva explained. "My son, her husband" — she nodded to indicate Helena — "is expecting us. He's giving a talk this afternoon at the Lutheran church," she continued, adding a patently irrelevant detail, and Helena nodded to confirm. The main thing was to come across as not particularly intelligent women, harmless, and primarily helpless. And a charming smile couldn't hurt either. "We thought we'd take a scenic drive along the country roads from Bremerhaven, to see the views," she chattered on, "and look what happened."

The young man had yet to utter a word. He looked at the two women facing him — elegant and dirty, and clearly foreign.

"Yes, I speak English. Are you from England?"

"No, no, from Prague," Batsheva replied, and broke into a stream of rapid-fire sentences in Czech. "Oops, you don't speak Czech," she eventually stopped herself and said, blushing, and switching to English again. "Will you help us? Please?" she added. Helena fixed the young man with her big, beautiful, trust-inspiring eyes.

"I don't have a vehicle that can tow you right now," the young man said. "What about calling a road rescue service? Do you have insurance?"

"It's a rental," Helena replied, "but it'll take half a day for someone to get here. Perhaps you could help us nevertheless? You look pretty strong," she added with a smile.

"Is the car far from here?"

"Not too far. We got a little mixed up at the crossroads and turned down the road leading here. It's very narrow, you know, that's how we skidded. I skidded, I mean, I may have been driving a little too fast," she said with an air of false contrition. Batsheva looked at her reproachfully, thus confirming that the mishap was indeed all Helena's fault.

"Stefan!" the young man shouted into the house. "Come here for a moment. We have a couple of damsels in distress at the door," he called out, his use of the flowery English expression leaving him obviously pleased with himself.

Stefan took his time, but eventually showed up alongside his friend. His disheveled hair appeared to indicate that he had just woken up, or hadn't planned on being in the company of others that day.

"Let's give these nice ladies a hand," said the young man who had opened the door for them, speaking cheerfully in English so they'd understand, and then adding softly in German, "So we can get them the hell out of here. We don't need them hanging around here for hours, not to mention calling in a tow truck and who knows what else."

"Thank you, thank you," Batsheva said, and Helena expressed her gratitude, too, with a sweet smile. "I'm Alenka," Batsheva said, holding out her hand to the young man. "And this is Suzanna, my daughter-in-law."

"Nice to meet you. Klaus. Stefan. Let's

see what we can do." He whistled and a large herding dog came bounding from somewhere deep inside the house to join them, wagging its tail, pleased to be going out for a morning walk.

The two young men slammed the door of the house shut and followed the women. The dog ran ahead of them, stopping to look back at the group every now and then, as if to make sure they were following him. *They're in for some hard work,* Helena thought with satisfaction. Even after they manage to get the car out of the ditch, they'll find out that it won't start. The fall into the ditch had caused the cable leading from the ignition switch to disconnect. They had taken care of that, of course. It would take Klaus and Stefan some time to figure out the precise problem. And then we really will get the hell out of here, she said to herself. Only then.

After watching the group leave the farmyard, Ya'ara signaled to Ann and Nufar to join her. "Remember," she whispered, "time isn't on our side. Be precise. We'll start with a quick sweep through the house. Make a mental note of everything that looks interesting. And then, look for computers, iPads, phones, paperwork. Don't touch a thing before you take a picture of its position in the room, so it can be put back exactly where it was before." They approached the back door of the house. Ya'ara reached into her pocket for a thin nail file and began fiddling with the lock. She had the door open within seconds. They began their systematic sweep. Room by room. First floor, second floor, attic. Ann's heart was pounding. This was a first for her. It's a good thing I studied breaking and entering skills at Oxford, she joked, to herself only. Mother would be so proud if she knew.

The house was filthy, and every single thing inside appeared to be covered in a layer of dust and grime. The beds weren't made and the rooms were stuffy. There were two beds in each room. Ya'ara was taken aback by the spartan conditions and shoddy upkeep, and particularly by the fact that the room of the two young women looked just like the other two rooms. She was expecting something different. Not because she believed that women would always be neater and cleaner than men; it was because of Matthias. The group's equipment appeared to have been thrown into several large backpacks and military kitbags. A single bathroom served the entire house, and it, too, was caked in a yellowish layer of dirt and neglect. She felt like throwing up. What had happened to Martina? she asked herself. Matthias couldn't have fallen in love with a filthy, neglectful young woman. Suddenly that seemed more serious to her than the knowledge that his young lover was involved in something sinister. But perhaps she, too, had succumbed to the barrackslike mood and living conditions.

They ended up finding two laptops and an iPad. The laptops were in one of the bedrooms, charging. The iPad was in the girls' room. There were no cellphones. And none of the papers appeared to be of any interest. One of the kitchen drawers contained a collection of receipts, from supermarkets, pharmacies, gas stations. Ya'ara took pictures of them with her phone. She then instructed Ann and Nufar to sit down at the laptops. "Get to work," she said. "Copy everything that's on them onto your portable hard drives. We'll do the sorting later. Quickly, but thoroughly. Don't worry. Helena and Batsheva will keep them busy. And Aslan and Assaf will warn us if the others are on their way back. In case we have to leave quickly, we'll do so via the back door, at a sprint, toward the woods. Get moving. I want us out of here within twenty minutes tops."

Ya'ara left the two cadets upstairs and

went back down to the first floor of the house. She took a chair from the kitchen and placed it under the door handle. That should delay them for a few seconds if necessary. She then went into the living room, where the final remnants of warmth were coming off the large iron stove that stood in the open expanse. She settled down alongside the window, hidden by a thick curtain, from where she could keep an eye on the dirt track leading away from the farm. If one or more members of the group were to return to the farm, they'd do so from there. She'd see them and be able to warn Ann and Nufar. She had chosen them for the task because of all the women in her team, they were the most proficient when it came to computers. And they both spoke German. That, too, was important when trying to find one's way around computers that were probably running on German-language operating systems. She was tempted to use the time to search the barn, but she wouldn't allow herself to abandon her lookout spot. And the restraint she was forced to exercise in order to maintain operational discipline caused her actual physical pain, as if it were twisting her arm. If she had had another team member at her disposal, she would have sent him in there.

Perhaps she shouldn't have left both Aslan and Assaf on stakeout at the crossroads. Assaf could have finally proven his worth to her, if he could just stop asking questions. But it was too late now.

When she answered the phone, Aslan began speaking without any unnecessary niceties. "The Golf's on its way back. At breakneck speed. We weren't able to detain them. They're on their way to you."

They'd be there in a minute and a half, two minutes at most. She walked toward the staircase and shouted: "Nufar, Ann. Shut down the computers immediately! Did you get that?"

"Got you," Nufar responded.

"Just a moment," Ann said.

"You don't have a moment. Now!"

"Okay," came Ann's voice from the second floor. "Coming down."

The blue Golf screeched to a halt alongside the small group of people at the side of the road. Klaus and Stefan were in the ditch, trying with all their might to push the small Polo back onto the road. They were very dirty, the edges of their trousers were covered in mud, and Batsheva and Helena were looking on anxiously.

"What's going on here?" asked the driver of the Golf, sticking his head out of the window.

"Come give us a hand," Klaus groaned, as he and Stefan braced themselves against the Polo in an effort to prevent it from slipping back into the ditch.

The two men in the Golf exited the vehicle in one smooth movement. *Like detectives in an American television series,* Batsheva thought. Their car was parked at an angle, blocking the narrow road leading to the farm. The front doors remained open.

"Who are the two women?" one of them asked.

"Two Czechs who don't know how to drive," Klaus moaned ungraciously.

"What are they doing here? How did they get here?"

"They're driving from Bremerhaven to Bremen, on country roads. Come help us, so we can get them the hell out of here."

The driver of the Golf descended reluctantly into the muddy ditch. He aimed a hostile glance at Batsheva before allowing his eyes to linger on Helena for a little longer. She smiled shyly at him and said in English: "It's my fault entirely, I'm the driver." He grumbled, kept his eyes on her, winked almost unnoticeably, and then positioned himself between his two friends, straining his muscles. "Come on," he said, "all together. One, two, three!"

The Golf had yet to arrive for some reason. *Perhaps it stopped alongside Batsheva and Helena's vehicle,* Ya'ara thought. "We've earned a few extra minutes," she said to Nufar and Ann, who were standing next to her. "Head for the woods now. Meet up there with Sayid and continue to the assembly point. I have one more small thing to do here and I'll join you right away. Wait for me, because I have no way of getting out of this shithole without you. Okay?"

The two cadets left the farmhouse, through the back door as planned, and broke into a sprint. Ya'ara watched them move off into the distance and admired the beauty and ease of their running. Ah, the magic of youth, she said to herself, as if her youth were a distant memory. The magic of youth. How long does it last?

She moved the chair away from the front door and returned it to the kitchen. She then cautiously opened the door and ran, crouching, toward the barn. She paused for a short while after stepping inside to allow her eyes to get accustomed to the darkness. A beam of light that shone through an opening in the roof was casting a golden circle on the ground, like a powerful spotlight. But the barn for the most part was in darkness. Anyone hiding something would place it as far from the entrance as possible. Instinctively. And Ya'ara looked around as if she herself had something to hide in the dark barn, catching sight of the ladder leading to an open platform, a raised loft of sorts, at the back end of the structure. But having to continually climb up and down such a ladder with targets and Kalashnikovs wouldn't be very easy. The hiding place had to be readily accessible and convenient. Piled up in the far corner were a collection of agricultural implements, wooden planks, and heaps of straw. As she approached, she noticed three large barrels standing there, too. There was a strong smell of gasoline coming off them. She felt them. They appeared whole and sealed, apart from the narrow plastic cap screwed to the top of each of them. No assault rifle was getting through an opening like that. She placed both her hands on the upper part of one of the barrels and tried to twist it. Clockwise and counterclockwise. Nothing. She moved on to the second barrel and did the same. When she tried turning the top of the barrel counterclockwise, as if she were opening it, nothing happened. When she applied force in the opposite direction, as if she were trying to close it, however, she felt something move. As if someone had made a cut around the entire circumference of the barrel, about two-thirds of the way up the side. She twisted the top part of the barrel until it detached from the barrel itself, leaving its contents exposed to her. It was actually a double-sided barrel, a cylinder within a cylinder. The outer cylinder was filled with gasoline. The inner cylinder was dry and contained a large leather bag sealed with a clasp. She removed the heavy bag, opened the clasp and examined the contents with the help of the thin flashlight she was carrying. She saw three assault rifles and a pistol. A large number of magazines. The gasoline was clearly there to help conceal the weapons from sniffer dogs. It was that understanding that had probably drawn her, somewhat subconsciously, to the barrels in the first place. She closed the leather bag and returned it to its hiding place. And then screwed the top of the barrel back on again. She noticed that the thin cut around the barrel was hidden by a sticker displaying the name of some fuel company. Someone had done a nice professional job there. She checked the third barrel. It, too, showed signs of opening, but she chose to leave it closed. She already had what she wanted. She examined the image of the barrel on her iPhone, and made sure that the corner of the barn looked exactly as it had when she first walked in. She cracked open the barn door. Through the narrow opening she saw the blue Golf pull into the yard at high speed before coming to a stop in the parking area. Out of the car stepped four men — three young and one older — looking grumpy and covered in mud and grease. The dog came running up behind them, panting, its ribs rising and falling, vapor rising from its mouth. Ya'ara smiled. Batsheva and Helena had tired them out good and proper. They walked by the barn and entered the farmhouse one after the other, turning on the electric lights in the living quarters. Long purple shadows were darkening the farmyard. The sun was sinking. The exhausted dog had fallen asleep under the car and Ya'ara hoped he wouldn't wake suddenly on picking up her scent. She slipped out of the barn, gingerly closed the door, and moved pressed up against the barn's walls until she no longer had a direct view of the farmhouse. The dog slept on. Walking crouched and at a quick pace she headed toward the earth embankment, climbed up and over, and then began making her way to the assembly point, on a small bridge near the grove of trees. The Glock pistol, which she had taken from the hidden leather bag and which was now tucked into her pants under her shirt, felt heavy and cold against the bare skin of her back.

31

They hadn't had a chance to copy the contents of the iPad. And one of the laptops they'd copied in full was a total disappointment. A tedious collection of academic papers on anarchism and radicalism and Marxism and countless other isms. Most of them in German and English. Some in Russian. The emails indicated that the computer belonged to Klaus. He also starred in a collection of photographs they found. Unable to crack his password, however, they couldn't get into his Facebook account. Although the chances of finding anything important there were very slim, Ya'ara had a hard time giving up. She angrily tried the name Trotsky before flailing her arms in theatrical despair. His profile was blocked.

The second laptop paved the way for them. Nufar got to work on the copied material. There wasn't much. A total of three folders bearing the names of three people. Bernhard Schlein. Peter Haas. Franz Mannesman. quick Google search revealed them to be three very senior bankers — the CEO of Commerzbank, the CEO of DZ Bank, and the deputy CEO of Deutsche Bank. Each folder contained photographs, some of which appeared to have been downloaded from the internet, with others — images of residences — seemingly captured in secret. Schlein and Mannesman, it turned out, lived in large, luxurious private homes. Photographs of a modern, elegant high-rise apartment block appeared in the Haas folder. A circle marked an apartment on the seventeenth floor. An arrow pointed to the entrance to the underground parking garage. Apart from the photographs of the residences themselves, the folders also contained pictures of the bankers, alone or with family members — wives and children, with the homes appearing in the background. There were also images of the streets that probably led to the respective homes. Security cameras and police speed cameras were marked with circles. Marked out on maps of residential neighborhoods found in the folders were the homes of the bankers, as well as the nearest police stations and suburban train or subway stations. Public buildings in the vicinity were also marked on the maps. In the folders, too, were larger maps that displayed the areas within a fifty-kilometer radius of the three homes. Marked out on these maps were the nearby highways and the exits leading from them to the homes of the bankers. Each folder also included photographs, from a wide range of angles and distances, of several vehicles. All of them large, black luxury vehicles. One Maybach and two large Mercedeses. Some of the images were close-ups of the license plates of the vehicles. In all likelihood, they were the bankers' official company cars. One of the pictures showed Schlein getting out of his ride, a driver in a dark suit opening the rear door for him.

Ya'ara went through the photographs of the receipts they found at the farm. Most of them were from stores and gas stations in the Bremen area. But almost half were from the Frankfurt area. Haas lived in the city itself. Schlein and Mannesman lived in small, affluent towns about a half-hour drive from the city. The receipts were conclusive proof that someone was covering the expenses of the group. Ya'ara hadn't believed to begin with that the sloppy occupants of the farm could be running the show all on their own.

"Do you know what these are?" Ya'ara

asked Aslan.

"Of course. Field dossiers."

There wasn't a shadow of doubt. The occupants of the farm had amassed intelligence on three subjects, in preparation for an operation — information on their residences, their vehicles, the roads in and out of the respective areas, the security measures in place in the vicinities.

All at once, the pieces of the puzzle slipped into place. Ya'ara looked at Aslan. The blood had drained from her face. She felt as if she was seeing ghosts. History never remains in the past, and here it was, coming back to haunt again.

"Do you realize what's happening here?" she asked, as if she were talking to herself. "It's looking like a rerun of Baader-Meinhof, but with smartphones and computers this time around. And the targets once again are the capitalist pigs. The bosses of the big banks, the despicable representatives of American imperialism. And the granddaughter of someone from the gang is at the very heart of the entire business, taking an interest in the dubious heritage of her grandmother from more than merely an academic perspective. And someone who is undoubtedly a Russian intelligence officer is mixed up with the group, and may even be steering them. And they're conducting shooting drills with Kalashnikovs and nine-millimeter pistols."

Aslan looked at her. He knew she might be right, but wondered at the same time whether it might not be a good idea to take a more cautious view of the situation. They were almost whispering, keeping their suspicions between the two of them.

"It could be other things too," Aslan said, trying to remind her that doubt, too, played an important role in their line of work.

"Yes, you're right," Ya'ara responded. "The circumstances are different, the Soviet Union fell apart a long time ago, and the collective dreams have also changed. Still, I have no doubt it's happening. That the Baader-Meinhof similarities and ties are not coincidental. You know, just like I do, that nothing is coincidental. I can't believe it's happening again." She clasped her hands to her head. "Unfathomable madness."

32

"We've got a positive ID on him!" Matthias excitedly exclaimed to Ya'ara. They were on a late-night call. "Your Ivan, as you call him, is a colonel in the GRU, the Russian military intelligence service. In the 1980s, he operated in Paris under the cover of a correspondent for TASS, the Soviet Union's news agency. And some ten years back now, he served as the press attaché at the Russian Consulate in Munich. The French security services were suspicious of him already back in the late 1980s, and a high-ranking GRU officer who defected to Britain a few years later went on to confirm their suspicions and expose him as one of their agents. When he arrived in Munich, our security service kept a close watch on him and tried to keep him in check. After completing his service in Germany, he disappeared off the radar, and we lost track of him. Considering all the upheaval in Russia, he could very well have been dismissed from the military intelligence service or may even have left of his own accord to become a businessman, selling remnants of the Red Army, like half of the KGB and other intelligence personnel who had worked abroad."

Ya'ara had yet to tell Matthias what they had found on the computers of the farm gang. She felt it was best to hold back that information from him, certainly at this stage. It was easy for her to keep things to herself, even if she hated doing so with Matthias. "How did you identify him?" she asked pertinently.

"I ran his image through various databases. The computer came back with four highly probable options. A long-serving desk clerk who happened to be passing by my desk at the time glanced at my computer, pointed at one of the images, and said, 'Hey, that's Colonel Denis Kovanyov! Where has he popped up from all of a sudden?' I told her that one of my sources had photographed someone in one of the Baltic states. The source, I said, believed the man to be a Russian intelligence agent, but couldn't prove it. And now the computer had thrown up four possibilities. 'Lucky you like to peek at other people's computer screens,' I said to her. She didn't appreciate the jab. 'You'd do well to take him seriously,' she said. 'He's a mean bastard, and did us a lot of damage when he was stationed in Munich.' Brigita, the desk clerk, was working at the time for the counterespionage unit that operated out of headquarters, in Pullach."

"Yes, I know a little bit about elderly desk officers with superpowers," Ya'ara said. "But, getting back to business, do you know what name he usually went under?"

"Brigita called him Alexander the Great and said he was probably as crazy as his namesake. That was his operational name — Alexander."

Ya'ara asked if Matthias knew how Kovanyov had entered Germany, and under what name, but he said he hadn't yet managed to clarify those details. "I assume he's using a forged passport," Matthias said. "He almost certainly didn't come in through an official German border crossing. In all likelihood, he made his way to Amsterdam or Copenhagen, and from there he continued by train or car to Bremen. A familiar modus operandi for the Russians."

"It's great that you've identified him, Matthias," Ya'ara responded. "I need to hang up now, but please, please be available in the morning. By then I may have something important to tell you."

■ ■ ■ ■

It was after midnight. Ya'ara left the noisy pub so she could speak from somewhere quieter. The temperature had dropped rapidly, well below zero. Her breath felt as if it was turning to ice, but perhaps for the first time since arriving in Germany, the cold wasn't troubling her.

She took an unused burner phone out of her pocket and called the number that Martina seemed to be using, the same number that had led them ultimately to the remote farm east of the city. She knew she was taking a gamble, and that the stakes this time were very high, but the cool, sharp clarity of her mind gave her confidence in her actions.

"I apologize if I've woken you, Martina," she said in English, in a thick Russian accent, after hearing a female voice answer with a groan. "My name is Nadia. Alexander asked me to call you. He needs to see you right away, tonight, alone."

"Who are you?" Martina asked, clearly somewhat sleepy still.

"It's important and urgent. It concerns the customs official in Hamburg, and he doesn't want the others to know." Ya'ara was betting that the Russian colonel was still using his old operational name. She had refrained from referring to Matthias by his name. Kovanyov surely adhered to secure communication protocols in his dealings with the German group, and he certainly wouldn't have mentioned specific names in phone calls. She was convinced by now that Matthias was merely a pawn in the hands of the young woman who was talking to her. She held her breath, waiting for Martina's response.

"So why doesn't he call me himself?"

"He needs to take care of a loan and has important meetings in the morning at three banks." Ya'ara was hoping that she had added an additional layer of credibility to her story. "If anyone else there is up, tell them that Alexander has summoned you for a final update. Take the Golf. It's less conspicuous than the Land Rover. Make your way to the truck parking lot alongside the entrance to the port. I'll take you to him from there. Martina" — she switched to Russian — "do everything quietly and calmly, but come quickly. It's important. And drive carefully," she switched back to English, "it's black outside like a night in December."

"That's exactly what it is," Martina responded in a whisper, sounding wide awake by this time.

Ya'ara breathed a long, quiet sigh of relief on seeing the approaching blue Golf. She motioned for the car to stop, directing it to the side of the road. Martina lowered the window and Ya'ara saw her up close for the first time. She didn't like the look of the young woman, and that certainly made things easier for her.

"Hi, I'm Nadia," Ya'ara said, still in her Russian accent, which came to her naturally, after all. "I'll join you, and show you the way. We'll be there in a few minutes."

She opened the car door and sat down alongside Martina. "Security needs to be tighter than ever during the final moments before an operation," she said. Martina glanced at her and began driving.

They drove alongside a seemingly endless array of shipping containers, turning right at the end of the road into an area of old warehouses. The headlights of the Golf revealed tall weeds growing out of the concrete surface on which they came to a stop. The darkness around them was truly heavy and opaque, almost solid. Ya'ara lit a flashlight and aimed it at the door of a dilapidated warehouse. "Come," she said, "he's waiting there for us." Ya'ara turned on the light when they walked in. Two pale bulbs cast a weak and somewhat deceptive light over the dusty expanse. In the middle of the large space, under the swinging bulbs, stood a plain wooden table with a bottle of vodka and three glasses on its surface. "Sit, please," Ya'ara said, "he'll be joining us right away."

"I don't like what's happening here," Martina said, her voice hostile and suspicious. "I'm leaving."

In a single smooth movement, Ya'ara pulled the pistol out from behind her back, cocked it, and fired a round into Martina's left foot. Martina screamed and collapsed. Ya'ara aimed the pistol at her head. "The next one will kill you," she said. "Lift yourself up, with the help of the table, and take a seat." Martina whimpered, a look of shock and hatred on her face. She grabbed the table with both hands and managed with a supreme effort to pull herself up, before standing there, shaking, on her good right leg. Her left foot was shattered and bleeding, with its Timberland boot horribly torn, revealing a mixture of flesh and bone. "Good, now sit, slowly, slowly."

Ya'ara walked around the table, stood behind Martina, pulled the chair closer to her, and pressed the tip of the Glock's barrel against the back of Martina's neck. Using a large roll of duct tape, she proceeded to wind a wide strip around Martina's torso and the back of the chair. Martina couldn't move. Ya'ara poured out a large measure of vodka for her and said, "Drink it, in one shot. It'll ease your pain."

"Who are you? Who are you?"

"We don't have much time. I'm an officer from the Security Division of the FSB, the Russian Federal Security Service. You and your friends have fallen victim to a plot hatched by subversive and reactionary elements in our intelligence services. The operations you've planned are liable to set all of Europe on fire. No responsible state can allow itself to play a part in such a thing. We are aware of your insane plans to murder three of the most senior bankers in Germany in their homes. We can't allow that to happen."

"But Alexander spoke to us about the need to shake the foundations of Europe again, a Europe that's become smug and cruel. That's alienating the oppressed who are trying to flee there as refugees. That's turning its Muslim populations into rejected and impoverished people and then wonders why they rise up against it." Martina's face was pale and drawn, her pain and rage ablaze in her eyes. "Our previous campaign ended in defeat, the authorities imprisoned my grandmother and murdered the defenseless Andreas Baader and Ulrike Meinhof in their prison cells. But in Europe today there are young and powerful forces that aren't willing to play a part in this bourgeois puppet show. More and more people know that they've seen the truth and have paid the price for doing so. And now you're telling me that you, too, are cooperating with them. Have they bought you, too?"

"Quiet!" Ya'ara hushed her, seemingly offended by Martina's words. She dragged back the chair to which Martina was bound. The motion caused Martina to feel the pain in her leg shoot to her head like a bolt of lightning. She moaned in agony. Ya'ara walked around to face her, leaning against the table.

"Listen to me good and proper, Martina," she said. "I'll blow your other foot to pieces, too, and then your left knee, and afterward the right, and you'll pray to the God you don't believe in and beg to die. I want you to tell me all you know about Matthias Geller, how you met him, and what Alexander instructed you to do with him." She picked up the Glock and aimed it at her legs. A look of terror flashed through Martina's eyes. She spat at Ya'ara, to the accompaniment of a poisonous hissing sound. Ya'ara put a bullet in her right foot. Martina yelled and screamed in pain and rage and helplessness. Ya'ara stared at her, her face blank.

"Alexander instructed me to get close to Matthias." Tears were streaming down her cheeks and long strands of snot dribbled from her nose. "He pointed him out to me at one of the bars near the port. He told me he was a real son of a bitch who worked for the German intelligence service. After we met, Matthias told me he was a customs official. He fell in love with me like a young boy. Did he really think someone thirty years his junior was going to fall in love with him like that? Alexander told me not to tell the others. It was my private assignment. I was supposed to go to him after the operation in Frankfurt. To hide out at his place. I had a whole story to tell him — why I had disappeared like that and why I was back. Like any infatuated teenager, he would have believed me. I was then supposed to kill him and leave enough clues and evidence behind to tie him to the assassination of the bankers. It would have made for an interesting twist in the plot, don't you think? Just imagine the suspicion and paranoia it would have stirred in the BND." She sighed, and briefly pursed her lips in pain. "You're a filthy fucking bitch," she said with the last of her strength, the pain from her shattered feet pounding and pounding in her chest and head. "A crazy fucking bitch."

Ya'ara fired two rounds into her head. She stepped out of the cold warehouse and into the freezing black night, adjusting the collar of her coat. She had one thing left to do.

When she reached the center of the city in the Golf, Ya'ara called the police. She spoke in English, with a pronounced Russian accent, from the same cellphone she had used to call Martina.

"Listen up," she said to the dispatcher. "If you don't deal with this call quickly and in earnest, your career with the police will be over and done with. Write down every word I say, and then report immediately afterward to the duty officer and make sure, too, that the Bremen police chief is wakened and informed. He, personally, will fire you if you spare his sleep. Understand?"

"I hear you, ma'am." The dispatcher sounded attentive and alert. Ya'ara knew that their conversation was being recorded, like all calls that come in to the police dispatcher.

"A gang of murderous anarchists, four men and two women, all Germans, are residing currently on a farm east of Bremen." She provided the exact coordinates of the farm. "They are planning the simultaneous assassination of the CEOs of Commerzbank and DZ Bank and the deputy CEO of Deutsche Bank. Schlein, Haas, and Mannesman. The killings are due to take place between Christmas Eve and New Year's Eve. You'll find weapons and ammunition hidden in gasoline drums in the farmhouse barn. Kalashnikovs and pistols. One of the computers at the farmhouse contains folders with detailed intelligence about the three objects, their vehicles, and their residences. I know all of this because backing the gang of anarchists is a department of Russian military intelligence that has gone insane. I serve in the GRU and I am not willing to lend a hand to madness that will leave us all wallowing in blood."

She spoke slowly, trying to create an impression of determination and despair and helplessness.

"Did you write down everything I said?" she asked. "Do you realize just how important and urgent a matter this is?"

"I understand, ma'am. Can you give me your name and a number on which to contact you?"

Ya'ara hung up. She had dumped the pistol she used to kill Martina on the drive from the port area to the city center. She had stopped by the river and thrown it with all her strength into the fast-flowing black current. She knew she hadn't left any fingerprints in the warehouse. The gloves had made sure of that. Now, she got out of the Golf, leaving the keys inside. She took off her gloves and removed the SIM card from the phone she had used, breaking it into little pieces and scattering them on the ground as she continued on foot. As for the phone itself, she slammed it down onto the sidewalk and crushed it with her foot. She then picked up the pieces and threw them into a drain at the side of the road. She and Aslan had worked together on the text for the call to the police. But the entire episode with Martina had taken place without the knowledge of anyone else at all. It was her initiative, her mission alone. She was painfully aware that Martina had joined the ranks of the people whose lives she had taken — her private Order of the Dead. All were justified, she thought, and immediately pushed the image of Martina's corpse from her thoughts. Ya'ara knew that the wound this killing would leave in her soul was hers alone. She felt as if she were cloaked in something black and heavy. But she was familiar with that cloak, and knew that at some point, ultimately, she would find solace. She would wrap Martina in it, too.

33

East of Bremen, December 22, 2014

As had happened many times before, the forces went into action in the small hours of the morning. A sleeping enemy is a defenseless enemy. At that time of the day, even the toughest of the tough allow themselves to drop their guard and sail away fast asleep into moments of childhood and innocence. The night is a friend of those who can see despite the darkness, of those with adrenaline rushing through their blood, of those primed for battle from head to toe.

Ya'ara's call did the trick. The decisions that followed in its wake were swift and decisive. No one suspected a hoax. The details were precise and corresponded with snippets of intelligence already in the hands of the German police and German security service — snippets that until that very moment had yet to come together to form a solid picture. With the consent of the

Bremen police chief, responsibility for the matter was transferred to the BKA, the Federal Criminal Police Office of Germany, and three hours before a pale dawn began painting orange streaks across the morning sky, members of the Police Tactical Unit, the elite counterterrorism squad, deployed around the farm, setting up surveillance positions and security perimeters. There was no movement on the farm itself. A four-by-four Land Rover was parked in the yard, and a weak glow was coming from inside the farmhouse, perhaps from a light above the staircase. The four helicopters flew in very low, almost noiselessly, and the commandos they were carrying alighted quickly and in precise order, before crouching and advancing slowly on the house. With perfect timing, they burst in through the front door and two second-floor windows, climbing up one after the other on aluminum ladders. The dull sounds of stun grenades could be heard from within the house, followed by a short burst of gunfire. A second team surrounded the barn, weapons at the ready. Two sappers dressed in cumbersome protective gear were sent inside, accompanied by a German shepherd trained to sniff out explosives.

The commandos removed five stunned

individuals from the living quarters — four men and one young woman. All of them barefoot. The faces of two, apparently injured in the raid, were bleeding slightly. Their hair was disheveled and unruly. All five were aggressively shoved into a van that sped into the farmyard and then roared out again. Within twenty minutes they'd be at the detention facility. A brief medical examination and then the start of a very prolonged interrogation.

34

The following day, the last day before Christmas Eve, three powerful explosive devices were detonated in three pubs in three cities in England — London, Manchester, and Birmingham. The attacks left twenty-three people dead and more than a hundred wounded. No one took responsibility for the blasts.

In Rome, the governor of the central bank was wounded in an assassination attempt just outside his home. He was struck in the stomach by two bullets fired from a pistol. According to eyewitnesses, a woman wearing a motorcycle helmet shot at him four or five times. After the governor slumped bleeding to the sidewalk, they reported, the woman ran to a waiting motorcycle on the other side of the street, its motor running, hopped on behind the rider, wrapped her arms around his waist, and the two raced off down the street and disappeared.

35

Hamburg, December 30, 2014

Matthias appeared thinner, Ya'ara thought, when they sat down together at the small restaurant in Hamburg. Thin and pallid and elderly, as if his years had finally caught up with him. It didn't matter to her in the least.

"They found Martina's body in an abandoned warehouse near the port in Bremen," he said to her, his painful gaze closely scrutinizing her.

"I'm sorry," she replied.

"She was tortured before they killed her. She was tied up, and someone shot her in both feet. She bled out for a few minutes at least before she was shot in the head. The person who did it used a Glock. We know from the ballistics results. Two more of the same pistols were found at the farm."

"Her Russian handler may have killed her. He may have thought she was endangering the others, and the operation. It's best not to think about it."

"Maybe." Her words clearly hadn't put his mind at rest. He wasn't simply a grieving lover, he was also a proficient intelligence official. Ya'ara wondered if he wanted to know the real answers.

She touched Matthias's hand, caressing it absentmindedly, tracing its contours with her fingertips. She had always thought his hands were beautiful and masculine, and now she wanted him to hold hers. But his hands remained limp. She was wearing a necklace of large pearls that shone like pale moonlight. Her fair hair was tied up. Her beauty took his breath away. But at the same time, and for the first time, he also noticed a sharp stab of iciness that pained him.

"They arrested the remaining five members of the group," Matthias continued. "And they found the computers with the field dossiers and the weapons, Kalashnikov assault rifles and Glock pistols. Based on what the investigators have learned thus far, the group was supposed to operate in pairs, simultaneously. The police received an anonymous call from a woman, a GRU officer, but you know that, of course. The conversation was very detailed and focused. Very convincing at least. Attested to by the fact that they acted that same night."

"Did Tomas, your friend at the security service, ask you anything?"

"Nothing. A good friend knows when not to ask, too."

"Matthias," Ya'ara softly said, "let's go away somewhere, for a week or two, just the two of us, you and me. We'll rent some cabin in the forest or, if you want somewhere warmer, we'll go to southern Italy. Sicily, perhaps?"

The look in his eyes that her blue-gray orbs encountered was primarily one of weariness. "I can't right now, Ya'ara," he said. "More than once I've thought to myself that I'd like nothing more than to be with you, just to be with you, no matter where, just to be there with you. But now I need to be here. With myself. Maybe they'll get to me during the course of their investigation into the entire affair, and I don't want them to think I've fled. And I also don't want them to draw a connection between us, certainly not in this context. And there's also Martina. Or who she was, in other words. We need some time, Ya'ara."

He saw the shadow of pain flash through her eyes, but he knew things had to be the way he said.

"You took some crazy risks for me. I know. You went to the ends of the earth for me. I appreciate it a lot more than I'm able to express. You know I'm not a man of words. I know you saved me. And you certainly saved the lives of three of the most senior bankers in Germany."

"We weren't able to save those who were killed in England. And it was nothing but luck that left the governor of Italy's central bank wounded and not dead."

"Are you positive that all the incidents are related?"

"They must be. Everything happened, or was supposed to happen, simultaneously. On the same day. Retro attacks in three locations. The IRA, the Red Brigades, the Baader-Meinhof Gang. Someone has a very creative and demonic imagination. Someone who's saying: Look what we can do. Look at the murder and mayhem we can spark at any given moment. Someone's saying: Look at me. You can't ignore me. I have the potential to cause enormous damage. And we all know about the ties to Russian intelligence."

"It's hard for me to believe that the Russians, as a state, are tied to the affair. That's simply madness on their part, if it's them. And they're very calculated and rational, after all."

"We identified Kovanyov."

"Maybe he's operating on his own account. Maybe he's a rogue agent who's out of control and out of his mind."

"Maybe. Anything's possible. But I don't think so. The Russians have taken several extreme measures over the past year. They truly are calculated, you're right, but they believe they can raise the risk threshold significantly. How would you describe what's happening in Ukraine if not as a calculated but daring move on the very edge?"

They sipped their wine in silence. When it was poured into the glasses, the red beverage looked almost black.

"Tell me, Matthias," Ya'ara asked in a soft but clear voice, "could the Russians have exposed you? Could they have identified you as an intelligence official? Perhaps they wanted to use Martina to implicate you, and the BND in turn, in this whole affair?"

"I have no idea. But having a source at any governmental entity in Hamburg would be enough for them to learn who I am. I'm well known to certain customs officials and the Interior Ministry and the police and the authorities at the port and in the free-trade zone and the Chamber of Commerce . . . The list is endless. When you're someone of my rank, you have no choice but to reveal your true position to your peers and affiliated organizations. So yes, I may very well have been made by Russian intelligence."

"I'm worried that you're in danger. Maybe you should ask for a transfer to a different role, somewhere else, to make a fresh start?"

"I can't run away. And if they take the ships and the port and the seamen away from me, I'll no longer be myself."

"There's always a moment when one has to move on, isn't there?"

"Right now, Ya'ara, I feel like I'm at my peak. I'm in the right place; the only way on from here is down. I can't sentence myself to a slow death because of an imaginary threat."

"Don't be melodramatic. It doesn't suit you."

"I feel very clear-headed actually. And besides, I can think of worse ways to die than by a bullet from a Russian-made Makarov pistol. Wasn't it Hemingway who said he wanted to die at the hands of a jealous husband armed with a shotgun?"

"Do you really think he said that? If he did, he was a perfect fool. And in the end, he shot himself. And there's nothing heroic about being liquidated by the Russians."

"Hemingway was a genius. And since when have you been such a big coward?"

"But I don't want anything to happen to you." Ya'ara sensed that something in her voice was about to break, so she stopped suddenly, taking a deep breath.

"Are those tears that I see in your beautiful eyes?" Matthias was genuinely surprised.

"I'm just tired and stressed. You're right. You know what you're doing. I can't be your mother." She thought for a moment. "And I really don't want to be."

"The thought of you as my mother makes me shudder. Come on," Matthias said softly, "we're both tired. Let's call it a night. Are you organized?"

"Of course." She smiled. "I'm at the hotel at the end of the street. Are you going home?"

"Maybe after a brief review at a bar or two. I need to make sure that the quality of their schnapps hasn't deteriorated."

"Go to sleep. Don't wander around like that in the middle of the night."

When they left the restaurant, wrapped in their thick coats, Ya'ara buried her head in his chest, and his large hands stroked her silky hair. Tiny snowflakes were drifting silently through the air, melting into tiny droplets of water as they landed on her head and sparkling like diamonds under the light of the streetlamps. He had the feeling that this would be their final embrace, that he had to let go of her.

"Happy New Year, Matthias," she said after emerging from his arms.

"Happy New Year," he said, and wondered if he meant to wish her a good life, a life that would always be lived far from his own.

36

Berlin, December 31, 2014

"I'd like us to raise our glasses and drink a toast to the New Year. You're all free this evening to celebrate however you like. Berlin is a great city for partying. Tomorrow you'll board your flights back to Israel, in keeping with the routes we've laid out. I hope you get some rest ahead of the next stage in your training. We'll meet here again on January 12. Monday morning. At ten."

Ya'ara looked at them one by one, her eyes locking momentarily with those of Nufar, Helena, Assaf, Ann, Batsheva, and Sayid. Affirming to each and every one of them that he or she was important, central, that the bond that had formed between them was unique. The cadets responded with looks of absolute concentration and readiness.

"We've been through some significant events together. I want to tell you that you were all wonderful. You're even better than I thought you'd be. You'll be even better than I thought you'd be," she corrected herself, "because you're just starting out. You demonstrated courage, and an ability to analyze and improvise, and you are good team members. What we did was take care of an emergency. And now you need to gain experience and learn in an orderly fashion."

"Are you certain we're worthy of praise?" Batsheva asked. "We were successful in Bremen, but dozens of people were killed in England."

"We can't take on the whole world single-handedly. Our mission was a success. Larger and more experienced forces will now enter the fray. This is a never-ending war."

Sayid wanted to ask Ya'ara where she had been all that night. She only got back to their hotel at four in the morning. He knew that because he had heard the door open and looked at the time on the screen of the phone that was charging on the bedside table. She went straight into the shower and stayed there for a long time. He could hear the water running nonstop. He thought he might have heard the sound of crying, too, but dismissed the thought almost immediately. Ya'ara wasn't one to cry. After emerging from the bathroom, she went straight to bed, curled up like a baby, tightly gripping the edge of the blanket in one hand. She didn't say a word, and he dropped off again. Now he wanted to ask, but he had learned by then that there'd be some questions that he'd never ask.

Helena looked into Ann's eyes. "Should we go for a drink?" she asked soundlessly. Ann's eyes smiled in response.

"L'Chaim," Ya'ara said. "To the lives of the cadets."

As they mingled together by the door on their way out, Batsheva turned to Aslan and asked, "Are you going with Ya'ara or coming with us?" She was referring to herself and Sayid. Assaf and Nufar had already announced that they were off to wander around Unter den Linden. Helena and Ann had hurried out together first.

"I think Ya'ara would like to be alone for a while. I'll join you, if that's okay."

"Of course. We invited you, didn't we?"

They lingered now at the door, as if they didn't want to part.

"Come on," Ya'ara said, "get out of here already. We'll meet in a week and a half."

"Bye, Ya'ara."

"Bye. Have fun. Happy New Year."

She hadn't asked Matthias where he'd be spending New Year's Eve. Maybe with his sister's family. Maybe with friends. Maybe alone, in front of the large fireplace, in his home on the outskirts of Hamburg. *It's actually not very far from here,* she thought for a moment. No, don't be so childish, she said to herself, pulling herself together. You're just feeling lonely.

She saw her as she stepped out into the street. A fair-haired woman, a little older than she was. A little taller. She caught a fleeting glimpse of her face, just as she turned right at the corner, a pleasant, pretty face, a large, strong nose, full lips, high cheekbones. And now she observed her from behind, the woman who was walking away from her, wearing a long, dark gray woolen coat, which came down to her ankles almost, like a robe. A silk scarf in shades of orange and gold around her neck. She knew it wasn't her, that it couldn't be her, and yet it felt as if she was looking at Tatiana. Her older sister. She expected her to turn around and call to her by her old name and jokingly scold her for being so far from home. Ya'ara closed her eyes, and the colors of the scarf, a glowing stain on her retinas for a short while, slowly turned dark. Enough already, enough, she berated herself, taking a deep breath of icy air into her lungs. You can't keep seeing her everywhere you go. When Ya'ara opened her eyes again, the street was full of people hurrying home on the eve of a new year. She felt a jarring pain, as if she had lost her sister all over again. Once again, Tatiana had disappeared and become a ghost.

37

Berlin, December 31, 2014

Due to the early hour, the revelers had yet to take to the streets. Helena and Ann were sitting at a corner table at what had already become their pub. They had drunk their first cocktail and were feeling comfortable and at ease. Helena's hair was tied back, and Ann restored a rogue strand to its rightful place behind her ear.

It was then that Helena noticed that Ann was wearing pajamas under her raincoat.

"I hate dressing to the nines," Ann admitted, giggling at the sight of the flannel pajamas she had on. "But that's what's always expected of me. As if a failure on my part to dress nicely, to put on makeup and to do my hair, is an offense to those who look at me. Funny, isn't it?" she asked.

"That's an odd expression — to the nines," Helena responded. "But you know you don't have to pretend to be someone else on the outside. You're not a store mannequin. You don't owe a thing to anyone. And certainly not in that way."

"I know, I know," Ann sighed. "Maybe it's got something to do with the fact that I always have to be the best at everything, the most educated, the most diligent, the most beautiful. Maybe it's because I'm a new immigrant."

"Not much newer than me."

"Nonsense, you were a child when you moved to Israel."

"That just means I've been a new immigrant for many years."

They went silent, sensing that something meaningful was transpiring between them, something beyond words.

"I hate Christmas," Helena suddenly said.

"Strange, me, too, ever since I was a kid. Apart from the presents," Ann agreed.

"What's happening at home?" Helena asked.

"I don't really know. I left Daniel a message to let him know I'll be arriving tomorrow evening. He didn't even respond. To be honest, we've hardly spoken since I've been here. He's busy, I'm busy. What about you?"

"It's complicated. These past weeks have left me pretty shaken. You know me a little. I'm fixed in my ways, organized. I need things to run smoothly. The next step was clear to me. Marriage in 2015. Eli is a great guy. He'll be done with his doctoral thesis within three to four months, so we could reserve a hall for the summer already. But I feel confused all of a sudden. Nothing seems logical any longer. My plans were so clear and now they've faded . . . And that's so not like me at all. To be confused, I mean. I'm not one to get muddled."

"We need to give all of this some time. These aren't normal circumstances. It's not the right time to make decisions."

"You're very right." Helena took Ann's hand and held it, under the table. They were sitting right next to each other now. Ann gently stroked her hair, and Helena rested her head on Ann's shoulder. Ann tilted her own head, her cheek resting on Helena's hair.

"Your hair smells like flowers," Ann murmured.

"For the first time in a long while, my head is in exactly the right place," Helena said in a whisper, her head resting in the crook of Ann's delicate neck, with her own neck curving softly and straining upward.

38

Berlin, December 31, 2014

Ya'ara wrapped herself in the thick comforter, her body stretched out diagonally across the double bed in her rented apartment in Berlin. She loved the apartment, and when the cadets dispersed and all went their own separate ways, she got the chance to go back there again. Two spacious rooms in a building erected before World War I, a gleaming and glistening wooden floor. Like many others in the neighborhood, the structure had undergone a refurbishment of late. It was located opposite a small square, with access to the square itself along a quiet road, lined with tall overhanging trees, that also featured an Italian restaurant, a Pakistani restaurant, a local pub, and a secondhand bookstore. Visible from the end of the street, in all its sobriety, was a red-brick church, topped by a bell tower, the heavy bells peeking through the openings of the double arches. She thought about the architect who had designed it three centuries ago, and wondered about the journey he had taken, months on end in Genoa, Lucca, Florence, Naples, descending from the north to the south, the skies gradually clearing, the heat rising, the flowers boasting bold colors, clouds of bugs humming in the scorching air, the waves of the blue sea crashing up against white cliffs, the light breaking on them bright and blinding.

For the thousandth time she watched a YouTube clip to which she was constantly drawn. A Beatles' song, "While My Guitar Gently Weeps," from a performance at the Albert Hall in London. Eric Clapton was leading a huge ensemble, with Paul McCartney at the piano, three drummers, one of them Ringo Starr, at least five guitarists, two back-up vocalists, one black woman and one white, neither of them young, and a hyperactive old man with dark sunglasses banging his hands on a set of bongos at a furious pace, and Clapton himself playing wonderfully and singing in his flat-sounding baritone voice. But she was drawn most of all by one of the guitarists, whom the camera keeps panning back to. He was playing a large acoustic guitar, to the left of Clapton and a little behind him, playing with breathtaking self-confidence, quite surprising, considering he was sharing a stage with some of the greatest musicians in the world. He looked just twenty-something, so thin, so beautiful, his eyes hidden by his hair, wearing a big white shirt made from an airy cotton fabric, and he was playing like an angel, sadness in his eyes, singing along now and then, present on the stage. The circular hall was filled to the brim, packed with a thrilled and seemingly electrified audience. This was clearly no regular performance. By now she knew the identity of the young, the beautiful, the fragile and self-assured young man, whom the cameraman returned to time and again. Something about solving the mystery had left her disappointed; she should have guessed herself. The song was recorded during a one-off performance in 2002 in memory of George Harrison, who had died of cancer a year earlier.

The young man was Dhani Harrison, George's musician son. Yes, she should have noticed for herself how much he looked like him, even though the famous father looked more dark and tormented and hermit-like than his beautiful son, and if she had realized that he was the son of George Harrison then she would have clearly understood what he was doing there on the stage with his father's friends, and why the camera kept focusing on him, not simply because he was young and attractive and mysterious and talented but because he was so reminiscent of his father, like some kind of ghost, but she chose to forget what she had found out, and wanted to ask herself time and time again who that young man could be. Twelve years had passed since that memorial performance, and she had seen recent pictures on the internet of Dhani Harrison, and he looked different now, more rugged, less beautiful, filling small arenas in Portland and Seattle. He would never be a superstar like the late George or John, or their friends.

She was here while Matthias was in his house in Hamburg just two hours away from her. She was cuddled up, alone in her bed, watching videos on the screen of the phone she should have used to report all that had happened in Bremen, but she was putting it off. She would be in Tel Aviv tomorrow, breathing in the smell of the rain and wet leaves, tasting a hidden hint of salt from the sea on the air.

39

Berlin, January 11, 2015

Nufar and Sayid ran into each other as they exited the terminal at Tegel Airport, on their way to the long line of taxis that was waiting idly, spewing fumes, for the few passengers who were arriving in ice-cold Berlin on a Sunday afternoon. Nufar arrived on a connection from Frankfurt, Sayid flew in via Amsterdam. Nufar was pleased to see him, and she allowed her emotions to brighten her face with a broad smile. "It's so good to see you," she said as she hugged him. "I've missed you. All of this." She gestured to form a wide circle with her hand, her movement designed to include the aircraft and the airline counters and the cold air and the low clouds that lay over the city.

"I'm happy to see you, too," Sayid said. "And to get back here. I've been restless over the past few days. I'm a little surprised by myself, but I'm missing the action. Me, an economist in the bank's research department, who's missing a few hours of surveillance in the swamps around Bremen."

Nufar laughed. "What you're saying is so true. Those brief and action-packed weeks have messed with our heads. I'm like some kind of a junkie now, craving more."

"How were things back in Israel? All good?"

"I spent time with my mother and sister. It's always nice, even if we start arguing about every issue in the world after a few days together. And yes, I wanted to get back here already. Everything seemed a little strange to me. As if I was seeing something in regular things that others couldn't see, like I had a third eye."

Sayid wanted to ask her about her father, but he didn't want to encroach on her privacy, which until now seemed to envelop her meticulously from all sides. And he didn't ask. "Yes," he said, "you've got a point there. As if the world itself is different, strange. You know, I was just hanging out one day at a café on Weizmann Street in Givatayim, enjoying the Israeli winter sun, thinking of the cold here with a shudder, and suddenly the entire street seemed different to me. Nothing was necessarily as it appeared to be. Is that electrician's van really an electrician's van? And that older woman over there wearing a headscarf and sunglasses and carrying a small dog, what is she really up to? To be honest, we need to keep things on an even keel. After all, most things are truly as they appear to be, right?"

"Sometimes a cigar is just a cigar," Nufar responded.

Sayid looked at her, and she couldn't tell if he had understood the Freud reference.

"Should we share a cab?" she asked, and immediately suggested he join her for dinner, if he didn't have other plans.

"Gladly," Sayid replied gallantly, "wherever you choose."

"I feel like Vietnamese. I've been dreaming about a bowl of noodles with chicken."

"Is that all?" he asked with a smile. "That sounds like a dream that's easily realized."

Nufar smiled, too.

As they walked side by side, dragging their trolley suitcases, there was something natural and simple between them, so much so that Sayid was required to remind himself just how much his life had changed. It's me, Sayid, he said to himself. The shy boy from Algiers. A cadet in a unit so secret that it still has no name. Going out to dinner in

Berlin with a young woman, so smart and beautiful. It's me, Sayid.

40

The cadets were kept busy over the following two days with intensive debriefings concerning their activities in Bremen. They had the chance now to analyze the events quietly and without any pressure, and to actually learn something finally. Ya'ara and Aslan reviewed the events with the cadets in a systematic and methodical fashion. They spoke to them in concrete terms and added background and context to moves that were carried out quickly and in such a manner that they had appeared to the cadets to be instinctive. They discussed planning, situation assessment, intuition. And with the aid of hindsight, they analyzed the various actions they had taken and tried to assess the risks involved in them and to identify the steps that had led to breakthroughs.

"We did a very good job," Ya'ara told them. "You did. We thwarted a very sophisticated and extremely cruel plot. We saved lives. At least three families were not destroyed because of your solid field work, your courage, and your devotion. And we managed to prevent an earthquake in the German banking system. And to help a good friend." She looked around, looking straight into their eyes, each and every one of them. "True, we had luck. True again, we were not able to do anything about the attacks in Britain and in Italy. But this war is a long one. We are not alone in it, although it seems that we have to lead and be in the front lines. All the time. And with perseverance and valor and faith we will win." She paused, slightly embarrassed. She resorted to talking business.

"Experience, legwork, and luck," Ya'ara concluded, but it was clear to everyone that this was just a very partial summation. What about creativity? And the ability to think on one's feet? And courage? But they decided to move on. Because Ya'ara had returned from Israel with new missions. None of those present knew who had given her the assignments personally, not even Aslan.

She and Aslan had talked about what was expected of them the night before.

"Look," she said to him, "the world is changing at a frightening pace right before our eyes. It's becoming chaotic and violent and incomprehensible, and we need to operate within this scope, to restore the balance a little. Islam is spiraling out of control, going back to some wild and primeval point in time. Think about the dusty expanses of the Middle East. About the endless convoys of fighters. Cruel, thin men with long beards, carrying assault rifles and swords. The pickup trucks racing across the wide-open plains, with machine guns fixed to their cargo bays. The insane freedom to kill and destroy. To behead.

"Something about this dark savagery, which appears to be more like a video game than the Quran, is attracting thousands of European Muslims, young men — and women, too — who were born and educated in Europe, who grew up in supposedly free societies, and who hate with all their might, with every ounce of their being, the societies and cultures in which they are living. And after they've affiliated themselves with this darkness, after they've experienced combat, after they've learned to spill blood, after they've fallen in love with or become addicted to the blood, they return home, to their European countries, to their frightening and disadvantaged neighborhoods, to their slim chances of fitting in. And they start killing. Again and again and again. And it won't come to an end just like that. It's not going to die out on its own."

"Do you want to take on millions of Muslims in Europe?"

"I want to fight because that's who I am. That, first and foremost. And yes, I believe we have a chance."

"Look, Ya'ara, I'm not an intellectual like you, and I, too, have sworn to fight my enemies, but even I know that the picture you're painting doesn't tell the full story. Those extremists call themselves Muslims, but Islam is not a murderous religion. What do you think — that you and I are going to rid the world of an entire religion? We're going to crush Islam with a bunch of cadets?" He added a smile at the end of his words, but he was clearly somewhat concerned about Ya'ara's zeal. He knew how quickly her thoughts could be translated into actions in the field.

"You're right," she said. "You're right. Let me explain. And of course we aren't going to triumph on our own. You know what? The ultimate winners, to be honest, will be the Muslims themselves. Who'll come to their senses and won't allow themselves to be led by a gang of murderous lunatics. Islam, after all, embodies a great deal of beauty, complexity, and wisdom. And there are good and wealthy and intellectually enriching places in the history of Islam that one can return to as sources of inspiration. But that could take a long time. Years, generations perhaps. And the Europeans, too, have to realize at some point that if they maintain their passive and hesitant approach, the barbarity will overpower them. And you'll slowly see their determination and fighting spirit growing ever stronger."

Aslan remained silent. He hated that word, barbarity, but waited for more to come from Ya'ara. He had already said way more than usual just moments before.

Ya'ara continued. "We can be the trigger. We'll show the way. We'll be the snake that slithers unseen through the grass, emerges, strikes, and vanishes again. Until the next time. And the time after that. That's how I envision the years to come." Ya'ara stopped. Observing herself, as always, from the outside, trying to understand the meaning of her own enthusiasm, as if she were some kind of a brainwashed military officer or zealous youth movement counselor. But she was not like that, after all, she was cool and calculating. Though she really did believe what she had said.

"That's a frightening image, that snake of

yours," Aslan said.

She couldn't contain herself, and her enthusiasm bubbled over again. "But it's an accurate one, too. Because that's exactly what I want to do. I want to frighten. To intimidate. To add another variable to the equation. To say: Look, here's something covert, deadly, that isn't going to show any tolerance. If you murder, if you incite and encourage murder, if nothing but pure hatred flows in your blood, you will pay with your life."

"And we're going to do all this with six cadets?"

She took a deep breath, regaining her composure and adopting a businesslike approach once again. "To begin with," she said. "And there'll be others to come. And I have an idea about how to increase our force significantly, in a relatively short period of time. But I want us to remain focused for now.

"And you know, Aslan," Ya'ara continued after stemming her flow of words, her flow of thoughts, for a moment, "we aren't like them, after all. We aren't about to embark on a massacre. If we operate properly, we'll get to select those who truly deserve to die, we'll strike and disappear without a trace, and our reputation will precede us. Isolated incidents, in succession, without any obvious modus operandi, will create waves, a reverberation, a long and blood-curdling whisper."

The similarity between Ya'ara's suggested course of action and the incident they had recently thwarted, the attack planned by the new Baader-Meinhof group, didn't escape Aslan, but he held his tongue.

"We'll be doing what we do for a good cause, a just cause," Ya'ara said, appearing to read his mind. "There's no reason to question the method. And we'll be focused. We'll strike only at those who deserve it. We won't be selecting random targets."

"So how do you want us to move forward?" Aslan asked. "What are we going to do tomorrow, with the cadets?"

"Osama Hamdan."

"Who?"

"Osama Hamdan and Anjam Badawi." Ya'ara continued without hesitating. "Hamdan is the man who murdered Yael Ziv at the central synagogue in Brussels. He's currently in custody in Belgium. Badawi is a Muslim preacher in London, as radical as they come. We'll be targeting both of them. We'll split into two groups. The mission will include intelligence gathering and the formulation of an operational plan for their assassination. After gathering the intelligence for the operation, if we manage to put together a real plan, we'll execute it, too. Tomorrow we'll divide the cadets into two teams. You'll accompany the one team to England. I'll take the second team to Belgium. We'll give ourselves a month. And see where we're at. I want us to eventually be in a position, with our existing force, to be able to put together a series of six to eight operations a year. But we'll get there only after we complete the cadets' training and are able to say that we're up and running from an operational perspective. We'll be constructing the force, meanwhile, in conjunction with actual field experience and learning."

"Hamdan is in jail already. Why do you want to kill him?"

"First, because he deserves it." An image from many years ago popped into her thoughts. Her own mother with her head bent over Yael, whispering something to her. "And Yael deserves to be avenged. And second, getting to someone who's in prison, with half the Belgian police force guarding him, is a unique professional challenge. And I want all those pieces of filth to know that if they hurt us, they won't die of old age. Plain and simple — they'll be liquidated.

Yes, the Europeans are indeed promoting various regulations and laws. And there's a Security Council resolution calling for action against what the council defines as foreign terrorist fighters. That's a good thing. It's important. And if they act decisively and systematically, they can make significant inroads. But at the same time, we need to be the rogue element, the ruthless element, which will add the required resoluteness to this war. This insane phenomenon can't be defeated by regular means only. We'll be the ever-present black shadow from which the lightning strikes."

"Do we have a mandate for all of this?" he asked.

Ya'ara looked at him with her bright eyes, responding in the affirmative with just a nod of her head.

"How can a girl like you be so fanatical?" Aslan asked with obvious affection, watered down with a certain degree of reservation.

"Don't know. That's just me."

"You know I love you just the way you are," he said, as if trying to convince himself. "And the preacher?"

"He is worse than a hundred murderers. He drives hundreds of young Muslims to make pilgrimages to the sites of murders and jihadi attacks. He's the most cold-blooded of them. He says the most terrible things in such a soft and gentle and sanctimonious tone of voice. He's asking for a bullet between the eyes, and we're going to grant his request. He sends out others to murder and be killed. We're going to give him the honor of being a *shaheed* himself."

The teams had already been determined — Aslan would work with Sayid, Helena with Ann, Ya'ara with Batsheva, Nufar with Assaf.

"We have nothing to go on aside from the names. We're starting from scratch. Think of ways to obtain information. The internet, obviously. We'll start from there, but find other ways, too."

"What about weapons?" Assaf asked. "We're eventually going to need arms. A pistol, hand grenades, something."

"Correct. But it's early days now and it depends a lot on the intelligence we secure. We'll have to equip ourselves with the means that best suit the operational plan we put together."

"But we may have to select an operational plan that suits the weapons at our disposal. If all we have in the end are knives that can be purchased at a store that caters to chefs, we'd need a very different plan than one for a situation in which we had, let's say, a sniper rifle," Assaf said.

"An important point, Assaf," Ya'ara said, her mind offering her an image of Assaf attacking terrorists with a large kitchen knife. She was impressed by his practicality, which had caught her attention already during the initial selection stage. "We'll work on the weapons question at the same time. Ultimately, we need to ensure that all our avenues of activity converge at a single point in time. That's part of the entire issue. To know how to plan and make progress on several different tracks, even when things are very uncertain. That's the world in which we're learning to operate. Sometimes we fall flat on our faces, and often, you'll be surprised to hear, it works. Provided that uncertainty doesn't scare you too much. We're scheduled to meet again in a month's time. Take care of yourselves," she said to the small team that was already gathered around Aslan. "And we'll take care of ourselves. Remember, no foolish suicide missions. We don't need martyrs, only serious individuals who want to stay in the business for many years to come."

Sayid remained silent while Ya'ara was talking. Now might have been the first time he fully understood that this was going to be his life over a long period of time. And the implications were staring him in the face. *How am I ever going to meet someone?* he thought with a sudden sense of anxiety. How will I ever have a family? A home? He pictured himself twenty or twenty-five years down the line. His hair graying, his face drawn, sitting in a dingy bar in Zurich or Delhi or Johannesburg, with nowhere to go. Where would his home be then?

"Sayid, are you with us?" Ya'ara asked.

"Yes, of course, I was just daydreaming for a moment."

"Good dreams, I hope."

"Not quite. A nightmare you couldn't even imagine," he responded with his pleasant smile.

"We're out of here, Sayid," Aslan said to him. "Our work begins."

Ya'ara assembled her team around her. "You'll be getting to work, too, Batsheva, Nufar, and Assaf. I want you to compile and organize all the information you can find on Hamdan on the internet by this evening. I want to see his name in the obituaries column within a month." Yael Ziv's pale face, her large dark eyes, her elusive smile, the foreign and gentle sound of her voice. She imagined them all. She could feel the sharp edge of her frustration and rage cutting into her, leaving her with a familiar sense of restlessness and disquiet, a powerful urge to act. There's a price to pay for the horrors you cause, she whispered to herself, unsure who she was talking to.

41

Frankfurt, January 2015

She didn't like Frankfurt. Germany had beautiful and pleasing cities, but Frankfurt couldn't be counted among them. For her, the city always aroused a sense of distaste. The filth and violence of the central train station area, the wretchedness of the sex district, the luxury stores fortified by security guards, bars, and heavy locks, the skyscrapers that had made the city more American than any other German metropolis. She was familiar, too, of course, with the city's redeeming features. The museums along the wide river, the old city, Fressgass — the culinary main street leading away from the stock exchange in the central business district, and the area around the university, bubbling with beautiful young people and their serious and optimistic energy of activism. But more than anything else, at the end of every visit to Frankfurt, a city that could have been a real diamond but somehow missed its opportunity, she felt a strong need for a long, hot shower.

Ya'ara arrived in Frankfurt this time in the late evening, on the fast train from Berlin.

He was waiting for her at bar of the Frankfurter Hof Hotel. A silent waiter relieved her of her long coat the moment she walked in. She was at her best that evening, statuesque, in high heels, her blue dress clinging to her body, two pearl earrings gleaming in her ears, her fair hair appearing even paler under the dim lights of the bar. There wasn't a single man in the shadowy expanse who failed to sense her presence. She never changes, the man waiting for her in the far corner of the room whispered to himself. Breathtaking and a danger on two legs. He rose from the deep leather armchair in which he was sitting as she approached, and she shook his hand formally, and then, abruptly shaking off the formality, she kissed both his cheeks. Goran Petrovich was a tall, strong man. His hair was graying, his blue eyes were cold and piercing, a white scar cut across his face from just below his right eye and down to his chin. A rare smile was the only thing that upset the menacing impression he made. He wasn't smiling now.

Ya'ara had met him for the first time a few years after the end of the civil war that had left Yugoslavia ripped to bleeding shreds. She and her team were operating in the Balkans at the time. Iran's Revolutionary Guard Corps, the exporters of Tehran's terror and fanaticism, wasn't about to forgo any potential stronghold, and the Iranians viewed Muslim Bosnia, which had emerged from the war scarred and bleeding, as easy pickings. Ya'ara's squad teamed up back then with international forces that had been deployed to expose the Iranian activity, and to sabotage and thwart it. That's the way it goes in war, she drummed into her cadets. It's a fight for every inch. A relentless battle. Matthias had been the one to hook her up with Goran, a tough and ruthless Serb fighter who, after the war, went on doing the only thing in which he excelled, and he was doing the same now for a high fee, in secret.

Welcome to the world of the mercenaries, Matthias had said to her at the time, before leaving her in a dingy bar that reeked of smoke, at just twenty-seven years old, in the charming company of the Serbian with the blood-soaked hands. The realization that Ya'ara wasn't intimidated by him in the least was the thing that had sold Goran. He could smell fear, discern the slight tremor that betrays anxiety, the shift of a gaze designed to avoid confrontation, the accelerated pulse. He didn't pick up on any of those things with Ya'ara. She was young, no doubt, but she knew exactly what she wanted, her tactical thinking was impressive, her humor tickled him, and her charm enveloped their encounters like the fragrance of an expensive perfume. Sometimes, when thinking about her, he wondered why in fact she hadn't been afraid of him. After all, anyone with eyes in their heads would have been somewhat fearful at least, and with good reason, too. Not Ya'ara, however. But, as he admitted to himself, that wasn't the only reason he enjoyed her company, and he treasured his connection with her like a warm secret.

And now, two years, or maybe more, after their last meeting, he was looking at her once again, her radiance still intense and moving.

They had their first drink at the bar, followed by dinner at the hotel's prestigious restaurant. She ordered wild quail in a cassis sauce, served on a bed of artichokes. Goran went for angelfish medallions on a barley ragout, with plump and spicy chorizo sausages on the side. They spoke like old friends who had lots of catching up to do. *How strange,* Ya'ara thought. *Here we sit by candlelight, sharing intimate details that even the people closest to us may not know, yet this entire connection is taking place in a bubble, nothing about it relates to our real lives, our true identities, our real families and friends. But still, within this bubble, whose existence we are both aware of, the connection is a real one. Maybe these bubbles are in fact our real lives, my life.* She smiled at Goran, who was telling her just then about the defining moment of his wild boar hunt in the black mountains of Montenegro before Christmas.

She spoke to Goran about the weapons she needed.

"Are you putting a small army together?" he asked with a smile, briefly running the tip of his finger along the white scar on his face.

"Something like that. And I'm going to need a few items in England, too. I won't be able to transport them from here. I'll need to get them there. Can you do that?"

"You know I can. For you, my darling, I'm willing to do special things."

"And that, too, for the right price."

"Of course. I'm a businessman," Goran

said, flashing one of his wolfish grins.

They skipped dessert and moved on to *Schwarzer,* a strong black coffee. Their silences, too, weren't uncomfortable ones.

"Tell me, Goran," Ya'ara said pensively, "how long will we go on doing this?"

"For a whole lot longer I hope. Does it look like we're suffering? Look at us now. A fine meal, good company, plenty money, spice in our lives. If we were to stop doing it, we'd die a slow death."

"Perhaps you're right. Perhaps it's our destiny."

"You're too serious, my darling. Come, let's have another drink. I don't like to see you sad."

"I'm not sad, they're just thoughts that run through my mind sometimes. Come, another drink at the bar. And then we'll head out. The night awaits us."

42

London, February 1948

Yosef Raphael closed the iron door of the studio and secured the heavy padlock. Both of them, he and Henry Moore, looked like silhouettes in the cold, wet air.

"Come, come, young man, let's warm our bones at a pub, and then you can escort me to a cab."

Raphael felt as if he were walking on air. Henry Moore had visited his studio, the studio that was also his place of residence. He had been his guest for almost two hours, reviewing his sculptures, his ink sketches, listening to his ideas. Raphael told him about his encounter with Constantin Brancusi, the great Romanian sculptor, at his studio in France. He felt his soul glide and soar to the heavens on seeing the abstract birds, their perfect beauty, depicted in the elderly sculptor's totem poles, which seemed to climb unendingly skyward. Moore said a few words, but Raphael sensed that his guest didn't want to discuss Brancusi at length. He curbed his enthusiasm somewhat. He was eager to hear Moore's opinion on his piece, *Absalom,* which he was in the midst of working on.

"He's very different from the rest of your work," Moore said to him, his eyes focused on the white marble statue. "Definitely not at all like your desert sculptures." Raphael had shown him photographs of warrior-like figures and wild animals that inhabited the age-old deserts of his imagination, sculptures he had left behind at his studio in Israel.

"I feel that *Absalom,* too, is belligerent and savage. But I have to see him as a classical figure, like a Greek statue almost. Thin and elongated, gleaming in its whiteness, anatomically perfect, strength contained within the marble. Look at the tragedy that it embodies, that will ultimately burst forth. Look at the arrogance and self-confidence, which will be his downfall. Look at how beautiful he is."

"There's something misleading about this piece," Moore said, his gaze sharp and thoughtful at the same time. "It looks initially like the work of a very talented student who's been given the task of copying a classical Greek sculpture. But little by little, one sees the elements you've just spoken of. The wildness, the hubris, the defiance. Very nice, my young friend," Moore said, eyeing Raphael with admiration. "Very nice. I'm curious to see the finished product. What I can already see before me is a great artist." Raphael was beside himself.

They were making their way now down the dark street, its edges dimly lit by an orange glow. When they entered the local pub, it was Raphael who received a nodded greeting from the publican behind the bar and several regular patrons. None of them recognized Moore, the renowned sculptor.

"I want to introduce you to a close acquaintance of mine," Moore said to Raphael as they warmed up with their second round of whiskey each. "There you go, some good things have come from Scotland, too," he added, gazing soberly at the heavy amber liquid. "He's an interesting man, a scholar of ancient cultures and an art collector, from a noble family, who lives on a large estate in the Oxford area. Splendid and tattered. Like England," he said with a bitter smile. "I'll send him a letter, and I'll ask him to invite you."

"Gladly," Raphael said. "It would be a

great honor for me."

They drank two more measures, wrapped themselves in their coats, and walked toward the small square, where you could always find a waiting taxi or two. Moore wobbled a little as he tried to get into the black cab, and he smiled contritely at Raphael.

"Farewell, my young friend. You're doing good things. Keep at it. Work hard. That's the plight of us sculptors. Hard work. Hard work! Keep in touch."

Raphael closed the taxi door and watched the vehicle move away, soon to disappear into the mist. He tightened his coat, tied his scarf firmly around his neck, and began walking in the opposite direction from his home, from his studio. He wanted to clear his mind, to allow the ice-cold air to clean his lungs.

43

Brussels, January 15

"I'm in."

Nufar was focused on three laptops that were connected to one another with a tangle of cables. Assaf and Batsheva were leaning over her, casting a shadow over the screens.

"Give her some space," Ya'ara said. "We can't afford to make any mistakes now."

The logo of the Belgian Prison Service appeared in the corner of the screen of the laptop on the left. Nufar had finally managed to hack into the organization responsible for the incarceration and security of Osama Hamdan, the murderer from Brussels's main synagogue.

When Nufar had suggested the idea of a cyberattack on the prison service's computer network, Ya'ara was skeptical.

"It's a state-run security organization of a European country, I'm sure its computer network is well protected," she said. "And how would we do it anyway? Do you know how to? To assess the risks? To avoid detection?" She thought she was asking rhetorical questions and expected to see Nufar hang her head in defeat on hearing them.

"Look, Ya'ara, it can definitely be done. I know this wasn't the reason you recruited me, but during my military service and then also as a student, I built on the computer know-how I acquired as a young girl. There isn't an economist or businessperson out there who knows their way around computers as well as I do. Well, that was the case at least during my time at INSEAD. And yes, I admit my know-how isn't systematic, but I can usually rely on my intuition to help me out. So I think I know how to approach this. We'll need to identity their system's weak spots. Someone always makes a cybersecurity error somewhere. And we'll need some luck, too."

"Luck is good. I'm all for luck."

"And I can't guarantee success." Following the brief speech she had just given, Nufar continued suddenly in a more cautious tone of voice. "But I should give it a try. We've been racking our brains for a week already in an effort to find a way to get the information we need. I think this is the way to do it."

Ya'ara nodded, hoping that her highly intelligent cadet wasn't going to expose them all due to some rookie mistake.

And now, from the business center of the Hilton Hotel at the Brussels airport, Nufar began wandering through the computer system of the Belgian Prison Service's central headquarters.

"It could take hours," Nufar said to them. "Give me some breathing room. I'll call you over when I come across something interesting."

"Coffee, anyone?" suggested Assaf, who had decided to contribute, in some way, to the war effort.

A few minutes later, he served two cups of coffee to Nufar and Ya'ara. Batsheva, for her part, was drinking hot chocolate in the hotel lobby, sitting with one leg crossed over the other, waiting for more exciting news.

Nufar turned up a piece of relevant information after a little more than two hours of searching. Hamdan was scheduled to appear in court in Brussels for a remand hearing in two and half weeks' time, on February 9, at eleven in the morning. The precise courtroom for the hearing had yet to be determined. But detailed sketches of the layout of the courthouse, which were found in a folder belonging to the unit responsible for escorting prisoners, showed exactly where the security vehicles entered the building, as well as the location of the detention cells in which the prisoners were held until it was time for them to be brought up to one of the courtrooms. There was a gap of about five or six meters between the closest parking spot for the security vehicles and the steel door leading to the detainees' enclosure. Ya'ara believed that if they could just find a clear line of sight from some elevated point outside the courthouse onto the few meters the prisoners were required to cross on foot before entering the building, they'd have their opportunity.

"Okay, guys," she said, "we'll go out into the field. Some things need to be seen firsthand. Assaf and I will go out together. Batsheva, you'll stay here with Nufar until she decides she's finished with the computer system. Help her afterward to pack up all the gear. Join us when you're done and have returned everything to the apartment."

They were renting a large and well-equipped apartment on Avenue Louise. Brussels, the capital of the European Union, excelled in the field of furnished apartments for short-term rentals. Expensive, but discreet and convenient. The city was always full of diplomats and experts who were there for conferences and seminars and debates that were part of the extensive and intensive activities of the Union's institutions. Ya'ara had even casually said, despite not being asked anything, that she and her group would be in the city for several weeks in the framework of a project dealing with European legislation on the environment. The girl at the real estate agency simply nodded her head politely and disinterestedly. The only thing that interested her was the credit card.

The court building overlooked the square. Its golden dome shone in the winter sunlight that was coming through a rip in the clouds. It was an immense and grandiose structure built of stone and marble when Belgium was still a small colonial empire, committing and concealing its crimes far from home, in the Congo. The building was surrounded in part by scaffolding, an integral feature of a round of renovation and maintenance work that appeared to be going on forever. Ya'ara and Assaf scanned the area around them in frustration. They weren't able to spot any tall building within reasonable range from which the inner courtyard would be visible.

"If you were thinking of a sniper operation," Assaf said, "I wouldn't bet on a distance of more than four hundred meters. And I can't see a single vantage point that comes even close to that range. We're going to need a helicopter."

"A helicopter is a little over the top," Ya'ara responded. "But what about a small model aircraft that can be remotely controlled?"

Assaf pondered Ya'ara's idea, while she let out a deep sigh of frustration. The idea, in theory, was a good one. It was her job, however, to explain to Assaf that they were reaching way too high. Yes, in Hollywood movies, multirotor drones that could stay in the air for hours instead of minutes were already operational, and served terrorists of all kinds. But the basic notion, in fact, requires development and training and, above all, absolute precision. It isn't something that can be put together in an instant without prior know-how, without a laboratory that could develop its own product, or, at the very least, could take a commercial product and adapt it for the purpose of carrying out an operational mission. It couldn't be done without achieving absolute control over the aerial vehicle, without intense training, mishaps, minor accidents, more training, more mishaps, tests, proof of feasibility, proof of durability — they were all essential elements. You wanted a small unit that would be starting from scratch, she told herself. This is the cost.

"We need to recruit a Q," she said. "We need a genius — male or female. A super-nerd with outlandish ideas and magical hands."

"First, finish with us, your cadets. And then we'll set up the tech division."

"Truth is I have someone in mind. The connection is a little tenuous — a friend of the brother of a girl who was on the team with me last year. Dima. He did a little work for us back then, too. Without being aware of its true purpose. We didn't tell him then that he was aiding the forces of darkness. I have a feeling he'd be an excellent candidate." *And he's the only candidate I have,* she thought. Nufar's skills were impressive, but Dima, as she had learned on a previous occasion, was truly the computer whisperer, and his abilities spilled over into other fields of technology, too. After deciding to contact him, she knew she had deleted one task from the long list that awaited her after the current operation.

They continued to walk around the court building, like two tourists, in the hope that the site itself would spark some kind of idea.

"How are things going for you, up to this point?" Ya'ara asked.

"The course? It feels like I'm on a roller-coaster. Yes. The world you've shown us is amazing. Amazing and very cold," Assaf responded, frozen drops of rain pricking into the back of his neck. The sun that had appeared earlier was just an illusion, and all trace of it was gone. Ya'ara wondered nevertheless if Assaf was talking only about physical cold.

"And home?"

"What about home?"

"Are you coping with the longing, the distance?"

"Look, this is a training period. I hope things will be a little more flexible in the future. That we won't have to be away for so long. Tali and I have agreed to give it a chance, to take a deep breath. It's working for now. I miss my children more than I thought possible, but when we were on that break just now, I couldn't wait to get back to Europe. I couldn't believe it, but I wanted to get back to what we had in Bremen."

"Yes, I felt the same. I started to lose my mind after four days. Come now, let's focus. We need to find another way. And when you have eliminated the impossible . . ."

"I know," Assaf interrupted, "whatever remains, however improbable, must be the truth. I love Sherlock Holmes," he added, almost apologetically.

"Nice," Ya'ara said. "But books are one thing and reality is another, and right now I can't see a way of taking him out from afar. Not in the framework of the timetable we've set ourselves. I can't afford to allow the operation to continue for an entire year. Our unit is supposed to function differently. To generate a series of incidents and continuity. And that you can't achieve with operations that go on forever."

Assaf nodded. They were walking down streets of gray, a cold, pestering rain coming down on them. Ya'ara tightened her coat around her body and her mind conjured up the image of a drone, a miniature flying saucer of sorts, like something out of a sci-fi movie from the 1960s or '70s, relaying all she could see in real time, armed with a tiny explosive charge, hovering almost soundlessly at a height of a few dozen meters, diving down rapidly onto its target.

It's not such an absurd idea, she thought. We'll set up a small tech unit. I'm sure that the PM will give us go-ahead to do it, and it'll be easy to recruit the personnel. They continued to make their way through the winding streets toward the Grand Place, Assaf walking beside her, watching her think. Intently watching her think.

44

London, Bethnal Green, January 2015

Belgium and England are separated by a gray and icy sea. And in keeping with the dampness and drizzle of Brussels, the weather in London, too, was wet and bleak and cold. For the past few hours, just as over the previous two days, they had been walking in pairs through the streets of East London's Bethnal Green, until recently a low-income district that had spent the last few years trying to powder its drab cheeks. The harsh neighborhood, home to a large Bangladeshi Muslim population, did have a certain charm, the cadets admitted. It's hard to believe that in the eighteenth century it was still a village of sorts that earned its livelihood from agriculture; and in the nineteenth century, the district saw the rise of a silk and textiles industry. Many of the area's Victorian homes were destroyed by the German bombing in World War II. And after the war, hastily built low-rise buildings, as part of immense and awful housing estates, were erected on the ruins. Over the past few years, the neighborhood had begun a very gradual and cautious process of renewal, in small and hesitant steps. Refurbished old houses now appeared here and there. A handful of art galleries had opened. Cafés and small restaurants were beginning to adorn the streets. Not just fish and chips shops and oil-splattered kebab stalls. It wasn't to everyone's taste.

Preacher Anjam Badawi's mosque wasn't far from Jesus Green. *A coming together of Muhammad and Jesus on the street corner,* Sayid thought ironically, *and now the Jews are joining the party.* Aslan and Ann, Helena and Sayid. Aslan wanted them to get to know the neighborhood, to let it get under their skin. This was their third day of wandering its streets, studying its traffic patterns, the parks, the cafés and restaurants, the public transport systems. Making a mental note of the churches, mosques, police stations, Underground stations. Badawi's image graced posters on the street inviting the faithful to a prayer session and sermon at his mosque. He was right there, so nearby. After reading his appalling vitriol on the internet, they could now feel his hatred creeping down their backs.

They met up at one of the pubs on the outskirts of the neighborhood, where they conversed in English. Speaking Hebrew, as it was plain to see, would not have been warmly received at that location.

"It's a combination of Dhaka and Charles Dickens," Helena said as she removed her coat and warmed her hands.

"You mix your metaphors in the most scandalous fashion," Ann remarked.

"I actually understood exactly what she was saying," Sayid said, coming to Helena's aid. He failed to notice the brief look of affection the two women exchanged.

Aslan returned to the table carrying four glasses of beer.

"Any thoughts?" he asked.

"It's better to be in a warm pub than out on the frozen streets," Helena responded, a mustache of beer foam adorning her upper lip. Ann looked at her and smiled.

"Something wrong?" Helena asked.

Sayid ran his finger discreetly across his lips, and Helena thanked him silently and licked off the beer mustache with the tip of her tongue.

"I think," Ann said, "that we should stop wandering these streets aimlessly. I think Sayid should attend the prayer session. That would be the simplest and most direct way to get close to Badawi, to see how this prayer and sermon business is run, if he has bodyguards, how he gets to the mosque, how he leaves."

"Can you do it?" Aslan asked, directing his question at Sayid.

"I'm familiar with the Quran and the prayers," Sayid responded. "Growing up in Algeria I was required to study the Quran. I'm not a religious Muslim, of course, and can't pretend to be one, but I could certainly play the part of a refugee who's looking to find warmth and meaning and something familiar at the mosque."

"Are you sure?" Aslan asked. "It's a risky play."

"Not for me," Sayid said. "I'm a genuine Algerian, I know Algiers and Constantine like the back of my hand, and miss it. I have no trouble talking of extremism and atrocities. I've read enough reports and blogs and I've seen a fair number of pictures. The world is focused these days on Syria, but the jihadists are active in North Africa, too. A large number of refugees come from North African countries. I just need a little time to prepare a precise and detailed cover story. With its focus, in fact, on my time here in London. Where I'm living, what brings me to Bethnal Green, whether I work, doing what, how I got to England, things like that."

"We'll help you," Aslan said, nodding his head to confirm it was the right move. "In any case, the story is mainly for your benefit. To bolster your self-confidence. After all, you don't have to answer to anyone. You only need to be ready."

I'm ready, Sayid thought, suddenly realizing for just how long he had been waiting for this moment.

45

Brussels, January 2015

"What we're looking for is a weak spot," Ya'ara said to her cadets. "Information that will allow us to get closer to Hamdan. And we probably have more chance of doing so when he's on the move, when he's not guarded by walls and fences and steel gates. Surprise and determination are the elements that will tip the scales in our favor. Our desire to take him out surpasses their will to protect him."

"I hope they know that, too," Assaf mumbled.

They were all dressed in designer wear, tailored in neat and clean lines. Batsheva also boasted a necklace of gleaming pearls, and she flashed a smile conveying both enjoyment and self-irony at her reflection in the mirror. "I could get used to this," she said with a sigh.

"It's not really that different from the way

you always dress," Assaf said, and Batsheva said yes, perhaps, without going into the small details of the line of the skirt and the name of the designer.

Ya'ara didn't miss an opportunity to offer them a brief lesson. "In truth," she said, "it's practical. These are the uniforms that make it easier for us to blend in. Elegance is a way to observe and not be seen."

"Okay," Nufar said, her eyes on the screen, "I need some quiet now. You wanted a weak spot, so give me a moment and stop talking about clothes."

Ya'ara wondered if she should remark on Nufar's chutzpah, but decided instead to alter course.

"Let Nufar work," she declared.

She finally found what they were looking for.

"Okay, look here," she said. "They're in the open while en route from the detention center to the courthouse. As a safeguard, they travel in convoy. A van carrying the prisoners, and two escort vehicles. And they travel along a different route every time. Here, look." Nufar pointed to a folder belonging to the unit responsible for escorting prisoners. "The computer marks out a different route for every trip, and then relays it to the GPS systems of the vehicles in the convoy. The escort teams don't have to memorize the route because the GPS directs them. The changes are random, there's a limited number of ways to go from point A to point B, but even the security personnel themselves are made aware of the route at the last minute."

"Aside from being able to see their computers, are you able to mess with them, too?" Batsheva felt Ya'ara's gaze focus on her.

"Go on," Ya'ara said to Batsheva.

"Because if we're able to override the computer and feed them a route of our choosing, we can separate the prisoners' vehicle from the escort vehicles, and lead the prisoners' vehicle wherever we want. I think that's what you were talking about earlier, Ya'ara, about the possibility of creating a decisive advantage at a specific point in time and space."

"That's an angle of approach with potential," Ya'ara said with restraint. "Provided Nufar can do it." Can you, her look inquired.

"Theoretically, I can actively override their system. It just needs to be done at the right time, and in a manner that can't be detected. If only I had some help here. I need to be able to take a more in-depth look into their system. And to do so with caution, to avoid detection."

"I want us to be able to run a pilot within a week," Ya'ara said. "So we can see if this whole concept works. Our goal for the pilot will be to divert the convoy of inmates traveling from the prison to the courthouse next Monday, and to see if things run smoothly, if we manage to pull it off without being detected, if the vehicles do in fact follow the route we've plotted for them. We have lots of work to do. Nufar needs to study the system, in depth. We need to get to know the routes and to prepare an alternative path that is going to make sense to them. And already now we also need to start planning the route Hamdan will take on the way to his encounter not with Belgian justice but with ours."

She couldn't fall asleep that night. She still didn't know whether Hamdan would be the only prisoner in the vehicle, or whether he'd be one of a group of inmates. According to the information they had gathered thus far, the vehicle would contain a driver and probably one escort, perhaps two. All armed. The fundamental planning principles for the operation called for no casualties apart from Hamdan himself. No prison guards and none of the other detainees. And still, the expected confrontation would see her and her team up against armed guards who were tasked with protecting their prisoners or preventing them from escaping.

That said, the element of surprise and the element of determination would play in their favor. The Belgian prison guards weren't going to be in any hurry to die defending their posts. Particularly if she and her team managed to show them that their lives weren't in danger, that the threat wasn't being directed at them. They might also have a small numerical advantage. There'd be four of them. Against three guards. And if Goran kept his promise, they'd be armed with stun grenades, too. But Ya'ara couldn't ignore the fact that she'd be leading an unskilled team. That they'd be operating in an environment that would soon turn hostile and dangerous. A manhunt for them would begin within minutes.

Should she be launching the operation under such circumstances? Her thoughts became clouded as sleep closed in on her. Before finally dropping off, she pictured a blurred image of the scene of the operation, tinged with the glowing colors of the sunset.

She saw the ashen face of Yael Ziv, her large dark eyes. She watched her spiral down into a bottomless pit right there in front of her. She closed her eyes.

46

England, April 1948

The letter sent to Raphael's studio arrived in a thick, fine-quality envelope that was embellished with a crest incorporating a dragon, a unicorn, and a rose. "Dear Mr. Raphael," read the letter in a green shade of ink from a fountain pen, "Our mutual friend, Henry Moore, has spoken to me at length about you. He admires you greatly, and informed me that your work and ideas may be of interest to me. I'd like to put his words to the test. I'd be pleased to have you as a guest at my home over the last weekend of the month. If you can make your way to Morning Meadow on Friday on the 11:43 train from Oxford, I will send a car to get you. We'll have the entire weekend at our disposal. You can return to your blessed work on Monday. Looking forward to your arrival, Alfred Strong, Viscount."

The day was surprisingly springlike. The

smell of blossoms hung in the air, and the budding young leaves shone as green as green could be. Raphael marveled once again at the incredible power of nature, bursting forth with new life. He was collected at the small village's train station by a courteous driver of few words. And it wasn't long before they had said good-bye to the confines of the community, leaving behind its small yellow-stone houses. Towering over the low structures stood the church steeple, gleaming far into the distance, as if an invisible hand were polishing it with gold.

They drove along a country road, lined on both sides by hedges, restricting their fields of vision. Raphael felt as if the perfumed air, thick with the fragrance of blooming flowers, was clinging to him. An avenue of ancient trees showed the way to their destination. When the avenue came to an end, the wide-open landscape was revealed suddenly in all its splendor, and before them stood a small palace, made of red brick, its façade adorned with tall columns. The car sped through a large iron gate and came to a stop in front of the residence. Standing at the top of the stairs leading to the sizable palace doors was an elderly man, his gray hair unkempt, his nose hooked and determined, his eyes twinkling with an inquisitive smile.

"Hello. I'm Alfred Strong. Welcome to Lion's Slope."

The name of the residence did indeed do justice to the place: There truly was a slope, a gleaming green stretch of lawn, dotted with thousands of tiny flowers, that trailed gently downward toward the small lake. Raphael wondered if there were lions on the estate, too, and thought he wouldn't be too surprised to catch sight of one of the majestic predators wandering lazily around the grounds.

"Hello, Sir Alfred. Thank you for the invitation. I'm pleased to be here."

"Alfred, Alfred. No need for Sir. What should I call you? Joseph?"

"No, Raphael. Just Raphael. That's best."

Dinner was served in the vast semilit dining room. Flickering candles glowed on the antique table, their flames reflected in the large wineglasses. A fire burned in the fireplace at the far end of the room, casting strange patterns of light and shade on the stone floor. Alfred Strong's young wife joined them.

"This is Lady Sarah, my beautiful wife," Strong said with obvious pride. Sarah's dark eyes surveyed Raphael with curiosity. She offered him a fair-skinned, delicate hand, and he couldn't decide whether to shake or kiss it. During their dinner, Strong told Raphael about his intense interest in the ancient cultures of the Near East. He had studied at Oxford and had even graduated with distinction. He was offered a position at the college he attended, but was forced, so he said, to leave the paradise of academe to take charge of the family's business affairs. He was a little vague about the exact nature of those business affairs, but spoke more than once about an ammunitions plant, and on another occasion he also mentioned something about financial activity in the City, in London.

Be that as it may, his passion focused on his travels to archaeological sites in Mesopotamia, where he had worked with youthful enthusiasm as a volunteer and self-appointed helper to learned delegation heads. When he spoke of his participation in the expedition to the archaeological dig at the Sumerian Royal Cemetery in the ancient city of Ur, his eyes shone with unconcealed pride. He joined MI5 immediately after the outbreak of the war, and served as a member of the secret team that handled the Nazi spies who were captured on British soil and subsequently used as double agents.

"It's a very closely guarded secret," he whispered to Raphael. "It was wonderful, like playing chess on a few dozen boards at the same time." Raphael was surprised to hear Strong tell him of such things with an air of nonchalance, as if he were discussing a sport or hobby. But he had already learned that the rules of the game by which members of the English upper classes played were quite different from those that applied to the rest of humanity.

On the way to dinner, they managed to pop into the magnificent library room for a few minutes. Laid out on display among the thousands of books were glass boxes containing small archaeological items. Despite his lack of knowledge on the subject, Raphael felt drawn to the items. He could sense they were unique treasures, memories of lost cultures frozen in time.

"There's a story behind each and every one of them," Strong muttered, and Raphael wondered whether his host was actually familiar with the stories, or whether the ancient artifacts, as far as Strong was concerned, were simply additional assets in the framework of all the wealth the family had accumulated over the generations.

"Come, have a look at something over here," his host said, pointing Raphael toward one of the large windows of the library's west-facing wall. The sun was casting a warm, rich light over the hills and sloping stretch of lawn, coloring the edges of the white clouds with a golden glitter. Visible from the window was a large stone sculpture, an abstract piece. It must have weighed a ton, yet appeared at the same time to convey a strong sense of lightness, elegance, as if it were an expression of an ideal of beauty.

"He knows what he's doing, our Henry, right?" Strong said in a low voice. Raphael wasn't able to think of the great Henry Moore as "our Henry," and besides, he was so moved by the beauty of the sculpture that all he could do was nod in agreement. Yes, he undoubtedly knew what he was doing.

"We have several more wonderful sculptures at this residence, in the garden," Strong said, waving his hand in a way that was characteristic of nobility, as if to suggest that all of this — this estate, these archaeological treasures, the books, the sculptures, the game meat roast that would soon be served to their table — was no big deal.

"Do you know David Herbert Samuel?"

Strong asked, his jaws chewing on the venison as he heaped another teaspoon of red currant sauce into his mouth.

"Do you mean Herbert Louis?"

"No, no, Herbert Louis Samuel was your first high commissioner," Strong said, and by "your" he was probably referring to the residents of the Land of Israel-Palestine.

"I'm talking about his grandson, David Herbert Samuel. He was born in Palestine and lived there until he moved to England to study. I met him at Oxford. He's younger than me, of course, but he studied chemistry with Sarah, and when I was courting this beautiful maiden" — he looked at Sarah with deep affection and a smile — "I was also forced to be dragged off to their stupid parties, and that's how I met him, too."

"We may have been young," Sarah said, "but the war made us grow up very fast. David, you know" — Raphael didn't know if she was addressing her husband or him — "abandoned his studies and joined the army. He saw action in the Far East. He returned to Oxford to complete his studies only after the war. He left England a short while ago. He said he was needed there with you, that there was a war going on."

Raphael was impressed by the image of David Herbert Samuel that his hosts' conversation had portrayed thus far.

"He truly is a wonderful young man. He's also very handsome and striking. You can't deny that, my darling," Sarah continued, smiling at Strong warmly. "Did you know he served as military governor in Sumatra?"

Raphael, who until then had never heard of the man, was unfamiliar with that detail, too. But he listened.

"That's one of the things he got to do during the war. Alfred played his part, too," she added, gazing at her husband and caressing his hand. "He did some great things, but I'm not allowed to know about them, and certainly can't breathe a word."

"Sarah, Sarah, there's no need to exaggerate."

"You aren't awarded the Order of the British Empire for nothing," she responded vehemently. "The war of minds you waged contributed greatly to the victory."

Strong absentmindedly caressed her hand.

"You know I'm a Jewess, right?" Lady Sarah casually said when they met in the large kitchen the following morning.

"No, I didn't know," Raphael responded, a large mug of coffee in his hand. "But it makes me happy."

"And why so?" she asked suspiciously.

"I think it pleases me to know that we share some kind of affinity. A bit like distant family, right?"

"It's a little pretentious to think that all Jews are one big family. It seems to me sometimes that we are bound by very little, actually. I'm an Englishwoman, that's my culture, that's my heritage. But," she added dolefully, "Adolf Hitler thought differently. Had he managed to get his hands on us, on you and me, all the differences, all the divides, would have counted for nothing. We would have met the same terrible end in no time. We would have been turned into smoke. A large family of incinerated people."

Raphael could see the sadness in her eyes. He wanted to console her, although he wasn't quite sure for what, but instead he remained rooted to the spot. Something in her proud posture stopped him from approaching her.

This woman was a collection of contrasts, but the look with which she was fixing him now, defiant and almost wild, brought them closer. He didn't feel at that precise moment that he himself needed sympathy and a comforting caress, even though most of his family — uncles and cousins, relatives, loved ones — had been murdered by the

Nazis. He and his parents had immigrated to the Land of Israel when he was a little boy. Two sisters and a brother were born there. Despite the loving and longing letters his mother would send to relatives who remained behind, letters that turned increasingly desperate, urging them to join the family in Israel, Salonika, which had always been their home, maintained its grip. The brothers, the sisters, their children, down to the very last one, were arrested by the SS and murdered in Auschwitz. Raphael knew the names of all his family members who had perished, their dates of birth and the dates of their deaths. His mother had made him memorize them all. And still, at that moment, all Raphael could feel was a deep sense of compassion toward Sarah, the young, sad woman in whose home he was a guest.

"Did you lose family members in the war?" he asked her, maintaining the physical distance between them.

"No, no. We are very deeply rooted here on English soil. The first members of my family came to this island more than three hundred years ago. At the end of the seventeenth century. Portuguese Jews who arrived here via Amsterdam, with the authorization of Cromwell. We've been safe ever since.

But the horrific pictures from the camps, the testimonies of our soldiers, the eyes of the people whose bodies had turned to skeletons. . . ." Her eyes welled with tears. She couldn't complete her sentence.

"And you?" she asked. "Did you lose family in the war?"

He felt the blood drain from his face. "My parents got out of Greece in time," he said. "Shortly after the Great War. The Land of Israel became our home. But those in my family who remained behind all perished." He stopped there, and his body, which had stiffened, clearly conveyed his unwillingness to elaborate.

"We won't talk about it anymore. Not now." Sarah smiled through her tears. "We'll have our tea outside, in the garden. Alfred went out early for a ride. He should be back soon. You can go on doing whatever it is you're doing . . ."

She doesn't bother completing her sentences either, Raphael thought. *As if things are clear and there's no need to make the effort. Whatever it is you're doing. Who does she mean by you? Alfred and me? You, the men?*

"So you studied chemistry at Oxford," he said to her as they sat down at the white marble table in the garden. "Are you involved in the field?"

"First there was the war, and afterward I needed time to myself," she responded, her eyes blurring again. "Although I studied chemistry, as one of just two women who were doing so at Oxford at the time, I've always been interested in the history of art. Lately I've been toying with the idea of combining the two fields, of studying restoration. Taking care of Alfred's collection. Helping perhaps at the churches in the district. There are quite a few important pieces of art around here that are crying out for repair and preservation. You know, things are sometimes more fragile than they appear to be."

The time passed quickly, and as he stood at the door of Lion's Slope on Monday morning, tightening the scarf around his neck, the driver was already patiently waiting for him alongside the open door of the black Bentley. He put his bag down so he could shake his host's hand.

"Thank you for a wonderful weekend," Raphael said.

"The pleasure was mine, ours," Strong replied, smiling at Sarah, seeking her confirmation.

"Certainly, it was my pleasure, too," Sarah

said in her deep voice, her dark eyes staring straight into Raphael's.

"I hope from now you're going to feel like one of the family," Strong said to him. "As we agreed, you can work in the hunters' cabin, turn it into your country studio. Every great artist needs the right conditions in which to work and create. But we've already discussed it all. We don't want to hold you up. You need to make your train. It's good to be here" — he smiled — "but you also have to maintain your escape routes."

Strong's handshake was warm and firm. The hand Sarah offered was limp, as if she had suddenly gone weak. "We'd love you to come back," she said. "You promised."

As the car pulled away, Strong and his wife were still standing at the front door of their home, he waving his hand, she with her arms folded and a piercing gaze fixed on Raphael.

47

London, Bethnal Green, January 2015

Their large eyes gleamed through the slits in the veils. Ann and Helena removed the fabric that was covering their heads and faces but remained dressed in loose-fitting black dresses that concealed their bodies from neck to ankle. Helena flopped into the shabby armchair with a sigh. The four of them were staying in an apartment rented by Sayid, who gave a Maghreb name, paid in cash, and told the landlord that his papers were still at the Home Office branch in Croydon, South London, awaiting final approval.

The apartment was located in the attic of a yellowish brick building from the early twentieth century. Living in the same block were six Bengali families, three families from Somalia, and one family of Egyptian origin. Small satellite dishes adorned the apartments' meager balconies. The attic apartment was small and run-down. A furnished flat, the Jamaican estate agent proudly declared as he gestured toward the shabby items on display, and Sayid, the refugee from Algeria, thanked his lucky stars. The realtor was unaware of the apartment's major and true advantage — an open line of sight to the exit door of the mosque at which preacher Anjam Badawi delivered his sermons. The range: 450 meters.

Sayid had already attended Friday prayers at the mosque on two occasions. He was taken aback by the warmth with which he was received. The regular worshippers embraced him but didn't trouble him with questions. He found a spot for himself in one of the last rows of worshippers, trying to occupy as little space as possible. Rather than be a burden on the others, he only wanted to find some peace of mind. But even from his position at the far edge of the mosque, he could see the enthusiasm that gripped his fellow worshippers when Badawi delivered his sermon.

Accompanying Badawi were three well-built young men who served as his bodyguards. Sayid found it hard to believe that they were armed. Carrying a firearm without a permit is a serious criminal offense in

England, but their self-assured and threatening demeanor, their alertness and obvious devotion to their duty, were certainly a deterrent. Who knows, they may have had knives and clubs concealed on their person. With them around him, it would be difficult to get close to Badawi. And it would undoubtedly be even more difficult to make an escape from the place if someone were to strike at him from close range.

After the first sermon, the worshippers left the mosque and took to the street. Sayid followed suit. Badawi and his henchmen also left the mosque, talking among themselves. A battered Rover was waiting at the curb to pick them up. Several fired-up youths walked alongside Badawi, asking him questions, trying to impress him. He wasn't in any hurry to get into the car, and spoke congenially with the group surrounding him, patiently answering their questions. Sayid witnessed the same ritual on his second visit, too. Badawi's powerful rhetoric continued to reverberate even after he had finished delivering his sermon, and his words, like a giant magnet, seemed to pull the young men out onto the street in his wake, looking to draw encouragement and meaning from his presence.

Ann and Helena sewed their dresses and

veils themselves. They realized it would be much easier for them to walk around Bethnal Green protected by their black clothing. No one dared to approach any of the veiled women in the street, and they certainly didn't attract the kind of attention they would have had they spent hours wandering through the neighborhood as attractive white women in jeans and jackets from Uniqlo or the Gap.

In fact, thought Ann, who had known London since birth, Bethnal Green was a deceptive neighborhood. Some of its streets looked no different from the well-kept thoroughfares of Islington or Fulham. But take just take one step beyond some imaginary borderline, and you step into another country. The neighborhood changed face in an instant, becoming hard and rough, and the people walking its streets suddenly didn't look the same, were no longer members of the English middle class, but immigrants and the children of immigrants, from those same countries ruled in the past by the empire on which the sun never set.

In keeping with Sayid's findings, an assassination from close quarters was ruled out as a possible course of action. As a result, Aslan decided to opt for a sniper operation from a distance. So they scoured the area to find a rooftop or apartment on a high floor that offered a clear line of sight to the mosque. And that's how they found the place in which the team was currently staying. They had already decided that Aslan would be the one to take out the preacher. He was the only member of the team with sniping skills and experience. The only thing they still needed was a weapon for the operation. That was a constant point of weakness when it came to covert operations abroad, and Aslan's stomach always churned ahead of an incriminating encounter with people he didn't know and who couldn't be trusted in the least. But he believed in Goran, and he was relying on him not to drop them in the shit knowingly. The connection between him and Ya'ara ensured that, insofar as one could be sure of anything at all in the world of mercenaries and arms dealers. He trusted Goran's contacts far less, however. And even if the connection with them amounted to nothing more than a money transfer to an anonymous bank account or stashing a sum of cash in a hidden location, they'd still know where the weapon could be found, and they could share that information with counterterrorism forces or the London police or MI5. And they would certainly do so if they were exposed or were cooperating with them. Ultimately, the weapon had to change hands. There was no getting around that.

Aslan and his team began planning their escape route from the apartment after the shooting. They discussed several courses of action. Escape in a rental car, on a motorcycle, via the Underground. Aslan wasn't happy with any of the options. Stealing a vehicle was an option, of course, but the theft itself could lead to complications, and his cadets had very limited experience with stealing cars. Zero would probably be a better word. The Underground, for its part, is a great place in which to blend in with the masses, but it is also one of the most photographed locations in the world.

"Why don't you dress up as a woman, cover yourself up in a black dress and veil, and make your getaway from the apartment on foot?" Ann suggested.

"Like Ehud Barak?" Sayid asked.

"And if you're going to be a woman," Helena interjected, "you should be pushing a baby carriage. We can prepare a doll wrapped in blankets for you. Who's going to suspect a mother with a baby carriage of being a dangerous sniper?"

"Not bad, but remember, with all those disguises and masquerades, I'm also going to need to get away from this place as quickly as possible."

"Bicycle?"

"Speak in complete sentences, please, Sayid."

"What about escaping the neighborhood on a bicycle?" Sayid suggested. "There's something innocent-looking about a bicycle. Unlike a getaway car or motorcycle that speeds off with a terrible noise. A simple bicycle. A woman on a bicycle. Covered in a veil. In a neighborhood in which half the women never show their faces in public."

"I want an orderly analysis of the various options," Aslan said. "You're cadets. You're here to learn. Let's do this properly."

48

Brussels, February 2, 2015

The pilot run was a success — its first stage at least. They managed to divert the convoy of prisoners to a different route from the one that had been set for them. Nufar was in front of her battery of computers at seven in the morning already. They were basing their alternative route on one that had served the convoy in the past. They wanted the escort teams to feel secure, to recognize the route they were taking. They decided therefore to insert a small deviation only at one specific point along a familiar path. Instead of driving through a traffic tunnel, the vehicles would be diverted to the upper stretch of the road. A move that would require them to stop or at least slow down at an intersection or two. Nufar fed the particulars of the new route into the computer of the operations officer. Two questions remained. One: Would it work? The other: Would the escort teams ask questions later about the route selected for them?

Nufar remained behind to keep an eye on the convoy's progress in real time, via the computers of the Prison Service, which she had already made her own. Assaf stayed with her, to deal with any possible disturbance. Ya'ara and Batsheva went out into the field, to observe the convoy with their own eyes. They took up a position at a café that offered a view of the intersection the vehicles were due to reach. They wanted to see if it would actually transpire. Would five vehicles really take the upper stretch of road rather than continue uninterrupted through the tunnel? They wanted to see if there'd be any sign of bewilderment or confusion stemming from the deviation in the familiar route, or if the drivers would simply follow the directions provided by the GPS device. It was nine twenty. Dawn had broken not too long ago. February's days in Brussels are dark and gloomy. But on the right side of the café's large window, it was warm and cozy. Two cups of coffee with that strong morning aroma, fresh and crispy croissants. A WhatsApp message from Nufar: "Convoy entering the tunnel. ETA two minutes." And arrive it did. A white patrol car with flashing blue lights emerged at high speed from the opening of the tunnel, crossed through the first intersection, and then stopped at the next one. A red light, pedestrians wrapped in their coats traversing the crosswalk with heads bowed against the icy wind. A prisoner-transport vehicle, with flashing blue lights, too, and bars to secure its windows, pulled up behind the first vehicle. And behind it, a second patrol car, another prisoner-transport vehicle, and then a third patrol car. The rearguard. They had a clear view of the entire convoy. *What a wonderful sight,* Ya'ara thought. The convoy waiting patiently for the light to change. Pulling off with the roar of engines as the red turned to green. Insofar at least as Ya'ara and Batsheva could tell, the slight change in the route prompted no reaction from the prison guards and security personnel. None of them exited the vehicles with their weapons drawn. The drivers didn't decide to keep going despite the red light. Nothing at all about the manner in which the vehicles in the convoy were traveling changed. A WhatsApp message to Nufar: "You did it, honey! Just like in the movies!"

If their manipulation of the route went unnoticed, without subsequent questions or queries, they would set the real operation in motion on Monday of the following week. The change they'd make to the convoy's route would be more extreme. In a week's time, they would separate the prisoner-transport vehicles from the escort vehicles. They would reroute the vehicle carrying Hamdan to a location that offered them a tactical advantage over the security guards, even if it was a temporary advantage only. And they would exploit their advantage quickly and aggressively. At that stage, whether the change in the route raised questions would be irrelevant. Because there would be far more difficult questions begging for answers.

49

Ya'ara had chosen to remain alone. She wasn't happy with the plan they had come up with. Had she been working with experienced fighters by her side, she would have taken advantage of the isolation of the prisoners' vehicle to create a significant numerical advantage at the scene. According to the most recent information they had gleaned from the computer system of the Belgian Prison Service, the vehicle carrying the prisoners would be manned by just two guards — the driver and a second prison guard sitting next to him. She assumed they would both be armed. The prisoners in the back of the van would be alone, with no guards. A guard in the back with them could very easily become a hostage. And if he were armed, the prisoners could seize his weapon. Security for the convoy, therefore, rested primarily on the escort vehicles. The guards manning them could respond quickly and efficiently to any incident. Diverting the escort vehicles and isolating the van carrying Hamdan would give them the advantage of surprise and the potential advantage of creating a superior fighting force in terms of size. They would be temporary advantages only, of course. The guards in the escort vehicles would realize that they had been cut off from the prisoner van, and were likely to backtrack to the separation point as quickly as possible. Ya'ara decided therefore to divert the prisoner van at a point along the route that would delay the return of the escort vehicles for as long as possible. A busy one-way street. They wouldn't be able to backtrack against the flow of the traffic. They'd have to circle around to the separation point, and doing so would take time. Not long, though. Ya'ara and Assaf had checked the route, and did it, without sirens and flashing blue lights, in two minutes and twenty seconds. Ya'ara assumed that the escort vehicles would do it in a minute and a half. During that time, she and her team would have to divert the van, stop it, disable it, neutralize the two guards, gain access to the prisoner compartment, identify Hamdan, kill him, and withdraw. And all of it without causing irreversible harm to the guards and without causing any injury to the other prisoners, if there were any in the van with their object.

But Ya'ara didn't have experienced fighters at her disposal. These were her cadets. Barely three months into their training. With the exception of the mission in Bremen, they lacked operational experience and had never found themselves in a face-to-face confrontation with professional armed guards. She couldn't put them at such risk. Assaf had indeed served as an officer and fighter in the Combat Engineering Corps, but that didn't make him an experienced assassin qualified to operate on the streets of Europe. Batsheva had already proven herself to be a competent actress and creative thinker, but Ya'ara struggled to picture her detonating an explosive device or firing a pistol in broad daylight, with or without Manolo Blahnik pumps on her feet. And the intelligent Nufar, she did great work as a hacker, but she, too, wasn't ready yet for an operation of this kind.

Ya'ara was at a pub in one of the narrow alleys that led off from the Grand Place. She was sitting alone, on the table in front of her a large glass of beer, one of the hundreds of varieties the pub boasted. All made in Belgium of course. The pub wasn't crowded, and the ice-cold look in her eyes was enough to repel the men who thought, for a fraction of a second only, of approaching her. Very beautiful, but dangerous and radiating about as much warmth as an iceberg. That's the impression she was giving off, and at that point in time, it was the exact impression she wanted them to get. Her thoughts drifted momentarily to Matthias, and she wondered what he was going through, what was happening with him. She felt a sudden longing for him, wanted to be with him, to feel the pull of his large, powerful body next to her. She shook her head and returned to the mental image of the scene of the targeted killing that appeared so clearly in her mind. Not for a second did she consider cancelling the operation. But she had to get through it without placing her cadets in the line of fire. She pictured herself emerging from the shadows of the street and moving toward the prisoner van that had been cut off from its escorts and had suddenly run into a dead end. Municipal excavation work had closed the street. This they knew from their patrols around the area, which had focused on the final kilometer leading up to the courthouse. Being so close to their destination, the escorts would have let their guard down a little by then, forgetting that the final kilometer was always the most dangerous. Only thinking, what now?

50

Brussels, February 9, 2015

To the guards sitting in the front of the van, the scene that unfolded before their eyes appeared to have come straight out of a horror film. A thin figure, wearing a black gas mask, came at them from out of nowhere. They were still struggling to figure out how they had ended up in a narrow dead-end street, with their path blocked by large yellow plastic barriers, and behind the barriers a deep trench dug into the road. The approaching figure had both its hands gripped around the handle of a pistol fitted with a silencer. They heard two soft pops and felt the front end of the vehicle sink as its two front tires deflated. The next bullet shattered the windshield and passed between them. The figure then pulled a hand grenade from the pocket of its coat, and a second one, too, before throwing them both into the cabin from very close range. The guards were convinced they were done for, that they were about to be blown into a million pieces. But no. One of the grenades slammed them with a painful ear-shattering noise, along with a bright and blinding flash of light. They felt the shockwave in their ears and their bodies froze. The second grenade emitted a steady stream of gas that immediately hampered their breathing, causing extreme pain to their eyes at the same time. They were no longer able to see the thin figure, which had moved around to the rear of the vehicle.

Ya'ara reached into her coat pocket and retrieved a rectangular object, the size of a Galaxy 6 cellphone. She fixed the device to the heavy lock that secured the van's two back doors and knelt down alongside the vehicle. The sound of a dull explosion rang out and the doors flew open, with one almost ripped off its hinges. Goran had added a little spice to the charge, she thought with a smile. The back of the van contained three prisoners, their wrists and ankles shackled. She recognized Osama Hamdan immediately. She could see the looks of fear and bewilderment on the faces of the prisoners. Had someone come to rescue them? To free them from the production line of the Belgian justice system? To kill them? Who had sent this slender warrior, wrapped in a large coat, with its face hidden by a monstrous mask? Ya'ara lifted the mask so that she could ask, in a calm and clear voice, in French: "Are you Osama Hamdan?" He nodded, extremely surprised that someone had come to his rescue. They hadn't planned this part of the operation in advance. Only the murder at the synagogue.

Ya'ara repeated her question, and added: "Answer out loud."

"Yes, it's me," he responded, his voice thick and strangled.

"See you in hell," she spat back with intense scorn and hatred, squeezing the trigger of her pistol three times in succession. The three bullets struck him in the face, ripping it to shreds, with particles of brain and bone splattering against the interior of the van and over the other two prisoners, who fell to their knees. A dark, wet patch stained the trousers of one of them. His friend covered his face with his hands and his entire body was trembling.

At the same time, the front doors of the vehicle opened and the two prison guards stumbled out, the one coughing, with tears streaming from his eyes, the other with his hands over his ears. The stun grenade must have ruptured his left eardrum — Ya'ara could see blood trickling from his ear down to his neck. One of the guards, the driver, still coughing and with mucus pouring from his nose, started to reach for the pistol in his belt. Ya'ara stared at him coldly through the visor of her gas mask, which she had replaced after seeing Hamdan blown to bits by the bullets she had fired into his head. She wasn't sure if the guard could see her eyes, but he could certainly see the gun in her hand. The two shots she fired in the direction of his legs struck the road just inches from his feet, sending small pieces of asphalt flying toward him. The message was clear. I don't want to harm you, but I am proficient enough with this weapon to do it easily. One threatening move and the next bullet will be in your neck, your jaw, either of your eyes I choose.

The guard cautiously moved his hand away from his gun holster, and the near-invisible and very slight movement of his eyes seemed to say: Got you, there's no need for anyone else to be killed here.

Ya'ara backed away slowly, before turning suddenly into a narrow alley and heading down a steep staircase leading to a one-way road that wound up the hill toward Louise Square. She could see the immense structure of the courthouse dominating the landscape, casting a giant shadow. Making her way down the stairs, she pulled out a department store shopping bag from her coat pocket, slipped the gas mask off her head in one smooth movement, shook out her fair hair, which was tied in a ponytail, and stuffed the mask into the bag. The pistol went back into her pocket. Batsheva was behind the wheel of the black Opel Corsa that was parked, with its engine running, exactly opposite the stairs Ya'ara came down in light, quick bounds. She signaled, as required, and was already pulling away from the curb before Ya'ara had closed the door. "Drive slowly," Ya'ara instructed her. "We have all the time in the world." Cleary the overstatement of the year, but Batsheva smiled at her and skillfully maneuvered the car into traffic.

51

London, Bethnal Green, February 13, 2015

Friday the 13th of February was clear and cold. Aslan rested the sniper rifle up against the window sill, the ice-cold air coming into the apartment making his body tremble. Sayid looked at him. Sayid had a dual role. First, as the tenant of the apartment, to deal with any possible disturbances, to respond to any unexpected knock on the door. Second, toward the end of the prayer service, to stand alongside Aslan with a sophisticated pair of binoculars, and to make sure that Aslan identified and fixed his sights on Anjam Badawi, the soft-spoken preacher who instilled hatred and madness in the hearts of his followers. Sayid had seen him from up close during prayers at the mosque, and if Aslan was in doubt, Sayid could point him out. Aslan, for his part, had adorned the windowsill with pictures of Badawi that they had downloaded from the internet, committing them to memory.

Collecting the weapon had gone by without a hitch. The sniper rifle and ammunition were left for them by Goran's men in a woodshed in the courtyard of an abandoned country house southeast of London. Aslan had left a sealed envelope with the payment for the weapon in the shed in advance. From a concealed vantage point some eight hundred meters away, Aslan then used a pair of high-powered binoculars to track the black Ford Focus that came down the dirt road leading to the courtyard, its tires spraying water and mud. A man who was sitting next to the driver got out of the car and collected the envelope from the shed. He stuffed it into an inside pocket of his coat and then retrieved a large kitbag from the trunk, glancing warily all around him. Within less than half a minute, the kitbag was resting in the shed, and the car had sped away on its muddy tires. As it disappeared around a bend, a cold silence descended on the scene. Two and a half hours had passed since Aslan sent the coordinates of the location. Goran's men were fast workers.

In theory, from the moment the mail was sent from Aslan to Goran's men, nothing was certain. The details could also have been in the hands of the police or security service. Aslan was faced with two options — to act immediately, in the hope of getting a jump on the enemy; or to wait patiently at the lookout point, and to ensure that there were no forces deployed around the structure and the shed. Both options involved a gamble of sorts. A weigh-up of risks and probabilities.

Aslan decided to wait. It was three thirty in the afternoon. The sun was already on its way down. According to Aslan's reading of the situation, if rival forces failed to show up before nightfall, they'd hold off deploying until first light the following day. He'd wait patiently for the small hours of the morning, and only then would he approach the shed. He'd collect the kitbag and navigate through the fields for some ten miles to a narrow country road, where Ann would be waiting to pick him up. The designated rendezvous point was well away from the abandoned house. If Aslan had been planning to ambush the gun buyer, he wouldn't have taken that narrow road into account. And that's exactly why Aslan chose that specific rendezvous point with Ann.

In the view of someone planning an operation, Ann was in a completely different sphere. Aslan's main problem was the cold. The bone-chilling iciness of February in the United Kingdom. It wasn't Aslan's first time on stakeout in the freezing cold, but the only advantage his experience offered was that he was familiar with the suffering that awaited him and knew how to equip himself. At least that was what he thought.

When my parents sent me with such intense pride to study engineering at the Technion, they certainly couldn't have imagined I'd end up like this, he thought, in a freezing cold trench, on a black night, in some shithole in southeast England. With hundreds of similar operations already under my belt, in and around Nablus and Jenin and Deir al-Balah and Nabatieh and Sidon and Marseilles and Zug and Manila . . . But he had chosen his path, and was proud of it, and hoped that over the years his elderly parents had also found a source of satisfaction and quiet pride in the little they knew of his activities.

When he got into the small car Ann was driving in the early hours of that morning, he was surprised to see her long bare legs stretching out from under a shiny red minidress, and expensive-looking, black high-heeled shoes on her feet. It might have been the stark contrast between her glittering appearance and his strenuous walk through the black fields. She noticed the look on his face.

"Something wrong?" she asked. "You said my cover story was that I'm on my way home from a party, right?"

"Absolutely, I did say that."

"So don't look so shocked," she said, straightening her dress so that it covered her thighs.

Aslan decided to change the subject. "Let's go straight to Bethnal Green," he said. "We have an illegal sniper rifle on the backseat. I'd like to be out and about with it there for as little time as possible."

Aslan surveyed the courtyard in front of the mosque through the scope. He moved the rifle slowly from left to right and made a mental note of the few individuals who were crossing the expanse, or who were lingering there, waiting for the prayers to end. Then he moved the rifle a few millimeters from right to left, breathing gently, regulating his pulse. Sayid thought he looked a little like a snake dozing in the sun, a dangerous venomous snake that could strike suddenly, in a burst of deadly energy.

Aslan's gaze was focused now on the mosque's large door, his breathing still gentle, measured, relaxed. The door started to swing open.

At first, just a handful of worshippers spilled out. They didn't hang around, seemingly hurrying off to their daily affairs. For a short while the mosque's doors remained open without anyone else stepping out. The courtyard looked almost deserted. But then a cluster of people emerged. A group of men, with Badawi, the preacher, in the center. Three burly henchmen made up the inner circle, their eyes surveying the surroundings, and around them was a group of fired-up young men, aiming admiring glances at the preacher. Badawi advanced slowly, and the group moved along with him. His hands flailed in the air, seeking to emphasize something he must have been saying. Even through the scope, the look on his face was welcoming, attentive, and soft, and Aslan couldn't help but think how much his outward appearance belied the cruel messages he delivered to his faithful followers.

"Can you pick him out?" Sayid asked, eyeing the mosque through the binoculars. "He's bearded. Wearing glasses. A white shirt, brown jacket. Gray woolen scarf."

"Got him," Aslan responded, his cheek resting against the butt of the rifle, one eye peering intently through the scope.

In Aslan's eyes, the scene laid out before him looked like something from a silent movie. All he could hear was the wind, as a cold gust blew past the open window, along with the sound of cars on the move in the distance. An icy sun shone its light onto the courtyard. A large shadow suddenly infiltrated the illuminated expanse, the wind carrying the clouds rapidly onward, toward the clusters of buildings and beyond them toward the park, and further still, to the hills on the horizon. Badawi was already just a few meters from the sidewalk, the old, battered car waiting for him. One of his bodyguards strode quickly toward the vehicle to open the door and usher the preacher inside.

The scope's crosshairs were on Badawi's chest. A headshot from that distance wasn't the correct option; the head made for too small a target. Sayid, who was keeping an eye on the group's progress through the binoculars, realized that Aslan had to take his shot without delay, right then, before Badawi disappeared into the car. Aslan's breathing rate remained unchanged. His finger squeezed the trigger. He fired one shot, followed immediately by a second. Through the scope he saw a red stain spreading across Badawi's white shirt as his body crumpled to the sidewalk. He saw a second red stain spreading across the light-colored coat of a small girl, who was already sprawled on the sidewalk, one arm stretched taut above her head, her legs motionless, a purple backpack tossed by her side, a stack of colorful notebooks peeking out from inside the bag. The youths gathered around Badawi dispersed at a run, trying to find cover from the shots. Two of the preacher's guards were kneeling over him. The girl was prone on the cold sidewalk, alone, an island of emptiness, surrounded by silence. And then a young man ran toward her and seemed to collapse over her, embracing her, concealing her small body with his own.

"What just happened here?" Sayid asked in horror. "What the hell . . ."

"Now's not the time for talking," Aslan responded. "We're getting out of here. I'm just dismantling the rifle and then we're gone like the wind." They had already wiped the apartment clean of fingerprints beforehand. Aslan's hand, too, the one that had fired the rifle, was wearing a thin driving glove, and he was now cleaning the weapon and the windowsill it had been resting on just moments earlier. The pieces of the weapon were stuffed into a sports bag, which was then wrapped in a large towel.

Aslan put on the black dress, the loose-fitting one that Ann and Helena had made for him, and covered his face with a veil. He had one last look around the apartment and then said to Sayid, "Say good-bye nicely, because you're never coming back here. Let's go. You first."

Waiting for them on the ground floor, near the front door, was an old baby carriage, which they had purchased at a market stall in a nearby neighborhood. Aslan placed the sports bag in the carriage and covered it with a woolen baby blanket. Sayid stepped out onto the street, with Aslan behind him, pushing the carriage, his face completely hidden, a bulky coat covering his dress. He tried to alter his gait, but no one seemed to be paying him any attention anyway. Ambulance and police sirens could be heard in the distance. They split up. Sayid headed for the bus stop, and Aslan turned right, moving away from the apartment, distancing himself further from the mosque.

Aslan spotted Ann and Helena at the far end of the alleyway, only their eyes shining through the slit in their veils. Leaning up against the crumbling brick wall next to them was a bicycle. Without saying a word to them, he abandoned the baby carriage, got on the bike, and started pedaling.

Helena assumed control of the baby carriage, with Ann by her side. Two anonymous women in black attire, a dismantled sniper rifle sleeping in their baby carriage, under a woolen blanket. Ahead lay a fifteen-minute stroll. Their car was parked on a quiet street. When they got there, the rifle and folded carriage would go into the trunk. A ninety-minute drive would then get them to a secluded forest in Kent, where the sniper rifle would be stashed away at a prearranged location.

They had come to the conclusion that it would be best, no matter what, to hide the rifle rather than get rid of it in a hurry. They'd remain in England for the time being. The security tension at the country's airports and marine border crossing was going to be sky-high during the first few days after the assassination. Within two weeks, as agreed, the team would meet up in Berlin. Until then, Ann and Helena would remain together in Liverpool. Aslan was going to embark on an exhausting hike along the length of Hadrian's Wall, in the north of England. And that very same evening, Sayid, the only one who could be linked to the apartment in which the shooting took place, would become a blond and take up residence in a room at a small hotel in

Oxford that he had already reserved, where he'd devote his days to research at the Bodleian Library, working hard on his study of Arabic poetry in the Middle Ages.

52

Newcastle, England, February 14, 2015

Aslan had been waiting at the café near the cathedral in Newcastle since the early hours of the morning. His face was pale and drawn, and he was drinking from a cup of already cold coffee. When he saw her get out of the taxi, dragging a small suitcase on wheels behind her, something in him moved. She smiled at him and hugged him as he rose to greet her. He appeared stiff and tired to her.

"Big shit, huh?" she said, taking off her coat and hanging it on a wooden stand near the table.

"Yes. Awful." He went silent. "I didn't see her at all. I have no idea where she came from. She wasn't there. And then that bloodstain appeared on her coat, growing ever larger, like some kind of a possessed flower. There was a girl there, Ya'ara, her name was Yasmin. I have no idea how it happened. What happened. I have no idea."

Ya'ara had read the BBC News website report about Badawi's assassination — and the fact that a seven-year-old girl had also been killed in the targeted killing operation — even before the telephone update from Aslan. Aslan made contact only after he had disengaged completely from Bethnal Green, dumped his clothing in a church collection bin for the needy in Hackney, and checked that no one was following him. When he finally got to King's Cross train station, he turned on his cellphone and reported to Ya'ara. She could hear death in his voice and knew she had to see him face-to-face. She asked him to make his way to Newcastle, while she boarded the first flight out of Schiphol Airport in Amsterdam, where she had spent the previous few days keeping track of the cadets.

The operation in Brussels had ended successfully, Yael Ziv's killer was dead, and her team had dispersed, with Nufar and Assaf taking a train to Cologne and Batsheva heading to Paris. She had followed Aslan's operation anxiously. She knew that the rules of the ops world didn't allow for successes only. The seed of failure lies in every course of action, and when it comes to targeted killing operations, the risk curve rises steeply. And still, every operation is carried out in the hope that if the gods of operational statistics choose to make something go wrong, it'll befall someone else. When pitted against the statistics, optimism wins the day. Because if one were to act in keeping with a sober assessment of one's chances, one wouldn't do a thing. Nevertheless, when a disaster occurs, it hits one hard, even if in theory it was expected.

"It's not good for you to be here, you know. To knowingly enter a crime scene when you can avoid doing so is a mistake. Or rash." Aslan spoke with obvious exhaustion in his voice. "This entire country is on the hunt now," he said. "Not only did terrorists kill a Muslim leader, thus sparking intense rage among the entire Muslim community in Britain, they also murdered an innocent young girl. A girl who was on her way home from school, who collected Barbie dolls, who wanted to be a doctor. No one is going to pardon that. And here you are, stepping knowingly into this entire mess. You're pushing your luck, aren't you?"

Ya'ara realized that Aslan had busied himself in the interim with gathering particulars about the dead girl. It couldn't have been very difficult. Her image adorned every newspaper in England. "I wanted to see you," she said. "And more important, I need to see Sayid. He can't be left alone after witnessing such a thing with his own eyes."

Aslan recognized the criticism implicit in Ya'ara's words. But he was dead tired and didn't say a word. He could picture the girl he had killed, her hands drenched in blood and reaching out to him. Ya'ara saw his eyes lose focus. The skin of his face appeared to be graying right there and then. He was the strong man, the experienced man, some twenty years her senior. He needed her now, and she didn't know how to help him. She rested her hand on his. It was ice cold.

"You couldn't see her, Aslan. She must have been hiding behind her father."

Aslan groaned.

"Look, you eliminated Badawi, that despicable man, whose incitement led to hatred and terror attacks and the murder of innocent people. We're at war, Aslan. Remember that."

"I murdered a little girl."

"Aslan . . ."

"That's what I did. You can spin the story however you like, but you can't justify that."

"You're right, it's terrible. But that's war. War exacts civilian casualties, too."

"Maybe. Whatever you say. I'm not even

sure it's our war."

For a long while she looked at him without saying a word. And then she gathered herself and said, "You're not yourself, Aslan. You're going to regret the things you've just said." Her eyes were frozen and hard as granite.

"Yes, you're right there. I'm not thinking clearly right now. A few days in the countryside will do me good. I'll walk and walk and focus on the cold and my aching muscles and maybe it'll pass. You can tell me about Brussels when I get back."

"I'll tell you now." Her report was concise and precise and devoid of emotion. She spoke as if she was undergoing a debriefing in the operations room.

"You're crazy," he said to her. "Taking on an unreasonable risk."

"I couldn't put the cadets in the ring. They're too inexperienced."

"Under such circumstances, you don't go through with the operation. You were right not to put them up against armed guards in such close quarters, but crazy to do it yourself."

"It was a calculated risk, Aslan. Look, here I am. I did it right."

"Risk management. That's a phrase that may suit a business administration course at

Harvard, but not a targeted killing operation. You were outnumbered, facing professional security personnel, in an arena under their control. You played Russian roulette, that's what you did."

"I had the element of surprise on my side." Ya'ara was taken aback by the anger she felt creeping into her heart. "I knew what I was going to do. They didn't understand what was happening to them. I wanted to kill Hamdan. All they wanted was not to be killed. I scared them. I must have looked like an alien with that gas mask."

"You played Russian roulette," Aslan reiterated. "You took a gamble and won. But the statistics even themselves out. If you keep flying off the track, you'll get yourself killed. And then you won't have a unit, and won't be waging a war, or doing anything at all. It'll all end before it's even started. Is that what you want? For it to end in nothing? In defeat?"

Her anger bubbled inside her. Her mission had ended in success. She was running the operation. In the unit they had set up, she outranked him. "Come on," she said, caressing his hand without real feeling. "Let's not argue now. We need to rest and process what happened to us.

"We managed to carry out two important

operations in a very short time. If we continue at this rate, with the same intensity, we'll make an impact. They'll start to run scared. They'll lose people, get into a panic, turn on themselves. And the European security services, too, will see that this war can be won, and they will also begin to take the initiative and mount operations. They'll be a lot more focused and aggressive, even if it means having to amend the laws in the framework of which they're required to operate.

"Aslan, we're doing something right. And we're good at it because we're doing it a little differently. We think differently. We're a little more daring. A little out of the box. And yet we're still working properly. Intelligently, with planning. That's why the unit was established. So that we can defeat these monsters. And that's what we've started doing."

Aslan stood up and placed a five-pound note on the table. "Walk with me to the bus stop. There are only two buses a day to the remote location I need to get to. Maybe you're right. But you have to look after yourself. Look, you can see that I'm okay. Just a little pensive and extremely tired. But it'll work out fine. It always turns out fine in the end."

Ya'ara wasn't convinced that Aslan was okay. But she knew him, and knew that the only thing he wanted right then was to be alone, in nature, his body warming from the physical exertion, the demons that had been troubling him pushed into a dark corner of his soul. She was relying on his inner strength, but knew that those reserves would run dry at some point, too — though probably not now. She thought about Sayid and mentally plotted the quickest route to get to him. She planned to see him no later than tonight.

Nufar and Assaf were in Cologne. Batsheva was in Paris. Ann and Helena were in Liverpool. Sayid was in Oxford. Aslan was here, by her side, the ice-cold air of Newcastle watching their breath turn into distinct clouds of vapor. She could picture the faces of all of them. They were her people, her unit. They were at war. This was what her war looked like.

53

Cologne, February 2015

"Can you fold this properly for me?" Assaf asked.

Nufar burst out laughing. "You mean to say you can't even fold a map?" she exclaimed.

Assaf shrugged his shoulders. "It's never been my forte," he responded.

The café at which they were sitting wasn't far from the Dom, Cologne's world-renowned cathedral. The tourist map of the city in Assaf's hands looked like a comedy prop. He spread it out across the table one more time, trying not to knock over the mugs of coffee or smear the paper with the remains of the butter and jam that had come with the croissant. He tried to reconstruct the correct order of the folds, and failed dismally once again.

"Come on, give it to me," Nufar said. "Pathetic. Are sure you were an officer in the Combat Engineering Corps? Don't you need to be able to dismantle mines and operate heavy engineering machinery for that? And you can't even fold a map!"

"Enough. Move on. You're humiliating me. And it's not my fault. It's you, you get me all flustered. I have to spend two weeks with someone like you in a big city in Germany and it's not easy."

"Tell me, Assaf, when are you going to stop with that? With your quick tongue, with the endless flirting? You don't need to make an impression on me. And that's certainly not the way to impress me. Okay?"

"You're right. That's not really who I am, it's tiresome for me, too. Let's try not to do it any longer. I'll try, I mean," he corrected himself.

"Really try, okay? A small town in Germany."

"What?"

"You said we're in a big German city, and that's true. Cologne really is a big city. But you know that just a few kilometers from here, down the river, lies Bonn, about which John le Carré wrote a book called *A Small Town in Germany.* It always amazes me — a city that was once the capital of an economic superpower, of an important country, of West Germany. And now it's becoming a mere footnote in the history books. All they'll have to say about it in a few years' time will be: 'Served as the capital of West Germany during the period 1949 to 1990.' "

"That's what they're writing about it already. Look at Wikipedia." He showed her the page he had opened on the screen of his phone. "The city's already a footnote. Have you read his books, le Carré's?"

"I have. A few. My father gave me two or three of them to read. He was the only author he read religiously, and I wanted to love the same things my father loved. To tell you the truth, I see his books as mementos from an era long since passed. Back then it was the Cold War. The wars these days are different."

"Yes, and we are the soldiers fighting this war, which is going on right now. Do you feel like a covert fighter in a global campaign? Tell me truthfully: Did you ever think you'd be in this position?"

"No, it never once crossed my mind. I studied at INSEAD, after all. My objectives lay elsewhere. But the fact is I'm here now. Assaf" — she hesitated for a moment — "how terrible do you think it is for me to be happy that we managed to kill that Osama Hamdan guy? For me to be happy about the death of someone?"

"I've seen the footage from the security cameras that were in the synagogue. The images were aired on television constantly. He appears so calculating and cool-headed in them. He plucked the submachine gun from his backpack and opened fire on innocent people. With such brutality. He deserved to die. If someone has to do this kind of work, it's good that we're the ones doing it."

"Yes, you're probably right. There's no point in agonizing over it, or feeling bad about not doing so. It doesn't even suit me." Her eyes glimmered, and she suddenly began to recite mournfully: " 'That's the nature of the Palmach, which leaves no work to anyone who is not one of us.' Do you know that old song?"

"Yes, yes, 'Their nation wasn't a mother to them' . . ."

"Exactly. 'She didn't know they were heading out' . . ."

"So you think we're like the Palmach?"

"Enough, Assaf," she said, turning impatient all of a sudden. "We're starting to talk like old-timers. Forget the Palmach and everything else. We are who we are. Let's go outside for a while. I need some air. Look at that cathedral. Can you imagine what this place must have looked like when it was first built?"

The dark turrets of the Dom towered above them. Ice-cold air was rising from the wide Rhine River that flowed below them, its waters murky and dark. They began walking in a southerly direction, against the flow of the current. A thin black dog was sniffing at the withered grass between the sidewalk and the fence.

They felt invincible. Two young and talented individuals who were in the right place at the right time. Nufar looked at Assaf, who was walking beside her. He had yet to find his place, she thought.

"That was very impressive," he said to her. "What you did there with the computers, in Brussels."

Nufar kicked at a stone.

He looked at her, uncertain if she had heard him.

"When we get back to the hotel," she said, "I think you should call home. It's important to keep in touch."

"What about you?"

"I'll do so, too," she responded, but she didn't know whom she'd call.

54

London, MI5 Headquarters, February 15, 2015

The silence in the conference room adjacent to the bureau of the director of MI5 was deafening. Sitting there side by side were the head of the Counterterrorism Division, the head of the East London Field Department, and the head of the Desk Department. The head of the Research Department, with a cup of hot tea in his right hand and a stack of cardboard files under his left arm, was trying to open the door to the conference room with his shoulder, and only the quick reaction of his personal assistant spared the faded carpet, the color of which was already something of a mystery, from another stain. There was plenty of room around the shiny mahogany table, which was covered with a greenish shade of leather with gold trim on the edges. They were waiting for the director to enter. They had taken a hard hit, and knew their boss was fuming.

The interleading door between the bureau and the conference room opened and the MI5 director's bureau chief walked in, greeting those present in the room with a glance. "Sir Robert will join you in a few minutes," he declared. "He's on a call with Number 10."

When he entered the conference room, the look on Sir Robert's face was more serious than ever. He sat at the head of the table and nodded to the head of the Counterterrorism Division, as if to say: Speak! The division chief motioned to the head of the Desk Department, Mary Clarkson, who clicked on her computer mouse.

"Good morning, gentlemen," she said, her voice as soft and refined as ever. The image of Anjam Badawi appeared on the screen. "This is Anjam Badawi, a radical Muslim preacher from a mosque in Bethnal Green. Here at MI5, he goes by the code name Winter Fox. We arrested him three years ago on suspicion of incitement and posing a threat to public security. During the course of his detention, we were able to turn and recruit him, and in time he became our most valuable agent among the Muslim extremists in London. One could say, in fact, that he was our most valuable asset in the entire United Kingdom. Two days ago, while leaving the mosque after Friday prayers, he was killed by a single shot from a sniper. A second shot struck, presumably inadvertently, a seven-year-old girl, who was waiting outside the mosque for her father, one of the worshippers that day." The screen displayed a picture of Yasmin al Hussein, sprawled on the ground, blood staining her white dress, her legs at an unnatural angle, one of her shoes tossed aside in the courtyard, the white sock on her left foot a stark focal point in the image.

"Do we have any idea who may have killed Winter Fox," the MI5 director asked.

Clarkson turned to glance questioningly at the head of the Research Division. Terry James looked like a professor from the University of London, complete with thick-lensed glasses and a worn corduroy jacket. His appearance wasn't a far cry from reality. James ended up at MI5 following an impressive academic career. He wasn't from London, though, but from York, in the north, and had devoted most of his life to studying philology at Durham University. Before beginning his studies, he served for seven years in the SAS, the Special Air Service, the British army's elite commando unit. He was older than everyone else in the room, even Sir Robert.

"No," he said, "we still have no idea who killed Winter Fox, but we can hazard a guess. More so than guess, we can evaluate. First of all, the hit was the work of professionals. Ballistic examinations carried out by the forensic crime lab have identified the bullets that killed Winter Fox and the young girl as rounds from a Russian-made sniper rifle, used by the Red Army's special forces, among others. According to the ballistic experts, the shots were fired in all likelihood from a distance of four to five hundred yards. The police are still searching for the precise location the sniper used. But they'll find it soon, and maybe turn up some evidence there, too. Or so we hope. In any event, it all points to the work of a highly skilled sniper. Someone entrusted to carry out a targeted killing successfully from such a distance has to be."

"Do you mean to say that the Russians assassinated Winter Fox?"

"No, Sir Robert, we have no reason to suspect them in particular. Russia's military forces aren't the only ones who use the type of weapon that served the sniper. It's been used in the war in the Balkans, and we know that arms dealers are selling it on the black market, too. Here, in Britain, over the past two years alone, Scotland Yard has seized four such rifles from crime gangs. We believe there are a lot more out there. Our suspicions, therefore, are not directed at the Russians in particular, even though they also view radical Islam as an enemy, and as far as they're concerned, combating Islamic terrorism is best done far beyond the borders of Russia. I believe we're dealing with an intelligence organization of a state, and not an internal conflict between rival Islamic factions. The targeted killing was too professional a job to be attributed to them. And as for possible state involvement, there are very few countries that fight terrorism in such an active and aggressive fashion. We, the Americans, and the Israelis. And the Russians, whom I've already mentioned. Naturally, we didn't liquidate the best intelligence source we had. And it doesn't have the look and feel of an American operation either. Despite all their arrogance and audacity, they wouldn't carry out a targeted killing operation like that on English soil."

"All you've said until now is mere guesswork," the MI5 director commented. "Okay, not guesswork, speculation. But do you have anything on which to base your assessment? Do you think Badawi's assassination is related to the events in Belgium a few days ago?"

"Exactly! Osama Hamdan, who perpetrated the attack at the central synagogue in Brussels, was assassinated in the Belgian capital. He was already in detention and was on his way to a court hearing. They killed him in a prisoner-transport vehicle, for God's sake! It wasn't a targeted killing. Plastered all over the operation in huge letters is the word 'revenge.' I'm convinced the Israelis killed Hamdan. And four days later Badawi is assassinated in London. There are no such things as coincidences in our line of work. It's starting to look like a finely tuned campaign with an Israeli signature. The Mossad. I don't know when and where they'll strike again, but my money would be on some time soon."

"It's been more than twenty-five years," Clarkson remarked.

"What are you talking about?"

"In 1987, the Mossad was involved in the assassination of that Palestinian cartoonist, what was his name . . ."

"Naji al-Ali," said the head of the Counterterrorism Division. "But Arafat's people were probably the ones who did the actual killing . . ."

"Yes, whatever, but the Mossad was involved up to its neck in the affair. They had an agent here who had the weapon stashed at his home. In any event, they've been holding back ever since, and haven't conducted any violent operations on British soil. Uncharacteristic restraint, considering it's the Mossad. It must have come to an end."

"Sons of bitches," said the director of MI5. "Tony" — he turned to his bureau chief — "bring Alan in here." Alan Foster was the agency's deputy director. "I want him on a plane to Tel Aviv by tonight, for talks with the head of the Mossad. We need to put a stop to this madness immediately. They can't be allowed to run wild here, to assassinate our assets and murder little girls along the way."

"Uh-umm" — the bureau chief cleared his throat — "it's Sunday and Mr. Foster is surely at his home in Exeter."

"So he can move his ass and get here. Right away. Fucking Sunday. Find out where he is and send a helicopter to collect him. I hope he's not out on a fox hunt or something."

"Sir," Tony said, "fox hunting is for the MI6 people only."

"And our fox has already been hunted," Clarkson remarked cynically.

55

Mossad Headquarters, Tel Aviv, February 15, 2015

"Can someone tell me what the hell is going on here?" The Mossad chief looked stressed and agitated. Contrary to the intelligence agency's hedonistic image, her bureau was modest and sparse. Daylight had no chance of making it down to level five belowground, and the filtered air that flowed into her office was cold and synthetic. Her bureau chief asked if she'd like a coffee. "Yes, please, but a strong one," she replied — their prearranged code that meant instead of coffee, it would be better to fill the ceramic mug with a generous measure of Irish whiskey, and just a drop of water. Some were aware that Caracal, as the Mossad chief was known, drank whiskey from time to time. But they had never seen her lose her flair for sharp thinking or absorbing data, processing it quickly and making tough decisions. If Caracal had lost anything just then, it was her cool and collected manner, but not due to the whiskey at all, and only because she didn't know what was going on. And not knowing made her aggressive and impatient.

"It's been a week since the assassination of Osama Hamdan in Brussels, and we still have no idea who was behind it," she said, looking coldly at her people sitting on the other side of her large desk. "And now the deputy director of the British internal security service has informed us that he's arriving tomorrow and demands a meeting with me without delay. Demands!"

The head of the Mossad's Foreign Relations Division shifted uncomfortably in his chair, as if he were responsible himself for the British official's impoliteness.

"Do you know what they want?"

"Madam Director, there has indeed been an adamant request for an urgent and personal meeting with you. And no, they didn't mention the subject matter. They assume we are well aware of what's troubling them. And we all know that a radical Muslim preacher by the name of Badawi was assassinated in London the day before yesterday. I can only surmise that the urgent visit by the deputy director of MI5 is related to the killing."

"Are you telling me they think we did it?"

"Yes, primarily because of the timing. And there was also a somewhat unclear remark that our representative in London heard from them and relayed verbatim in a cable. They said: 'Thatcher and Shamir are no longer with us, but their signatures are still valid.' "

"And do you know what that means?"

The head of the Foreign Relations Division shifted uncomfortably in his chair again. "Not exactly. . . . It rings a bell but . . ."

"Well, let me tell you," Caracal said in an icy tone. "Almost thirty years ago, twenty-eight, to be precise, the British shut down our station in London, expelling everyone there. From the station chief down to the last of the secretaries. They claimed we were involved in the murder of a Palestinian cartoonist who used to make fun of Arafat on a regular basis. He was sharp and amusing, but apparently Arafat failed to appreciate his sense of humor. He ordered the hit. We, of course, had nothing to do with the assassination. Why would we be interested in a cartoonist? But the British claimed that one of our agents was involved in the killing. He had kept a suitcase containing the weapons in his apartment for three weeks. He didn't say a word to us about it, and we weren't professional or smart enough to ask. But what could we tell the British? That we had behaved like amateurs? In any event, they didn't believe us, and expelled everyone. And after the scandal, there was an exchange of letters between the Israeli and British prime ministers at the time, Shamir and Thatcher, and the Israeli prime minister signed an undertaking to never again operate on British soil without their knowledge and approval. Never to assassinate, God forbid, never to conduct a clandestine operation. So, you're right. They think that we assassinated that preacher, Badawi, and have thus blatantly violated the commitment we made three decades ago."

"But it wasn't us, Madam Director. You know that."

"Yes, but what I don't know is who did it. And who killed Hamdan. And that bothers me a whole lot. Any ideas, anyone?"

"I'm guessing it wasn't the Swiss intelligence service," one of the meeting's attendees commented lightheartedly.

No one laughed. The Mossad chief didn't even smile.

"When you come up with any ideas, let me know. And those ideas better be based on information."

The brief meeting, as everyone in the room understood, had come to an end. "Ido," Caracal said to her bureau chief before they left room, "get me Aharon Levin on the phone. I have an idea. I need to pick his brain."

Aharon Levin had served as head of the Mossad for almost a decade, ending his term in office at the beginning of the new millennium, shortly before the attack on the Twin Towers in New York. He was viewed as one of the Mossad's best directors ever, and was well-known for both his original approach to operational strategy and his personal ties to men and women in politics and intelligence around the globe.

Aharon came across as an absentminded professor and made a conscious effort to uphold that impression, and those who were fooled by his harmless appearance paid a heavy price. And now he was walking into the office of the current Mossad chief, an office that was once his own, accompanied by her bureau chief. He fished two cellphones from his pockets and placed them in the trustworthy hands of Ido. "Just a moment," he said to him, rummaging through his bag, pulling out dossiers, a folded umbrella, and a copy of *The Economist.* "Here you go," he declared triumphantly, "take this phone, too." Ido stood there holding the three phones, his wealth of experience the only thing stopping him from rolling his eyes in despair. Caracal invited Aharon to join her in the small seating area at the far end of her bureau. Her bureau chief had already suggested replacing the armchairs several times, or reupholstering them at least, but Caracal said she liked them just the way they were. Comfortable, shabby, full of character.

"Aharon," she said to him, typically direct, "I hope we're not watching a rerun of the Cobra affair, or perhaps I should say a sequel to it . . ."

Aharon fixed her with a look of pure innocence.

"Please, Aharon, neither of us was born yesterday."

Cobra was the KGB's code name for Alon Regev, the prime minister's political strategy advisor. A year and a half earlier, Regev had been exposed as a Russian spy by Aharon Levin and a small team working closely with him. Aharon had been operating at the time without the knowledge of anyone else in the security establishment, with the state president the only other person party to the secret. Regev was ultimately killed in a mysterious car accident north of Ashkelon, on his way to fleeing the country by sea. Aharon's team was rumored to have killed him, but she'd never been able to confirm it. Aharon never once breathed a single word about the incident, and the members of his team dispersed and disappeared back into everyday life, each returning to his or her own affairs. Of the current exploits of Ya'ara and Aslan, who were part of the original team and had since established a covert operational squad answering to the prime minister alone, Aharon Levin knew absolutely nothing at all.

"What was, *was,*" Aharon said nonchalantly, "there's no need or point in delving into the past. We did what we had to do, and we operated in a compartmentalized fashion because we had no idea where he was hiding. We've already discussed this, Anat. Even if you didn't like what happened, I think you understood that we had no choice."

"Maybe there is no point in delving into the past, but when the past comes back to haunt us, then it's vital that we deal with it. Aharon, someone is running amok in Europe and I need to know that it isn't you. Forgive me for being so direct and blunt, but things have spun out of control and it needs to be stopped immediately."

Aharon knew she was talking about the assassinations in Brussels and London. He, too, had wondered who was behind them, and if the Mossad under Caracal was starting to go off the rails. From his perspective, in an era of international cooperation and the establishment of alliances for a coordinated onslaught on radical Islam, carrying out wild assassinations in the very hearts of the capitals of Europe was the epitome of madness.

"Let's pretend that you didn't ask me that question," Aharon said in the tone of a Polish nobleman deeply hurt by being doubted. "Of course I have no part in this madness. And not for a second have I thought that it was the work of the Mossad," he added, even though the notion had crossed his mind.

"I truly appreciate that," Caracal said.

"Nevertheless, Anat, we both see an Israeli fingerprint on those operations. And I'm referring first and foremost to the assassination of Osama Hamdan in Belgium. That was retribution. That's the only possible motive. Revenge."

"Revenge, or a move to silence him. We discussed the possibility that he was killed by the jihadist organization to which he belonged. I'm not going to say Al Qaeda, that would be too amorphous and inaccurate. Hamdan belonged to a Muslim gang that identified with Al Qaeda. That doesn't make the gang part of a global organization. In any event, whatever the case may be, there's no need for a thesis on the organizational affiliation of that piece of filth. He may have known secrets that someone didn't want exposed ever."

"To me that sounds like a possibility in theory only. If he had any secrets, he could have already given them up during his questioning. He was interrogated, after all, for weeks on end. And if he didn't divulge any secrets, then why kill him? Besides, according to the media reports at least, the individual who carried out the hit sent him on his way to the next world with a farewell greeting that went something like: 'May you burn in hell.' Someone killed him out of hatred."

"Look, Aharon, I despised him, too. He acted with terrible cruelty and coldness, and it just so happens that the woman he murdered had served the country all her life. And he also wounded another five people in the same incident. Jews, of course. But he was in a prisoner-transport vehicle when he was killed. On his way to court. From the perspective of the State of Israel, justice had been done.

"We would never initiate a strike on a terrorist who is already in custody and facing legal proceedings. We certainly wouldn't undermine the sovereignty of an ally in such a manner," she said. "And I can't think of an intelligence agency of any other normal country that would mount such an operation. And soon thereafter, that preacher was killed in the very heart of London. And the little girl who was murdered, too. It's terrible. And I'm convinced that the two incidents are related. Brussels and London were carried out by the same party. That's my working assumption. And it's a strong working assumption. The savagery of the hit in Brussels could be a clue toward solving this madness. Aharon, this thing is causing us extensive damage, and it'll get a whole lot worse if we don't put a stop to it."

Aharon was lost in thought. Something about the Mossad chief's choice of words had caught his attention. He tried to parse out what had caused that spark to flicker in his brain. "Are you thinking of something?" Caracal asked. "Do you have an idea?"

Aharon delayed his response. The savagery of the hit in Brussels, the savagery of the hit in Brussels. "Perhaps. I'm not sure. I need to check out a few things and then get back to you. I may need your help with clarifying a number of things. Border control records, SIGINT data . . ." His words were left hanging in the air.

The Mossad chief knew that there was no point in pressing him to share his thoughts. Aharon Levin had always done things his own way. At his own pace. "My bureau chief will give you all the assistance you need. I'll ask him to coordinate the handling of any request you may have. But please, Aharon. Quickly. We can't afford to allow this to get out of hand."

After leaving the Mossad compound, Aharon pulled over to the side of the road. He found the number he was looking for only after a search through his third phone. "Hello, hello," he said, surprised by the call, even though he was the one who had placed it. "Hello, Michael, hello. How are you? Excellent, excellent," he added, before receiving a response of any kind. "Are you busy now? What, you have a meeting in twenty minutes? So apologize. Cancel and apologize. I need to see you now. Yes, in the usual place. You're in Nahmani, right? At our apartment?" Michael Turgeman had served as a Mossad field operative for twenty-five years. Now, he was a free citizen, or so he believed, at least. When the hunt for Cobra began, the team set up by Aharon, with Michael at his side, had used an office on Nahmani Street as an ops apartment where they held their meetings. As a base from which they set out on their various missions. So it was "our apartment." It was serving now as the offices of Michael Turgeman & Partners, Law Firm. "The usual place" was the Arcaffe branch at the Ramat Aviv Mall. Aharon liked to hold his meetings there. Fortunately for Michael, the congestion on the roads was restricted to the traffic pouring into Tel Aviv. The road north was relatively open.

56

Ramat Aviv Mall, February 15, 2015

Aharon didn't beat about the bush. "It has to be her. That combination of professionalism and irresponsibility has her name written all over it," he said in anger. By "her," he was referring to Ya'ara Stein.

Michael took affront. "You're dumping this whole thing on her without a shred of proof. You're still mad at her about the Cobra assassination, and you know as well as I do that the hit on him was the right thing to do ultimately."

"I don't want to argue with you. In any event, what she did was a gross violation of my instructions. When she gets an idea in that head of hers, she runs with it without regard for anything or anyone. She's arrogant, your friend. And reckless. Arrogant, wild, and irresponsible."

"You're angry, Aharon, and anger offers bad counsel."

"Do you know where she is? Have you spoken to her in the past few days?"

"We don't have that kind of a relationship. I haven't seen or spoken to Ya'ara since the Cobra affair. And run it by me one more time: What's your connection to this whole story? And more important, what's mine?"

"The Mossad chief summoned me. She thought I was doing something behind her back again. And when I'm involved, you are, too. And I'm telling you now, Israelis were the ones who carried out those targeted killings, highly professional and with a very personal agenda. We need to stop it. And first things first, find Ya'ara."

Ya'ara didn't answer Michael's call. She might have changed her number. He wasn't aware of her current address. He managed to get hold of her father in Kiryat Haim, and he said she'd been spending a lot of time overseas recently, in Berlin, doing something in the film world. She had a German phone number, he said, but he doesn't call. He didn't want to bother her. She called from time to time, and mailed him, too. If Michael wanted, he would email Ya'ara to tell her that someone by the name of Michael Turgeman was looking for her. No, his daughter had never mentioned him.

No, he couldn't give him her address in Israel or phone number overseas. And not her email address either. If she wanted to, she would contact him.

Aharon had told him that Ido, the bureau chief, was coordinating the handling of the matter on behalf of the head of the Mossad and would help him with whatever he needed. Michael asked Ido to check the Interior Ministry's records to see if Ya'ara was in the country or abroad somewhere. He asked for her border-crossing history, in and out of Israel, for the previous six months. He asked for wiretaps on her father's phones, and for a number for Ya'ara's German phone, and maybe other phones she was using, too, based on her father's incoming and outgoing call records, from both his landline at home and his cellphone. He asked for a wiretap on Ya'ara's Israeli phone and a location for the phone over the past six months. If they were able to identity foreign phones that Ya'ara was using, he wanted them to try to locate them, but without asking for assistance from outside elements. In no way were they to involve foreign intelligence officials. Ido said all his requests required the approval of the head of the Shin Bet security service, and Michael said Ido wasn't the Mossad director's bureau chief for nothing and should do whatever needed to be done. He knew he was asking a lot, and he, too, wasn't sure if anything would come of all the inquiries. He was hoping with all his heart that Ya'ara had nothing to do with the assassinations, but feared his hopes would be crushed. But he knew at the same time that if Ya'ara was in some kind of trouble, he should be on her side. Should be. Wanted to be.

When it is called for, the Mossad and Shin Bet know how to work very quickly. That's how Michael learned that Ya'ara had spent the majority of the past six months overseas. She was abroad now, too, with her last departure from Israel a month earlier. Her Israeli phone went with her, but remained switched off for most of the time. Berlin was the only place in Europe where she had used that phone. They also identified two German phone numbers from which she had called her father several times. They must have been her phones. One of them was located the night before in Oxford, England.

"Is she connected somehow to this whole business — that young woman?" Ido asked.

"It's something I need to check."

■ ■ ■ ■

When Michael updated Aharon Levin, he stressed that he had come up with no information linking Ya'ara to Brussels or London, and certainly not on the dates the assassinations took place.

"I want you to go to her," Aharon decided. "Even if it's a shot in the dark. Yes, you could simply call her German phone, but if she has something to hide, she'll feel under pressure and disappear on you. She'll also wonder how you got her number, and you definitely won't want to tell her that there's a tap on her father's phone. That's all we need."

"Why would she think of a wiretap? I'll tell her I got her number from her father."

"She'll check with him and he'll deny it, of course. You won't get away with that story." Aharon paused for a moment, deep in thought. "Unless," he continued, voicing the idea in his mind out loud, "unless we have him arrested and thus unavailable for forty-eight hours."

"I'm going to forget you suggested that," Michael responded. "You can leave the Mossad, but apparently the Mossad never leaves you. Excuse me for saying so, Aharon, but that's an abhorrent idea. It wouldn't work anyway. There's nothing to justify arresting him like that, and as someone with so much experience under his belt, you should know it."

Aharon didn't like Michael's tone. He would never have dared to speak to him like that in the past. "Reasons of state security would justify an arrest. Far more serious things than holding someone in custody for two days have been done in the name of state security." But he knew Michael had a point. "You know what? The best thing would be for you to get yourself to London, and then straight on to Oxford. We'll try to guide you to her by tracking her phone location, if possible. You used to be an excellent field operative. You'll find her. That's the best way to go about it. Something like this can't be handled from afar. You need to look her in the eyes when you speak to her."

57

Oxford, February 16, 2015

After landing at Heathrow, Michael received a message that Ya'ara's phone was still in Oxford, and a second update came in when he arrived in Oxford on a train from London's Paddington Station. The experts at the Mossad had managed to narrow down the location to the city center. The Mossad director's bureau chief also passed on another piece of information that left Michael momentarily stunned and breathless. "Fuck," he said to himself out loud. "Fuck."

The day was gray and damp, and his clothes were no match for the wet cold. He had left his suitcase in a locker at the Oxford train station; there was no point in wasting time settling into the hotel room that had been reserved for him.

He set out on foot from the train station without any fixed ideas on how to go about finding Ya'ara. He wandered aimlessly and veered off in the direction of the Covered Market, where the remains of holiday decorations still adorned some of the stores. Dead animals, hanging from hooks, stared at him. Game meat on offer at the butcher stalls. Wild boars, rabbits, deer, and pheasants with their dead heads turned to face the paved walkways. Resting on plastic leaves in the illuminated displays were wild fowl, quails, and ducks, some skinless, some adorned with a few festive feathers. He hadn't eaten meat for a year already, and sights like the ones before him only strengthened his resolve.

He passed by the shops quickly, hoping against all odds to catch a glimpse of Ya'ara's fair face in one of them. He went out into the open street, and a cold, murky gust of wind slammed him in the face. He walked on, his eyes scanning the street. Across from St. John's College he spotted the Eagle and Child, the pub frequented by J. R. R. Tolkien, the author of *Lord of the Rings.* Or was it C. S. Lewis?

He remembered Aharon Levin, the Anglophile, telling him about it. At the center of the pub sign, the red eagle's wings appeared proudly spread across the sky-blue backdrop. Across the street stood the rival pub, the Lamb and Flag. It was a gloomy afternoon, and both pubs were practically empty. He went into the Eagle and Child and ordered a whiskey, drinking it standing up, in one gulp. The alcohol burned his throat and made his eyes tear. He felt the warmth spreading through his chest and offered a nod of thanks to the photo hanging on the wall of Colin Dexter, the creator of the magnificent and morose Inspector Morse. *This city overwhelms me,* he thought, feeling a pang of sorrow and regret. He would never be a young student at Oxford. Another of those paths that might have been open to him in the past had closed, and suddenly he regretted ignoring them with such reckless abandon. Perhaps it was a matter of age that caused him to look back at the past with remorse.

Out on the street again he tightened the cashmere scarf around his neck. He thought about his good friend, Tamar, whom he affectionately called Professor de Vuitton. She really was a professor, an expert on classical studies at Tel Aviv University, but he called her de Vuitton because of the beautiful bag that formed an inseparable part of her look. *It's a modest little bag,* she'd always say to him, and Michael had laughed — every time.

Tamar had studied at Oxford for five

years, and he thought of her walking through the same streets, reading the age-old books in the Bodleian Library, listening to one of Bach's fugues in the college church. *If I sat down for a few hours at Blackwell's,* she had once told him, referring to the city's huge bookshop, *half the people I knew would pass by.*

Michael decided to view the memory as a sign and took off in the direction of the well-known store. He was sandwiched at the store's entrance between a woman with bags in her hands who was making a concerted effort to leave and two teenage girls dressed in school skirts, their knees blue from the cold, who were trying to get in. He climbed the spiral staircase to the second floor, and there she really was, as if she'd been waiting for him. But she wasn't alone. With her fair hair gleaming and her neck gracefully tilted, she was sitting next to a young Arab man with bleached hair, a large cup of tea clutched between her two hands.

Fortunately for Michael, Ya'ara was focused on the young man sitting next to her and didn't see him. He moved on, taking care not to stop abruptly, trying to mix in among the shoppers. He kept his distance. He didn't want to approach Ya'ara in the presence of the guy she was with. They seemed to be friends, and were engaged, as far as he could tell, in a relaxed conversation, their heads tilted slightly toward each other, her hand touching his for a moment. He decided to leave the large store, find somewhere to settle down and keep an eye on the exit, and try to follow Ya'ara to a spot where he could intercept her on her own. He knew that an effort to keep track of her in such a manner was doomed to almost certain failure. All it would take would be for her to get into a car, or a taxi, or even a bus. In any event, he wouldn't be able to get close to her without exposing himself. And if he kept his distance, chances were he'd lose her. But he didn't have much choice, and couldn't think of a better plan. He had been incredibly lucky to find her so easily, and he, as was his wont, was aware of his good fortune but took it for granted at the same time, too. Perhaps it would keep smiling on him.

He waited for more than an hour for Ya'ara and her friend to leave Blackwell's. They put on their coats and shook hands, parting ways with a slightly odd sense of formality. He turned to the left and she turned in the opposite direction, retrieving a woolen hat from one of her coat pockets and placing it on her head, covering her ears, protecting herself against the damp cold. Ya'ara then set off down the darkening street, and he followed in her wake. She was heading in the direction of the city's central bus station when she suddenly turned sharply and entered a pub that seemed rather remote to him. He walked in a few minutes after her, expecting to see her sitting at the bar or one of the tables. But she wasn't there. He went straight into the women's bathroom. The doors of the two stalls were open. All he found in the men's room was one old man, swaying and groaning over the urinal. He returned to the bar and spotted a narrow staircase, dimly lit, leading to a second floor. Black Gothic lettering on a wooden sign read "Hotel." The stairs were covered in a faded red carpet, stained with black patches. He approached the counter and asked the publican: "Do you rent out rooms?"

"Yes, darling," she replied, "but they're all taken."

"Do you have a guest, a young woman, blond . . . ?"

The publican looked at him suspiciously. She didn't like the question.

"I suggest you go drink somewhere else," she said. A middle-aged man, his arms covered in tattoos, approached from the far end of the bar.

"The gentleman's leaving now," the publican said to him. "It's okay."

Michael left the pub and moved away to a point from which he could still see the entrance, but wasn't exposed to the gaze of the bartender, whose piercing eyes he had felt on his back until he closed the door behind him. He pulled his phone out of his pocket and called Ya'ara's German number. He heard her low voice answer: "Hello."

"Hi, Ya'ara," he said. "It's Michael Turgeman. Don't panic. Everything's okay."

He had the feeling that nothing was okay.

58

"You can't stay in this dump," he said to her. "Drive on to the Old Bank Hotel, please," he instructed the cab driver. "Stay with me. There must be a sofa in the room," he continued, addressing Ya'ara again. "I can sleep on it, and you'll have a normal bed."

"Michael, you can't act as if we've met up here by chance. I need you to explain to me what's going on."

"I think it's you who has a lot of explaining to do, but not right now. We'll get there, settle in, sit down together in the hotel library in front of the burning fire, drink something. I need to warm up. And I'm pleased to see you. I was worried about you and have missed you."

When she sat down next to him in the back of the Oxford taxi, their hands almost touched. Suddenly she squeezed his hand affectionately. "I've missed you, too," she said. "It's been quite a while since I've been with someone normal."

Michael wasn't sure if he should take that as a compliment. "So I'm just some sort of family friend to you then?"

"There's no need to take offense at everything. Just because you're a settled person, with his feet on the ground, who can be trusted, that doesn't make you an uncle, or anything like that."

Michael wanted to tell her that he really didn't want to be either her uncle or even best friend. But he forced himself to hold back. He needed to maintain some degree of authority over her, although he doubted whether there was anyone in the world who could tell her what to do. He shifted slightly to the left, toward the cab door.

"You're moving away from me," she said. "Don't."

She washed her face in the bathroom of the large, plush room. And yes, there was a very big bed in the room, and a sofa, too, which Michael didn't view as particularly inviting. *She looks tired and tense,* he thought, turning to look at Ya'ara's pale, washed face.

"Should we go down?" he asked.

"Yeah, sure," she replied, trying to brush aside the tension in her voice.

A large fire was indeed blazing in the library fireplace, and they settled into two comfortable armchairs in front of it. A silent waiter served them two glasses of cognac. Ya'ara inhaled the sharp alcohol fumes, steeped in rich and intoxicating scents of oak and vanilla and leather.

"There's a reason I'm here, Ya'ara," Michael said. "I didn't come here out of longing for you. There are bigger things on the go than my personal wishes . . ." He felt he was getting a little tongue-tied, and started over. "In all honesty, I wouldn't have found you without the Mossad exercising its capabilities. People there are very concerned, very very concerned, about a few things that have happened, and I'm here to ask you — straight up, no games — if you've had any part in them."

"What are you talking about?"

"Two targeted killings were carried out in Europe in recent days, and both have left the country up to its neck in shit," Michael said. "A Muslim preacher who spewed hatred to his followers was assassinated right here, in England, but a young girl was killed in the incident, too. Moreover, this preacher was also a British security service source. That you didn't know, did you? The individual who killed him didn't just run wild in the heart of one of the capital's neighborhoods, but also severely compromised the Brits' war on Islamic terrorism."

He paused for a moment, trying to figure out what impression his words were making on Ya'ara. When he was informed that to top all the trouble, the preacher was also an MI5 asset, he didn't want to believe it. And it was clear to him that whoever had killed the preacher couldn't have known they were shooting at a rare and particularly valuable intelligence source. With that in mind, however, the entire operation, with the dead child, went from being a sad mishap to being a terrible farce. The expression on Ya'ara's face remained unchanged, her eyes inquisitive, waiting to hear the rest. "The British are convinced that we assassinated Anjam Badawi. That we violated all our commitments to them, and that we're the ones who turned London into the Wild West. And in the process, we killed an innocent child and took out one of their assets."

"You know," Ya'ara said, "if he was indeed a source, he may have been exposed and killed by a Muslim terror activist who wanted to avenge his betrayal."

"If and if and if. That's just a guessing game. It was a sniper kill from very far away.

It was the work of a professional, experienced assassin."

"And Al Qaeda or Islamic State or whoever else doesn't have experienced snipers?"

"Enough, Ya'ara, be serious. The incident here is connected to the assassination of Osama Hamdan. The two killings are related; none of us believe in coincidences. And Hamdan's assassination was an act of revenge. Someone really wanted him dead, and wasn't going to make do with seeing him sentenced to life in prison by a Belgian court. Someone was very angry about the murder of Yael Ziv. Making it highly likely that the assassination was the work of an Israeli squad. And the close proximity indicates that the same team killed Badawi, too. The Mossad wasn't behind this madness, and I want to be sure that it wasn't you."

Ya'ara looked unfazed. He felt she was absorbing and digesting the things he was saying to her with interest, like an intellectual, aloof and at ease. "And because the Mossad tells you that they didn't do it, you come running straight to me?" she said. "Do you have any grounds for doing so? Is there something linking me, directly or indirectly, to these assassinations? Does it seem reasonable to you to come all this way based on . . . I don't even know what. Are you here as a result of guesswork or male intuition?"

For a moment, the suspicion cast on Ya'ara appeared to Michael to be unfounded. What actually tied her to the killings? The ferocity and daring with which they were carried out? Because she was overseas when they occurred? It could have been mere coincidence, after all. Clearly she couldn't have carried out the operations on her own. And running a team costs a lot more money than she had. And what was her motive? She was no longer a part of the system. Why would she assume responsibility and take action? He knew her, wild perhaps sometimes, crossing red lines, but no, she didn't have delusions of grandeur. And in any case, two targeted killings are worthless on their own. Without waging a widespread campaign, there's no chance of winning anyway. And in order to conduct a prolonged campaign, you need people and infrastructure and money. In an instant, his entire trip appeared misguided and unnecessary.

"You've been lost in thought," she said with a smile. "Tell me," she asked, "who sent you to find me? The Mossad? Or Aharon Levin, in one of his bouts of paranoia?"

"The director of the Mossad approached Aharon, and he suggested that I find you. He thought you might listen to me. He wasn't surprised to learn you were out of the country. And he believes you're tied to the killings. And I don't have to tell you that his gut feelings are usually accurate. You know that he rarely misses the target."

"Stop admiring that old man. He got things wrong just as much as he got things right. And I'm not convinced the years have been good to him. He used to be determined and ruthless. But he didn't dare to go all the way in the Cobra affair, as he should have, as was called for. There truly was no other way. And he didn't have the balls to finish the job. So I suggest you stop looking up to him. You're not a kid anymore, Michael. You're a man in his fifties. It's time to stand on your own two feet. Go home and report to him that you found me, and that I'm fine, and that I've moved on. Your world no longer interests me."

Despite the calm, collected manner in which she spoke, her measured tone, the relaxed expression on her face, Michael doubted her last statement. He knew her. He didn't believe that she was fine, just as he didn't believe that she had moved on. Despite the composure she was showing, she appeared caught up in something and was troubled. He noticed the shadow that passed fleetingly through her eyes. He could see something in her now that reminded him of a defiant teenage girl, compensating for her anxieties and insecurities with a display of a mixture of coldness and audacity. And that's exactly what made him want to protect her. To shield her from herself. He had the sense that she had gone too far.

"Do you want to go up to the room?" he asked.

"Yes. And I'd like to ask you to do something for me."

"What?"

"I want you to sleep in the bed with me. To hold me. We won't do anything. I'm exhausted anyway. But I want you to be right up close to me. Is it okay for me to ask?"

He hesitated for a moment. "Sure, let's go," he said.

59

When he woke the following morning, Ya'ara was still fast asleep. Her arm was draped across his chest, and he gently moved it aside. Her soft hair lay over her face. *She looks like a little girl,* he thought, almost drowning in the T-shirt and sweat-pants he had given her. When he returned from the shower, she opened one eye and smiled at him sweetly. "I'm going to sleep a little longer, okay?" she said.

"I'll ask them to send breakfast up to the room."

"Just like in my hotel," Ya'ara said after she was up, her mouth full with a bite of croissant, strawberry jam smeared across her upper lip.

"How did you manage to end up in a dump like that?" Michael asked, pouring orange juice into her glass.

"It was the first place I saw."

"Doesn't suit you."

"You know I get by anywhere. But that one was probably over the top. What a shithole." She noticed his gaze, and cleaned the jam off her lips with her tongue.

"Who's the Arab guy you were with at Blackwell's?" Michael asked. She smiled to herself. Yes, Sayid could certainly appear to be an Arab student, thin, a little tormented, a dreamy and intelligent look in his eyes. "Ah, he's my sister's son." Michael knew she wasn't answering him seriously. It didn't fit, not in terms of the young man's age, and not in terms of his appearance.

What Michael didn't know was that Ya'ara's sister had disappeared at the age of sixteen, and was never found. He knew that every individual carries a heavy burden on his or her shoulders, but despite the fact that he had known Ya'ara for so many years, he was unaware of that crucial event, which remained a bleeding wound in her soul. And had he found out then what he hadn't known for all that time, his heart would have agonized over his blindness. He had read through Ya'ara's personal dossier at some point in the distant past, but the story of the disappearance of her sister was tucked away in the classified section of her file. Their working relationship, accompanied by mutual affection, didn't bring down the walls Ya'ara had erected around herself. Ya'ara's inner smile turned now into a stinging grimace. She hadn't said the word "sister" since telling her cadets the story of Tatiana's disappearance, at their first meeting in Western Galilee. And suddenly, unintentionally, for no other reason but to lightheartedly evade Michael's questions, the word "sister" had come out of her mouth. She hated herself for it.

Michael decided not to press her. He couldn't decide whether to believe her claim to have no ties to the two assassinations, but she hadn't offered any explanation for her presence in Oxford. "You have beautiful feet," he said to her, his eyes on her bare toes.

"They're more frozen than beautiful, feel," she said, lifting her left leg and resting her foot on his knee. He clutched her foot in both hands. She dipped the croissant into her coffee and popped the pastry into her mouth. Take it easy, Michael, he said to himself. And felt like a fool.

"I want to sleep a little more," Ya'ara said. "And then I need to move on. Would you like to join me?"

"Where are you going?"

"To Liverpool. I'd like you to come. Can you? I'm asking nicely."

He nodded. He needed more time with her, it made no difference where they spent it. She released her foot from his grasp and went back to bed. Curled up under the thick blanket, with her eyes closed, she reminded him again of a young girl. "Wake me at eleven-thirty, okay?" she asked, her knees tucked up to her tummy, her figure almost hidden in the large bed. "Watch over me, okay?" she said, her words coming in a whisper this time.

60

The intercity train raced northward at a speed of two hundred kilometers an hour. Ya'ara was very quiet and Michael sat next to her, in silence, too, sipping the tepid coffee he had purchased from the refreshments cart pushed by a young girl who, despite her tender years, appeared drained, tired of life. Ya'ara was glad he had joined her; she didn't want to be alone and preferred knowing where he was rather than having him follow her.

She had plans to meet up in Liverpool with Ann and Helena, and she still hadn't figured out what she was going to tell Michael. But she knew she'd manage. Michael wasn't a real threat. Yes, she had been taken aback when he told her that Anjam Badawi was an MI5 asset, but it didn't cause her to doubt herself. She had no way of knowing about Badawi when they were formulating their plan to kill him. She asked herself if she would have changed her decision had she known he was a British source, and didn't know what to say. She acknowledged the damage done inadvertently to British intelligence as a result of his assassination, and admitted that had she known in advance, she probably would have let him slip and moved on to the next piece of filth on the list. But what happened wasn't her idea. She was given a free hand in all matters relating to the planning and execution of the operations, but the list was passed on to her by the prime minister, in the convoluted manner they had arranged ahead of time.

I wonder, she thought, *how the prime minister selects the targets he's given me. He must receive material from Military Intelligence and the Mossad, by way of his military secretary.* Osama Hamdan wasn't on the list of names she had received. He was at the top of her private list. A savage beast who had killed her mother's good friend without a second thought, without a moment's hesitation. She had decided that as the commander of a secret team of cadets, she deserved that bonus.

The relationship between her mother and Yael had been one of the basic facts of life to Ya'ara. The two women came from very different worlds — her mother was a new immigrant from Siberia who lived in the suburbs of Haifa, and Yael Ziv was a third-generation Israeli, from a plush home on the summit of Mount Carmel. Their mutual love for literature brought them together. Ya'ara didn't know how they had met, and when she did ask, her mother evaded the question. But the initial contact was made, and Yael, who used to host a literary club gathering at her home, invited Ya'ara's mother to join them, to speak about the Russian books she loved so much, to read extracts from them, if only for them to hear the melodic beauty of the Russian language rolling off her tongue, and to read and get to know the books of the Israeli authors whom the club members would discuss in all earnestness, with excitement but also fiery criticism.

Her mother used to invite her to tag along, and Ya'ara did, but only occasionally, both drawn to and repelled by the well-to-do and educated world she was exposed to, a world that projected self-confidence and quiet arrogance. The relationship between the two women blossomed into a profound and quiet friendship. They shared the kind of closeness that exists between sisters. And when her mother fell ill, Yael more than anyone else was there for her, holding her hand after a long day of treatments, bringing over a pot of meat soup on Saturday mornings, faithfully on the other end of the line for a long and quiet phone call. But Hamdan's assassination wasn't only personal revenge.

As Ya'ara understood things, his killing conformed with the prime minister's perception that rampant Islamic terror could only be defeated by means of a hard-fought and bloody war, from close quarters, with continuing and relentless violence, without balking, in order to surprise, to catch the enemy unawares, to rattle his confidence and sense of security, and to sow fear in his heart. And carrying out a hit on a murderer inside a prisoner-transport vehicle was exactly the kind of move a strategy like that called for.

That was why she wasn't moved by Michael's shock. There'll be many more such killings to come, she promised him silently. And the organization that sent you should be aware of that, too. She knew she couldn't triumph alone. Combating such madness required a global campaign. A campaign in which the Mossad would also have a role to play. And even that wouldn't be enough. Military forces would have to emerge victorious in the battles that take place on the ground, in the vast deserts now controlled by the fighters of the Islamic caliphate. But she and her people could be the catalyst for the campaign, the wild and dangerous variable that shows the way, like a tornado that wreaks havoc along its path.

She thought about the young girl who had been killed in the Badawi operation. She regretted her death but refused to wallow in sadness. She wasn't Aslan. Sometimes even little girls have to die for causes greater than themselves. After all, it was impossible to bring her back to life, and as far as she was concerned, forgoing Badawi's assassination would have been too high a price to pay for the purpose of saving her.

Where was her God when it was time to protect the life of a young girl? she thought defiantly. She felt like a drawn sword in a continuing campaign. She herself was the spark. And her serene outward appearance served her, as always, as a shield. Who would imagine that the light-eyed, fair-haired woman with the map of Europe spread out in front of her was planning her next operations? No, no one knew what she had in mind. Certainly not Michael, whose suspicions had already drifted off to sleep, with the sight of a bare foot leaving him unable to think straight. She rested her head on Michael's shoulder and allowed her eyes to close. The train continued northward, the landscape flashing by on both sides in a blur.

61

Liverpool, February 2015

They both woke at the same time, their faces almost touching, the soft thick blanket covering them to their necks, the dreams of the night yet to fade completely from their memories, their soft hair spread across the pillows. Ann smiled and Helena gently caressed her face. Ann's fingertips weren't slow to respond and trailed along the line of Helena's thigh, pausing at the delicate join between her upper leg and calf.

"Good morning," Ann whispered.

"Good morning." Helena stretched, her hands now above her head. "It really is a good morning," she added, rolling over and bringing her face up close to Ann's, a huge smile on her lips.

"That was my first time with another woman," Ann said. "Well, if we forget about that one clumsy night at boarding school. In any event, that doesn't really count."

"I'm sure my high school was very different," Helena said.

"We're not in high school now," Ann responded. "I'm married and you have a boyfriend."

"Yes, but I heard once that different rules apply when you're overseas," Helena remarked.

"As two people who came from abroad . . ." Ann started to say, but then fell silent.

Helena glanced at her sideways, wondering what Ann was thinking through their light chatter. She was painfully aware of her naked body. Ann had touched a place buried deep in her soul, a place made up of nothing but fragile truths.

"Okay, you may be right," Ann concluded, brushing the blanket off herself. "Let's not talk about it. Not yet, okay?" she said, looking at Helena imploringly now.

"Sure. Shhhhhhhh. No talking." The silenced words were soon replaced by Helena's arms reaching out and drawing Ann toward her.

In the late afternoon, at the café at the Tate Liverpool, the northern branch of the renowned London art museum, three women sat and stared at one another in silence. To an onlooker from the side, they might have appeared to be old friends. A keen-eyed observer would have been able to recognize the tension between them.

When Ya'ara told Michael she had to meet someone, he didn't ask questions. He was still carrying a hint of Ya'ara's scent, as if their shared slumber was imprinted on his person. He let her go, knowing that if he were to follow her himself, she'd have no trouble spotting him. Ya'ara left the hotel and headed to her meeting with Helena and Ann only after making sure she was alone.

For her part, she was pleased to see them. She viewed Ann and Helena as leading cadets on her team — quick, sharp, cosmopolitan. She was surprised by the cold reception she encountered from them. Offended, actually. She couldn't work out where the tension in the air was coming from, but quickly gathered herself. It doesn't suit you, she scolded herself, you're their commander and they're just cadets. Don't be so sensitive.

"Even though it wasn't a clean operation, and yes, despite the young girl who was killed," she said to them, "your mission achieved its objective. All in all, you did great work." She tried to read their faces.

Helena's face was blank. Ann's lower lip was trembling slightly. "How can you say that?" Helena asked, seemingly speaking for both of them. "An outcome like that means we didn't plan things well enough. That you didn't plan things well enough. We adopted a course of action that ended in disaster. We've just begun our training, and we're relying on you. And look what happened!"

"What happened," Ya'ara said quietly, voicing each syllable in a manner that clearly testified to her pent-up anger, "is that a hate-mongering preacher was liquidated. The world is a better place without him. Your planning of the operation was exemplary. What happened was unavoidable. Tragedies occur sometimes, but you have to move on from them. There's no such thing as a sterile war."

"Those are empty words," Helena responded. "How many more tragedies are we going to encounter? Is that what awaits us?"

Ann lightly touched Helena's hand, trying to quiet her.

"I'm not sure I'm suited to this business," Helena continued, ignoring Ann's touch. "I'm not sure it suits us."

"Do you feel the same?" Ya'ara asked, focusing her gaze on Ann. She realized a new bond had formed between the two cadets, and she wasn't convinced of its benefit to the cause.

Ann shifted uncomfortably in her chair. "I don't know. It's normal for us to feel a little down, right? I need some time to take it all in. To lie low. To allow these two weeks to pass quietly."

Ya'ara wondered if Ann was being evasive. From an operational perspective, the decision to keep the team in England was the right one, but from the moment she made the call, she feared it could exact a heavy price. Ann and Helena were very green cadets, not experienced fighters. Sayid was in a similar position, despite appearing to be holding up pretty well. He was very pleased to see her when they met up, and seemed at ease and well-balanced. When she asked him about the death of the young girl, he gazed up into space but his words confirmed he was okay. These two weeks, cut off completely from the other cadets, could undoubtedly undermine the motivation of the two young women, their sense of duty, their willingness to cope with year after year of the never-ending seesaw between the elation that comes with the operations and the disheartenment that follows in its wake. And still, insofar as Helena was concerned at least, there was clearly something more. She showed Ya'ara a photograph on her phone of the young Yasmin wrapped in the arms of her father.

"See that?" she said. "That's a living girl. That's what she looked like when she was alive." Ya'ara told her to turn off the phone and please calm down.

She didn't know what else to say. After all, they weren't children. They were dealing in matters of life and death; there was no room for unnecessary drama.

"Look," she eventually said, her gaze shifting back and forth between Ann's lowered eyes and Helena's defiant expression, "this thing we've got ourselves into really is a serious and taxing affair. There's a price to pay when you're on the front line. It's the real thing. And coping with it isn't always easy. We'll have a lot more time to talk about what happened, but our mission now, your mission now, is to deal with the coming days. To get through them peacefully and quietly, without making a fuss or falling apart.

"We don't have to — can't — solve every problem or answer every question right now. And I can't tell you what to think or how to think. That's your responsibility, to make the best of everything you've been through.

Because ahead of us lies a long road that only very few can follow. I've already told you, it's a great privilege to be selected, but no one can force you to follow that road. And personally, I've no interest in anyone who doesn't want to follow that road. All I can say is that there'll be more ups and downs, more victories and, yes, more crashes. And just as I am, you, too, will be accompanied throughout by that same sense of mission and duty that gives me meaning and allows me to feel, despite all the pain, that my life has a reason." Ya'ara smiled. "There you have it, just the kind of grandiose statements I didn't want to make. They must sound meaningless to you."

Ann looked at her with her big eyes, attentive and serious. She felt she had gotten to her. "We'll be okay, Ya'ara," Helena said. "We'll meet up in Berlin as arranged. We can make all our decisions then."

It was as if a door had been slammed shut in her face. Her cadets were looking at her, forming a united front. Something had happened between them, and Ya'ara knew she had to think out her next move carefully after they had been the ones to decide to end the conversation.

Evening had fallen, and dismal yellow lights were casting a weak glow over the street visible from the café's windows. She thought of Aslan walking along the length of Hadrian's Wall, pitching his tent somewhere sheltered from the wind, snuggling into his sleeping bag, waiting for the long night to pass. She tried to think of what Aslan would say to them and remembered his well-known penchant for silence. She thought about Michael. She hadn't planned on being a parental figure for her two cadets. It was not what they needed and wasn't something she could offer.

She stood up and left, nodding farewell to the two women. Ann responded with a faint smile; Helena looked at her blankly.

Standing there in a foreign city in the cold evening air, after closing the door behind her, Ya'ara suddenly felt incredibly lonely.

62

"I'm leaving tomorrow," Ya'ara said to Michael. They were sitting opposite each other in Ya'ara's hotel room. Even before she spoke, Michael had noticed her suitcase in a prominent place on the floor. Ya'ara had already packed the few clothes she had.

"I need to get back to Germany."

Michael looked at her pale, drawn face.

"I don't think you should go," he said. "You're traveling on empty. You need to rest."

"You're not my father, Michael."

"I don't know where you went this afternoon, but you were wiped out when you got back here. Let's stay in the hotel for a few more days. We can sleep late, we'll find nice places for lunch, we'll go to shows in the evening. This place is full of music spots; maybe we'll discover the new John Lennon."

She smiled at him wearily and a wave of affection washed over Michael.

"Listen," he said, "whatever's waiting for you in Germany can wait a little longer, can't it? And if you need to do something to postpone things, perhaps I can help . . . Ya'ara, your eyes are telling me that you need to stop for a while. Do you know who you remind me of?"

She looked up and gazed at him questioningly.

"You remind me of myself. This itinerary of yours, from Oxford, to Liverpool, to Germany. That's what I used to do when I was in service."

Ya'ara tensed up, wondering just how much Michael knew about what she was doing. She allowed him to continue nevertheless.

"And I remember something else." Michael knew she was listening to him, but also noticed the hint of an arrogant smile, the shadow of the condescending look she was giving him.

"I remember, too, that each and every one of them needed something from me. And everyone I met with took whatever they needed. A piece of my experience, a piece of my courage. A piece of my optimism. And then there'd come a moment when I'd feel drained. That I had nothing more to give. And the worst part of it was the sense I got that they could see it, too. That their faith in me and regard for me were faltering. And then I had to take a time-out. Had to take a step back. Had to stop giving of myself. Even for a limited time only. But I needed that space to myself. Because in those moments, I no longer had anything to give."

He knew Ya'ara thought that she wasn't that type of person. That her reserves would never run dry. That was the source of her strength, but a source of grave danger, too. It was plain to see that something had sapped her of her strength and left her vulnerable. As if her core temperature had dropped drastically and she wasn't aware of it, despite the intense distress signals her body was trying to convey to her.

"As I see things," he continued, despite getting no response from her, "the right thing to do now would be to cover you with a thick blanket, turn out the light, and let you sleep. Tell me when you were planning to fly out tomorrow and I'll cancel your ticket for you. If you need to let anyone know, I can do that for you, too. Don't worry."

Ya'ara reached out to him, touching his fingertips. "Maybe you're right. Even though you and I are very different people. But I really don't have to leave tomorrow."

She gave him the details of the flight she had booked to Cologne. "I'd appreciate it if you could let them know about the cancellation," she said.

"Can you sleep with me tonight again?" she asked quietly. "Like at the hotel in Oxford?" He wondered how many nights he could sleep in the same bed with her without feeling humiliated. But he knew she needed him, and knew, too, that he was making progress, even if he wasn't aware of where it would lead. He knew that Ya'ara was struggling with strong forces, and thought he was beginning to understand.

"Yes," he said to her. "I'll be with you. Don't worry."

63

They walked toward Strawberry Field. Once a wide-open stretch of land. Closed in today by ugly redbrick housing estates. But some green space remained, surrounded by a rickety fence with a layer of peeling paint. Just the gate, made of intricate ironwork, was painted a bright red. These were strawberry fields forever. It was a surprisingly warm day, the kind of day that leads people to remark gleefully to one another about the good weather. Ya'ara walked along with her head bowed, her fair hair covering her face, her hand almost touching Michael's.

"Look," she said to him, raising her head, her eyes squinting in the sun. "Just us and the Japanese tourists."

The visitors from Japan were taking photographs alongside the sign displaying the name of the location, Strawberry Field, grinning at the camera lens each time someone from the group snapped his friends.

"Should we get our photo taken, too?" Michael asked.

"You know I don't like to be photographed."

"I thought you had stopped working a long time ago."

"You're right. Let's ask them to take a picture of us with your iPhone. How come after knowing each other for so long we don't have a single photograph of us together? We're a little screwed up, right?"

"No, it's just habit. Are you sure you don't want a selfie?"

"There's a limit to everything, Michael."

A smiling Japanese girl was happy to photograph them. She waved them closer to each other. And then motioned with her arm for Michael to place his own around Ya'ara's shoulders. And gestured a little more to tell Ya'ara to tilt her head toward him.

"A real Antonioni she is," Michael muttered, grumpily, tugging Ya'ara closer to him at the same time. Ya'ara played along with an air of softness.

"Good that she's an Antonioni and not a Tarantino. Otherwise there'd be a massacre here by now."

"We'd look like figures in a Francis Bacon painting."

"I'm not sure he painted women at all," Ya'ara remarked, and Michael told her in response about the first time he saw a Francis Bacon self-portrait and felt as if someone had managed to capture the essence of humanity.

"Maybe there are some of his works on display here, at Tate Liverpool. It's worth checking out," Michael suggested.

Ya'ara wondered if he was trying to tell her something. Just yesterday she had met at the Tate with Ann and Helena. But his face revealed nothing.

"And while we're on the subject," he added casually, "maybe we should take a trip to Leeds tomorrow? It's where Henry Moore studied, and some of his pieces are on display at the municipal gallery. Up for it?"

"Gladly. Why not? I'd forgotten that you're such an art lover. And maybe we'll find a good place to eat there, too. Let's pretend we're tourists."

Michael looked at her and wondered when she wasn't pretending, when she was really telling him the whole truth. But Ya'ara was standing there next to him, tall and erect, beautiful and happy, as if there wasn't a single worry in the world weighing her down.

He decided he'd make do with that for now.

64

Tel Aviv, Liverpool, February 2015

Michael had met up with Ronit late in the evening before his flight to London. Ronit had once been a combatant in the same squad in which Ya'ara had served. So they were friends, but he didn't know if they were still in touch. As talented and daring as she was, Ronit was also viewed as a strange bird. Maybe that's what had drawn Ya'ara to her, he thought. She had left the squad and the Mossad, and Michael had heard that she was doing something obscure in the hi-tech field. It took her a few moments to recognize his voice when he called, but she agreed to meet him right away. "But you'll have to take a walk with me and Nora," she said.

"Nora? Your daughter?"

"My dog, dummy." A slight faux pas only, but it flickered in Michael's head like a warning signal.

They met across the road from Ronit's house on Be'eri Street. It was dark and wet, and Michael closed his coat. Nora was bounding around them energetically, and Ronit let her off the leash, remarking that it was a quiet street and not a problem. Nora circled around them excitedly and sped off down the empty street, savoring the freedom and space that had opened up to her.

"Is she a purebred dog, or what?"

"No, Michael, she's not purebred. She's a mixture of so many kinds that I have no idea what she is. Is this what you called me for after so many years? To talk about my dog?"

"I wanted to ask you about Ya'ara Stein. Are you still in touch?"

"Unfortunately not. I left the squad and two years later Ya'ara went on unpaid leave. Went off to study film. We slowly lost touch. It just happens sometimes. Although I think about her a lot." She paused for a moment. "She's okay, right?"

"I have no reason to think otherwise. But there's something important that I need to clarify. Do you know if she had any connection to the late Yael Ziv?"

"I'm not sure I know who you're talking about, although the name sounds familiar . . ."

"Yael Ziv was murdered in a terror attack

in the central synagogue in Brussels."

"Ah, right. Of course I've heard about her." They had reached the public park, with the dog right behind them. Tall trees swayed like black shadows against the cloudy sky. "I don't recall any ties between her and Ya'ara." She hesitated for a moment, quietly trying to sift through her memory. "No," she said. "Is it important? Why do you ask?"

"I'm looking into something at the request of Aharon Levin. It would be easiest to try to inquire via the Mossad, but the truth is I don't want to involve them. Doing so could put Ya'ara in harm's way, and I want to protect her, if possible."

"Are you still with the Mossad?"

"No, no. I've been out for two years already. I opened a law office. But I get asked to do various things sometimes. I never say no."

"Maybe it's time you started. I have to ask: Did anything ever happen between you in the end?"

"Between who?"

"Who are we talking about? Between you and Ya'ara."

"No. Never."

"You worked together on several operations," she said. "And she spoke about you in a manner that got me thinking, and getting information out of her . . . Oh, well, never mind."

"I value her greatly. She's an exceptional fighter and an interesting woman. But nothing happened between us."

"You have paternal feelings toward her, right? A feeling of wanting to shield her."

"Yes," he said, impressed by her sharp senses. "Most of all, I don't want anything to happen to her."

"She has a tendency to reach into the flames and then wonder how she got burned," Ronit said. "Fortunately, that doesn't happen to her much. She's too smart. But sometimes she's more hardheaded than smart."

Michael smiled softly, sympathetically. He felt that she needed to talk, that his role in their conversation was that of a listener to things she wanted to get off her chest.

"I miss her," Ronit said. "I really do. More than I'd like to admit, in fact. I miss her even though I doubt the feeling's mutual. I'll try to find out for you if she had any connection to that woman. Hold on. Hold on. Do you think . . . ?"

Michael realized that Ronit had connected the dots and seen the link between his questions and the reports published about the assassination in Belgium.

"I don't know anything for certain and there's no reason to jump to wild conclusions. But now you understand my concern. So a few discreet inquiries on your behalf would be to her benefit. I'm worried about her. Don't go through any official Mossad channels. I'm going away tomorrow morning, but I'll call you in a day or two, okay?"

Ya'ara was still sleeping when he called her from the small garden across the road from the hotel.

"Hi," Ronit said, careful not to use his name, still maintaining the habits acquired during the years she spent as a field operative. You can never know what name the person on the other side of the line is using. "I spoke to her father. He remembered me and was happy to hear from me after so long. I visited her parents' home with her on several occasions, and was even their guest once at the family's Passover Seder. It turns out it was her mother who knew Yael, actually. They were very good friends, they shared common interests, and Yael was a big help to Ya'ara's mother during the family's initial years in the country. And later, when Ya'ara's mother fell ill, Yael was her angel, so he told me.

"He got very emotional talking about his wife. Naturally, of course. I apologized to him for stirring such charged memories, but he said that speaking about her allowed him to remember her best. He said that the news of Yael's murder had left him broken. He went to the funeral, but there were so many people there and he didn't have the courage to speak to her husband and children. He didn't really know them anyway. The friendship, he said, was strictly between the two women. A private friendship. Does that help you at all?"

"It's a big help. Thanks. Don't discuss this with anyone, okay? Keep it to yourself. There's no need for people to start telling stories to themselves."

"Send her my warmest regards if you see her. And tell her I miss her. And when you get back to Israel, perhaps we can get together for a coffee, you and me. Nora's been asking about you."

Michael sat down on a bench in the garden. He sighed, took a cigar out of his jacket pocket, and lit it, losing himself in his thoughts as he inhaled the thick, fragrant smoke.

65

Paris, February 2015

Batsheva peered out into the street through the café's glass wall, waiting for Claude's figure to emerge from around the corner. The glass was distorting the shapes outside and she felt as if she was in a movie; at that precise moment, she was the viewer watching the scene unfold, but at any minute she could step into the shoes of one of the main characters. She recalled the missions she had been given as a teenager, missions that had led her, ultimately, to this moment, the crisis she had chosen not to share with Ya'ara and the other cadets. Becoming a cadet enabled her to find meaning in her life again. She felt as if she had been reborn. And in the end, she overcame everything, the slight depression, the sense of meaninglessness. She was in Paris, and not simply for the pleasures it offered. She had a reason for being there.

Across the street, through the incessant rain, the fringes of the Luxembourg Gardens looked like a grayish-green stain, wet and blurry. She was hoping desperately that the rain would stop.

When he walked through the door, Batsheva couldn't help thinking that he looked like a street mongrel, almost pitiful, his hair wet and shaggy. His face, with its look of misery and suffering, lit up when he saw her. She stood up and embraced him gingerly, to avoid getting wet. He was a head shorter than her, his dripping-wet hair plastered to his scalp, his shirt hanging out of his trousers, his umbrella inside-out and broken.

"Once again you chose one of the most expensive cafés in the city," he said. "The price here of a café au lait is outrageous. You could have had something to drink at my place for free."

But Batsheva had chosen this time not to have to forge a path among the piles of folders and mountains of paperwork that cluttered the musty system of rooms composing his office, one of the oldest insurance agencies in Paris. The last time she was there she was served a turbid lukewarm coffee, and along with the coffee, she was also subjected to the overtly hostile looks of

Madeleine, Claude's personal assistant, who was clearly in love with him. A normal café was a better option, she thought.

In spite of his clumsy, shabby appearance, and notwithstanding the dreariness of his profession, Claude was one of the most learned and brilliant people she knew. He spoke fourteen languages and apologized for being able to read and write in only ten of them. He had a phenomenal memory and oozed personal charm, the moment you gave him a second chance. He once had plans to pursue an academic career in the United States; he believed he could become a world-renowned historian, a historian of ideas. But when his father fell ill, he was summoned back to Paris to provide for the family. You should never rely on first impressions, he had once told her. Ya'ara had said the same. But Batsheva recalled an American saying she had heard many years earlier, that you never get a second chance to make a first impression. Thus, despite the gross injustice of having to do so, you should invest a great deal in the initial impression you make. That's what she had said to Ya'ara, and Ya'ara, who always left a dazzling first impression, said, You're right, Batsheva, even if I've never put it that way myself.

She had met Claude for the first time in the late 1980s, at a wedding in Jerusalem. He had come especially from France; she was the bride's cousin. His dry humor appealed to her from the very outset, and the closeness that developed between them continued through the years, even when the marriage they celebrated back then fell apart in the form of an unpleasant divorce. He taught her ancient proverbs in French, and she offered him snippets from her life, anecdotes, incidents in part, enough for him to want more, and not enough to cause him to ask for something he couldn't get. In any event, he became her permanent way station in Paris. Thanks to his unrelenting inquisitiveness and unlimited connections, he often helped her to locate artworks and family members and heirs pertinent to her legal affairs. "You're making me walk the streets like a hooker," he protested affectionately. "I'm a reputable insurance agent and you're turning me into a miserable private detective."

"You love it," she responded. "And besides, every job dignifies the individual who performs it. And this detective work contributes much more to your wife's alimony than does your insurance business, which has seen better days, as far as I understand."

She loved his company, his frenetic energy, his wide, comprehensive knowledge. He enjoyed her wit, her sharp tongue, her passion for a juicy piece of gossip. He used to look at her with a sense of wonderment that hadn't faded with the years, surveying her tall stature, allowing his eyes to feed on her beautiful face and looking at her expensive jewelry, and then he'd whisper to himself: Is that really me? Claude?

"Listen, Claude," she said to him after two more cups of tea were slammed down onto the table in front of them, in the typical style of Paris's grumpy waiters. "I'm expanding my business dealings a little, and I'm going to need your help with other matters in the future. I still don't know when I'll be calling on you, but I want your help, discreetly of course, with setting up an infrastructure that I can use here if necessary. We'll need a small apartment, a bank account in the name of a company you'll open, a technical translations company, let's say, or something like that, and I also need you to get me two 9mm pistols, and ammunition, of course."

"Of course, ammunition, too, of course," he mumbled, making no effort to hide his astonishment. "When you say you're expanding your business, does that mean you're joining the ranks of organized crime?

Because it suits you really well, and I want to congratulate you on your initiative and wish you luck with your new endeavors." Batsheva's request had indeed caught him by surprise, and he knew for certain: She'll always surprise me.

"Don't be cynical, Claude, it doesn't really suit you. You know I'm not a gangster. I'm working here for the State of Israel, for Zion. There are some things that need to be done. For our homeland. You can see for yourself what is happening here in Paris, what's happening in France, throughout Europe. There's a real war starting here, and no one's going to leave the Jews out of it. They've already dragged us in, after all. Hypercacher isn't far from where you live, right?" Hypercacher was a Jewish supermarket that was attacked by Muslim terrorists. "And we need to prepare for a long, harsh war, which will be conducted in secret, for the most part. As you must realize, I've become a part of it and you'll be a part of it, too. I need a friend, and I need someone I can count on. And if need be, you'll show everyone who is the best racing driver among the chubby Jews, or who is the most successful insurance agent among the racing drivers. Whichever you prefer."

Claude didn't conceal his pride. Among

his other occupations and pastimes, he was also an amateur race car driver, secretly proud of his driving skills as well as his intricate knowledge of the streets of Paris. He claimed, in fact, to know his way very well around the streets of several cities in the world, and would always say that if his insurance business were to crumble completely, he could always work as a taxi driver in ten different capitals around the globe. Batsheva was well aware of his weakness for fast cars, and had even accompanied him once to an amateur competition somewhere near Antwerp, Belgium, where he finished a very respectable fourth.

"Tell me now," he asked, lowering his voice, "where am I going to get the pistols for you?"

"Don't whisper, it'll make people think we've got something to hide," she instructed. "Didn't you tell me about that criminal, the one who turned religious? What's his name? Lucien something."

Claude nodded.

"So tell him you need two unregistered guns for a group of young individuals who've decided to band together to protect the community. Give him the sense that he's doing something important for his brothers. Believe me, that's the way to get the best goods on the market. I don't know when we'll need them, but it wouldn't be a good idea to start looking only when the need is urgent. It's always best to be prepared in advance."

"Without doubt," Claude said. He imagined the meeting with Lucien, the man's surprise, and the understanding smile spreading slowly across his face.

Batsheva looked at Claude sitting there in front of her, his eyes appearing to be shining all of a sudden like those of a child. She knew his brain was already intensively and excitedly at work on the secret task she had given him, and she thought that with soldiers like him, smart and loving and faithful, not only could one go to war, but victory was an option, too.

66

Liverpool, Leeds, February 2015

She was holding the big cup of coffee in both her hands, a huge pile of scrambled eggs and bacon resting on her plate.

"Are you really going to eat all of that?" he asked with genuine astonishment.

"Yes, of course," Ya'ara said with childlike glee as she grabbed her fork. "I'm starving."

Michael looked at her and couldn't reconcile the two faces of Ya'ara, her playful and childish side and her cold and calculating one. His heart told him they were both real, and yet he could never foresee which would override the other. He recalled their shared experiences. They had had a good day yesterday. A typically gray Leeds made them feel welcome, and he thought Henry Moore's sketches were no less captivating and beautiful than his large sculptures. Ya'ara gave each piece of art a long, thoughtful look, and circled the sculptures, her body seemingly ready to spring into action, like a tigress seeking out her prey's weak spot. There were times when she leaned against the wall, sinking slowly to the floor, her gaze fixed unwaveringly on the sculpture, studying it in earnest, a line of concentration across her brow, her beautiful lips slightly accentuated, her eyes focused.

That morning, at breakfast, Michael noticed Ya'ara repeatedly checking her emails on her phone. "Are you expecting something important?" he asked. "No, no," she replied, "simply having trouble getting hold of someone." She had lost contact over the past few days with the prime minister's confidant, the esteemed lawyer who took care of relaying the prime minister's instructions to her and also arranged the transfer of funds that allowed her and her cadets to operate. She knew that breaks in communication were always a possibility. They had happened before. She was dealing with a very busy man, who would disappear himself from time to time, slipping under the radar to carry out secret missions for his master. But she wondered now if the silence was related to the suspicions and hostility of the British, who were outraged by the targeted killing carried out in their capital, the liquidation of a highly valuable intelligence source. Ya'ara recalled what the prime minister had said to her, that a day would come when he'd be forced to deny any ties with her. Had that day come already, and was the break in communication a sign of that denial? Is this what you feel when they disconnect that thin cable that keeps you tied to the mother ship? "Fuck them all," she said in a flash of rage, imagining she was addressing the members of her team, who weren't there with her, who didn't even know that the person running things was none other than the prime minister himself. "You know what," she said defiantly, picturing them sitting in front of her, the six cadets, "it actually suits me to drift freely like this, without a home. And I'm sure it'll suit you, too."

Later that same day, while they were strolling along the piers at Liverpool's old port, wrapped up snugly in their warm coats, still pretending to be on holiday, Michael turned to Ya'ara and asked, "Are you familiar with Yosef Raphael?"

"I think so," she responded. "He was a sculptor, right? I think I saw one of his pieces in Tefen, made from rusted sheets of iron. Weighing a good few tons I'm sure, but floating there like it was weightless. What about him?"

"Raphael passed away in the early 1980s. He truly was a wonderful sculptor, a trail-blazer. He was identified initially with the Canaanite sculptors, although I don't know if he was an actual member of the Canaanite Movement. He then moved on to abstract sculpting, primarily in iron. Think of Yechiel Shemi, of Yaacov Dorchin. He's up there with them."

Ya'ara raised an eyebrow in admiration that was only partially faked. Michael continued.

"You know I have a fondness for historical affairs. Especially our secret history. So even when serving in very senior positions, I would also conduct projects on the side for Kedem, the History Department. That's how I learned that Yosef Raphael used to work for SHAI, the Haganah's espionage and counterintelligence arm, and then for the Mossad. He lived abroad for almost a decade, in England for the most part. Up until 1954, when he returned to Israel. For almost the entire period he spent abroad, in addition to studying art and working as a sculptor, he was also involved in various covert activities. He purchased weapons, handled assets, relayed funds. Whatever they gave him to do or asked of him. He had the perfect cover story, and he was brave and creative and dedicated."

They stopped and sat on a bench overlooking the gray sea, which showed itself between the large warehouses, made of cheerless, dark-red bricks, that had been renovated a few years earlier and had already taken on the appearance again of old, blackening structures, seemingly from another era, in which greatness and misery had served in the mix. Michael went on.

"And now for another hero in the story. Because I'm not boring you with all of this for nothing. Allow me to introduce you to David Herbert Samuel. He was an extraordinary man, or so all the evidence indicates, at least. The grandson of the first British high commissioner in the Land of Israel. He was also a gifted chemist, studied at Oxford, enlisted in the British army during World War II, and went on to complete his studies after his discharge. He returned to Israel ahead of the War of Independence, to fight. After the war, he went back to his scientific work. By the way, he inherited his grandfather's title, and that's how we had a real English lord at the Weizmann Institute. Can you believe it?"

"I believe everything you tell me," Ya'ara said. "You know that." Michael continued.

"When I served as head of the Special

Relations Department, I wanted to conduct research into the activities of SHAI abroad, the same activity that the Mossad kept going as part of the transition that Ben-Gurion led from an era of underground movements to an era of statehood. In any event, one of the files I retrieved from the archives contained records of a conversation in 1953 between someone from the Mossad and David Herbert Samuel. At the time, Samuel claimed to have received a message from the wife of a British chemist who had told him that a scientific paper that could prove critical to the national security of the fledgling State of Israel had been passed on by her husband to a colleague of his, so that he could send it on further, to Israel. Samuel didn't elaborate on his relationship with the woman in question. Anyway, he understood from her that the paper was intended ultimately for him, or his department. But it failed to arrive. Or at least he never saw it. I tried to look into the matter and asked a long-serving official at the Defense Ministry if he recalled our getting a particularly important document from England during that period, but he — and he really doesn't forget a thing — wasn't able to recall anything of the sort. Not that it means anything. For old-timers like him, the very mention of the words SHAI or Irgun is tantamount to divulging state secrets."

"But where does Yosef Raphael fit in with all of this?"

"Adi Peretz, the intelligence officer who worked with us on the Cobra affair, did some private research for me. I asked her to try to find out if that British chemist, by the name of Siegfried Edward Jones, was connected to Israel in any way. Adi soon discovered that Jones, who studied chemistry at Oxford before World War II, had disappeared. He appears in the university's records, of course, and in the 1930s he also published several scientific articles in important journals, but she couldn't find a single reference to his scientific activity after the war, no publications, no membership in scientific societies, nothing. Except for the date of his death in the early 1960s.

"Adi then looked into all the members of his chemistry class at Oxford to see if one of them may have had ties to Israel. She focused initially on the men, because Samuel had spoken about a colleague who had a way to relay the document to Israel. She found nothing. But if the conversation with Samuel was conducted in English, there would have been no grammatical distinction between male and female, and the colleague could just as easily have been a woman. When she reviewed the names of all the students in his year once again, she came across that of Sarah Gold, and Gold could definitely be a Jewish name. A look through the Marriage Registry revealed that Sarah Gold had married Alfred Strong, who, I won't bore you with details, was a former MI5 official and the owner of several weapons manufacturing plants. Sarah Gold, who was now Sarah Strong, did indeed study chemistry, but she was involved in the field of art, primarily the preservation of ancient Christian works. She and her husband had an important art collection, sculptures mostly, that even included works by Henry Moore."

Ya'ara realized that their visit to Leeds yesterday had not been accidental.

"In any event," Michael continued, "Adi located a report published in a local Oxford newspaper about an exhibition under the patronage of Sarah and Alfred Strong of works by a young sculptor from the Land of Israel, one Yosef Raphael. The centerpiece of the exhibition was a spectacular marble sculpture by the name of *Absalom.* The newspaper report doesn't include a photograph of the piece, but the art critic describes it as breathtaking."

"And . . .?" Ya'ara asked.

"That's all. That's the possible tie between the missing chemist, Jones, and Sara Gold, who became Sarah Strong, and Yosef Raphael, who, as I said, used to carry out assignments for the Mossad on a regular basis."

"But they're all dead now."

"No. Just before I left to meet you . . ."

To locate me, to interrogate me, to keep an eye on me, to watch over me — that would be more accurate, Ya'ara thought.

"I asked them to make some inquiries for me."

Everyone keeps working for him, Ya'ara thought.

"And it turns out that Sarah Strong is still alive. Ninety-five years old. Living in a remote village in the Torridon Hills of Scotland."

"And what needs to be done about this exciting discovery? It's something that happened more than sixty years ago, after all. Even if you've managed to connect the dots correctly somehow, it's all ancient history. What are you trying to tell me?"

"I want us to find Mrs. Strong. I hope it's still possible to talk with her. Perhaps she could lead us to the lost document. I think it could still be of value today."

"What value could it have? It's just a foolish fantasy. I have more important and more urgent things to take care of."

"I thought you were on vacation," Michael said, and Ya'ara shrugged her shoulders and said, "Producing movies is work, too. The Mossad isn't the only place where work gets done."

Michael wondered when she would tell him the truth. "Come with me. We'll give it a week, you can get back to your affairs in Berlin afterward. At best, you can do something that would restore the Mossad's faith in you. It wouldn't do you any harm at all, considering the situation you find yourself in now. And at worst, we took a trip to one of the most beautiful regions of Scotland."

Ya'ara ran a quick check on the particulars of his proposal. When she looked up from the screen of her phone, she said, "Do you know what a remote place you're talking about, those Torridon Hills? Look, they're in the middle of the Highlands. The winter there is horrendous. The roads are narrow and are surely blocked by the snow."

"That's not what I see." Michael showed her a picture on his phone of the Torridon Hotel and Inn, a luxury hotel with an extensive bar and a large fireplace. "Since when have you been afraid of traveling on narrow roads and driving in the snow? And when have you ever said no to such a prestigious collection of single malt whiskey?"

"We'll do it this way," Ya'ara said, wondering if she was giving in to Michael too easily. "I'll try to talk to Sarah Strong. We'll see if there's any point in visiting her at all. If she's still lucid and is also willing to welcome visitors she doesn't know in the middle of winter, we'll go. Why not? After all, you're pretty good company, and I wouldn't mind lazing about in front of the fireplace at that hotel."

Sarah Strong answered the phone in the voice of a young woman, albeit a stern one. She was courteous and pleasant, and became genuinely curious when Ya'ara mentioned the name of Yosef Raphael.

"Oh, that extraordinary man," she said. "He was truly a wonderful sculptor. Very unique. I understand he died many years ago. Did you say you wanted to make a film about him? If so, I have something interesting to show you." Ya'ara said she was in the initial stage of collecting material. As usual, she managed to lull her conversation partner into a relaxed sense of security, and Sarah Strong didn't come across as suspicious in any way at all. It might have been her loneliness talking when she invited Ya'ara to visit without delay, or maybe her memories. Ya'ara said she'd be coming with a good friend. They had already been to Leeds, she explained, to the birthplace of Henry Moore, who had befriended Raphael. If it suited her to have them, they'd be happy to come to the Torridon Hills to visit her, in her small village, on the shores of the frozen lake.

"Just dress well, my dear," Sarah Strong said. "It's as cold here as in Birnam Wood in midwinter. I only hope the trees don't come marching against you."

67

Scotland, Torridon Hills, February 2015

Ya'ara was stunned by the beauty of the old woman, Sarah Strong. She was thin and stood erect, her brown eyes clear and deep, her gray hair thick and sleek. She was wearing an old-fashioned dress, in a shade of Prussian blue, and even Ya'ara, who had no particular interest in the subject, could recognize the quality of the fabric and stitching. Pinned close to the edge of the dress's modest bustline was a magnificent brooch inlaid with a large blue stone, a sapphire probably, shining bright in the middle of an entanglement of white gold filaments studded with tiny diamonds.

"Thank you, Annie," Sarah said to the woman who had greeted them at the front door before leading them to a sitting room overlooking the lake and the high mountains beyond, their peaks hidden by low clouds.

"I'm no longer a young woman," she

explained. "Annie's from around here, and she's been living with me in recent years." Annie must be about seventy, Ya'ara guessed, her imagination already weaving a story about how Annie had moved in to take care of Sarah, after she, Annie, had lost her husband. Her three adult children had long since moved to one of Scotland's main cities, Glasgow or Edinburgh, and her position with Lady Sarah Strong provided her with a small income, something to do, and, primarily, an escape from the loneliness that had made each year increasingly difficult, particularly during the bleak winter days that appeared to go on forever.

"I'm Ya'ara Stein," she said, introducing herself and reaching out to offer Sarah her hand, which was met with a surprisingly firm and stable handshake. "Thank you for your invitation. This is Michael Turgeman, a good friend of mine." Michael bowed his head, maintaining his distance and silence.

"Sit, sit, please. How was the journey?"

"Truly breathtaking," Ya'ara said. "I was so struck by the beauty of the mountains. Due to the narrow roads, we drove very slowly, and I just wanted the drive to go on forever." Sarah smiled at her and Ya'ara continued with a degree of enthusiasm that left even Michael surprised. "The world outside is almost white and black, like in a Japanese ink sketch, but here, you, and your house, everything is bountiful and saturated with colors."

Ya'ara felt as though she had stepped into a wonderland kingdom and was standing before the palace guard. She couldn't help but admire everything she saw, the Prussian blue of Sarah Strong's dress, the thick rugs in deep shades of brown and red, the fire ablaze in the fireplace, the green fabric wallpaper that covered the room's walls, a bouquet of roses in the large vase in the corner of the room, handcrafted silk roses, she assumed, the glimmer of the glass and silverware that Annie brought in on a tray, the smell of strong tea brewing in the pot. She felt as if she had come home, even though the place she was in was a very far cry from the house in which she was raised.

"If you allow me the same candor," Lady Sarah said, her eyes sparkling mischievously, "you've come bearing a whirlwind of youth, which we probably need around here a great deal. You've come a long way. I hope you won't think you've driven all this way for nothing. We'll have some tea first. And then I want you to see something."

Ya'ara poured tea for the three of them from the silver pot, adding sugar to Sarah's cup, and some milk, too. "I understand from the research I've done that there was a connection between you, the two of you, and Yosef Raphael, that you and your husband supported him while he worked here, in England, I mean."

"Yosef was an artist of great talent. He was also a very charismatic and handsome man. But I think my husband was drawn to his good looks more so than me. Henry, Henry Moore, was the one who suggested that we meet the young artist from Palestine. And because Alfred had been a collector of Henry Moore's work from the very beginning, he gladly agreed to do so. Yosef was a guest at our home in Oxfordshire, and Alfred didn't leave him alone for a second, as if he were his younger brother. He offered him the use of the estate's hunting cabin, suggested that he turn it into a studio and work there whenever he wanted to get out of London and enjoy the quiet of the countryside. You're aware I'm sure that Yosef worked slowly; the hours he spent thinking most definitely exceeded the hours he spent holding a chisel and sculpting. That's why he has so few pieces, from those years at least. But he had a unique fingerprint, which is something that all artists seek. His sculptures were original, defiant, very different to the kind of things other artists were doing around the same time. He had a free spirit. Being so far from his homeland may just have been the very thing that allowed him to create sculptures that in my eyes were an inseparable part of his country, of the way in which I pictured the Land of Israel. I always thought they embodied some kind of deep, primeval link to ancient times."

"When did you see him for the last time?"

"In the mid-1950s, I no longer recall if it was '54 or '55. Yosef had decided to return to Israel. He spent some time with us at our estate two or three weeks before he left. He sorted out and packed up the contents of his studio in the hunting cabin, put all his sketches and notes in a large bag, and mostly just wandered around the estate's extensive grounds with Alfred for hours on end. I remember sitting together with him in the evening on the home's large balcony. The weather was warm, and when the sun went down, long purple shadows stretched over us. We didn't talk much, but there was a warm and familiar sense of kinship between us. Yosef looked particularly handsome to me that evening, and his features, which were always bold and resolute, appeared more so than ever. I remember thinking to myself that he was no longer with us. In spirit, he was already across the sea, in his new country. His old new country."

"You're Jewish. Have you ever been to Israel?"

"No, I've never been to your country. But I don't travel much anyway. Certainly not now, but even when I was younger, I rarely traveled to other countries. Alfred and I were so different. He traveled around the world. He'd turn up anywhere and everywhere he could find an archaeological dig. Especially in the ancient Near East. That was his passion. That's what took him to Israel, too. At least twice, three times perhaps. I'm not sure. He participated in the digs carried out by General Sukenik — General Yadin was his name, actually. He used to return from his visits filled with wonderment."

"Did he meet up with Yosef in Israel?"

"No. I don't think so. He disappeared from our lives somehow, but not entirely, as you'll see. The day after our last evening together, he asked us to join him in his studio. In the middle of the studio was a sculpture covered with cloth. When he removed the cover, it appeared as if the sun was shining from within the exposed statue.

It was a white marble sculpture, very unlike his other pieces. I wasn't even aware that he'd ever worked in marble. It was the figure of a warrior prince, with a chiseled face and long, beautiful curls. 'This is *Absalom,*' he said. 'I want him to be yours, Alfred's and yours, Sarah.' I remember my surprise and how moved I was by the sculpture, which despite its classical lines conveyed something remarkably contemporary, too. And not some kind of ornate and embellished neoclassicism that I absolutely can't stand. His work on it started at his studio in London, and he had it brought to the studio on the estate so that he could complete the piece. On the rare occasions we visited him there, he used to cover it with a cloth, so we didn't even know of its existence until then. He must have wanted us to see *Absalom* only once it was complete. And it really is one of the most beautiful sculptures I've ever seen. Come, come," she said to Ya'ara and Michael, "I want you to see for yourselves."

Sarah led them toward a small patio, protected by a glass ceiling, a climbing plant thickly entangled around its walls. The climber was bare of leaves in the winter, with only its branches and sprigs pressed close to the walls like an ever-expanding network of arteries and capillaries. Standing in the center of the patio was a gleaming-white marble statue, a daring and arrogant warrior figure, brave and reckless, his lean body muscular and graceful, his eyes gazing straight ahead with self-confidence, his lips parted with the hint of a dismissive smile, entirely aware of his enslaving beauty, the youthful energy emanating from his person, his long, curly hair caressing his shoulders and back, his muscles in a relaxed state of readiness, his body tilted slightly in motion, completely indifferent to the destruction that awaited him, unaware of the tragic outcome that lay just ahead. Sarah was right, there was something entirely contemporary about the piece, despite the fact that it also embodied gestures to the classical Greek form of sculpture. It stood almost two meters tall, conveying both a captivating sense of lightness and the knowledge of the heavy crash to come.

"It's spectacular," Ya'ara said in a whisper. "Gloriously beautiful," she continued in Hebrew to Michael. "Truly so." Sarah observed the amazed faces of her guests with a sense of satisfaction and pride. Few people had seen *Absalom,* but those who had had been exposed to an experience, a spiritual experience you could call it, that stemmed from his breathtaking beauty and the certain tragedy accompanying the splendor of his youth.

"I see him as a relative, distant, but a relative nevertheless, of Michelangelo's *David,*" Sarah said. "Absalom, after all, was David's son. Picture the figure of David at the Galleria dell'Accademia in Florence. And as an adult now, no longer the youth who defeated Goliath, but a king, a man at the height of his power. And now he's grown older. Become corrupt and weary. And his young son is rebelling against him. More than four hundred years and one thousand miles apart, here stands a creation that I view as a true product of David's loins. And yet, it is totally original." Her eyes gazed at the sculpture with a mixture of profound familiarity and rediscovery.

In that very instant, the years appeared to drop off Sarah. As if Yosef Raphael was lifting the cloth draped over *Absalom* right before her eyes. As if her husband were standing beside her, his hand resting briefly on her shoulder, the internal light of the marble sculpture casting a dazzling glow over all of them. "I know, it's a crime that I'm the only one who gets to look at it. It's an old woman's privilege. After I die, I'll leave it to be enjoyed by the public at large."

Ya'ara looked at her. "I'd love to talk to you some more about Raphael," she said to Sarah, "and if you allow me, I'd like to make notes, too."

"We can speak now before dinner, and afterward, too," Sarah said. "You'll sleep in the guest room, and we can talk tomorrow as well. And of course you're welcome to stay too, Michael."

The exchange of looks between himself and Ya'ara was enough to tell him that she wanted to stay there with Sarah alone, to tackle the question of the missing document in an atmosphere of mutual trust. Something like that can't be done in a trio. When delving into an area of secrets and crimes, it's best to do so one on one. It's not a whorehouse. It's true intimacy. "Thank you for your generosity," he said to Sarah. "But I've booked a room at a hotel on the other side of the lake. I'll be happy to rest a little after the long drive. I can come back tomorrow to get Ya'ara."

"I'm aware that we've yet to get to know each other, but you look a little sad, my dear," Sarah said to her as they settled down in front of the fireplace after dinner. Annie added more logs to the burning fire and said she was going to her room, to sleep.

"Just thoughtful mostly," Ya'ara replied. "I'm not sure where my life is going, if anywhere at all."

"You make films. Do you not see a future for yourself in the field, in cinema?"

"I don't know. I make films about life and get the sense that I'm not living life myself. And I'm always on the move. I spend most of my time in Germany, but it's not my home. I don't know where home is. How can a person not know where his home is?"

Sarah placed her slender hand, its skin like parchment, on Ya'ara's hand and caressed it gently. "I've always believed that home is the place you always want to go back to. Is there a place like that for you, a place you want to return to?"

"I want to go back to the house in which I grew up. But it's gone now. My mother died a long time ago. Along with the apartment I'm renting in Berlin, I also rent a room in an apartment in Tel Aviv. But if you were to pack up all of my belongings — and everything I have fits into two suitcases and a backpack — and move them to a different apartment, I wouldn't even notice."

"And what about this young man, Michael? He seems like a very decent fellow and is clearly in love with you."

"I wouldn't call Michael a young man."

Ya'ara laughed. "He's fifty already."

"To me, he's a young man, and you're just a little girl. Never mind. But are you a couple?"

"He wants to look after me. He's always taking care of me. Trying to save me from myself. But no, there isn't anything between us. And I'm not so sure he's in love with me. He just gets confused sometimes and thinks he is."

"You're a heartbreaker and you aren't even aware of it. Surely you must know that there are men out there who'd be willing to kill for you."

"I'm not heartless. And yes, sometimes I think there's someone in Germany whom I'd like to be with. But it seems so impossible. I may just be fooling myself. Perhaps I'm meant to be alone. I know how to do it. To live like that."

"I've been alone since Alfred died. And that was thirty-nine years ago."

"Do you have any children?"

"No. We had a little girl, but she died when she was still a baby. Joanna. And then I went through two miscarriages, and gave up afterward. I couldn't face more heartbreak. But life was good, too. Alfred was an extraordinary partner. Life with him was interesting and enriching. He gave me a sense of security that stemmed from the knowledge that I was loved. And for almost forty years now, I've been walking around with that void he left in my life. Sometimes I get the sense that I even manage to make friends with that hole he left behind. I left the estate near Oxford. It got too big, and I felt I was wandering around there like a ghost. I wanted somewhere small and beautiful and remote. And I found that here. Don't you think?"

Ya'ara looked around. "Yes, I think you've come to a perfect spot. I hope there's a place like this waiting for me, too."

"I'm sure you'll find it in the end. But the road there may be a long one, and somehow I don't believe you choose particularly easy roads for yourself." They talked some more, drinking cup after cup of strong black tea. "It's known as builder's tea," Lady Sarah said to her with a smile. "We're like two construction workers," she added.

"I don't need much sleep at my age, my lovely girl," Sarah said as the flames in the fireplace died down, "but you're still young and need yours." She accompanied Ya'ara to the small guest room. A large, soft towel was lying on the bed, courtesy of Annie before she retired for the night, and Sarah placed a round bar of lavender-scented soap, wrapped in tissue paper, on top of it. "They're made here in the village," she said. "Here you go, you can add another touch to the marvelous bouquet of scents that envelops you. You have no idea how wonderful you are. Come closer for a moment, darling." Ya'ara clasped Sarah's two hands in hers, and Sarah kissed her on the forehead. "There, there, no need for that," Sarah said to her softly, wiping silent tears from Ya'ara's cheeks. "Good night. Cover up well."

"Were you in love with him?" Ya'ara asked when they sat down together for breakfast, faint rays of sunlight streaming through the kitchen window, breaking against the beautiful copper utensils hanging over the sink.

"With Yosef? Not at all. Yes, he was foreign and mysterious. But there was an air of arrogance about him that put me off, and I only wanted Alfred anyway. And after my Joanna died there was no room in my heart for anyone else."

"I want to tell you something," Ya'ara said, and moved her head a little closer to Sarah's. "This may come as a surprise to you, but my research into Raphael also took me to the archives of the Haganah, one of the Jewish underground movements in Palestine during the British Mandate period.

In fact, it was the largest and most important underground movement in operation back then among the Jewish community."

Sarah nodded her head like someone who knew. "I ended up at the archives thanks to a lead I received from an elderly man who didn't want to go into any details but referred me to the documents. He must have assumed that if they allowed me to see them, then the particulars they contain were no longer classified." Sarah remained silent.

Ya'ara continued. "I didn't know what I was looking for in the Haganah archives. Raphael, after all, was abroad during the decisive years of the struggle. But according to a long-serving archivist I spoke with there, a man who had spent his entire life reading and rummaging through old documents, 'The man wasn't merely a great artist, he also played his part in the struggle.' "

Sarah raised her eyebrows in an expression of surprise, but Ya'ara spotted the spark of amusement in her eyes.

"To make a long story short, I'll simply say I was surprised to learn that Raphael had served as an undercover agent of sorts for the Haganah overseas, for the organization's intelligence division. And following the establishment of the State of Israel, he continued to help in a manner that could only be described as discreet."

"Are you trying to tell me he was a spy?"

"First and foremost, and above all, Raphael was an artist. But the Jewish people were at war back then, and whoever could do their bit and be of help did so, even at the cost of putting themselves at risk and making sacrifices. According to the files I saw at the archives, Raphael helped from time to time, as much as he could. He transferred documents from here to there, arranged meetings between people who needed to make contact, things like that. Tell me, Sarah" — Ya'ara lowered her voice a little, moving almost imperceptibly closer to her host at the same time — "did you sense any of that? Did you know of anything that Raphael did for the State of Israel besides create sculptures that became an important part of its culture?"

Sarah closed her eyes.

"You know, my dear," she said, "there are things that are best left unsaid even today. If I knew anything, it was very little, and only implied. I came to realize as the years went by that I didn't truly know Yosef. We had lengthy conversations, we discussed art, we spoke about trivial matters, too. But those were my years of sorrow. I was sad and withdrawn, grieving for my daughter, for my people. I felt bound by both types of sorrow. I'm not sure if I really managed to reach him, Yosef. And he was too focused on himself, his work. We spoke of course about the tragedy that had befallen us, our people, during that terrible war, but all we did was beat around the bush. We didn't openly touch on our personal pain. That's how we were back then, during those years. And because of that restraint, that lack of openness, our conversations didn't broach the subject of politics either. Each of us wanted our peace and quiet. The solitude that protected us. So I didn't really know what he was doing."

Ya'ara remained silent and attentive.

"Once, however, someone I had studied with contacted me. I hadn't been in touch with him for years and the only thing I had heard about him was that when the war broke out, he was engaged in some kind of classified scientific research. But everyone was involved in secret activities in those days. He sent me a letter and asked if we could get together in Oxford. He suggested a day and time and implored me to come to the meeting. For old time's sake, he wrote, and looking back I don't know if he really meant it or simply wrote it so that it would appear to anyone else reading the letter that perhaps the proposed encounter was of a romantic nature. I really don't know. When we met, I saw that the years had taken their toll on him. He was bald and had aged a lot; his skin was pale and his face was drawn. He greeted me with a smile and he was clearly pleased to see me. Nevertheless, he got straight to the point right away. I've heard, he said, that a young Israeli sculptor works sometimes in a studio you have made available to him on your estate. I'd like you to give him this envelope, and to ask him to make sure he passes it on to David, who studied with us. You remember David, right? David Herbert Samuel. He handed me a thick yellow envelope. It's very important, he said. Give him the envelope, and tell him to transfer it to David. I tried to ask him questions, but he simply said: Sarah, it's important. Please pass the envelope on to him. When I asked him what he was doing at the time, if he was married and had a family, questions like that, he said something along the lines of — ultimately everyone does what they have to do. And as for my wife, he said, everything I do, I do for her. It was only then that I realized how much he had changed. He was no longer the funny chap whom I had studied with, but was now a stressed-out man who appeared to be carrying the weight of the world's woes on his shoulders. It's odd that I remember it so clearly. Things that happened just a year ago are far more obscure to me . . . Anyway, he bade me a polite but hasty farewell. Our driver came to collect me at the prearranged time and that's it. I returned to the estate and never heard from him again."

"And what did you do?"

"I did what he asked of me. I gave the envelope to Yosef and he simply said thank you and that he'd take care of it."

"Do you know if he did take care of it, as he said he would?"

"I have no idea. We never spoke about it again."

"It was never mentioned?"

"No."

"Did you tell Alfred about the whole incident?"

"No. Never."

"Why not?"

"I don't really know. Perhaps I thought it was best that way. We didn't speak about everything. No one speaks about everything. Each and every one of us has secrets. Everyone deserves to have their own secrets. Don't you agree? I get the feeling that you actually have quite a few secrets tucked away yourself."

Ya'ara ignored her remark. "Do you know what was in the envelope?" she asked.

"I can only guess. I made up an entire story about it. You might laugh, but I didn't tell myself the story until just before falling asleep, with my eyes already closed and my mind sinking into a world of oblivion. Only then did I think of it, a moment of clarity of sorts appearing suddenly from within the fog."

"I think I understand," Ya'ara said. "What did you tell yourself?"

"Oh, it doesn't matter now. Just something that seemed to be connected to something else. I don't remember anymore. It's been so long since then."

68

Oxfordshire, February 2015

Ya'ara stopped about a kilometer and a half from the boundary of the estate and parked the rental car so that it couldn't be seen from the road, at the start of a countryside hiking trail alongside a cold and fast-flowing stream. Someone seeing and taking an interest in the car would assume its occupants were avid nature enthusiasts who had gone out for a winter stroll. Even in the throes of the icy season, the landscape was still beautiful in its own harsh and bleak way, and the air was clear and painfully crisp.

Two days had gone by since she said good-bye to Lady Sarah Strong. She promised to be in touch and thanked her for opening her heart and home to her. As she was walking down the driveway toward Michael, who waved from the car, Ya'ara turned around and ran back to her host. She reached into her bag to retrieve a tiny bottle boasting a precisely simple design. "I want you to have this, to remember me by," she said to Sarah. "It's my favorite perfume, made in a very special store in Paris. Here, it's yours, I think it suits you." She hugged her and kissed her on the cheeks. Sarah remained standing at the door to her home, her brown eyes warmly following the car as it moved off into the distance.

Ya'ara told Michael that they had come up empty-handed. Sarah had indeed passed on the message and envelope she was asked to convey, but curiosity obviously wasn't one of her attributes. She didn't look inside the envelope and couldn't say what had happened to it. "That's the way it goes in our line of work," she said, with an air of flippancy that seemed put on to him. "Always chasing ghosts. Never mind," she continued, the tone of her voice cheerful and uplifting, "we had a lovely trip, we met a fascinating woman, and most important, you managed to take care of me. I'm okay now." Michael gave her a dubious look. "Yes, I'm just fine now. I needed a friend, and you came, just like an angel." She grasped his hand and squeezed it. "Promise you'll always be by my side when I need you, okay?" she said, before adding after a moment's thought: "And call for me when you need someone like me by your side. No matter where I am, I'll come. Promise."

Michael didn't like what he was hearing. He didn't like her promising him things as if he were a little boy, and he didn't like her cheerful tone, which he believed was a mask for a complex, dark, and violent soul.

"And reassure Aharon, and the Mossad, that there are no grounds for their suspicions. There's a war going on in the world. People are being killed. It's madness to point a finger at me." She told Michael she was going to remain in London for a few more days. Alone. He could go back to his law firm with his heart at ease. Could go on with his life. And shouldn't allow Aharon to keep calling on him whenever he needed someone to do his dirty work for him. And yes, of course, she would call when she was next in Israel and they would get together. Coffee on a warm and sunny winter's day in Tel Aviv.

Michael knew that Ya'ara was involved, in one way or another, in the targeted killings in Brussels and London. He couldn't figure out whom she was working for, what her next moves would be. But he was good when it came to knowing things. He had seen her crash momentarily, and then saw her bounce back. The signs were already coming together to form a picture of reality that didn't bode well. But what choice did he have but to leave when she asked him to do so? He had no authority with her, and apparently his influence over her wasn't as strong as he had thought. And he didn't like the place she left him in even during those moments in which she sought his closeness and support. It's not a relationship that serves me well, he admitted to himself, there'll always be a power struggle between us, and she will always come out on top in the end. *It isn't love,* he thought, trying to convince himself. Addiction perhaps, but not love. She doesn't make me a better man. And even as the large Boeing 777 accelerated and its wheels disengaged from the thawed runway at Heathrow Airport, and London's western suburbs appeared before him in their full winter's gloom, he could still sense the sour taste of his self-loathing. The unease and disquiet, the bitter longing for Ya'ara's daffodil scent.

Ya'ara had no trouble scaling the property's wooden fence. She knew that the large estate was empty. When Lady Sarah decided to move to Scotland, she asked her lawyers to arrange for the estate to be transferred to English Heritage, an organization with the goal of preserving palaces and country estates and opening them to the public, as reminders of Britain in all its glory and greatness. In keeping with her vision, the main building would house workshops for artists and an exhibition hall displaying the magnificent collection of sculptures and antiquities that Alfred had built up through the years. But the process was a long and exhausting one, and in the end, due to funding difficulties, the estate was open to visitors and guest artists only during the summer months. But it was winter now, and Ya'ara wanted to get a look at the cabin that had served as Yosef Raphael's studio. She couldn't explain why, but sensed nevertheless that she needed to see it, that the place in which the spectacular sculpture of Absalom was shaped and polished would tell her something she had yet to learn.

The ease with which she picked the lock of the cabin's heavy wooden door was almost embarrassing, but Ya'ara was pleased with herself nevertheless. The excitement and illegal act heightened her alertness and focus. She explored both floors of the small cabin, as well as the hollow of the stylish turret that adorned the roof. She then returned to the room that had served, undoubtedly, as Yosef Raphael's studio.

Sarah had told her that since Raphael's departure, the cabin had remained empty. And indeed, the stone floor was worn and shiny, giving off an intense chill. Several logs and large pieces of wood were piled up in the corner of the room, a large, heavy table was positioned alongside one of the walls, an easel covered with a length of thick, dusty fabric stood by the window. Ya'ara looked around and took stock — an old and cracked leather armchair, an empty bookcase, a small AGA stove, an aluminum kettle, an iron stove heater that still contained a heap of crumbling newspapers. The newspaper at the top of the pile displayed the front page of the *Daily Telegraph* from October 12, 1954. The room was ice cold, and Ya'ara wrapped herself up in her coat and sat down on the leather armchair. She tried to imagine what the room had looked like when Raphael had worked there, particles of dust swirling in the rays of sunlight streaming in at an angle through the window, the blows of the chisel on the block of marble, steam rising from the kettle, warmth radiating from the stove heater, a length of colorful fabric tossed carelessly on the leather armchair, a young Sarah sitting in the armchair, her large brown eyes keenly following the dancing muscles of the handsome sculptor. Ya'ara sat there like that for a very long time. She then walked around the room, alongside the cold walls, running her hand over them, a thoughtful look in her eyes. She went over to the large wooden table, examined it from all sides, and bent down to inspect it from underneath, too. And after that, she began rolling the logs of wood toward the center of the room. She arranged them side by side, studied them intently, gently felt them with her hands. She then returned to the armchair, her eyes still focused on the lengths of wood. When she got up again, she went over to one of the thick logs made distinctive by its light-colored, peeling bark, which was covered with greenish blotches. She felt it thoroughly with her hands before revolving it slowly and carefully examining every centimeter of the bark. She then retrieved a set of precision screwdrivers from her backpack, selected one of them, and gently inserted its tip into a tiny round hole she had found in the bark, no more than a millimeter or two in diameter. The shaft of the screwdriver slid in to a depth of about five centimeters, disappearing almost entirely into the log. She pushed down hard on the screwdriver and heard a click. The log split into two before her eyes, as if it were a book just waiting for its faithful reader. A small space had been hewn into the center of the log, and in it was a yellow envelope. Without a moment's hesitation, she removed the envelope and placed it in her backpack, closed the log with a click, and rolled it along with the others back to their place in the corner of the room. She then left the hunting cabin without looking back. She was a trespasser, and it was never a good idea to feel too comfortable in that capacity. After scaling the fence again and setting out quickly back to her car on foot, she could feel the blood pumping through her veins. She didn't stop along the way to open the envelope, and didn't do so when she got into the car either. She opened the yellow envelope only in the room she had booked for herself at a country inn, some fifteen kilometers from Lion's Slope Estate. From the envelope she carefully removed a thick paperback booklet, bearing the seal of the realm. Printed across the top of the cover were the words "Top Secret, for the eyes of classified H.E.R. associates only," and in the center of the page, in thick black letters, the title read: "Operation Hurricane."

The thick booklet was in surprisingly good condition. It was numbered and contained

227 pages, most of them filled with what appeared to her to be long, complex mathematical formulae in clear, precise handwriting. She didn't understand the formulae at all, and could only partially decipher the segments of text in English. But the brief, businesslike introduction offered her a general understanding of what she had in her hands. And after a brief check on the internet, she knew she was holding a bomb. Operation Hurricane was the code name the British gave to their first-ever detonation of an atomic bomb. The test was conducted on October 3, 1952, in a lagoon off the coast of Western Australia. The British nuclear program, so she learned, kicked off during World War II. Two exiled German scientists, Otto Frisch and Rudolf Peierls, prepared a preliminary memorandum on the subject for the British Ministry of Aircraft Production, which went on to establish a secret committee tasked with the ultimate goal of producing a weapon never before seen by humanity. After the war, and after the United States declined to continue its cooperation in the field of nuclear research, Britain decided to resume its independent development efforts. The project earned the code name, H.E.R. — High Explosive Research. Britain's first nuclear

device was detonated in the Monte Bello Islands, inside the hull of an abandoned frigate, the HMS *Plym.* A second test was conducted a little more than a year later, in November 1953, when a nuclear device known as Blue Danube was dropped from the air in the same region. The booklet she was holding in her hands, Ya'ara realized, was a detailed scientific summary of those tests.

69

Thames Valley Police Station, February 2015

Staff Sergeant Barnes looked at his watch. It was four thirty-five. Just another twenty-five minutes until his shift was due to end. He thought of the dinner he hoped his wife, Patricia, was already busy preparing, and wondered how everything would look in less than two years, when he reached retirement age and took his pension. John, a jittery young man with acne on his face, arrived from the post office, pushing a cart laden with a stack of envelopes. In this day and age of the internet and emails, Barnes thought, one would think there'd be less regular mail, but there seemed to be as many envelopes as ever on the cart. John stacked the mail on a worn table that stood perpendicular to Barnes's desk.

"Watch out for the cup of tea," the staff sergeant growled at him, and John just mumbled, "Yes, sir," and ran for his life.

Barnes had already decided that Donaldson, who'd be coming to replace him on duty, would deal with all the mail. He had no desire at all to do it himself. But one large, ocher envelope caught his attention. Written across the front of the envelope in large black letters made with a marker pen were the words: "To be opened by a chief inspector or higher only." There was no sender's address, and the postal stamp was from the central post office in Oxford, with the previous day's date. Barnes felt the envelope and it appeared to contain a stack of paperwork, a thick booklet perhaps, or maybe documents from a law firm, he thought, but those usually came by registered mail and clearly noted the address of the firm. Something made him rise laboriously from his chair and pass the envelope through the X-ray machine. Apart from five large, thick staples, arranged in a single line, he saw nothing. He returned to his desk, sighed, and dialed an internal number at the station.

"Sir," he said when he heard the voice of Superintendent Lewis. "We've just received an envelope in the mail that I think you should see."

Superintendent Lewis opened the envelope

in front of Barnes. The staff sergeant watched as the expression on his commander's face went from one of impatience to one of perplexity, and he remained standing in front of the large desk until Lewis gave him a look that clearly said: That'll be all. Barnes wanted to ask him about the contents of the envelope, but decided against it. His shift was coming to an end, and besides, Lewis had a reputation for being a grumpy and arrogant character. After Barnes left the room, Lewis called a number at Scotland Yard. "Hello, Henry," he said. "You're not going to believe this, but a highly classified document from more than sixty years ago has just landed on my desk. Apparently someone thought it was time to return it to official hands. No, it's not the kind of document that should be forwarded through the internal mail service. I will bring it to you personally tomorrow afternoon. It'll remain in my safe until then. I suggest you invite a senior representative from the Defense Ministry's Department of Information Security to attend the meeting, too. Someone who has clearance on nuclear issues. Yes, certainly, I can stay for a short while after the meeting. Good beer, memories from the Oxford days, constructive gossip. Could it get any better than that?"

70

London, March 2015

Ya'ara stared intently at the paintings hanging in Room 31 of the National Portrait Gallery. The competition was tough, but Ya'ara knew ultimately that it was her favorite museum in London. When she had walked into the modest gallery just off Trafalgar Square for the very first time, still standing in the small, gloomy vestibule, she had done so primarily to escape the cold, stinging rain coming down outside. She expected to encounter hall after hall of portraits of princes in dark clothing with white batiste collars, of kings named George the third, fourth, and fifth, and of heavy-set and unattractive high-born women, their hair a light shade of blue and their cheeks far too rosy. Ya'ara was surprised to discover that the gallery was filled to the rafters with paintings and spectacular photographs of artists and athletes, of scientists and poets, of kings and prime ministers, of industrialists and theater actors and opera singers. Men and women, painted in the style of precise Realism or bold and colorful Expressionism. Textile designer Paul Smith, looking inquisitive and experienced, is immortalized sitting on a chair with a roll of shiny green fabric standing between his legs; a young and determined Queen Elizabeth is wearing an elegant robe adorned with fur trimmings; a black-and-white video clip shows soccer star David Beckham tossing in his sleep, his exposed body a model of perfection; Seamus Heaney, the Irish poet and Nobel laureate, his face plowed with wrinkles, his gaze bold and piercing, a stormy whirlwind of thick layers of paint splashed onto the canvas creating his image out of the chaos. And now she was in the large hall, Room 31, which housed paintings of the greats of the British nation from the first half of the twentieth century — leaders, actors, war heroes, aggressive industrialists, renowned scientists who broke new ground in the world, a black boxer, a beloved children's authoress. Her breath was taken away by the human richness, the greatness, the immense talent of the heroes and those who had immortalized their images.

This time, however, she wasn't simply moved by what she could see. She was troubled in fact, very troubled. Again she had entered the portrait gallery to escape. Not from the rain, but from a continuing sense of unease, from the doubt that was starting to eat away at her from the inside. It had been too long since she last managed to contact the lawyer who was supposed to coordinate between her and the prime minister. It no longer appeared coincidental. True, the prime minister had told her that if forced to do so, he would deny any ties with her. But when it appeared to be actually happening, she felt betrayed and hurt. She hurt all over.

She read a report on the Ynet news website about a special meeting of the Knesset Foreign Affairs and Defense Committee to which the prime minister was summoned to address the accusations that the State of Israel had carried out the assassinations in Brussels and London. "Israel is closely monitoring the events," the prime minister was quoted as saying by sources on the committee. "Although we weren't saddened by the news of the deaths of an extremist preacher and a cruel murderer, Israel has nothing to do with the incidents. We were of course very saddened to hear of the death of the young girl in London. Israel respects the sovereignty of its allies and would never launch an operation on their soil without coordination and approval." Ya'ara didn't know why the prime minister's words, expected and called for under the circumstances, offended her so much. Obviously he was going to say such things. Could he have said anything else? But she felt abandoned and alone.

You need to be stronger, she told herself. Why is this temporary break in communication troubling you so? It's an inescapable part of the job, after all. Who promised you that it would be easy? But it was a break that had gone on for another day and then another and then another. All she wanted to do was sleep. But there wasn't a bed in the world that felt as if it was really hers, in which she could close her eyes peacefully and wake up somewhere safe and familiar. Only temporary beds in hotels, and a bed in an apartment she was renting in Berlin for the time being, and a bed in an apartment with a roommate in Tel Aviv, where she had never been able to feel at home.

Where is my home, she asked herself, aware of her own misery, and aware, too, of the fact that the only thing she could do was to let the time pass and play its healing role. And in the meantime, she'd have to suffer, and deal with it. It wasn't the first time. The excitement she had felt on seeing the magnificent portraits had subsided, replaced by the feeling of emptiness spreading inside her. She wanted Michael by her side, Matthias, Hagai. It been so long since she last thought of the man with whom she had shared her life in the past. But she knew that none of them was thinking of her at that moment, not one of them had any idea just how much she needed him. She felt alone in the world.

With the last of her strength, she sat down on a bench in the hall and leaned forward, doubled over, a sour taste rising from her throat into her mouth. Her eyes closed tight, and black and red spots pulsed on her eyelids, inside her head. "Are you okay, my dear?" She heard the muffled voice of the elderly guard who had approached her. Ya'ara groaned out loud, but forced herself to sit up straight and open her eyes. "Yes, yes, everything's fine," she said to her. "I'm just fine," she added quickly, before getting up and leaving the room, still a little unsteady on her feet, and heading toward the stairs. She didn't have the strength to deal with the guard's kindness. She just wanted to get out of there.

71

London, March 2015

Had anyone asked her, Ya'ara wouldn't have been able to say how and under what circumstances she had made it to her hotel room in Paddington. It was a small, old-fashioned hotel, one out of a row of shabby guesthouses adjacent to one another in a long trainlike structure. When she got there, the reception desk was unmanned, and she struggled her way up the steep stairs to the third floor. She flopped onto the narrow bed still in her clothes, managing to position her head over the trash bin squeezed between the edge of the bed and the rickety writing desk, and threw up a bitter yellowish liquid. Her body was bathed in sticky perspiration. She sank into a fitful sleep, tossing in her bed, covering herself with the thick blanket.

When the chambermaid knocked on her door in the morning, Ya'ara shouted from the other side of the door that she wasn't to come in, and the chambermaid relented. Ya'ara knew in her stupor that her clothes were damp and her hair wet and sticky.

It wasn't until evening, when darkness had fallen, that she managed to get up and drink some water from the plastic cup in the small bathroom. She undressed and left her clothes in a dirty pile in the middle of the room, her bare feet recoiling from the cold feel of the white ceramic flooring. She rinsed her mouth out with the ice-cold water she collected in the palm of her hand, remains of toothpaste she had applied with her finger still smeared on her face, and collapsed naked onto the bed, onto the sour-smelling sheets, her eyes closed and burning.

She asked the chambermaid not to enter the following day, too, fending off her anxious questions from behind the closed door and declaring that everything was okay. She was just a little tired.

Only on the third day did she sit up straight on her bed, wrapped in a thin, worn-out towel that had been washed far too many times, her body smelling of the cheap liquid soap she had found in the bathroom. She felt better. At least that awful, bitter, metallic taste in her mouth was gone. She checked her email again. A blue dot suddenly appeared. Mail from the production company in Israel. Attorney Ben-Atar had renewed the contact that had been inexplicably broken.

72

Berlin, March 2015

Aslan looked thinner than she remembered. She had seen him, after all, in Newcastle just a little more than two weeks ago. His winter quest across the breadth of England must have been demanding and harsh. But his eyes smiled at her. They settled into the two comfortable armchairs positioned in the far corner of the café, near the door leading to the establishment's small courtyard at the back. During the summer, the yard was filled with people, bursting with music and an exuberant joie de vivre. It stood empty of people now, filled only with heaps of dirty snow that refused to melt.

"I have something for you," Ya'ara said, retrieving a wrapped package from her backpack and handing it carefully to Aslan.

"Should I open it?"

"Of course."

He tore off the wrapping paper and then

the layer of bubble wrap protecting whatever lay underneath. He revealed a large beer mug, long and slender, made from painted blue clay and bearing the crest of a noble house drawn by the hand of an artist.

"For your collection." She smiled at him.

"Wow! It must have cost a fortune. It's beautiful."

"From the eighteenth century. Seventeen hundred and something. It's written on the bottom. Enjoy!"

Aslan stood up and kissed her on the cheek. He had no idea how she knew about his collection. In all the years they had known each other, she had never been to his home.

"Tell me," he said, sitting back down in his armchair, "have you had any contact with the management?" They had yet to decide how to refer to their relationship of sorts with the prime minister. Aslan liked to speak of "the management"; she preferred the language of movie mobsters, like in *The Godfather.* "The consigliere did in fact disappear for a few days," she said nonchalantly, without a hint of the sense of spiraling out of control and waywardness that had befallen her. "But the contact has been renewed. And the boss wants to see me in the coming weeks. You should come along, too. We can give him an update on the cadets. We'll get some guidance from him."

"Perhaps you should meet in private. Apparently you speak the same language. I don't do that well in those situations."

"I can't think of a single situation in which you don't do well. I thought it would be good for you to meet him face-to-face, too. To be there to keep me on an even keel. You of all people know that my responses can sometimes be a little too hasty. And besides, if something were to happen to me, and you know as well as I do that that's entirely possible, it's important for there to be continuity, for there to be a way to press on with this thing that we're doing."

"What's going to happen to you? You're like a cat with nine lives."

"I still haven't worked out how many I've used up already," she responded, smiling but thoughtful, "and besides, you always think the worst. What would happen if I were to get married and go to the Caribbean for three months? Would that be it? Would our unit be left without a commander? Or do you not think I'm good enough for that?"

"Okay now, I couldn't even begin to imagine such a catastrophe. The poor guy, the poor guy," Aslan said, thinking that there were very few men capable of being a worthy partner for Ya'ara. Men who wouldn't only be dependent on her, but whom she'd need, too; men she'd treat as equals, whom she could devote herself to and allow herself to be imperfect around. "Have you seen Michael Turgeman recently?" he asked out of the blue, wondering if there could have been something between them. If there had been.

"No, don't be crazy," she responded, lying without hesitation, and wondering why she was doing so and not telling Aslan, in general terms at least, about Michael's trip and their encounter. "But maybe I'll give him a call the next time we're in Israel." She paused for a moment. "You can't imagine that . . ."

"I don't imagine a thing. But he's a very serious man, you should know. I think very highly of him. If you need someone to back you up in this matter, of the squad, perhaps you can bring him on board. I'd be very happy to work with him. He may add a touch of levelheadedness and responsibility to what we're doing."

"That's exactly the thing that worries me. He has too many red lines, restraints," Ya'ara said, thinking she was fortunate not to have shared more than she had with Aslan. As Sarah had told her, everyone needs a few secrets.

"He's exactly the kind of person we need," Aslan said. "Maybe it would be a way of extending our shelf life. We'll get to carry out more operations. You can look at it from that angle, too."

"All the cadets returned to base safely," Ya'ara commented with a dryness that replaced the light mood between them. She understood that Aslan had yet to forgive her for the operation in Brussels, for the assassination of Hamdan. He had told her that she had taken unreasonable risks, and she knew deep down that she had operated on the very edge. But that's how you win, she retorted to herself in defiance.

"You know what," she said to Aslan, "maybe there is something to what you're saying. Let me think about it. In any event, Michael Turgeman is an interesting candidate. Do you have any idea what happened with his plans to open a law firm?" Aslan shook his head.

During all the time she had just spent with Michael, she hadn't spoken to him about his life at all. In his company, she had been like a little girl, needing only his embrace, his protection. She tried to push her memories of those days, in Oxford and Liverpool, to the back of her mind. Only in the mountains of Scotland, with Sarah Strong, had she felt herself again, like the woman she really was. Aware of and open to the world. And suddenly she realized why Michael had led her to the Torridon Hills, and it wasn't only because of his ancient intelligence mystery. He had helped her to emerge from the shell into which she had crawled, to find interest and passion, to remember that the world is a wide-open place and the layers that compose it are alive and kicking. Don't underestimate him, she berated herself, that's your mistake. After all, there are things he's forgotten that you've yet to learn. And in her mind, she bowed her head in appreciation before Michael. Appreciation and esteem. If she felt anything more than that, she was quick to expel the emotion. It never was and never could be. That was not the kind of relationship they shared. She brushed aside the image in her thoughts of Michael looking into her eyes and giving her one of his cautious smiles. She returned to Aslan.

"So what do you think about the cadets?" she asked. "It's time to get them certified, right? To complete the course and start working."

"They're all getting through as far as you're concerned?"

"At the end of the day, yes. Everyone is getting through. I'd take any one of them along on a mission. But they're obviously not all at the same level. The men, actually, Sayid and Assaf, are the ones who are lagging behind a little. They're less independent at this point, and less creative. But Sayid displayed a great deal of courage by going into the mosque undercover, and I think the work is allowing him to find a side of himself that's new to him, and that he wants to adopt. And he's got the perfect cover story, of course. And Assaf, Assaf's a good guy, and decent, and you can count on him."

"The way you put it, it sounds like a list of drawbacks."

"No, not at all. He has a very good foundation. I'm sure that when it comes to military combat, he's brave and professional, and that people follow him. Our challenge is to complete his transformation to a covert fighter."

"You know yourself that there's nothing trivial about that transformation. And it doesn't always work."

"I know. But I want to run the process through to the end. I see him as a late bloomer of sorts. I believe in him."

"And the women?"

"What do you think?"

"I think they're excellent. Helena is a war machine. And Ann, she'll be a great combatant. Her seriousness, that English composure."

"Nufar? Batsheva?"

"You were with them in Brussels, so you have a broader perspective. But as far as I can tell, they're both undoubtedly exceptional. Nufar is very skilled with computers, she's certainly outspoken but accepts authority, and she's a very, very quick thinker. She radiates intelligence. She's too competitive, but that can be toned down, I think. And Batsheva, she's a character. She's already fully formed. Brave, independent, takes responsibility, original, interesting. She's come to us to learn the technique only, the professional skills. That aside, she's already fully cooked. But" — Aslan hesitated — "I get the sense that under all the glitter, there's also a dark and somber side to her."

"I agree," Ya'ara said. "She hides it well, but it's there. Personally, however, I prefer people who have some of that darkness," she concluded. Aslan nodded, despite having very different thoughts on the subject. The darkness in Ya'ara, particularly that revealed to him in recent months, deterred him.

"Yes," she said. "We have an excellent team. They need to get a little more polished and then we can add a second batch of cadets. Apart from that, we also need to set up a technology team. We need special equipment and means, specifically suited to our tasks. We can't keep using only the kind of things you can find on a shelf, or get from Goran and his people. I've been thinking about bringing in two young guys I know, two engineers. She's a mechanical engineer and he's an electronics engineer. I want us to try to recruit them when we're in Israel. He works in hi-tech these days, I think she works for Rafael, the defense technology firm. We need to find a way to convince them that we can offer them something more interesting."

"I can see we won't be getting much rest in Israel. And I'm assuming you remember that I'm going away for a month in April?"

"Of course I remember. I just can't recall which mountain you'll be climbing this time."

"Kilimanjaro."

"Do you know the song, the French one?" Ya'ara started humming the tune of Pascal Danel's "Les Neiges du Kilimandjaro."

"You couldn't hold a tune to save your life," he said to her affectionately.

"That's true," she replied, "but I love that song. I think I was born thirty years too late."

"You were born right on time."

"Right on time or not, we need to hold some kind of a ceremony, don't we? And find a name for our unit. We can't go on like this without a name."

"Any ideas?"

"I don't know. The name Sirocco keeps playing in my head. Does it sound like a suitable name for a unit of covert fighters? It reminds me of intense heat, the desert, an easterly wind, a storm from the east, something that scorches everything in its path, that kind of thing."

"A little bit of heat in this freezing cold Europe wouldn't hurt at all," Aslan said. "Sirocco is good. It could also be an acronym, perhaps. For example, S — service, security, stealth."

"Savagery."

"I — intelligence, initiative, innovation."

"Impunity."

"Come on now, Ya'ara. Lucky we don't have psychologists in the unit. They'd have ruled you out a long time ago."

"Lucky indeed. R — revenge, retribution, risky."

"We don't have to decide now, right?"

"Okay, I get it. We'll keep thinking. It's only for them, so they can feel they're a part of something bigger. We'll start tomorrow with the debriefings regarding the operations in Brussels and London. We'll put everything on the table and discuss it all. The tactical disadvantage with which I carried out the mission in Brussels, the death of the young girl in London, the risky association with the arms suppliers, the selection of targets."

"And you think our cadets are ready for such openness?"

"I don't know of any other way. It's the only way to learn, to get better. If it's tough for them, they need to deal with it. They aren't children."

Aslan thought of the long way the cadets had come in such a short time.

"I suggest we conduct the debriefings here, in Berlin," he said, "but that we conclude the course in Israel. Perhaps where we all met up for the first time. In the Galilee. Being abroad is a little like being in a movie. But ultimately we need to go back to having both feet on the ground. Our ground."

Ya'ara nodded with a sense of relief. Aslan had found the exact right words, the thing she was missing. He reached over the armrests of the chairs, found Ya'ara's hand, and gave it a small squeeze of affection. She responded with a smile, strands of light hair hiding her eyes. She brushed her hair back, sat up straight, and said: "Let's get out of here and go to some fancy bar with women wrapped in fur coats and men in evening suits. We'll drink a toast to the end of the course and the fact that we're here. Alive and well with plans to live full lives and more."

"We deserve it, that's for sure. I'm with you, let's go."

73

Berlin, March 2015

After two and a half hours of debriefing, everyone took a break. The cadets milled around the coffee machine, and Helena motioned to Ya'ara that she'd like to speak to her.

"So let's talk," Ya'ara said to her.

"No," Helena responded. "Not here. Let's talk in your office, if possible."

Ya'ara, out of habit, settled into the chair behind her desk, but Helena remained on her feet. She was standing there wonderfully upright, and something about her posture reminded Ya'ara of a Roman soldier. And there was something else there, something she couldn't quite put into words for herself. She invited her to take a seat, but Helena said she'd rather stand. They both looked at Ya'ara's bare desk, which was completely devoid of any picture, any item of a personal nature. Ya'ara folded her arms in front of her, and Helena thought for a moment that they, too, appeared to be props, just like the desk. In some way, it made things easier. Helena shared Ya'ara's penchant for privacy.

"I don't think I can continue," Helena said.

"Has something happened?"

"It's something to do with me."

"Is it because of what happened with the girl in London?"

"You brushed over it very quickly during the debriefing, didn't you?" Helena asked, lifting her chin a little. Here we go, the debriefing isn't over just yet, Ya'ara thought to herself. She calmly repeated what she had said to the cadets just an hour earlier. "You know as well as I do that it was an accident," she said. "And accidents happen."

A tense silence fell over the room. Helena was the first to break it. "In any event," she said, "I've already told you. It's something personal, unrelated to the course."

"You know," Ya'ara responded, "I have to admit I'm disappointed. I expected more of you. I saw more in you. To tell you the truth, I saw myself in you at your age." Only after voicing the words did Ya'ara realize that she wasn't trying to be manipulative, she was speaking the truth. Helena reminded her of herself; they shared that same sense of detachment from the crowd.

Helena replied quickly. "I don't think we're alike," she said.

Ya'ara ignored her last statement. She stood up from her chair and approached her cadet. "I need you to know that you're truly excellent," she said. "You'll be a great combatant. But only if you want it. No one's going to force you to do anything you don't want to do. And no one can. And if you need help with anything, tell me. I suggest we take a look at what's bothering you. And then we'll see if there's something we can do about it. We'll break down this whole thing, whatever it may be, into small pieces, and we'll see how we can deal with them one by one."

"It's nice of you to say we'll see, we'll break down, and we'll understand. But I'm not so sure that it's a matter for the two of us. It's first and foremost my issue. Something I need to figure out. I may be able to share it with you. But first I need to understand what I'm feeling."

Ya'ara realized that the conversation was over. Strange, she thought, that at the end of it all, Helena had remained a sealed box, whereas she, Ya'ara, who had faced far more complex situations than a talk to clear the air with a closed and stubborn cadet, had found herself at a disadvantage. Yes, she could have made her continue, but didn't want to do it like that; that wasn't the way to go about it. It's a job you're married to, that you breathe, that you go to sleep and wake with. If Helena wasn't the person she thought she was, there was no point in trying to persuade her. And if she was that person, she needed to come back of her own accord.

The first day of debriefings came to an end only when evening fell. Everyone felt spent. The intensity of the discussions drained them of energy. With hindsight they knew how they could have planned better, operated safer, caused less collateral damage, an ugly word for killing an innocent young girl. But one never has the benefit of hindsight when things are happening so fast, sometimes at the speed of a bullet. They would do better next time. They had done quite well this time. They were tired but content.

Ann approached Helena, who was lingering at the door. "Should we go get something to eat?" she asked, her hand touching Helena's for a moment. "Feel like it?"

"More than anything else," Helena said, her tone more serious than Ann's. "And besides, I don't know when we'll have another opportunity." They walked side by side down the wide steps of the old, elegant building, which was built at the beginning of the twentieth century and somehow had survived the war. "It hurts me to say good-bye to you like this," Helena said simply.

"Maybe we don't have to say good-bye."

"You're more naïve than I thought," Helena said with a pained smile. She didn't say a word about Daniel, Ann's husband. There was no need to. They had already guessed each other's thoughts, and Helena knew that her feelings didn't match those of Ann. She felt that for the first time in her life she was exactly where she was meant to be, with the woman she needed to be with. But for that same reason, in fact, she had to leave and walk away.

The cold mercilessly penetrated their open coats, and they both quickly tightened the scarves around their necks.

"This is fun," Ann said simply. "I'm happy when I'm with you." She linked arms with Helena.

Helena tried to tone down her feelings. She also wanted to say she was having fun and felt good. She tried a different approach. "You know," she said, "perhaps we're taking advantage of the fact that we've disappeared from our real world, and in the bubble in which we've been living for the past few months we've allowed ourselves to experiment . . ."

"Is that what you think?" Ann asked, her beautiful eyes wide-open and gazing at Helena, who whispered to herself to be brave. She couldn't expose her true feelings to her. She knew she'd panic, she'd recoil. For Ann, this was all a game, nothing more. And very soon, each of them would return to their real lives. *It's better to walk away than to have someone walk away from you,* she thought, reiterating what her mother had told her again and again. And that's exactly what she intended to do.

"Of course it's experimenting, sweetheart," Helena said to Ann in a calm tone. "You're the most exciting thing that's ever happened to me. And it could never have happened in any other way in my life. It's not the kind of thing that happens in the mapped-out life of a Russian girl destined for greatness. It could only have happened here. And here it will remain, too."

They made their way along the Ku'damm, the main street of the western part of Berlin, up close to each other, indifferent to the hordes of people pacing briskly all around them.

"The most exciting thing that's happened to you is this course, not me," Ann responded. "I don't even want to think about what would happen if you were forced to choose between this work and me." She smiled weakly at Helena. And Helena didn't tell her that she had already made her choice, that she had chosen her, the lovely and enchanting Ann, and that's exactly why she was leaving her.

When they were sitting together at the small restaurant, too, allowing themselves to hold hands, Helena continued to try to maintain her relaxed façade, but a voice in her head kept telling her softly to remember every detail because this was the last time they'd be sitting together like this, the last time she would be seeing Ann just inches away from her, breathing her in. And maybe it was the last time, too, that she'd be a part of the team, under the command of Ya'ara, who had both angered and amazed her, a part of the calling that had fulfilled her wildest and most daring dreams. The pain of parting burned inside her, but she smiled at Ann and turned her attention to the smell of flowers that hung in the restaurant air. At that exact moment, they both thought of springtime.

■ ■ ■ ■

Ya'ara turned out the lights in the production office and locked the door behind her. Helena and Ann were long gone, but Ya'ara could still sense the electrical pulses that lingered in the narrow space that had separated them. She was concerned. She felt as if she had allowed Helena to slip through her fingers, but she didn't know how to stop her or whether to do so at all. She didn't have answers regarding her. She wanted to be with Aslan, but he had disappeared on her and she didn't call him. It wouldn't be good for him to think she needed him. She was alone, and she'd be wise to get used to it. She walked down the wide stairs and vanished into the darkness.

74

Berlin, March 2015

Nufar and Assaf went out walking by the river again. The Spree this time, in the heart of Berlin. They felt drained after the long day of debriefing.

"You know something," Assaf said, appearing to edge closer to her with every step, "today was the first time I understood the extent of the risks involved in the plan we adopted for the Brussels operation. Like walking on a razor's edge."

Nufar looked at Assaf with an amused smile, and he felt obliged to defend his choice of words. "Yes, it was a wild gamble," he added. "And though it succeeded, it could also have failed."

"You're wrong," Nufar responded. "Ya'ara took advantage of the element of surprise, the ability to terrify and intimidate, to the very fullest. She wore a gas mask not only to protect herself from the tear gas, it was psychological warfare, too. And she must have looked like an alien monster to them at the time. And she managed to clearly point out to the Belgian prison guards the balance of forces between them. She was there to kill, but Hamdan only. They mostly just wanted to go home. She planned a brilliant operation, and created a situation in which she had an excellent chance of coming out on top. Nothing less. A little like David and Goliath."

"So who's who in this story?"

"Ya'ara is David, and the Belgian prison guards are Goliath. But in my opinion, Goliath didn't stand a chance. When David went out to fight him, his victory was guaranteed, and not only because Goliath underestimated his strength. David was quick and light on his feet, he was out of Goliath's range, he used a weapon that made Goliath's armor and shield ineffectual. You see, it really was a battle between enemies of unequal strength. But the stronger of the two, in fact, was David. That's clear. It's clear to me. He's the future. Goliath went to battle guaranteed to lose."

Nufar stopped talking and started to laugh.

"What, what's up?"

"Look at us," she said, "walking along the river on a freezing cold night in Berlin, big stars shining in the sky, and we're conducting a biblical discussion. A bit of a strange situation, is it not?"

"I've been in stranger," Assaf responded with a smile, and Nufar tensed.

Assaf continued. "I suggest we do what men and women who like each other do," he said. "As long as we're here, we're neighbors. So your room or mine?"

Nufar gave him a stern look, mixed with affection. "It's time I told you something in that regard, Assaf, but not out here in this cold."

"You're scaring me a little," he replied, smiling, trying to test how serious she was.

"I really want you to hear me out."

They sat down together in a neighborhood bar with a large fire ablaze in the fireplace at the far end of the room. Nufar was pleased that Assaf couldn't disappear on her into the grim darkness that characterized several of the bars in which they had spent long hours during their two weeks together in Cologne.

"If I wanted to fuck you," Nufar said to him, "I would have done so a long time ago."

Assaf recoiled. He didn't like the blunt language, the expression on Nufar's face, but he listened.

She looked at him intently. "You're a sweet guy," she said, "and good-looking, too, I'll admit that, and I've felt over the past few months that I'd like to be with someone, someone I can have fun with, without things getting too complicated. And if I'd made the first move, you'd have rushed into things without thinking twice."

Assaf wanted to protest but knew she was right. If she had just hinted at the possibility, he would have followed her without a moment's hesitation.

"I held back not because I wasn't attracted to you. On the contrary. But I stopped myself because I know you love your wife and that you miss her and your children. You told me about her yourself, and you showed me pictures of all of you and the drawing they sent you. You're alone now, and far from home, and you think there won't be any consequences for what we do, but that's not true. And if you're incapable now of acting responsibly, I'll do so for you. Because I know you, and I like you. And I don't want to do it to Tali either, I don't want to wrong her, too, because you don't do things like that. I, at least, don't do things like that, or more accurately, I try very hard not to ruin the lives of other people."

She took a sip of her whiskey sour and continued. "We're supposed to continue doing what we're doing for the coming years. This kind of work is demanding and requires focus and perseverance. I want us both to succeed. To be focused. To do nothing stupid that we're going to regret. To be able to work together and rely on one another without complicating everything in an impossible way. And if you're wondering, I hope to find someone who really loves me, not who wants to be with me because it's easy. And you have something you've already built and that is precious to you. That you need to safeguard. So don't ruin it. And let's not ruin what we have. I need you in this unit with me without complications and without any riots."

Assaf hesitated for a while before responding. "I think I understand," he said. "I didn't mean to offend you in any way. I would never hurt you. You know that's not what I wanted."

Nufar nodded in confirmation and Assaf leaned toward her, brushed her hair aside, and kissed her lightly on her right temple.

"You're amazing, Nufar," he said. "I'm glad you're my friend."

75

Berlin, Tiergarten, March 2015

Ya'ara recoiled at the sight of Sayid's pale face appearing suddenly through the freezing morning fog. She hadn't expected to see him when she went out to the Tiergarten for a vigorous morning run.

"You gave me a fright," she admitted. "What are you doing here?"

"The same as you, apparently. I've come to run."

Ya'ara looked at him with a smile on her face. "Very trendy, Sayid," she said. "In which part of town did they sell you that?"

He looked at her in surprise, and Ya'ara tried to tear her eyes away from his odd running suit, which was a mixture of purples and murky browns and zippers everywhere, and wondered if it was worth taking him on a quick shopping spree in sporting goods stores. She decided against it.

"You're usually very conservative when it

comes to your clothes. Conservative and elegant," she quickly added.

"You're right. But I've decided to let myself go. To spread my wings. To discover the new Sayid."

If this is the new Sayid, they may have to rethink all the training that had led him to the point in time at which he purchased that unsightly running suit, she thought, knowing very well that she would never voice such superficial thoughts out loud. Everyone's entitled to their own taste, even a taste as shocking as Sayid's. And he, despite everything and without doubt, was her favorite cadet.

"Follow me!" she called out to him, and set off at a quick pace, leaving him behind. He gathered himself and raced after her, but she moved farther away from him, as fast as the wind.

"I'll wait for you by the monument," she shouted to him.

The mist seemed to swallow her up and hug her coldly to its bosom. Sayid imagined seeing the dust clouds she had left in her wake. But the problem was, he thought, that they were in a country where there was no dust in the winter. Sayid cursed himself. He was doing too much thinking and clearly not enough exercising. And anyway, how come he had bumped into Ya'ara of all people so early that morning, in the middle of a huge park, with no chance of running at her pace, of being as fast as she was, as determined as she was. He pictured his slender body in his beautiful new running suit, and despite the pain in his side that was getting increasingly worse by the minute, he derived a brief moment of pleasure from the thought of himself bounding gracefully through that German park in his magnificent sportswear.

When he arrived breathless at the monument, Ya'ara was already coming to the end of her stretching exercises. She was bent over supplely, her hands gripping her ankles, and she peered at him through her mane of hair, seeing him upside down. *What a miserable sight I must be,* he thought, still trying to regulate his breathing, his body tilted to the left, his right hand over the area of pain above his waist.

"Don't stand still," she said to him. "Keep walking, and then do some stretching."

He walked around her in circles.

"Enough of that, Sayid," she said. "Only dogs walk in circles. See that tree, over there? Walk there and back."

After he returned, Ya'ara approached him and gave him instructions on what he needed to stretch and how to do so. He could feel his hamstrings stretching to a point at which he feared they were going to snap like strings on a guitar, and he eased up a little. "That's great," Ya'ara said. "Listen to your body. Only you know exactly what you feel. Don't do more than you're capable of doing. And just so you know, every day you run, you'll be able to do more." He nodded, barely able to utter a word. "This is your first run in a very long time, right?"

He confirmed that with a wobbly nod of his head. *There's no hiding from that witch,* he thought in an outburst of hostility. "To think I slept in the same bed as her," he whispered to himself.

"Did you say something?" she asked.

"No, no, nothing at all," he responded, his face turning red.

"Well, how is it?" she asked?

"How's what?"

"The course, everything we're doing, the things you've been through, the other cadets."

They were walking slowly side by side, in the direction of the park gate.

"Incredible, for the most part. Half the time I can't believe the things I'm doing, that I'm with this group."

"Is it a good incredible, or do you ask yourself: What am I doing here at all, how did I end up in this thing, how the hell do I get out of here?"

"You said if someone wanted to leave, they could, right?"

"Yes, I did."

"I don't want to leave. I haven't for a second, even after what happened to us in England. I hope I'm good enough to stay. I know I still have a lot to learn, that I'm not good enough yet, not quick enough, even my running suit . . . But this course, and what awaits us in particular, means a great deal to me. Do you get that? I have to stay."

"No one wants you to go, Sayid. On the contrary, I see great things ahead for you. You've shown us that you have capabilities and courage. You may feel sometimes that you're different from the others, but if you take the time to notice, we're all different."

He smiled at Ya'ara but she noticed the shadow that passed him across his face.

"What's up, Sayid? What's troubling you?"

"Look, you're familiar with my story. I don't have a family, and I'm willing to think of this unit as my family, and still I can't figure out how, with this kind of lifestyle, with all the long trips we can expect and all the secrets we need to keep, how I'll ever find someone. You know I'm not a child any longer, and I want to have a home. And a family of my own."

"Those things work out in the end. Or so I hope, at least. Otherwise, you and I will end up sitting next to each other in a retirement home somewhere, our shaking knees covered with blankets, staring into space, with the knowledge that at least we have each other.

"Yes, that's the exact scenario that frightens me," Sayid said, deciding that the conversation needed a lighter tone. "I don't think you'll be a very sympathetic old lady," he continued. "And to tell you the truth, I can't picture you in a retirement home. And besides, I have a relative who lives in a retirement home and she doesn't sit around and stare into space at all. She's like the Energizer bunny. Didn't you once promise me that kind of a future? In another conversation we had?"

"I have this same conversation with myself all the time. You may have been party to one once . . . And yes, I don't think it's normal for a young woman of thirty and a bit to think so much about growing old. I met someone a short while ago, a woman in her nineties. She actually made me feel optimistic. You can still be fascinating and interesting and beautiful even at a very old age. It's just a matter of luck, that's all you need."

"We still have a few more years to go. And don't forget you promised things would work out."

Work out, work out, sure they'll work out, Ya'ara thought. *How the hell am I supposed to know?*

76

Berlin, March 2015

She was surprised to see that Michael had written to her. He didn't do so very often at all. Almost never. But that was definitely his email address that appeared in her inbox with a message bearing the title: "A letter to Ya'ara." He wrote:

> I was driving yesterday along the road up to Jerusalem. The sky was covered with clouds, but golden rays of sunshine were piercing through them, like spotlights in a giant theater. Tu BiShvat is just around the corner and the mountains were indeed filled with almond trees. Beautiful almond trees in full bloom. And every year I'm amazed anew by just how beautiful and perfect those blossoms are. I swear to you, Ya'ara, it's the most beautiful landscape I know. The terraces all around were green, a kind of light green, almost

phosphorescent. And furrowed fields of wild mustard plants. And standing in this sea of colors were large gray boulders, which were here before us and will still be here long after we have gone, wet from droplets of rain or dew, the films of water glistening far into the distance, like patches of ice. The road was open and the air turned misty all of a sudden, but I could still see the view, because a soft light was dripping through. And growing, too, along the side of the road were bushes in bloom, with dark yellow flowers, a deep and beautiful yellow, like honey. Like your hair. I don't know what they're called, maybe I'll check it out, or maybe I'll leave them nameless. And those almond blossoms again, pink and red, more and more of them, growing on the very edge of an abyss. And pink cyclamens among the rocks. If I were a romantic man, I'd write: Bouquets of cyclamens, and every single one for you, Ya'ara. Instead, I'll say that I'm thinking of you over there in that cold, bleak winter, and think you should come home.

77

Israel, Western Galilee, March 2015

The spacious holiday cabin looked exactly as it had when they all met there for the first time. They left Berlin separately, with some of them flying directly to Israel and others stopping for a day or two in another European city. They had already grown accustomed to the never-ending practice of trying to break common patterns.

They were sitting in a circle again, all eyes on Ya'ara and Aslan by her side.

For several minutes the room remained silent. It was a peaceful silence, but also contained a dimension of solemnity and festivity.

"Today we come to the end of months of exhausting training," Ya'ara spoke, her voice low and soft. "Like most of the things we did, the training wasn't routine. You were thrown into the deep end from the very beginning, and you proved to be great swimmers. I'm proud of you. There's no one else I'd rather have by my side for the task of carrying out operational activities. From today, you are all combatants in a semiofficial and highly classified unit, a special ops unit. We don't exist anywhere. There are no records of us anywhere, there's no law that recognizes us, there's no clause in the state budget that's earmarked for us. But it's time you knew just how high up the chain of command this thing goes. The unit was set up in keeping with a personal directive of the prime minister, and we are conducting missions he assigns to us for the purpose of safeguarding the security of the State of Israel. I have no idea what this unit will look like further down the line, but we're going to make every effort to stave off its institutionalization for as long as possible. For as long as you and we are here" — she gestured to include Aslan among everyone else — "we'll continue in this manner. We'll maintain the ability to act quickly, forcefully, and aggressively, emerging out of nowhere and going back to nowhere when the job is done."

The eyes of the cadets displayed stern intentness and pride. Ya'ara focused her gaze on Helena and recognized a deep sadness in her face, overlaid, however, with determination. Helena had disappeared for two weeks, and she was different when she came back. She didn't offer any explanation and Ya'ara didn't ask for one. But she knew that her cadet had finally found her place, even if she had been forced to make some hard decisions to do so. Forced to let go. She believed she knew what it had entailed. She could see the distance that had opened up between her and Ann. She could see that Helena was making a concerted effort to keep as far away from her as she could, positioning herself at the farthest point from the person who had once been her best friend on the team, and maybe even more.

"Despite the fact that we don't exist anywhere, it's only fitting that we have a name. It's my and Aslan's joint decision. You recall we spoke about it at the end of the debriefing in Berlin, and I'm pleased you agreed to the unit name we proposed, Sirocco. We'll be the fiery hot storm that lays waste to whoever rises against us. It may sound poetic and dramatic, but it's the truth. Today, we, you, are joining a long line of Hebrew warriors, and we will play our part in the struggle to ensure the existence of our people and our country with the utmost dedication."

Ya'ara leaned toward her backpack and

pulled out a large crystal, in shades of brown and silver, with a touch of purple in each.

"This crystal is from a quarry in the Jerusalem mountains. A specialist jeweler has set eight small cuttings from it into gold pins. The pins are similar but not identical. Each pin is slightly different from the others. Each pin is a unique creation, a combination of prehistoric nature and the hand of an artist. This crystal contains sufficient material for the pins that will be given to every individual who joins Sirocco over the next hundred years. And today, each and every one of us will receive such a pin. They won't be worn outside Israel. Due to security considerations, and also because it's a kind of oath." She opened the black box resting next to the crystal. Glittering in the light, on a dark piece of velvet, were eight gold pins set with a shard of the crystal. She passed the open box to Batsheva, who was sitting to her right. Batsheva selected one of the pins and handed the box to Helena, who chose one of the pins almost at random and aggressively jabbed it through the fabric of her blouse. The box went from one to the next, and ended up back with Ya'ara. She took off the thick sweater she was wearing and pinned the piece of jewelry to the T-shirt she had on underneath, on the left side. "Near the heart," she said with a smile, and put on her sweater again. Just then, there came a loud knock on the door. "Excuse me a second," Ya'ara said, before standing up and going over to open.

"Have I come at a good time?" the prime minister asked.

"You couldn't have picked a better one," she responded. She saw the prime minister's bodyguard staying back, signaling to her that it was fine, he'd remain outside. "Friends," she said, returning to the center of the room, her guest by her side, "please welcome the prime minister of Israel."

The prime minister and Ya'ara walked slowly down the narrow road. A thick fog had settled, and visibility was very limited. Tiny rivulets of water trickled and wound their way along a ditch by the side of their path. The strong, clean smell of an Israeli winter enveloped them, dense clusters of short oak trees adorned the slope, and cyclamens painted touching pink patches of color among the rocks.

"How can they allow you to wander around like this?" Ya'ara asked, referring to the heavily manned security detail that accompanied him wherever he went.

"I'm stepping out on a limb today. They've allowed themselves to back off a little. No one knows I'm here. You have no idea of my sense of freedom."

"You said some good things to them, to the cadets. I think your words will resonate with them. Thank you for the effort. I appreciate it.

"I have to tell you, Ya'ara, you've surprised me in a good way. And my expectations of you were high to begin with. I didn't think you'd be ready to conduct operational activity so soon. I know how long it takes to train combatants."

"As I reported to you, we did it the other way around. We started with the operational activity, and then we learned from it, we dealt with conceptualization and theory, and we put things in order."

"Keep thinking outside the box. We need someone who thinks like that, too. Do you recall our discussing it? But do me a favor, take care of yourself. I understand what you did in Brussels, you created a situation in which you had the upper hand, the initiative, but if something had happened to you, I would have found that very hard to swallow."

"I'm a combatant. That's my job."

He nodded in agreement and Ya'ara felt ready to ask the question that had been bothering her.

"Prime minister," Ya'ara asked, "for a time I thought you had washed your hands of me. Was I wrong?"

"No, you weren't wrong. There was an outcry about the operations you carried out and we were forced to remain silent and suspend all communication with you. A few of the old foxes guessed you were involved."

One particular old fox, Ya'ara thought. For how long would Aharon Levin continue to keep track of her, she wondered.

"You've made yourself quite a few enemies in high places."

"I know," she said.

"I'm pleased to tell you that you have a friend in an even higher place. I have no intention of giving up on you. I sent you out there, after all. But don't do anything stupid. That's an order."

They walked alongside each other in silence. The prime minister took a pack of cigarettes out of his pocket. "Do you mind?" he asked. Ya'ara shook her head.

The prime minister lit the cigarette, and in the distance Ya'ara spotted the figure of a bodyguard standing at the precise point where she expected to see him, along the line of a closed perimeter. She was pleased. The security guards were doing their job properly. She and the prime minister turned around and started heading back.

"Isn't it hard for you sometimes?" she asked.

"Yes, it's hard sometimes."

"Do you ever think of quitting? Of passing on the burden to someone else?"

"It never enters my mind." The prime minister laughed. "It's my life. It's why I came into this world."

For as long as you get elected, Ya'ara thought, but kept that to herself. And asked out loud instead: "How can we know why we came into this world? I, for example, don't know. I simply exist."

"You know. You know. When you come across your calling, you know."

"So you think my calling is to be a combatant?"

"Your calling is to bring light to the world."

"I've found a very odd way of doing that," Ya'ara commented gloomily.

"I'm getting to know you, Ya'ara, and I think that's what you're doing. You have a special path to follow, and I know it's a tough one. But I also know you're going to do significant things in this world. You already have."

"You're enjoying that cigarette, aren't you?"

"You have no idea. I don't smoke in closed spaces, and I'm in closed spaces almost all the time. I don't always feel like it either. And I admit I don't allow myself to smoke in places where there are cameras. But now I want to and I can, and you were nice enough not to say no."

"Who dares to say no to you?"

"If there's anyone, it's you."

"Truthfully, my father smokes, too. It reminds me of home."

They were nearing the cabin. The cadets had already dispersed and Ya'ara knew that this was only the quiet before the storm. Because a storm was going to come.

"Ya'ara Stein," the prime minister said, looking her straight in the eyes, "we only just started. You have lots of work to do. You know where I'm aiming for. I'm patient. I'm not afraid of taking the long road. What did you say was the name — Sirocco?"

"Yes, Sirocco. Wherever needed, always."

The prime minister shook her hand and then grabbed hold of her two arms, in some kind of clumsy embrace. And then he shook his head, in surprise of sorts, and walked toward the car that was waiting for him, its headlights on and its engine growling softly. He got into the backseat, and a bodyguard shut the door behind him and got into the front. The vehicle sped off. Ya'ara stood outside for a few more minutes in silence. On her way to her room, she saw Sayid and Nufar having a chat. "Hey, you two," she called out to them, "wake me up when Assaf's soup is ready."

78

Israel Museum, Jerusalem, April 2015

Several dozen people were gathered in the foyer of the Israeli Art wing. It was seven fifty in the evening. The museum had already closed its doors to the public. Most of the place was in darkness, with the lights on in that particular wing only. To the select group of visitors, the works of art appeared to be glowing in a light emanating from within themselves. From afar, the broad strokes of turquoise in the huge Zaritsky painting seemed to be moving. On display at the entrance to the hall was Yitzhak Danziger's sculpture, *Nimrod,* his hand behind his back, gripping the hunting slingshot, and sitting on his shoulder — as if it were a natural continuation of his strong, slender body — a falcon. Despite its modest dimensions, all who laid eyes on the piece could clearly see why it in particular had become the shining example of Israeli sculpture, had turned from sculpture into icon. Standing opposite *Nimrod* was a tall object covered with a length of white cloth, with two museum guards in position on either side, and the group of visitors milling around it. In attendance, too, were three television crews and several journalists, along with representatives of the museum's board of trustees who had been invited by the institution's director, who had refused to tell them anything, and who were willing nevertheless to brave a surprisingly rainy and stormy Jerusalem evening. A small table nearby displayed an array of tall wine glasses, already filled. Accompanied by three of his people, the museum director, who had a fondness for dramatic occasions, hurried to join the group of men and women standing between *Nimrod* and the cloth-covered object.

"Ladies and gentlemen," he said in English to his audience, "thank you for responding so kindly to our urgent invitation, which wasn't, I admit, without an air of mystery. I appreciate the courage you have mustered to leave your homes on this rain-drenched Jerusalem evening. But I don't want to take up too much of your time with words. Allow me to present to you the new delightful treasure that joined the museum collection just today."

He motioned with his hand toward the covered object. The two guards removed the length of cloth, and right there and then, before the astonished eyes of the guests, the sculpture *Absalom* was revealed. The white marble piece stood on a block of light Jerusalem stone, meticulously carved, towering in all its height and rare beauty above the small crowd of people.

"Distinguished guests," the director continued, clearly enjoying the effect the piece was having on those seeing it for the first time, "this sculpture is the work of renowned artist Yosef Raphael. He never spoke about it during his lifetime, and we, with the exception of one enigmatic remark, were unaware of its existence, although there were those who had searched for it. Raphael did in fact mention it in a single sentence in the diary he kept during his years in England, but because it received just that one mention, and due to the fact that no records were found of any preparatory notes or other documentation relating to the piece, scholars of Raphael's work assumed that if the sculpture was indeed made, it was lost somewhere in England after World War II, more than sixty years ago. And lo and behold, it turns out that this spectacular work, of which one can already clearly say that it represents one of the high points of Israeli sculpture, does indeed exist, and in perfect shape, too. What we have here is the missing link in Israeli sculpture, offering a thought-provoking interpretation — a wonderful interpretation, if I may — of one of the tragic heroes of the Bible."

The television cameras focused on *Absalom.* So full of life was his marble body that one could almost hear the blood pumping through his veins, flowing furiously through the cold stone, while his face expressed arrogance and impatient defiance, along with the acknowledgment of his inevitable fate.

"The statue of Absalom was a gift from Yosef Raphael to Sir Alfred and Lady Sarah Strong, his close friends who gave him the use of a studio on their country estate in the area of Oxford. Sir Alfred passed away many years ago, and Lady Sarah Strong, already in her nineties, approached us a few weeks ago and requested to donate the sculpture to the Israel Museum, so that the people of Israel and visitors to the museum will be able to enjoy it from now on and forever."

The museum director sipped from a glass

of water handed to him by his assistant.

"Lady Sarah Strong insisted on completing the process of moving the sculpture to Jerusalem as quickly as possible. Although she wasn't able to come here herself, she wanted to know that *Absalom* had found his new home during her lifetime. We wish her, from here in Jerusalem, many more good years to come, and we thank her for her generosity from the bottom of our hearts."

The director reached into the inside pocket of his jacket to retrieve two pieces of paper.

"I want to read to you from a letter sent by Lady Sarah Strong and delivered to our chief curator of Israeli art. This is what she wrote: 'I was visited at my home a few days ago by a young Israeli filmmaker who was conducting research about the sculptor Yosef Raphael, a close friend of my dear husband and myself many decades ago. Her presence in my home reminded me of a wild and beautiful storm, and she left a bold impression on me. It's rare for a young woman to be able to touch the soul of an old woman like me in such a manner. Her connection to Israel awakened a long-dormant chord inside me, causing me to regret all the years during which I viewed

Israel only from afar. I'm too old to travel now. I'm happy where I am. But I wish to return the thing most precious to my heart to the place in which it truly belongs. I have spent many years enjoying life alongside great works of art. And now I'd like to share that privilege with others.' Distinguished guests, you won't have to listen to me for much longer. I'm sure you're all wondering about the young Israeli filmmaker who reminded the honorable lady of a beautiful storm, but I'm afraid we were unable to locate her. Maybe it's a mystery for you to solve," the director said, gesturing toward the journalists, who shrugged their shoulders. "Apparently there are still some things in this world of ours that are destined to remain hidden from our eyes. Let me thank you again for your spontaneous participation in this small but significant celebration, and I invite you all to raise a toast to the esteemed artist, Yosef Raphael, may his memory be blessed, to Lady Sarah Strong, who has enriched us with her generosity, and may she be blessed with many more good years to come, and to the mysterious filmmaker, the beautiful storm who unknowingly caused this masterpiece to end up here."

■ ■ ■ ■

Ya'ara and Michael were standing a little to the side, outside the crowded circle of people who had erupted in applause, which then turned into lively conversation. Ya'ara gazed at *Nimrod,* and at the look of disdain he was aiming at the impulsive and beautiful prince who was now standing in front of him.

"I hope things turn out well," she said quietly to Michael. "I can't see them getting along with each other."

"That's what it's all about. Two sons of royalty, and now there's this magnetic field of beauty and competition and stormy emotions between them."

"Are you talking about Danziger and Raphael or about *Nimrod* and *Absalom*?"

"I'm talking about us."

"Stop it, Michael. You say foolish things and manage to embarrass me."

"There isn't a person in this world who could embarrass you."

"I embarrass myself all the time."

"I don't believe you. You found the document, right?"

Ya'ara didn't hesitate. "Yes. I found it."

"And what did you do with it?"

"Exactly what needed to be done. I returned it to its rightful owners. We don't need things like that."

"Do you know what it contained?"

"Yes."

"And you took it upon yourself to decide that the Mossad, the State of Israel, has no need for it?"

"Yes, it isn't ours and never was ours."

Michael sighed, Ya'ara's sense of justice had a tendency to rear its head at the strangest times. In fact, he thought, Ya'ara was no less arrogant than the two statues standing before them, and he could clearly picture any artist who tried to cast her image in bronze or sculpt her in marble. Any such statue would fail. She was beyond the reach of artists. In any event, she must have realized that he was trying to get the Mossad to pardon her, and she had nothing but deep-seated scorn for that forgiveness, for the thought that she needed to be forgiven for something. *Sometimes I wish I could be a little like her,* he thought, *and sometimes I thank God that I'm so not.* He knew there was no point in pressing the issue. He knew, too, that he would always think about her and him. About her. Ya'ara.

"Let's get out of here," he said. "Before anyone realizes that the storm is right here."

They reached the exit door, the echo of their footsteps seemingly in pursuit.

"Ready?"

Instead of answering, Ya'ara zipped up her coat and hooked her arm around Michael's, smiling at him, as unattainable as ever.

79

Hamburg, April 2015

The evening was surprisingly pleasant, the sky clear and filled with stars, which were reflected in the still waters of Alster Lake in the heart of the metropolis. Ya'ara and Matthias wandered aimlessly through the city's magnificent streets. In less than an hour, the stores would close, the people would disperse to their homes, and quiet would fall over the large city. They stopped alongside the window of an elegant jewelry store. On display behind the armored glass were just a handful of spectacularly beautiful pieces of jewelry.

"Is there anything there that you like?"

Ya'ara peered intently through the glass. "Those earrings: I've never seen anything like them. But would I wear them? You have to be a princess to do that." Ya'ara was looking at a pair of earrings adorned with rare rubies. Set into each earring was an oval ruby with lightly polished edges. The stones were deep red in color. And set alongside each ruby was a circular diamond, too. "Those are very high-quality stones," Ya'ara said. "The color is perfect. It's called pigeon blood. And they're huge. I wonder what it feels like to wear earrings like those. True works of art."

"Come," Matthias said, "let's see what they look like on you."

They entered the store. An elegant middle-aged woman, with her long hair tied in a bun on the top of her head, greeted them with a pleasant expression.

"Good evening," Ya'ara said. "We saw the ruby earrings in the window. They're astonishing. May I try them on?"

The store assistant hesitated for just a moment. She knew she wasn't going to sell the earrings to the young woman standing in front of her, but for some reason she wanted to see what they'd look like on such a beautiful creature. She could sense Ya'ara's unique wildness under her icy façade.

The store assistant carefully removed the small velvet cushion with the earrings from the store window. Ya'ara held her light hair back, and the store assistant slipped the earrings into place. Ya'ara sat down and stared at her reflection in the small mirror that was standing on an antique wooden table. For a moment, she pictured herself living a completely different life. With earrings like the ones she had on, she could have been the daughter of a noble family, living on a magnificent estate, discreetly hidden from the watchful eyes of passersby. She could have been a northern princess.

"They're spectacular, and you are breathtaking. The earrings suit you so well. You're a very lucky man, sir," the store assistant said to Matthias. "Hold on to her."

"Could you tell us, please, how much they cost?"

The store assistant named a figure. The price left Matthias practically gasping for breath. "If you're taking them out of the European Union, you'll get a VAT refund," the woman said.

Matthias pulled himself together. Ya'ara smiled at him and then turned to address the store assistant. "It's a little out of our price range," she said. "But thank you. They're truly wonderful."

With some regret, she removed the earrings and returned them to the store assistant. "You were very nice and generous, Mrs. . . ."

"Mrs. Zeidel. Stephanie Zeidel."

"Thank you, Mrs. Zeidel. Stephanie.

Perhaps a day will come when I return. You've made me happy. And I wish you a particularly good evening."

Ya'ara hooked her arm around Matthias's again and they went back out into the street. She appeared cloaked in uncharacteristic cheerfulness. "You were a real hero for not fainting when she named the price," she said. "But I knew it would be something like that. I was required once to learn a little about the field of precious gemstones. And I knew those were particularly rare rubies. That color? It really is like blood. Who knows, maybe I'll be able to buy myself jewelry like that one day."

"You're an undercover princess, Ya'ara."

"Come, let's go eat. I'm leaving tomorrow and I feel like having some fun."

Two weeks had gone by since Ya'ara called Matthias and asked if she could come to him. "I won't disturb you," she said. "You don't have to make time for me. I simply need a little rest and I want to be with you. I can sleep on the sofa in the library room, okay? Tell me I can come."

Matthias wasn't sure. He felt very indebted to her, but he also had too many unanswered questions. And her presence always left him feeling shaken. She was smart and funny and beautiful, but she was also dangerous, unpredictable, and very young. He didn't know what to do with her, how to behave toward her, and that lack of knowledge caused him embarrassment and discomfort. Moreover, his unfortunate adventure with Martina Müller was enough for him. "Matthias," she repeated, hearing his silence. "Please."

He consented, and he knew two weeks later that he had done the right thing. She brought color and freshness to his life. He continued working, and left the house while she was still asleep on the sofa. But there were mornings when she woke early and sat with him in the small kitchen, the two of them drinking their strong morning coffee in silence. There were nights when he'd come home late, and find her awake sometimes, reading a book or listening to music, her face lighting up on seeing him walk in, and together they'd drink a glass of whiskey or schnapps before going to bed, each in his or her own room. He admitted to himself that if she were to ask to come to his bed, he wouldn't say no. But when she didn't do so, his nights didn't turn into long hours of painful longing. There was something calm and quiet about her presence, and he wondered where she hid all the aggression and violence he knew she had in her. He decided to give her what she wanted. Tranquility and a home and warm friendship.

On the last morning of her visit, she drove with him downtown, and he dropped her off at the central train station.

"Take care of yourself, Ya'ara, and keep in touch," he said. "Don't disappear."

She asked him to get out of the car for a moment, too. "I want to hug you and I don't need the gear lever poking into my ribs. I want to give you a tight squeeze," she said.

"These were the best two weeks I've had in a long time, and I'll be back, Matthias," Ya'ara said as they stood there with their arms around each other. "I feel sometimes that you are my home."

Matthias hoped that she wasn't saying such things too lightly, irresponsibly.

"I don't say things like that very casually," she said, as if his thoughts were an open book to her. "I've never met any other man like you."

We'll see, he thought, and ran his hand through her soft hair. "You're a princess even without those rubies. And seriously, look after yourself. Be careful. I want you to be my friend when I'm an old man, too."

"I'll always be your friend."

She dragged her trolley suitcase behind

her and walked into the huge station. He remained standing outside the car, its engine running, his gaze following her light head of hair.

Suddenly she saw her. A fair-haired woman, like herself, but a little older than she was. A little taller. She caught a fleeting glimpse of her face, just as she turned right toward the platforms, a calm and pretty face, with a large, strong nose, full lips, high cheekbones, and in her earlobes a pair of red earrings, stunningly beautiful and surprisingly familiar. And now she stood and watched as the woman walked ever farther away from her, a silk scarf in shades of orange and gold around her neck, the red glint in her ears. A thought flashed through her mind for a fraction of a second: It's Tatiana. Her older sister. And then in her mind's eye for a moment, the woman's face took on the face of the young girl who was killed in London. But Ya'ara shook her head, brushing aside the childish face that lay in wait for her on the fringes of her consciousness.

The next moment she was sure it was Tatiana, just her. Her forever-missing sister, the gaping hole in Ya'ara's chest, the real reason why she had never been able to love anyone, become attached to anyone. And then she closed her eyes, and the colors of the scarf, which were like a glowing stain on her retinas, turned into a black, all-absorbing surface. Enough already, enough, she berated herself, breathing the cold air into her lungs. It isn't her, you can't keep seeing her everywhere you go. When Ya'ara opened her eyes again, she could no longer locate the woman on the train platforms. They were crowded with people hurrying home. Once again, Tatiana Stein, her older sister, had become a ghost.

ABOUT THE AUTHOR

Jonathan de Shalit is the pseudonym of a former high-ranking member of the Israeli Intelligence Community. He is the author of *Traitor.* His books must pass a rigid vetting process, including the approval of a special Governmental Ministers' Committee. De Shalit has translated into Hebrew the American novel *A Sport and a Pastime* by James Salter and *Defectors* by Joseph Kanon, as well as John le Carre's autobiography, *The Pigeon Tunnel.*

The employees of Thorndike Press hope you have enjoyed this Large Print book. All our Thorndike, Wheeler, and Kennebec Large Print titles are designed for easy reading, and all our books are made to last. Other Thorndike Press Large Print books are available at your library, through selected bookstores, or directly from us.

For information about titles, please call:
(800) 223-1244

or visit our website at:
gale.com/thorndike

To share your comments, please write:
Publisher
Thorndike Press
10 Water St., Suite 310
Waterville, ME 04901